"...e?"

She den... a low voice.

"I kissed you."

She shook her head and felt the knot at the nape of her neck give, the heaviness of her hair loosening to tumble down her back. For some reason it signaled a final betrayal, a surrender she neither wanted, nor could avoid. A loss of the worst sort...of herself.

Their kiss couldn't have lasted longer than a moment or two and yet look at what he'd done to her. Or rather, look at how he'd caused her to come undone.

She'd always taken such pride in her cool poise, knowing that others might want, but could never take, not while she held herself at a careful distance.

But with one touch, Gabe had stripped all that away.

Dear Reader,

This will be my final Desire™ title, and I'd like to sincerely thank all the readers who have supported my career and been so encouraging over the years. It's been a true pleasure to share my stories with you and develop relationships with so many who have taken the time to email me. Some of my books have been a direct result of your comments and suggestions.

I would also like to thank Mills & Boon for seeing something in my first book, *Jinxed,* and helping to launch a career that's spanned so many years. I couldn't have asked for a better first home or better editors to assist me along the way. They have all been fabulous and I thank them all, particularly my current editor, Mary-Theresa Hussey!

I hope you enjoy *Becoming Dante,* part of the ongoing DANTE LEGACY series. I have to tell you I totally fell in love with Gabe Moretti, one of the forgotten Dantes, who struggles to find his way home and become what he was always meant to be. And I hope you'll look for my next story. I guarantee you'll be delighted with where I take you from here!

Unfortunately, the time has come for me to leave Mills & Boon, at least for now, but I hope you will continue to follow me and the new books I'm in the process of writing, many with characters and storylines we've both come to love, such as the Dantes.

Please visit my website, www.dayleclaire.com, where I'll have a list of upcoming releases, along with personal comments and information to keep you in the loop. Do drop by and let me know what you'd like to see from me next.

Love,

Day Leclaire

BECOMING DANTE

BY
DAY LECLAIRE

MILLS & BOON

Published in Great Britain 2013
by Mills & Boon, an imprint of Harlequin (UK) Limited,
Eton House, 18-24 Paradise Road, Richmond, Surrey TW9 1SR

© Day Totton Smith 2012

ISBN: 978 0 263 90464 2
ebook ISBN: 978 1 472 00085 9

51-0213

Harlequin (UK) policy is to use papers that are natural, renewable and recyclable products and made from wood grown in sustainable forests. The logging and manufacturing processes conform to the legal environmental regulations of the country of origin.

Printed and bound in Spain
by Blackprint CPI, Barcelona

USA TODAY bestselling author **Day Leclaire** has sales of well over five million books. She is a three-time winner of both a Colorado Award of Excellence and a Golden Quill Award. She's won *RT Book Reviews* Career Achievement and Love and Laughter Awards, a Holt Medallion and a Booksellers' Best Award. She has also received an impressive ten nominations for the prestigious Romance Writers of America RITA® Award.

Day's romances touch the heart and make you care about her characters as much as she does. In Day's own words, "I adore writing romances, and can't think of a better way to spend each day." For more information, visit Day at her website, www.dayleclaire.com.

To Diana Colpitts,

No.1 Dantes fan, and a soul-sister who loves *Star Trek, Star Wars* and NASCAR as much as I do.

Thank you for keeping me entertained with all your family stories and wild Dante dreams. Hugs, sweetie!

One

Gabe Moretti's office door slammed open and one of the most beautiful women he'd ever seen swept in. At her appearance, an odd sizzle raced through him, something he'd never experienced before, something that jarred him from complacency and threw all his senses on high alert.

She's yours, came an insidious whisper. *Take the woman!*

Gabe shoved aside the bizarre thought and focused on her, his brows drawing together. She was tall, or rather her three inch heels gave the illusion of height, and emphasized her delicate, almost fragile bone structure. Despite her slender frame, womanly curves filled out a charcoal-and-white suit that could only be Christian Dior. A black wool coat framed the outfit. Hair the color of banked embers fell away from a sculpted face and formed a heavy twist at her nape. But there was more to her than mere beauty. Character and sheer force of will melded with her appearance, while intelligence glittered in eyes a pale, startling green, eyes that were haunting…and haunted. They gave her an almost painful vulnerability, one Gabe reacted to with unsettling intensity.

Get. The. Woman.

The primal demand overcame thought and reason, the visceral tug almost more than he could withstand. Time slowed, stilled, stealing his intellect, his icy control, all that drove him and made him the man he'd fought to become. Desire honed into one imperative…this woman, in this place, captured within this moment. And all the while, the insidious whisper lashed at him. *Take her. Make her yours. Brand her with your touch. Your possession.* Heat crackled, unbearable in its intensity, ungovernable in its strength. It slipped deep inside, infiltrated his veins with each beat of his heart. It took root, sending out endless tendrils that blossomed within his soul. And then time sped up, thrusting him back into the here and now.

The woman checked her forward motion as though sensing some disturbance. She hesitated, her gaze locking with his. Clearly, he wasn't what she'd anticipated and his curiosity grew. Who or what had she been expecting? Or was she simply reacting to him in the same way he reacted to her?

"Gabe Moretti?" she asked in a deep, husky voice that threatened to fry sense and sensibility.

She's the one!

"I'm sorry, Mr. Moretti." His assistant, Sarah, hurried into the office. "She refused to make an appointment and demanded to see you immediately."

Gabe flipped closed the file he'd been reviewing and stood. He pinned the mystery woman with the sort of steely look that had earned him the nickname "Iceman" among both competitors and adversaries. Maybe he reacted so strongly because of the inner voice hammering at him— one he'd never heard before and hoped never to hear again. Or maybe it was to hold instinct at bay, one that insisted he ignore civilized behavior and take what he wanted, regardless of consequence. She simply returned his look with one of her own, the expression in her crystalline eyes as brilliant and fierce as Dante fire diamonds.

Ice versus fire, an intriguing combination.

"Why don't we start at the beginning?" he suggested. It impressed the hell out of him that he could speak so calmly while desire fomented within, splashing through him in hot, messy waves. "Such as, who are you?"

"Don't you recognize me? You should." Amusement filtered through the statement. "I'm Kat Malloy."

The simple statement impacted like a punch to the gut. So much for some fool, intuitive voice. Not only was this woman not *the one*, she could *never* be *the one*. No matter how badly he wanted her on a physical level, she was the last woman in existence he would take to his bed—or ever want in his bed. He'd seen her only once before in his entire life. Even then, he'd felt a similar reaction, though nowhere near this strong. Perhaps his earlier reaction had been mitigated by the fact that she'd been in another man's bed—her cousin's fiancé's, no less.

Gabe glanced at his assistant and gave a subtle jerk of his head.

The instant he and Kat were alone, he approached and delivered the first salvo. "Maybe if you weren't wearing clothes, I'd have an easier time remembering you."

Irritation flashed through her gaze like emerald lightning. "How kind of you to bring that up. Ever the gentleman."

"I wouldn't advise going down that road," he said, very, very gently. "Otherwise I'll be forced to discuss how well you fit the definition of a lady."

She dismissed his warning with a casual shrug, though based on the sweep of color darkening her cheekbones, his comment hit home. Good. So long as he kept their relationship adversarial, it wouldn't allow for any other emotions to creep in—like lust. Or passion. Or the need to rip her clothes off and imprint himself on her, body and soul.

"You've refused every attempt to make an appointment," she said. "The very least you could do is have the courtesy to hear my proposition before throwing me out."

He simply stared at her. Something in his demeanor must have penetrated her annoyance and she stilled, eyeing him warily…a succulent doe scenting a hungry predator. About damn time. He maintained his silence, allowing it to grow until cold, raw bitterness settled between them. And all the while that hideous voice hammered at him, making demands about Kat Malloy he had zero intention of listening to, let alone following.

"I owe you nothing. Maybe my late wife did. After all, you were Jessa's cousin," he said at last. He paused a beat before adding in a conversational tone, "Did you know she loved you like a sister? Even after what you did, even after your little fling with Benson Winters, she still spent the last two years of her life grieving over her lost relationship with you."

"Did she?" Kat raised a sleek eyebrow. "She certainly had a peculiar way of showing it, especially considering she turned our grandmother against me and vilified me in the press. For some reason that just doesn't strike me as very sisterly."

He saw red. "Maybe because you slept with her fiancé. And though I ultimately benefited since she turned to me for consolation, it was a despicable thing to do."

The Malloy woman rallied with impressive speed. "So everyone keeps telling me. For some strange reason, I have a slightly different take on what happened that night."

She gave his office a cursory glance, noting the generous sitting area where he often entertained clients. Ignoring the chairs, she chose the couch. She shrugged off her coat, tossed it over one of the arms and made herself at home, crossing her legs—gorgeous, shapely legs, he couldn't help but notice. Legs he would give almost anything to have wrapped around him. Of course, even a viper had a sinuous shape. That didn't mean he'd get close enough to feel the sting of her fangs or be infected by her poison. Not that his inner voice gave him any peace on that front. Apparently, it didn't care about fangs or poison, only about those legs, and how tight they could hold him.

Regarding him with remarkable self-possession, she said, "Before you throw me out, you should be aware of one vital detail." She smiled her siren's smile. "I have something you want."

He waved that aside. "You have nothing I want, now or ever."

She folded her hands in her lap. So proper. So decorous. So bloody classy. And every bit of it a lie. "Actually, the detail I'm referring to is Heart's Desire."

He froze. *Son of a bitch!* He'd spent years attempting to purchase his mother's fire diamond necklace from Matilda Chatsworth, without success. Kat's grandmother knew damn well how badly he wanted it, that he'd literally do anything necessary to get it back. Granted, not the best negotiating tactics for someone with his skill and experience. But he'd been far younger then, and lacked the ability to maintain a poker face, especially when it came to something that carried so much emotional baggage.

The necklace had been created by his mother, Cara, when she first started working for Dantes as one of their jewelry designers. During those early, heady days, she'd met and fallen in love with Dominic Dante, the owner's son. Their affair had been passionate and all-consuming, teetering on the brink of marriage. But instead of choosing his mother,

Dominic had taken a wife with a bank account balance that would assist Dantes' bottom line, no doubt at the urging of his parents. After his betrayal, his mother had accepted a position at Dantes, New York, and moved on with her life—until Dominic had swooped in years afterward and, unable to resist, she'd indulged in a one-night stand with him. That one night resulted in Gabe's and his twin sister, Lucia's, conception, causing Cara to leave Dantes permanently.

According to Dominic, he'd never forgotten Cara, his love never dying. He spent years attempting to find her, frustrated by how successfully she'd fallen off the grid. Eventually, fifteen years later, he tracked her down, and discovered she'd borne his twins. This time he proposed to her, despite still being married to his wife, Laura. He gave Cara a necklace she'd created for the firm, one he named Heart's Desire in her honor, along with a ring as a promise that he'd come to her after his divorce, marry her and legitimize his bastard twins by adopting them and bestowing the Dante name on them. Of course, that had never happened and all Cara Moretti had been left with were empty promises and the dying flames of the fire diamonds Dominic had given her.

Gabe had been twenty when his mother became ill and, desperate for money to care for her, he'd sold the fire diamond necklace to Matilda Chatsworth. The money had also provided him with a start in life. Despite knowing he'd had no choice but to sell the necklace, he'd always hoped to buy it back. It had taken him a long time to realize why it had become so vital to have it in his possession once again.

Eventually, he'd been able to acknowledge what the necklace represented—the symbolism it held for him, one that continued to burn in his heart. It stood for the man who'd created him. The family that had rejected him. And the mother and sister who had always been there for each other, through the good, the bad and the unbelievably ugly.

Unfortunately, by the time he had the financial where-withal to purchase Heart's Desire, Matilda refused to sell. Even when he'd married her granddaughter Jessa, the necklace remained just out of reach, a promise, but never a reality. What he didn't get was why, after all these years, had Matilda decided to give her wayward granddaughter the necklace instead of selling it back to him? Why would she turn on him like that, especially when she'd despised Kat for betraying Jessa?

Gabe focused on Kat, aware she'd become an obstacle in his path, one he'd do anything to remove. A blistering fury lapped at his control. "You have it?" Just those three words, but they contained an emotional history that spanned his entire life. That went to the very core of who and what he was.

Kat hesitated and answered indirectly. "My grandmother contacted me recently, asked me to return home. She's not well. She promised to give me the necklace after she..." Something painful shifted across her expression before vanishing. "Afterward."

"In that case, come see me when you actually have it. Now if you don't mind..." He jerked his head toward the door. "I'm busy."

"I'm afraid there's a little more involved than that." She glanced around, her gaze coming to rest on the nearby wet bar and her voice acquired a husky quality. "Is it possible to have some water? I'm dying of thirst."

"Planning to play the role of grieving granddaughter over the impending loss of your grandmother, Kat? Complete with crocodile tears, I have no doubt. Sorry, sweetheart, not buying it."

He caught a flicker of pain before her expression closed over. "Any tears I shed over my grandmother will be real. After my parents died when I was five, Gam raised me. I owe her more than I can ever express. But you don't have to worry about my breaking down in front of you. I never cry. Ever."

Gabe didn't bother to beat around the bush. "How much? How much for Heart's Desire?"

She didn't so much as twitch. "It's not for sale."

He shot to his feet, swearing beneath his breath. "You're a piece of work, you know that? First you sleep with Benson Winters, Jessa's former fiancé. Now you've found a way to wriggle back into Matilda's good graces and get your hands on that necklace. Why? What's your game?"

Her response came just as promptly. "This isn't a game. It never was."

He honed in on the bottom line, at least what he considered the bottom line. "I'll pay you full value for the necklace. More than full value. Money is no object." As usual, when it came to that damn necklace, every business skill and tactic he'd learned over the past decade vanished like mist beneath the rays of a hot summer sun.

"My price isn't money." She waved the discussion aside as though it were of little consequence and offered a cool smile. "I believe you were going to get me a drink?"

Damn, damn, damn. He'd spent no more than five minutes with the woman and she'd already managed to demolish years of effort to curb his emotions, to keep them walled off and under tight control. It had to be because he wanted her. Because she belonged to him. He stiffened in disbelief. Dear God, what the *hell* was happening to him?

Without a word, he crossed to a wet bar. "Flat or sparkling?"

"Flat."

"Ice?"

"Thank you. It would make a nice change."

"That's right." Ice sang against crystal. "You've been hiding out in Europe for the past five years."

"I haven't been hiding," she instantly protested.

Interesting. It would appear he'd managed to hit another hot button. It surprised him that a woman like Kat didn't have her weaknesses better fortified. "Bull. You hightailed it out of the country within days of the news breaking that you were having an affair with your cousin's fiancé, senatorial candidate Benson Winters. And you've stayed out of the country ever since, not even returning when Jessa and I married, let alone for her funeral." He handed her the glass, noting with satisfaction that it trembled ever so slightly in her grasp. "But the minute you figure out how to get your hands on Heart's Desire, you manage to find your way back to Seattle."

She took a quick sip of water, no doubt to give herself a precious few seconds to regain her equilibrium. "Is that why you've repeatedly refused to see me? Because I didn't attend Jessa's funeral?"

"It's as good a reason as any, wouldn't you agree?"

"If it were true." She took another restorative sip, before meeting his gaze. "Which it isn't."

Maybe if he focused on his anger, the desire would go away. Or at least, ease up. That's all he needed, a few minutes of respite from the fierce wave of need lashing at him, eroding his control with every passing second. He didn't understand it. The only emotion he should feel toward her was utter contempt. And yet... That wasn't what he felt. *Why?*

"Which part isn't true?" he bit out. "That you couldn't be bothered to attend your cousin's funeral, or you returned only in order to get your hands on Heart's Desire?"

She gave a careless shrug. "Jessa wouldn't have wanted me there."

"No question about that. And yet the second Matilda tells you she's ill, you return to circle like a vulture. Or am I mistaken about that, as well?"

She flinched, the movement barely perceptible, bringing a hint of vulnerability to those brilliant, haunted eyes. Of course, considering all he knew about her, she'd patented the look and incorporated it into her current scam, something he found far easier to believe than the alternative—that she possessed so much as a modicum of true vulnerability. He couldn't trust his instincts when it came to this woman, not when they urged him to make her his.

A ray of late morning sunshine shafted across the room, losing itself in the trace of red buried in the sooty darkness of her hair. "You're not mistaken. I'm here because my grandmother is ill."

"That's not why you're sitting in my office though, is it?" Cynicism ran rampant through the question. "I believe you're sitting here because you know how much I want Heart's Desire."

Her chin lifted an inch. "You're right. I am. I'm betting you'll do anything and everything to get your hands on it."

"Then name your price."

"I don't want money. What I do want in exchange for the necklace is quite simple and well within your ability to offer me." When he didn't reply, she continued. "I've heard you're one of the best negotiators in all of Seattle. Possibly in the entire Northwest." She set her glass aside and interlaced her fingers, the knuckles blanching white and betraying the nervousness lurking behind her calm façade. "Care to put it to the test?"

"Take your best shot."

"My grandmother is a very traditional woman. Naturally, she's concerned about me, and about my…" She hesitated, before adding delicately, "Shall we say, my unfortunate choices to date? Right now, she isn't open to a reconciliation. She's simply informed me that she intends to honor her promise to give me the necklace and to let me know that's likely to happen sooner rather than later."

"I gather giving you the necklace isn't good enough for you?"

Kat shook her head. "No. I want more. A lot more."

"Your grandmother is a wealthy woman. Let me guess. You feel entitled to a generous portion of that wealth."

She lifted a shoulder in a negligent shrug. "What I want is a reconciliation. My reasons are my own."

"And how do I fit into the picture?"

"Gam has made it clear that she needs proof of my respectability. I believe her exact words were…" She wrinkled her brow in reflection. "'I will need to see for myself that you've settled down with a respectable man who won't put up with any of your nonsense.'"

"Good God," he said faintly.

"Yes, that was my reaction, too. But, if I do what she asks, I believe Gam will welcome me home. That brings me to the aforementioned respectable man." She fixed her spring-green eyes on him and smiled. "Hello, respectable man."

He stared at her, appalled. "You're proposing marriage? No. Absolutely no way. You're insane to think I'd agree."

The flat statement didn't come close to mirroring his profound distaste for her outrageous proposition. Or his profound desire. Marriage. The marital bed. The wedding night. He recalled the first time he'd seen Kat and his hands balled into fists. She'd been nude, sprawled across satin sheets, her youthful face so falsely innocent. Sleeping Beauty well after the prince's "kiss" had wakened her.

Even then, he'd been knocked sideways by her, had felt the initial, confusing stirrings of what had exploded into something far more this time around. He'd assumed all those years ago it had been a natural male response to the sight of a beautiful, naked woman, though he'd never been able to explain why the image of her had been branded into his memory for the past five years, while images of his wife, who died two short years ago, had already faded away. No wonder he hadn't recognized the older, more stylish version of Kat who'd swept into his office. The two couldn't look more different—the buttoned-up sophisticate versus earthy temptation.

She laughed in open amusement. "Relax, Gabe. I'm not proposing marriage. I'm proposing an engagement. Granted, a prolonged engagement. One that will prove to Gam that I've settled down. You'll help make her final months happy ones."

"As if you give a damn about that."

"Actually, I do give a damn. Despite all that's happened, she's still my grandmother." She paused to allow that to sink in, before continuing, "Besides, who could be more perfect? Since you were Jessa's husband, our engagement takes me from infamous to respectable in one easy step. You're renowned for your honor and integrity. For being a powerful man who, though fair, isn't a pushover. You're exactly the man Gam has in mind to…" Her amusement grew, encouraged him to join in on the joke. "To keep me in line."

"No."

"Think of it, Gabe." She used her siren's voice on him, along with those leaf-bright eyes and sultry smile. All of it bent on seduction. "I'll be at your mercy. Forced to toe whatever line you draw. And in exchange, you get your Heart's Desire. Win-win."

He hesitated for a long minute, debating how to handle a proposition he should turn down flat, but found more tempting than he could have believed possible. What was that line from the TV show he'd watched as a child? *Resistance is futile.* He crossed to his desk and pressed a button on his phone. "Sarah?"

"Yes, Mr. Moretti," his assistant said immediately.

"Cancel the rest of my appointments today. I'll be leaving the office and won't be back until the usual time Monday. Reschedule everything for next week. Give the Atkinson project top priority."

He didn't bother waiting for a response. He turned his attention to Kat and gestured toward his office door. "Shall we?"

"Shall we…what?"

Her amusement faded, replaced by a wariness that caused Gabe to smile, though he suspected it lacked any semblance of humor. "Shall we see if we can consummate our future business agreement, of course. Assuming we're able to reach an agreement."

"Consummate," she repeated, stiffening. Nerves jittered across her expressive face. Nerves and something else, something he couldn't quite place. Dread?

He couldn't explain what prompted him to provoke her this way. Perhaps it was that damned vulnerability he'd picked up on, the need to determine whether or not it was just an act. Or maybe he sensed a weakness, something he could exploit in order to gain the upper hand in their battle of wills. More likely it was the lust that had dogged him since the moment she stepped into his office.

He lifted an eyebrow. "Isn't that the end result when a proposal is accepted? The parties consummate the agreement. I suggest we go somewhere more private where we can do so. After all, you've just said that part of the deal was having you at my mercy, forced to toe whatever line I draw. Well, sweetheart, consummating our agreement is my line. So, I suggest you plant the toes of those sexy Valentinos along my line and start begging for mercy."

"You must be joking." She shot to her feet, outrage lacing

her words. Not exactly flattering, considering most women were quite eager to…consummate with him.

Maybe that was why he didn't instantly reassure her. Or maybe it was that damnable inner voice driving him on. Whatever the cause, he gave her another verbal shove. "No, I'm not joking. I am open to conversation beforehand. Perhaps a call to my lawyer to draft something nice and legal so you can't default on our agreement. After that…" He moved in on her, stopping mere inches away. The sizzle between them increased to almost unbearable levels. "Well, let's just say you were right. I'll do whatever it takes to get my hands on that necklace."

"Even bedding me?" The question sounded almost bitter, which roused his curiosity.

"If you insist."

"I don't insist. In fact, I don't want to sleep with you or any other man." Her carefully constructed façade cracked and passionate intensity lashed through her words, increasing his curiosity. "All I want is to satisfy my grandmother's request."

"And all I want is Heart's Desire. You were the one who suggested an engagement as a means to achieve our mutual goals."

"That doesn't mean we have to—" She broke off, her lashes sweeping downward to conceal her expression. One of distaste, if he didn't miss his guess.

"I believe that's something we'll need to negotiate. And as you mentioned, I'm an expert negotiator." He leaned in, his voice barely above a whisper, yet filled with dark demand. "You put yourself in my path. You possess something I want. Why act surprised when I take what you so foolishly dangle in front of me, even if it means you get more than you bargained for?"

"That wasn't my intent," she protested. A hint of panic edged her words. "You know it wasn't."

"But it is the result. Now we're going somewhere private, somewhere we won't be overheard or interrupted, and we're going to figure out precisely what it will take to seal this devil's bargain. Because nothing—not our engagement, not consummation of our engagement and definitely not my late wife's infamous cousin—will stand in the way of my getting that necklace. Are we clear?"

Kat's uneven breathing shattered the sudden silence between them and her creamy complexion grew stark. She stared at him, her brilliant eyes dark with frustration. He expected her to cave. She didn't. Somehow she found the presence to gather her self-control and confront him with a look of total defiance. "No man tells me what to do. Not even my future fiancé."

In that moment Gabe realized he would do whatever it took to have this woman, regardless of who and what he knew her to be. How was that possible? His late wife had gone into explicit detail about her notorious cousin. He'd witnessed Kat's fall from grace with his own eyes. She was precisely the sort of woman he avoided at all costs. He attempted to put his attraction down to the superficial resemblance between the cousins—both fine-boned and sable-haired. But Jessa had possessed eyes as black as ink, her hair equally so, lacking that hint of fire buried deep within the dark strands. And her features were cheerleader pretty versus elegantly stunning. She'd also lacked the womanly curves that gave Kat's Dior suit such eye-catching definition. In addition, his late wife's sweet, compliant personality couldn't have been any more dissimilar from her cousin's prickly defiance. Not that who—or what—this woman was made the least difference. Only one thing mattered to him and nothing would come between him and his Heart's Desire.

"If you want to squirm your way back into Matilda's good graces as much as I want my family's necklace, you'll do whatever is required. And if that means a legally consummated agreement, than that's what you'll do." She started to protest and he cut her off without compunction. "Anything you have to say can be said in a more private setting than this."

"But—"

"Not. *Here.*"

She folded her arms across her chest. "Well, I'm not going to your place. So, it looks like it'll have to be your office, or nowhere."

"Fine. If you want to do it in my office, my office it is. Just let me lock the door and we can get this over with. Which do you prefer, desk or couch?"

She backed up a telling step. "Neither."

"Then I suggest we go somewhere private in order to discuss the situation. And that would be my place. It has the added advantage of giving the impression that my future wife has just flown in from overseas and we can't wait to be alone to…consummate our engagement."

"Which I have no intention of doing," she shot back.

He gestured toward the door. "Shall we?" She hesitated and he fought for patience. "By all means stand up for yourself. But I suggest you choose your battles. Fighting over every single issue is going to be exhausting, and frankly, it's pointless. If we can't agree on something as simple as where to hold our discussion, we might as well put an end to this farce right now."

"Fine. We'll go to your place. But all we'll be doing is talking."

"An excellent place to start."

He didn't give her time to come up with any further arguments. He ushered her from the office, then from the building, and into his car for the drive to Medina. They accomplished the vast portion of the trip in taut silence, whatever slumbered between them seething just beneath the surface, slowly intensifying until it reached almost unbearable levels.

They pulled into the drive of the sprawling estate fronting Lake Washington and Kat spared him a swift, startled glance. "It's beautiful," she murmured. Could she sound any more surprised?

"Wait until you see the views of the lake."

He led the way to the front door, entered his code and, without giving Kat warning, swept her into his arms and carried her over the threshold. The instant he set her on her feet, she attempted to pull away, but he didn't give her the chance.

"Welcome to my home, Ms. Malloy."

He could never explain what happened next, what sort of insanity seized him. He heard the voice in his head again, the dark, insidious voice that echoed with unmistakable demand. *Take the woman! She's the one.* Maybe he caved to temptation because he'd wanted her from the instant she'd walked into his office on those sexy peep-toed Valentino pumps with their "screw the world" siren-red spike heels. Or maybe he did it because she so clearly didn't want him. Or maybe it was to make a statement about who would be in charge of this unholy union. Whatever the reason, he took her hand in his to yank her into his arms. At the same instant, he lowered his head and took her mouth in a kiss of sheer demand.

The moment their hands and lips touched, passion exploded, a spark that flared to life, followed by a burn of need that flashed between them, melded them, connected them in a way he'd never experienced before. It flashed from mouth to fingertip before centering in his palm and sinking inward, straight through to his bones where it became part of the very fabric of his being. Desire crashed down on him, so insistent and undeniable that it took every ounce of the ice-cold discipline he was renowned for to keep himself under some semblance of control. To stop himself from carrying her off to his bedroom and consummating her proposal in every conceivable way.

And in that moment Gabe discovered that he couldn't maintain his self-control. Didn't want to. He deepened the kiss and allowed the insanity to consume him. More than anything he was driven to put his mark on her, brand her with his possession. To claim her for his own.

His woman. His future fiancée. His mate.

The one.

Two

Kat had no idea what Gabe Moretti had done to her.

A kiss. Just a simple kiss. That's all it should have been.

But the instant his lips touched hers, desire crashed down on her, a desire unlike anything she'd ever experienced before. One minute she'd been her own person, and the next she'd become someone else, someone who burned. Who needed. Who wanted with every fiber of her being.

No man had ever touched her like this. Not physically. Not emotionally. She'd worked so hard to protect herself, to build barriers that resisted all attempts to get too close. And yet, with one kiss this man—her soon-to-be fiancé—had swept away those barriers as though they were no more than flimsy tissue paper. How was it possible?

Even more distressing was the kiss itself, a kiss that actually sparked and burned, as though she'd touched a live wire. A kiss that had her sinking into him, opening to him, giving herself without thought or hesitation. If he chose to strip her naked right there in the foyer, she wouldn't have lifted a finger to stop him. Wouldn't? *Couldn't*. She could no more control her reaction to him than she could control the ebb and flow of the tide or the rising and setting of the sun.

He deepened the kiss and she yielded to him, allowed the insanity to consume her. She wanted him to put his mark on her, brand her with his possession. Claim her for his own.

He was her man. Her future fiancé. Her mate.

The one.

The instant the thought settled, she fought it. With a sharp cry, she wriggled free of Gabe's arms, even though it felt as though she were ripping away part of herself. She took a stumbling step backward. Then another and another until she felt the solid wood of his front door pressing against her spine.

No. Oh, no, no, no. How could she start over, wipe the slate clean, if she gave herself to this man? He belonged to an unwelcome past, along with Jessa and the scandal. Kat's plan from the start was to cut those ties and knot each and every dangling thread. Becoming engaged to Gabe had been part of that plan, but a temporary part, discarded as quickly as possible with no emotional involvement. Instead, those ties wrapped around her, tightening until she strangled beneath their pull and drag. Somehow, she'd lost who she was and who she'd meant to become, trapped within a web of Gabe's making, one of dark desire and need.

"What did you just do to me?" she demanded in a low voice.

"I kissed you."

She shook her head and felt the knot at the nape of her neck give, the heaviness of her hair loosening to tumble down her back. For some reason it signaled a final betrayal, a surrender she neither wanted, nor could avoid. A loss of the worst sort...of herself. Their kiss couldn't have lasted longer than a moment or two and yet look at what he'd done to her. Or rather, look at how he'd caused her to come undone. She'd always taken such pride in her cool poise, knowing that others might want, but could never take, not while she held herself at a careful distance. But with one touch, Gabe had stripped all that away.

"That was no kiss." She lifted trembling fingers to her mouth, where palm and lips both throbbed in tempo. "It burned. How did you do that?"

Something flickered in his golden gaze, almost as though he'd made an unexpected connection. "It just happened. I don't know how or why."

"Did it…" She moistened her lips. They felt warm and swollen…and delightfully sensitive. "Did it happen with Jessa? Is this a Moretti thing?"

A sooty eyebrow shot upward. "A Moretti thing?" he repeated, amusement lacing the question. He shook his head. "No, I suspect if it's anything, it's a Dante thing."

"Dante?" Did he mean the same Dantes who'd created his mother's necklace? The Dantes she one day hoped to work for? That didn't make any sense. "I don't understand."

"I don't either, but I will." He took a step in her direction and she tensed. To her relief, he didn't come any closer. "I don't know about you, but I need a drink. And I don't mean ice water."

"It's barely noon," she protested.

"I need a drink," he repeated. He gestured toward a room that opened off the foyer. "If you'll wait for me in the study, I'll arrange for lunch."

"I'd like to freshen up." She glanced around, an unwelcome helplessness settling over her. "Where…?"

"There's a bathroom off the study."

Praying that her shaky three-inch heels would hold her for the length of time it took to cross the wooden foyer floor, she headed in the direction he indicated and entered the study. It was a surprisingly charming room, beautifully appointed. As much as she'd have liked to linger and admire the heartwood floors and antique furniture, she continued on to the bathroom. One glance at the mirror confirmed her worst fears.

She didn't just look like a woman who'd been kissed senseless. She looked like a woman who'd been stripped bare. Exposed. Left utterly defenseless. That had happened only once before and she'd sworn she'd never allow it to happen again. And yet it had. Somehow Gabriel Moretti had found a way in and unlocked the Pandora's Box she kept buried in the deepest, darkest part of herself. And he'd done it with a single kiss. How was that possible?

And what was that bizarre heat that had flared between them? It hadn't been passion alone. Something more burned there. Something she didn't have a hope of controlling, that instead directed and ordained, as though fate had seized hold of her life and set it on a new and unalterable path. She didn't have a single doubt that path led straight into Gabe's arms, the one place she had no intention of going and the one place she most wanted to explore.

Lucky, lucky Jessa.

Kat lifted a hand to her mouth, stricken at how her fingers trembled. And her eyes... Dark, filled with pain. A window to her every thought and emotion. With her hair tumbling around her shoulders and her mouth ripe and swollen she appeared— Oh, God. *Ravished*. And with one kiss. What would happen when he took the embrace farther than a single kiss?

She shoved the thought away. This would never do. She simply wouldn't allow it. Opening her purse, she swiftly rebuilt the feminine barriers women through the ages had used to protect themselves. With her hair once again ruthlessly knotted at her nape and her makeup impeccably applied, she felt better. She'd feel a whole lot better if she could somehow shield the expression in her eyes.

She closed them and remembered. Remembered all she'd gone through, all she'd achieved to date. All she intended to accomplish in the future. She remembered the past, and the immense debt she owed her grandmother for taking her in after her parents' deaths. Of her struggle the past five years and how she'd ruthlessly pinched every penny of the inheritance she received from the trust account her parents set up. Life had been beyond difficult until her finances had taken a swift upward swing eighteen months ago, enough of a swing to indulge in a few excellent pieces of designer clothing and shoes.

But most important of all was her desperation to reconcile with the woman who'd been her entire world until five years ago. Not to mention her ultimate goal and eventual destination…San Francisco and the shot at a job as a jewelry designer for Dantes. It steadied her as nothing else could.

When she checked the mirror again, she saw a woman in charge of her own destiny. A woman who could resist Gabriel Moretti. She took a deep, calming breath, praying that's what Gabe saw, as well.

She returned to the study to discover him pouring drinks. He glanced at her and a knowing gleam shot through his distinctive gold eyes. "Feel better?" he asked.

"Much."

"Drink?"

She shrugged. Why not? "Thanks. Neat, please."

"I've arranged for lunch. It should be ready shortly. I also put a call in to my attorney. I'll have Tom Blythe pull together some sort of agreement. I can assure you he'll be discreet." Gabe approached and handed her a leaded crystal tumbler. Their fingertips brushed, intensifying the faint sizzle and burn that hummed between them. For some reason, it centered in her palm and in her lips. Odd. Very odd. And very distracting. "So, why don't you present your proposition and we'll discuss how we should go from there?"

His businesslike attitude helped steady her, earning her gratitude. "It's fairly simple. We make a point of a first meeting, somewhere public so it's both noticed and notable. We date for a set number of months. Announce our engagement. Allow the engagement to run its course until…" She took a quick drink, the burn of liquor helping to keep her composed and focused. She repeated the word, with more finality this time. "Until." She still couldn't bring herself to say the words, words that threatened to break her heart. *Until Gam died.*

"I think there's a little more involved than that," Gabe warned.

She lifted an eyebrow. "Such as?"

"The venue for our meeting. How long we should date. How and when to announce the engagement. How best to handle Matilda. At what point the transfer of property occurs." His voice dropped and his gaze heated. "Not to mention, the…consummation of our agreement."

This time he didn't even have to touch her for her to come undone. She took another quick drink before speaking, praying her voice didn't reveal any hint of her inner turmoil. Why him? Of all people, why Jessa's husband? "I suggest the most trendy, public venue possible for our initial dates. I'm a bit out of touch these days, so you would know better than I where that would be."

"Acceptable."

"As for announcing our engagement, I suggest we wait three to six months."

"One."

She shook her head. "No one is going to buy that."

"I believe they will." He smiled in a way that caused nerves to skitter along her spine and the tug of desire to intensify. "Especially when they see I can't keep my hands off you."

"Three," she bargained desperately. "Three months."

"One."

Her mouth tightened. "People won't believe it. And I need them to believe."

"People will believe I'm merely a fool in love," he stated matter-of-factly. "Unfortunately, your reputation precedes you, so I'm afraid they won't be quite so generous in their opinion of you. And when I end our engagement and cut off all contact with you, I suspect your flirtation with respectability will also end."

Kat got it then. Every ounce of color drained from her face and the breath stuttered in her lungs. "When you end the engagement, you hope to confirm the general consensus, don't you?" The question escaped in a thready whisper. "Why? Why would you do that?"

His tarnished eyes burned like the fires from hell. "Let's call it an engagement gift from Jessa. Of course, you can refuse, take the moral high ground and walk away from the deal. But something tells me you won't, even if it means finding yourself in the middle of another scandal with your reputation, once again, ripped to shreds."

"If you destroy my reputation, how am I supposed to convince my grandmother I've changed?"

"I don't plan to destroy your reputation while Matilda is still alive. In the meantime, she'll believe whatever I tell her. If I put my stamp of approval on you, she'll go along with it, mainly because she wants to believe. But we'll know the truth, won't we, Kat? And eventually, so will the rest of Seattle."

Pain tore through her. *Leave,* a small voice insisted. *Go now. Nothing is worth this.* Maybe she would have if it hadn't been for one unfortunate detail. Something happened when he'd kissed her. Something that changed everything. She couldn't explain it. Didn't understand how or why it altered the playing field. She simply knew it did.

Somehow, some way, he'd forged a connection between them, one she couldn't escape. Didn't want to escape. Oh, she knew it wouldn't last. Of course it wouldn't. But it compelled her to stay until that connection broke, or dissipated, or ran its course, no matter how painful that course might be.

She'd come to Seattle with one purpose in mind—a reconciliation with Gam. Nothing else mattered beyond that, especially now that their time together was so terribly finite. Or so Kat thought until her meeting with Gabe Moretti, until she'd walked into his office and been knocked sideways by a desire so paramount, nothing else seemed to matter. She closed her eyes. Okay, fine. So, she'd just proven to herself that she had base desires like every other woman in the world. That didn't change her goals, not really. Once that desire ran its course and once she'd made Gam's final days as happy as possible, she'd be free to move on and start over with a clean slate. The thought hovered before her like a golden dream. A dream she'd spent the past five years believing impossible to achieve.

"Well?" he demanded "Do you agree to my proposition?"

She struggled to conceal how much the small growl rippling through his question unsettled her. "Let's say I'm open to further negotiation."

If he felt any triumph at the concession, he didn't show it. If anything, his tension grew. "I insist on a legally binding agreement that you'll give me Heart's Desire."

"One that goes both ways," she shot right back. "I need you to promise to stay engaged to me and treat me appropriately while my grandmother's alive. Trust me when I say I intend to spell out in explicit detail just what 'appropriately' entails."

"Fair enough."

"Then we're agreed?"

He shook his head. "I expect you to consummate our agreement."

Heat stormed across her cheekbones. She turned on her heel and paced the room, pausing to examine a small free-flowing statuette, the dark polished wood exquisitely carved. She ran a finger along the smooth lines, wishing just once her life could run along equally smooth lines. A fruitless wish since it never had.

Even as a child her life had been one of turmoil, her grandmother the only steady, unwavering influence in her life. From the tender age of five, when her parents had died from a virus while on a humanitarian mission, her grandmother had been her world. Her rock.

Until Jessa changed all that.

She turned from the statuette and faced Gabe. "I suspect 'consummate our agreement' is your not-so-subtle way of telling me that you want to sleep with me."

"Not at all."

Confusion swept through her. Had she misunderstood? "Oh. Then what do you mean?"

He silently approached. "Sleeping won't be involved in our consummation. Sex will."

She didn't dare agree to that. It offered the possibility for far too many pitfalls. She assumed he wanted the necklace as badly as she wanted to reconcile with her grandmother. That didn't mean she'd risk everything on that one assumption. She forced herself to throw a quick, amused glance over her shoulder. "Sorry. That won't happen."

"You think not?"

She turned to face him. "Let's just say I'm saving myself for marriage," she said, perfectly serious. Not that he believed her.

Laughter escaped, the sound dark and rich and sliding through her veins like the sweetest of wines. "I like your sense of humor."

She fought to keep her barriers strong, to ignore the sensations lapping at her in ever increasing waves. "I didn't realize I'd said anything funny."

His eyes darkened, the color a tawny antique gold. They held her, warmed and warned her, made promises that filled her with longing and dread. "Fine," he said at last. "If you insist on waiting until you're married, I'll accept that."

But she knew he didn't mean the words, that he thought she'd cave to her baser instincts. Sadly, it was a strong possibility. "Then we have a deal?" she asked.

"We do." He tipped his glass toward hers. The crystal touched, releasing a soft, sweet note, the purity of it at odds with their unwholesome agreement.

He waited until they'd both taken a drink before setting the two tumblers aside. Then he reached for her, tugging her into his arms. Alarm shot through her. "What are you doing?"

"Consummating our agreement."

She struggled to free herself without success. "But, that's not what you said."

"I agreed to wait if you insisted we do so. That didn't mean I couldn't tempt you to change your mind." He lowered his head until his mouth hovered just above hers. "Are you tempted, Kat?"

He'd thought this kiss would be different.

It wasn't.

If anything, the bond created between them the first time they kissed intensified. Heat flared and splashed, rushing through his veins, sinking into his bones, and spiking his desire to an unbearable level. With a soft moan, her lips parted beneath his, allowing him to slip within and savor the honeyed warmth. Never had he tasted anything so delicious. It was as though her flavor had been specifically designed for him, designed to please and arouse, to tempt and satisfy. He couldn't seem to get enough. He wanted more.

He found the buttons to her suit jacket and released them. The edges parted a tantalizing few inches and beneath he found a scrap of black lace that revealed almost as much as it concealed. Her skin was a lovely shade of cream, so soft and pale against the darkness of her bra. The tops of her breasts rose above the fragile cups and her breath quickened beneath his gaze. Gently, tenderly, he shaped her breasts in his hands, recalling how they'd appeared when he'd found her in Winters' bed.

Stunning. Utterly stunning.

Her nipples tightened within his palms, pressing against the fragile lace in response to his caress and signaling her arousal. Fair enough. He was equally aroused, tight and heavy with the need to make this woman his own. He guided her backward toward the sofa, the imperative to take her and make her his beyond anything he'd experienced before. She bumped into the couch and with a startled cry, fell backward. She lay there against a deep green background, her jacket open, her hair once again free of its tight knot and tumbling like black fire around her pale shoulders. She stared up at him, her eyes picking up the color of the fabric and echoing its forest-shadowed hue.

He expected to see the knowing look of a woman who'd found herself in this position innumerable times in her checkered past. Instead, an innate feminine defenselessness gleamed there, a bewilderment he couldn't quite accept. Even so, he didn't sense any deception on her part, though he'd be a fool to believe anything this woman said or did. She played people, he reminded himself. She lied more easily than she told the truth. She was a woman who'd mastered the art of deception and manipulation, no doubt while still in the cradle.

And yet, still he wanted her.

He followed her down, planting his arms on either side of her head. His hands sank into her hair. The thick strands flowed through his fingers like silk, the slumberous fire within a fitting match for the fire that burned in her pale green gaze.

"Why do you wear it tied up in knots?" he asked.

"To keep it under control."

He offered an understanding smile. "You like control." It wasn't a question.

"Of myself," she conceded. She shifted against the cushions, a wry smile flickering across her mouth. "Not that I seem to possess any. At least, not with you."

"Seems we're in the same boat." He hadn't meant to concede so much. But this woman stripped him of control. Control and barriers and the ability to think straight. His reaction to her was as visceral as it was overwhelming. "But there's an easy solution."

"If you mean making love, I don't consider that an easy solution."

He couldn't prevent a cynical laugh. "Making love?"

Her lashes drifted downward and she shrugged. "Having sex?" she suggested dispassionately.

"Closer. And trust me…" He feathered a kiss across her jawline. She shuddered in reaction and he smiled, nipping at the soft, tender skin. "It's the simplest solution there is when you consider all the problems between us."

She stiffened ever so slightly. "This just adds another layer of complication."

He skated lower, along the long line of her neck. He could

feel her pulse against his mouth, practically taste her pounding need. "A delicious complication." Her breath escaped in soft little gasps, the sound fueling his arousal, the imperative to make her his building toward an overpowering desperation. If he didn't have her soon he just might go insane. "Not to mention a necessary one." Very, very necessary.

"Why is it necessary?" she asked.

Was she joking? His mouth settled in the satiny crook between neck and shoulder and he planted a series of kisses there. "We need to give the impression that we're crazy about each other. That we can't keep our hands to ourselves. That all we want is to get through whatever social function we're attending so we can escape to the nearest dark corner in order to get naked as fast as humanly possible."

She squeezed her eyes closed. "That doesn't mean we have to actually do it."

He swept her suit jacket off her shoulders and halfway down her arms. "I don't want there to be any question about the fact that we're lovers. Not a single doubt. It's the only way to explain the swiftness of our engagement. Women have a knack for sensing these things. They'll know if we're faking it."

"We're not faking our attraction. Maybe that's enough."

He levered upward. "You've been intimate with a man. You know damn well that changes things."

Her eyes opened and she gazed at him with an odd defiance. "Do I?"

"Oh, please. Don't try to play the innocent with me."

"I guess that would be pointless, wouldn't it?"

"Considering I was the one who found you with Winters? Yes." He didn't want to go there, didn't want to allow the shadow of another man to ruin the moment or slip between them. Not now. Not when he finally had her where he wanted her. "Be reasonable, Kat. You've had lovers. Think about how it is with them. The way you speak to him. Those small caresses and looks that only lovers exchange. The knowledge you gain when you've shared a bed. When you've been stripped bare and possessed by a man. It comes through in everything you do and say. In how you react on both a conscious and subconscious level."

"And we need to build that level of familiarity?"

How could she doubt it? "Yes. I want to touch you and have everyone watching sense that I've touched you just that way in bed. I want the same expression on your face and in your eyes, so everyone in the vicinity can tell that the last time you looked at me that way, our bodies were mated in the most intimate way possible."

She shuddered again and he knew his words had seduced her almost as much as his touch. "I don't want to do this." But somehow he suspected her words were meant for herself, rather than for his benefit.

His drew his fingertip along the edge of her bra, and a soft flush colored the tops of her breasts, while her breathing kicked up a notch. He lowered his head and caught her pebbled nipple between his teeth through the black lace, dampening it. The air burst from her lungs on a small cry that had him tightening in reaction, the urge to take her beyond anything he'd ever experienced before, the demand pure and elemental and unceasing. Hooking his fingers into the cups of the bra, he dragged them downward, exposing her.

She was every bit as lovely as he remembered, maybe more so. Full and round, her breasts were tipped by nipples the same shade as the skin of a ripe peach. More than anything he wanted to taste them, to see if they were as succulent as the fruit they resembled. He suspected they were. Before he could put thought to action, a brisk knock sounded at the door.

"Mr. Moretti? Lunch is ready."

Kat froze, passion transitioning to utter horror. She stared at him in disbelief. "What are we doing?"

"I believe it's called foreplay," he offered helpfully. He glanced down at her breasts. "Possibly an appetizer."

"Not any longer, it isn't." She dragged her bra into position before shoving at his shoulders. "Please, get off me."

"No appetizer?" She simply stared at him and he sighed. "I gather that means dessert's out of the question, too."

"I don't eat dessert."

He grinned. "I'd be happy to have yours."

"We're not talking about food, are we?"

Gabe spared a final glance at her breasts. "I guess it depends on your point of view." He stood and held out his hand. To his surprise, she accepted his assistance. "I assume you want to freshen up again."

She released a sigh. "Is there any point?"

"Not really." He ran his fingers through her hair, combing out the tangles while she tackled the buttons of her jacket, then attempted to smooth out a few of the creases without much success. "Besides, I like your hair down. It makes you appear more human."

A swift smile flashed across her mouth—a mouth naked of any artifice and still swollen from his kisses, he noted with satisfaction. "Human? Versus what?"

"Something unreal. Remote. Untouchable and untouched." He gave the hem of her suit jacket a gentle tug, amused to realize that the buttons weren't in the right holes. He should mention it. He really should. Or maybe not since it added immeasurably to that "human" quality. "And we both know that's not the real you."

Her expression closed down. "Since you know so much about me."

"I know enough." He gestured toward the door to the study. "Shall we?"

"I'd really prefer returning to my hotel. I'm still rather jetlagged."

He draped an arm around her waist and urged her forward. "Food will help. Dennis is an excellent chef. I'm sure you'll appreciate a good meal before I drive you to your hotel."

She didn't protest any further, following him into the informal dining room, a small, intimate area that overlooked the sprawl of green grass that tumbled toward the lake. She paused by the windows and seemed to relax infinitesimally.

"Like it?" Gabe asked.

"Who wouldn't?"

Jessa, he almost said, before catching himself in the nick of time. "Some prefer city life."

She lifted a shoulder in a quick shrug. "It has its advantages. Personally, I get tired of all the noise and constant press of humanity."

"Which is why I bought this place last year. That and the view."

She glanced at him over her shoulder. "You've owned it for only a year?"

"We lived in an apartment near my office," he answered the unspoken question. He gestured toward the table. "Shall we?"

She took her seat without another word, avoiding his gaze. Maybe it was because he'd mentioned Jessa, the ghost of his late wife creating an uncomfortable silence. He should despise Kat for the hell she'd put her cousin through, for her overall disdain toward right or wrong. For taking whatever she wanted, regardless of who she hurt in the process. At least in his mother's case, she'd attempted to do the right thing by leaving Dominic when he married another.

That didn't change the fact than when he held Kat in his arms, nothing mattered except making her his own.

Need—a need far greater than any he'd experienced with Jessa—stripped away every other impulse. There had to be an explanation. There had to be a reason he'd allow this woman to demolish lines he'd made an unwavering commitment to keep inviolate.

And he had no doubt where to place the blame. His father had been a Dante. Immoral. A cheat. A liar. Gabe had fought the Dante genes with the first breath he'd taken, and would no doubt continue to fight them until he gasped out his last. From the time he'd first understood the devastation his father had wrought in his mother's life, he'd made up his mind that he'd never become his father. Never turn into the man who'd caused his family so much suffering.

And yet… Somehow, some way those Dante genes were responsible for what had happened when he'd first touched Kat. There couldn't be any other explanation. Oh, he'd heard the ridiculous stories from his mother, though he'd never believed them. But now he wondered if there weren't some small grain of truth to what she'd revealed. Because judging by his reaction to Kat, the inner awareness coupled with the electric spark when they'd first touched, he'd been hit by the infamous Dantes' Inferno. He'd heard it described as a sort of itching burn experienced when future lovers first touched—or so his mother had claimed. As far as Gabe was concerned it was nothing more than a fairy tale his father had used to get his mother into bed.

He released his breath in a frustrated sigh. He'd hoped never to have to approach his father's family. Despised them, one and all, for their part in his mother's heartbreak and sorrow. But this Inferno business was too bizarre not to pursue. Tomorrow he'd get details, lots and lots of details, before cutting himself off from the Dantes once more. And then he'd figure out what to do about this Inferno nonsense, and more importantly, how to eradicate it.

Dennis entered with their salads before making himself scarce. Kat picked at her food for a few minutes before returning her fork to her plate. "This is ridiculous," she stated. Her gaze flashed to Gabe's. "Why am I here? I mean, seriously. What's left to discuss? You've wrung just about every possible concession from me. Can't you just let it go at that?"

He sipped the Chablis accompanying their lunch while he considered his response. "If we can't share a simple meal that doesn't bode well for our engagement."

Her mouth tilted upward in a dry smile and his gaze settled there, that blasted inner voice urging him to take those lush lips in an endless kiss and the hell with everything else, including food or consequence. "What doesn't bode well for our engagement is that you despise me."

He forced himself to look away from her mouth and focus instead on his salad. "You'll have to find a way to live with it, I'm afraid."

"Or you could cut me some slack."

He couldn't help laughing. So she wanted to be let off the hook already, did she? "Not a chance in hell, sweetheart."

She regarded him in silence for a few moments. "We're not engaged yet, which means that I still have choices available to me—including leaving."

He shrugged, unimpressed by the threat. "You can try, but we both know that you want your grandmother's inheritance too much to walk away."

"I want to reconcile with my grandmother," she corrected. "I want it very much. But not enough to spend endless months with someone who plans to make our time together so painful. Nothing's worth that."

Gabe lifted an eyebrow. "I gather we're negotiating again?"

"Yes."

Interesting. "What offer are you putting on the table?"

"I'd like to start over. Clean slate."

He shook his head. "That's not possible. You can't change what happened. What you did."

She hesitated before responding. "But we can choose to put it behind us and move on. I won't spend endless months with you, endure an engagement and...and pretend in public to be something we're not, all the while being punished by you over past events. I can't handle that."

"And if I don't agree?"

She tossed her napkin to the table. "Then you'll have to decide how badly you want your mother's necklace." She stood. "Apologize to Dennis if you would, please. I'm sure he'll understand if you explain that jetlag has finally caught up with me—which it has."

"I'll drive you back to Seattle." He could see her budding refusal and cut her off before she could say anything more. "I'll drive you back," he repeated.

She nodded, though he suspected it was more a result of exhaustion than because she saw the sense in accepting his offer. "I'll be at my hotel all day tomorrow. Feel free to call and give me your decision."

"Clean slate and a polite engagement?"

"Or I return to Europe and neither of us gets what we want."

"We don't need to wait until tomorrow. I accept your offer."

She didn't show the slightest relief. She simply nodded again and started toward the front door. He stopped her there. Unable to explain why he did it, he rebuttoned her suit jacket so the buttons and holes were properly aligned, then dropped a gentle kiss on her forehead. Hell, next he'd be tucking her into bed. Alone, no less. His mouth tightened.

He didn't have a clue what was going on, but first thing in the morning he intended to find out.

And then he intended to fix it so he could get his life back to normal.

Three

Early the next morning, Gabe left Kat a voicemail to warn he'd be out of touch that day. He took his private jet from Seattle to San Francisco, the flight proving uneventful. A car awaited him at his destination and he used the transit time into the city to finalize details on the Atkinson project. Several times he caught himself rubbing his palm, a burning itch centered there, one which had appeared the moment he first touched Kat, and continued to throb ever since. It was downright bizarre.

Since it was Saturday, they didn't experience much traffic and, in record time, pulled in front of the head office for Dantes, the jewelry empire that specialized in the one-of-a-kind Dante fire diamonds. As hoped, the place was deserted, nary a Dante in sight. Bad enough that he needed to speak to the family patriarch—his grandfather, Primo—without running into any of the legitimate side of the family. Most of them didn't even know he existed, which was precisely how Gabe preferred to keep it. He signed in at the front reception desk, accepted the guest pass and crossed to the bank of elevators that led to the executive offices. He exited on one of the upper echelon floors of the high-rise building and stepped into a foyer where even the air exuded luxury and opulence.

From the end of a long, shadow-draped corridor, a woman approached, no doubt to escort him to the office Primo still maintained, though Gabe's research indicated that his father's first legitimate son, Sev, ran Dantes. The patriarch and founder of the firm semi-retired not long after Gabe's father, Dominic, had died in a sailing accident which also claimed his wife, Laura, orphaning Sev and his three brothers. Primo's health had taken a serious hit due to the death of his eldest son, forcing him to hand the reins over to Sev. Of course, the Dantes pretended not to know about the existence of Gabe's mother, the twins, or that Dominic planned to marry her after divorcing his wife. Not that Gabe believed his father actually would have. Like all Dantes, his father liked to have his cake and eat it, too. Why else would he have been sailing with his wife?

He returned his attention to the woman and froze, instantly recognizing her hair, a distinctive blend of varying shades of brown. "What the bloody hell are you doing here?" he demanded.

She shot a quick, nervous glance over her shoulder. "Hush. I don't want anyone to hear you."

"You haven't answered my question, Lucia." Every protective instinct he possessed flared into life. He snatched her into his arms and gave her a swift, hard hug, one she returned with equal ferocity. "What are you doing here?" he repeated.

She stepped free of the embrace and offered an impish

grin, though he sensed a deeper emotion seething beneath her cheerful exterior. "I work for Primo."

"Damn it to hell." Gabe shot his hands through his hair. "Does he know who you are?"

A hint of familiar fire sparked to life in her eyes. "Of course not. I wouldn't do that without warning you first."

"*Why?*" he asked roughly. "Why, by all that's holy, would you want to have anything to do with the Dantes, after what *he* did to Mom?"

"*He.* You mean Dad." That single word contained a world of heartbreak and cut Gabe to the core. Of the three of them, his twin, Lucia, had held out the longest, certain that someday Dominic Dante would ride in on his white horse and sweep them off to live in his castle. Even after his death, she'd thought the Dantes would claim them as their own. Needless to say, that had never happened. Eventually, the fairy tale shattered, leaving nothing but devastation in its wake. "You can use the word, Gabriel. *Dad.* I swear it won't set your tongue on fire."

"Don't be so sure," he retorted. "And he wasn't our father. He was *their* father."

An all too familiar expression swept across her elegant features, one that would have done the most stubborn mule proud. "He was ours, too. Just because you don't want to know our family doesn't mean I don't."

His head jerked back as though she'd slapped him. "They are *not* our family."

"You may not want them for family, but that doesn't change the fact that they—"

Lucia broke off and for a split second her chin quivered, while tears burned in her distinctive blue-green eyes. Their mother's eyes. That, more than anything else, nearly sent Gabe to his knees. His sister, his strong, resilient twin, the woman who faced every adversity with a brave smile, hovered on the verge of tears. Without a word, he gathered her close and simply held her.

"Does it really mean that much to you?" he murmured.

"Yes." Her voice held a firm, if muffled, note. "They're all the family we have left."

He flinched. "We have each other. We'll always have each other."

"There's never been any question of that." She pulled back and cupped his face, her gaze brimming with adoration. "You're my big brother, even if it's only by four minutes."

"Five."

She laughed through her tears. "Okay, five. You've always been there when I needed you most. If you hadn't come to my rescue when—"

"Don't." It had been a brutal time, even worse than learning of their father's death. He smoothed back a lock of his sister's hair, the color so different from his own, a glorious mix of browns, from the very palest shade to the deepest. In appearance, they couldn't be any more different. But at heart… "There's no point going there."

She nodded her agreement. "You're right." Pulling free of his arms, she frowned. To his relief, she'd conquered her tears and appeared almost normal again. Almost. "So what are you doing here? I mean, since Primo isn't family."

Gabe spared a swift glance down the deserted hallway. "I have a question to ask him, one only he can answer."

She tilted her head to one side, avid curiosity sparkling in her gaze. "What question?"

"A none of your business question."

Her eyes narrowed, sharpened, and she took a step closer, catching his hand in hers. It had always been that way between them. Maybe it was because they were twins. Or maybe because they'd grown up fatherless. But there'd al-

-ways been a deep, emotional connection between them. "Something's happened. What is it?"

"Nothing that concerns you, brat." He gestured in the direction she'd come. "I'd like to get this meeting over with, if you don't mind."

She lifted her shoulders in a quick shrug. "Fine. Be all brooding and mysterious. You know you'll tell me eventually." She tossed him a teasing grin. "Admit it. You've never been able to resist me."

He wrapped her up in a quick embrace and dropped a swift, affectionate kiss on her brow. "True enough." He shot another glance toward Primo's office. "Before I meet with him, tell me what to expect. What's he like?"

She started to respond, then hesitated, shaking her head. "No, I don't believe I will. I think you should figure that out for yourself."

Aw, hell. That wasn't the least like her. She'd always been the most unguarded of all of them, her heart open to anyone and everyone—which had led her to fall in love with a bastard who'd ripped her to shreds. After that she'd grown more cautious, but never with Gabe. Her secrets were his. Until now, apparently.

"What's wrong, Lucia? What are you hiding?"

To his concern, distress peeked through, warning she hadn't fully regained her equilibrium. "I'm not hiding anything, other than my identity. I wanted to meet my grandfather in order to see what he's like without his knowing that I'm Cara Moretti's daughter. So, I'm using my married name."

"As far as I know they're only aware of my existence," he attempted to reassure. "I don't think they've discovered I have a twin."

"No, they haven't," she confirmed.

"He's hurt you somehow." He cut her off before she could speak. "Don't deny it. I can tell when you're in pain."

Lucia started to protest, but must have realized the sheer futility of it. He simply knew her too well. She released her breath in a sigh. "Okay, fine. But, just so you know, it isn't due to anything Primo's done."

"Then, what is it?"

She turned on her heel and headed down the corridor, pausing outside the door leading to Primo's suite. She kept her back to him, her spine a rigid line. "I'm his employee," she confessed in a low voice. "He's very kind to employees."

"But?"

She glanced at him over her shoulder. This time she managed to control the tears, to keep her expression calm and pleasant, which only made it all the more tragic. "That's not who I am. It's not what I am." She took a moment to gather herself, before confessing, "Oh, Gabe, I don't want to work for him. I want to be his granddaughter. I want what we never had. Family." Before he had a chance to respond, she shoved open the door and swept inside. Crossing the outer office to a second door, she knocked briskly before opening it. "Mr. Moretti is here to see you."

"Send him in."

The voice was deep and rich, flavored with his Tuscan origins. It contained an irresistible lyricism, a haunting song that felt almost familiar, striking a visceral chord within Gabe, tugging at him. Drawing him in where he most resisted going. He hesitated, torn between comforting his sister and meeting his grandfather.

Lucia took the decision from him. She stepped back and shook her head. "I'm okay." Then she held out her fist, her index finger extended to form a small hook. He did the same, linking their fingers the way their mother had taught them from the time they were babies. It was a game the three of them played, a show of unity. A way to say "I love you." A wordless code to offer strength and support. "Go," she whispered, breaking contact.

If he lingered, he'd blow her cover, and he couldn't do that to her. "This isn't over," he warned in an undertone. Then he stepped into the room and came face-to-face with a man who revealed what Gabe would look like in another fifty or so years.

Primo slowly stood, drinking him in. "You look so much like your brother Severo, you could be twins," he marveled.

Gabe fought not to flinch. "I don't consider him my brother."

Primo shrugged. "This does not surprise me. It is understandable you would feel this way about all of us. What your father did was wrong."

Okay, that surprised him. "I agree."

His grandfather released a husky laugh. "You did not expect me to say that about my own son, eh?" He flipped open an intricately carved humidor resting on his desk and selected a cigar. He gestured toward the box. "Would you like?"

"I believe it's illegal to smoke those in an office."

Primo snorted. "What? You are going to call the cigar police on me?"

"That depends on how our conversation goes."

The two men stared at each other for a split second. Then Primo broke the silence with a loud laugh. He circled the desk and approached Gabe. Sweeping his grandson into his arms, he gave him a long, hard hug, slapping his back with an iron hand. "I never thought to see this day, Gabriel." He gave the name its Italian pronunciation.

Gabe stiffened, totally unprepared for both the embrace and how to handle it. Finally, he gave the old man a thump

on the back. Based on Primo's gusty sigh, it seemed to satisfy him. He released Gabe and stepped back.

"I don't think you understand why I'm here," Gabe began.

Golden eyes, identical to his, stared at him. They were
wise, ancient eyes, filled with understanding and sadness,
joy and resignation. "I thank you for contacting me, even if
it was not in order to meet your *nonno*."

Gabe lowered his head. "Aw, hell." This was definitely
not going the way he'd intended.

"This is not going the way you intended, no?"

Crap. The Dante patriarch could even read his mind.
Gabe looked up, deciding to be direct. After all, for better
or worse, that's who he was. "No, it's not."

"You think…I come, I force myself to be polite to the
old man. I ask my question. And I leave before he can touch
my heart or infect my mind." Primo's index finger thumped
first against Gabe's chest, then his temple. "But it is too late.
There I am, like a…a—" He broke off with a frown. "What
animal burrows in where it does not belong?"

"You, apparently."

Primo barked out another laugh. In a practiced move, he
trimmed his cigar and lit it. "We keep the cigar a secret between the two of us, yes? Nonna will nag me into little pieces
if she finds out. Then she will report me to my *dottore*."

How had it happened? How had this canny old man managed to get to him? Because he was right. Gabe had planned
to show up, hold himself at a careful distance, ask his damn
question and then get the hell out. Instead, he stood there,
fascinated. Is that how it had been with his mother? Had
Dominic been equally charming, burrowing through his
mother's defenses until she'd given her heart and soul to the
man who'd fathered her two children?

"I'm not like him." He had no idea where the words came

from. They were out before he even realized he intended to speak them.

A deep sadness flickered across Primo's expressive face. "No, you are not," he agreed softly. "Any more than Severo or Marco, Lazzaro or Nicolò are like him. You all possess a moral compass he lacked. I am sorry for what he did to you. And I am sorry I did not find you sooner."

Find him sooner? Was it possible the rest of the Dantes *didn't* know about him and Lucia? No. Not a chance. Not that he'd confront Primo over the issue. There wasn't any point. "It doesn't matter. I had no interest in knowing any of you."

Primo brushed aside the comment, refusing to accept it. "You are here now, are you not?"

Gabe caught himself rubbing the itch centered in his palm again, a gesture that drew his grandfather's attention and prompted an odd smile. "I'm only here because I have a question."

Primo settled a hip on the edge of his desk and blew out a stream of smoke, eyeing his grandson through the haze. The Cheshire Cat, all grin and knowing eyes. "Many questions, I would think."

"Just one."

"Fine." Primo gestured with his cigar. "You ask your question. I will answer if I am able."

"Something happened recently." Now that the time had come, he realized he didn't quite know how to phrase what had happened without sounding crazy. "Something…odd."

Laughter deepened the lines in the old man's face, one that contained a peculiar understanding. "Did it? Interesting." He examined the glowing tip of his cigar. "This odd thing that happened recently, I do not suppose it occurred with a woman?"

Gabe froze. "Son of a bitch," he whispered. "You know, don't you?"

"Know what?"

Gabe spun on his heel and stalked the length of the room, struggling to contain his anger. How was it possible? For years he'd perfected his iceman reputation, right up until Kat had swept into his office and utterly decimated it. And now his grandfather... Between the two of them, he was lucky to retain any control at all. More than anything he wanted to walk out and never return. But he couldn't. Not until he uncovered the truth.

He turned to face Primo, surrendering to the pressing demand for answers. "Okay, what the hell was it? All I did was touch her and—"

"And you burned for her." His grandfather gestured with his cigar. "Your palm. It itches, an itch that will not go away."

"Yes! Yes, damn it." He yanked at his tie, the knot threatening to choke him. "That's precisely what happened. What was it?"

"The Inferno, of course. Did Dominic never tell your mother about it?"

Gabe hesitated. "He told her some sort of fairy tale about Dantes being able to tell their soul mates with one touch."

"There you are, then. Your question, it is answered." Primo lifted a snowy eyebrow. "Is there anything else?"

"What do you mean, *is there anything else?*" His temper blew, scorching through the last of his iciness. "The Inferno? Are you serious? That's not real. It's simply another fairy tale, one told to our mother and exaggerated in the scandal sheets after Marco's little media stunt. But it doesn't actually exist."

"I assure you, *nipote*, it does exist. The Inferno is no fairy tale. You ignore it at your own risk."

Gabe's eyes narrowed. "Explain that. What risk?"

"You touched a woman." Primo's voice softened, yet the lyricism intensified. It wove a web with words, the music of his Tuscan origins wrapping around Gabe and sinking into him until it became part and parcel of who and what he was at the very core. "You felt the fire of The Inferno. Felt this itch and burn that will not stop. That is because this woman, she is your soul mate. Now you must marry her or suffer the consequences as your father did when he refused to marry his Inferno mate."

"What consequences?" Gabe demanded.

Primo's grip tightened on his cigar. "I told my Dominic to marry your mother." His accent deepened with raw emotion and his hands danced through the air, their sweeping movements leaving graceful swirls of smoke in their wake. "I warn him, do not turn from this woman. But he thought he could have it all—your mother, an Inferno soul mate, and the wealth Laura could bring to their marriage."

Primo encouraged his parents to marry? No. No, his father had claimed Primo had prevented the marriage. Had forbidden it. "I don't believe you."

Primo shrugged. "You may believe what you will, *nipote*. It will not change what happened. You see this marriage of Dominic's, how poorly it worked out for him. It has always been so with The Inferno." He kept his unwavering focus on Gabe, his calm sincerity giving weight to his claim. "We are different, Gabriel. Dantes only love one woman for all of their lives. We must follow where it leads, take the woman it selects for us, or suffer the consequences. And there are always consequences if we turn from The Inferno. Your father, he discovered the truth of this."

Gabe froze. That's when it hit him. Kat Malloy. If Primo was right, *she* was his Inferno mate. No. Oh, hell no. "I am *not* a Dante," he stated. Insisted. Or—*damn it*—did he beg? "This has nothing to do with me. It can't. I won't let it."

Sorrow tarnished Primo's eyes. "You have always been a Dante. You always will be a Dante."

"You're wrong." He rejected the premise with a cutting sweep of his hand. "I am nothing like Dominic. I refuse to be like him. Like any of you. I'm a Moretti."

"If you truly were, you would not experience The Inferno. But you have." Primo knocked ash off the end of his cigar and approached. He dropped a hand on Gabe's shoulder and gave it a hard squeeze. "I understand this resentment you feel for us. How you must despise us. But do not think for one moment that Dominic represents the Dantes. He is a Dante despite what he did to Cara and Laura and all his children. That is not how we raised him. The choices he made, they were his own, just as your choices are your own. You can choose to listen to what I have told you, or you can follow in the unfortunate footsteps of your father and ignore what I have said. The Inferno, it will have its way, no matter which you choose."

Okay. Okay, he could handle this. Of course he could. After all, he and Kat were planning to become engaged. Inferno condition sort of met, right? Maybe enough to skate by? "I plan to become engaged to her. That takes care of The Inferno problem, I assume?"

Primo inclined his head. "If you marry her, yes."

"And if we don't marry?"

His grandfather replied with a silent shrug, one that seemed almost ominous.

"What does it matter whether or not we marry? Married or engaged, I plan to end our relationship as soon as this Inferno runs its course," Gabe informed his grandfather. Or was it more in nature of a warning?

"Excellent."

Gabe's brows shot upward. "Really? I'm surprised you agree."

Primo shrugged. "If you wait until The Inferno runs its course, you have a very long wait. Nonna and I, we have been married for sixty years and I am still waiting for The Inferno to run its course. I am sure it will not last very much longer. Maybe next year my palm, it will stop itching, yes?" He shot Gabe a wicked grin from around his cigar. "Then again… Maybe not."

Kat despised her public dates with Gabe, though she did her best to hide her reaction behind a calm, remote façade. Christmas hung in the air, just two short weeks away. It scented everything with cedar and cinnamon, and danced in every store window. Santa and his reindeer, along with stylized Christmas trees, and pretty winter scenes decorated the outside of colorful packages slung over shoppers' arms, clear evidence of the seasonal spending spree. Despite that, she hadn't quite found her Christmas spirit. Maybe it had something to do with how painful her dates with Gabe had become.

Even after more than three weeks and a dozen or so similar engagements, their arrival at any given venue never failed to stir a wave of interest. Kat hoped the attention would rouse a response from her grandmother. Approval. Disapproval. Something. But so far, she'd remained pointedly silent, neither phoning nor responding to calls. At least Kat had been able to confirm that Matilda's silence wasn't a result of her illness.

The fascinated whispers followed them to their table, one that couldn't have been more centrally located if they sat on a spotlighted dais. This is what she'd experienced after the scandal with senatorial candidate Benson Winters broke. The avid attention. The nasty comments, made just loud enough for her to hear. The press hounding her. The shame and embarrassment. It had marked her, leaving painful scars, even after five full years, just as it had ruined Benson's shot at a Senate seat. Of course, the scandal had only been part of the reason, the other being the tell-all book his ex-wife released immediately afterward.

Gabe bared his teeth in a parody of a smile. "If you don't stop looking at me as though I were a meal you regret ordering, people will never believe we're falling in love."

"We're not falling in love."

"No, we're not," he agreed. For some reason the promptness of his reply hurt. "But we're attempting to convince others that we're not just falling, but have fallen deeply, passionately, madly in love. At the very least, a smile would be an excellent place to start."

"Fine." She made an effort to relax and smile. "Maybe if we exchange normal, casual conversation it will help."

"Anything is worth a try if it means you stop looking at me like you're on the verge of bolting." He tilted his head to one side. "How about this… Tell me about your time in Europe. Where did you live? What did you do?"

Okay, that was more comfortable ground, at least for the most part. "I lived in Italy, Florence to be exact. I worked as a barista, among several other jobs, and attended school."

"What were you studying?"

"Jewelry design."

So much for comfortable ground. For some reason her response caused Gabe's expression to close over. It figured. It would seem they couldn't even manage casual conversation. The only time the two of them experienced any sort of accord was in each other's arms.

"Jewelry design," he repeated.

"For two years." His reaction caused her to proceed with caution. She tiptoed a tiny bit deeper into the conversational landmine. "Then I apprenticed for the next three, determined to learn as much as I could in order to have a shot at working for the best of the best."

"And who do you consider the best of the best?" he asked softly.

For some reason, she stiffened, going on high alert. She couldn't explain it, her reaction was so immediate and visceral. One minute she saw a normal, rational male sitting across from her. The next she saw a fierce predator, ready to rip her to shreds at the first wrong word. "Dantes." And there it was. The wrong word. She broke into hurried speech. "I fell in love with Heart's Desire years ago, was always begging Gam to show me her necklace. I wanted to learn how to create jewelry just like it. From…from the best." She trailed off. "What's wrong, Gabe?" Because something was wrong. Terribly wrong.

He stared at her through narrowed eyes, as though attempting to see all she kept hidden from him. "An interesting coincidence, that's all."

"What's an interesting coincidence?" She hesitated, then asked, "Does this have something to do with your necklace?"

Instead of answering her question, he changed the subject. "What do you say we leave the restaurant, find the nearest bed and get naked? Maybe then we can establish a workable connection."

The total non sequitur caught her off guard and it took her a split second to recover her balance. Heat flooded through her and—if she were being brutally honest—so did blatant hunger. "I have no intention of leaving the restaurant and finding the nearest bed, let alone getting naked," she informed him, inordinately pleased with the crispness of her tone.

Granted, her voice tripped a bit over that last word, tripped enough that she reached for her coffee cup, changing her mind the instant she saw the telltale tremor of her fingers. Instead, she folded her hands in her lap and rubbed at an itch centered in her palm. For some reason it had been driving her crazy over the past few weeks.

Gabe shrugged. "Fine. If you're not hungry for food, we can always get the hell out of here and spend our lunch consummating our agreement."

Of course, she wanted to do just that. She wanted to consummate with every fiber of her being. Her toes curled in her Fendi slings at the very suggestion. She simply did not plan to follow through on her base desires. Still... If only he hadn't used that particular word. No, not consummate, although that sent her respiratory system into overdrive, as well. The one he'd used earlier. *Naked.*

That single word thrust amazing images into her head. Shocking images. Images she had no business painting, especially in such vibrant, glorious colors. It was wrong, wrong, wrong. Not that all that wrongness changed a damn thing. More than anything in the world, she wanted to see Gabe Moretti naked. Then she wanted his lovely nakedness poured over and into her like warm, creamy butter. She snatched up her cup—trembling fingers be damned—and buried her nose in the steam rising from the coffee, praying the warmth sweeping across her face would be attributed to heat, rather than sheer, unadulterated lust. No such luck.

His laugh held a dark richness that also reminded her of butter. "What *are* you thinking, Ms. Malloy? Whatever it is, it's gotten you all hot and bothered."

She kept her attention focused on her coffee. "It's irritation. Having to pretend to want you irritates me."

His laugh grew. Deepened. "Liar. You can't even look at me. I wonder why? Could it be that you're not pretending, that you really do want me?" He leaned forward and took the cup from her, setting it aside. He laced his fingers with hers so their palms bumped together. Somehow the bubbling heat intensified from a low simmer to just shy of a rolling boil. "I have no objection to skipping the foreplay and getting straight to the consummating, if that's what you prefer."

Four

Kat's gaze snapped to Gabe's. Big mistake. Huge. Desire flooded through her, throbbing with painful insistence, making it nearly impossible to force out a laugh, though she gave it her best shot. "Leaving the restaurant, finding a bed and stripping off our clothes is your idea of foreplay?"

His slow smile threatened to melt her into a puddle of molten desire. Where had her cool and calm gone, let alone her collected? Straight into that puddle of lava, if she didn't miss her guess. The waiter arrived just then and placed their orders in front of them. To her intense disappointment, Gabe released her hand. How was it possible that something so ridiculously simple as his withdrawing his touch could stir such an intense sensation of loss? She really was losing it.

He waited until they were alone again before responding. "Yes, getting the hell out of this place, sweeping you off to the apartment above my office—which conveniently has a bed—and stripping you out of that elegant, though unnecessary dress, is my idea of foreplay. Allow me to explain."

Kat drew a deep breath. *Focus, woman. And great, big postscript... Not on sex!* "This I have to hear."

He leaned toward her and lowered his voice. "Once we're done picking at our food—because who can eat when all we can think about is—"

"Consummating?" she inserted dryly.

"Exactly. We wait for the bill to come. Anyone watching can tell we're impatient to leave. We can't keep our hands off each other. Nothing overt, of course. Just glancing brushes. Little strokes and caresses."

Palms bumping.

Kat set her coffee aside and deliberately folded her hands in her lap. "Funny. My hands have informed me they're perfectly happy right where they are."

"They're lying." He lifted an eyebrow. "I can prove it, if you'd like."

Kat shrugged. "You can try. And you can fail."

That last comment might have been a mistake. Gabe's eyes brightened, flashing with a wicked light. "Ah, a challenge."

"That's not what I—"

"Too late to take it back now. I accept."

"But, I—" She glared at him. Okay, how bad could it get? They sat at a table in a public venue, with countless diners and staff looking on. They were both properly dressed and coiffed. Unless he planned to dump her on top of her *moules marinères* and have his wicked way with her, she was quite safe. How hard would it be to resist his brand of foreplay? "Fine. Do your worst."

His smile returned, slow and seductive. Uh-oh. Maybe she shouldn't have said that. He reached for her fork and scooped a mussel from its shell, offering it to her. As much as she wanted to refuse, she couldn't bring herself to do it in front of a roomful of diners. Determined not to be seduced, she accepted the bite. The flavor burst across her tongue while his gaze locked onto her lips so that she could almost feel his mouth on hers. For some reason, the cream, butter and garlic became spiced with the memory of his kisses.

"That's not fair," she complained.

"Tempted, sweetheart?"

If she were the type to pout, which she most definitely was not, she would have pouted. "Only for more mussels."

"What a terrible liar you are. You just don't want to admit that I'm seducing you in a restaurant. That everyone watching knows precisely what I want to do to you. What you're hoping I'll do to you."

Her lashes swept downward. "I have no idea what you're talking about."

He didn't bother arguing the point. Instead, he proved it by taking her hand in his once again and stroking his index finger in a tantalizing circle around her palm. A palm that itched and throbbed, and had ever since the first time he'd touched her. How did he know? She'd never considered her hand particularly sensitive before. But ever since meeting him… His index finger stroked her palm and every bone in her body liquefied. If he didn't stop, she'd end up sliding under the table where she'd let him consummate their deal. Several times.

Kat shuddered, well aware that her expression revealed every amoral thought and desire. "I can't believe this. Why you? Why now? I mean, this is insane."

"Agreed. Not that it changes anything." He tilted his head to one side. "Are you ready to concede that I win the first round?"

"Only if you agree it ends here."

Clearly, he didn't like the sound of that. "Explain."

She wanted him more than she'd wanted any other man she'd ever met. But there were lines she refused to cross. Lines she'd drawn to protect herself from the sort of pain she'd experienced five years ago. Lines that were an indelible part of who and what she'd become as a result of all she'd been through.

Kat released a sigh. "I don't want to go to bed with you. I won't sleep with anyone until I'm married."

"It's that important to you?"

She nodded, picking at her food, just as he'd predicted. For some reason, her appetite had evaporated. "Yes, it is."

"Why?" he demanded in abject frustration.

Kat hesitated, shrugged. "I won't have sex with you because—whether you believe me or not—it's who I am."

"And you think we can ignore this…?"

Gabe took her hand for the third time, lacing their fingers so their palms mated, one to the other. Heat flared, flashing from his hand to hers and she barely controlled the shudder that threatened to rip her apart. What the hell was that? Where did it come from? Why had it happened? Why Gabe Moretti of all people, when he was the last person in the entire universe she should sleep with?

She attempted to tug her hand free, to escape whatever held them, bound them. But he refused to let go. She closed her eyes, battling the wash of emotions that poured through her. "What is that?" she demanded between gritted teeth.

"The Inferno, or so I've been told."

"I don't understand. What is The Inferno?"

"Desire. Need. Lust."

She looked at him, even though she knew her look told him far too much. "Please," she whispered, not above begging. "Let me go." To her everlasting relief, he did so. She dragged air into her lungs, and sat back in her chair, her spine a rigid line. But at least she could think straight again. Somewhat. "I still don't understand."

"A restaurant isn't the best place for this conversation." He fished out his wallet, removed a couple sizeable bills and tossed them onto the table. "Let's go."

"Go where?" It was a foolish question. She knew. She knew precisely what he wanted and where he intended to take her.

"Anywhere with a bed," he said, confirming her suspicion.

Oh, God. If he attempted to take her to bed, she'd surrender to him…and he knew it, agreement be damned. Indelible lines be damned. Both of them damned by this churning, endless, inescapable want. All he had to do was touch her and she lost all ability to think straight. All he had to do was kiss her and she found herself on her back with her clothing half removed, offering herself like the sort of woman he believed her to be.

"Gabe, you promised."

"No, I didn't. I'm not sure I'm capable of making such a promise. I always believed I could control this sort of thing." A muscle in his jaw tightened. "Now I'm not so sure. But I do promise to try."

He held out his hand. Aware of all eyes on them, she took it, allowing him to draw her from the table and assist her with her coat. Unfortunately, no one else thought they would try to control themselves. They already saw the fall, an inevitable one. Amused whispers escorted them toward the exit. They almost made it to the door when disaster struck. The hostess led a party into the dining room, two women and two men. One of the men paused and caught her hand in his, spinning her around.

"Kat? Kat Malloy? Is that you?"

She paused, startled. "Benson?" Oh, no. Of all the people

to run into, today of all days. And in front of so many witnesses, all still watching with avid interest. She regarded him warily, not quite sure what to expect. When the scandal broke he'd loudly declared his innocence and had insisted she set him up, claiming he'd expected to find Jessa in the suite, not Kat. That she'd attempted to trick him in an effort to seduce her cousin's fiancé. Not that anyone believed him, any more than they believed her, especially once his ex-wife's tell-all hit the stores. "How are you?" seemed the safest comment to make.

He didn't appear to notice anything amiss. He was a tall, gorgeous man, hovering within shouting distance of forty, his blond hair, brilliant blue eyes and rugged build clear evidence of his Norwegian ancestry. The smile he aimed at Kat held both charm and sincerity. "I had no idea you were back in town. If I had I would have called." He gave her hand a squeeze. "I need to talk to you when you have a free moment. There's something I'd like to say. Will you call my office so we can arrange a convenient time to get together?"

Gabe came to stand directly behind Kat, resting a possessive hand on her shoulder. "Winters," he said, his voice as cold as the man's name.

Benson glanced at him, a wrinkle of confusion ridging his brow before clearing as he made the connection. His smile faded. "Moretti, isn't it?"

"Yes." His gaze settled on Kat's hand, still held in Winters'. "I strongly recommend you let go of my fiancée." Silence settled over the dining room at his comment.

Benson instantly released Kat. "Sorry, I didn't realize…" He frowned. "Did you say *fiancée?*"

Kat stepped free of Gabe's hold and turned to face him. "What are you talking about?"

"I'm talking about our engagement."

"There is no engagement."

"Yet," he corrected. "There is no engagement, yet. That's where we were going." He spoke to her, but the full power of those tawny eyes remained focused on Winters. "To discuss our engagement before I carry you off to bed."

His comment seemed to echo across the room. Kat closed her eyes, praying the earth would open beneath her feet and simply swallow her whole. No such luck. The silence stretched. Benson finally broke it with a quick laugh. "Well, congratulations, Moretti. You picked a real winner this time."

Kat caught her breath in dismay. They needed to leave, now, before that little shot struck home. She offered Benson a brilliant smile, slipped her arm through Gabe's and made tracks for the exit. They had just swung through the heavy wood and glass doors when the words impacted, slapping at him with the same harshness as the brisk, late December wind sweeping through the city's cement canyons.

"This time?" Gabe's eyes caught fire and he attempted to do a swift one-eighty. Kat clung to him and forcibly ushered him away from the restaurant. "What the bloody hell did he mean, *this time?*"

Damn, damn, damn. "Nothing. I'm sure he didn't mean anything by it."

"The hell he didn't."

"I'm sure it was just a figure of speech."

"It wasn't Jessa's fault their engagement ended."

No. Full blame rested on Kat and Benson's heads, or so Gabe believed, especially after witnessing the affectionate interaction between the "guilty" parties. His beloved Jessa was the innocent victim, whose name and reputation he'd protect at all costs. It was a battle Kat couldn't win, not here and now—or anywhere else, for that matter. So instead, she towed Gabe down the sidewalk and past the beautifully decorated storefront windows dressed in Christmas attire, biting her tongue the entire way. She could only hope he didn't force the issue and return to the restaurant to insist Benson explain the crack. The faint strands of "Silver Bells" slipped from a nearby department store, along with a crowd of laughing customers. Maybe it would have a soothing influence on Gabe's subconscious.

"Bastard," he muttered. So much for a soothing influence.

"Let it go." Kat scrambled for a way to divert the conversation. "We were going somewhere private so you could explain this Inferno thing to me, remember?"

To her relief, she succeeded in distracting him. "No, we were going somewhere private so I could seduce you. Or, attempt to seduce you."

"No, thank you," she said politely.

He shot her a grim smile. "You can try to say no, but I don't think either of us are having much luck with that."

"No seducing." *Please. Please seduce me.* No! No, she didn't mean to think that. Ever. "Maybe we should discuss the engagement you just announced."

"That will definitely be one of the topics under discussion afterward."

"Afterward?" A full-blown picture erupted in her mind of the two of them curled together, gasping out their sexual release, his parts so entwined with her parts they were almost impossible to distinguish. Between her crazed imagination and her grip on Gabe's arm, happy signals flooded prime areas of her body, areas that hadn't known any happiness in a very long time. She hastened to release him and step away, a bitter-cold chill settling into the gap. "There will be no afterward because there won't be a beforeward. There will only be a discussion, and that held at a distance. A safe distance."

"Again, we can try." He scratched the palm of his right hand as though attempting to ease an itch centered there.

"Not sure it'll work considering The Inferno's 'unsafety' perimeter extends to at least San Francisco without any signs of diminishing."

She didn't quite get the San Francisco comment, but the way he scratched his palm was all too familiar. She'd been doing the exact same thing. And near as she could trace it back, the itch began at his Medina home when he'd first taken her hand in his and set off that bizarre burn that raced from her palm, straight through to the core of her. What the hell was going on? Somehow he'd contaminated her. Infected her with whatever infected him. She struggled not to scratch at her palm, too. One way or another she intended to get answers, though perhaps not in the middle of a bustling, downtown sidewalk, with the Christmas rush swirling around them.

"You are aware you've informed a key segment of Seattle we're engaged to be married after just three weeks of dating," she thought to mention.

Gabe stopped mid-step and scrubbed his hands over his face. "I did, didn't I? What the hell was I thinking?"

"I have no clue." She reached for his arm, catching herself at the last second. Best not to touch the pretty, sexy man again or let him touch her. Last time he did, she found herself flat on her back, decadently splayed, displayed and turned into a tasty appetizer. "Gabe, no one is going to believe we decided to get married after such a brief acquaintance."

He continued toward their destination, forcing her to keep up or be left standing in the middle of the sidewalk. "We wanted people talking." He shrugged. "This will do it."

"True, though I suspect the sort of talk they'll be exchanging won't work in our favor."

He opened the door to his office building and ushered her inside. Nodding to the receptionist, he headed for the elevators. "Let's go upstairs and discuss how we want to handle this. Come up with a game plan."

The elevator doors slid open and Kat stepped inside. "How about this for a game plan... How about you stop telling people we're engaged until we actually are?"

Gabe stabbed the button for the appropriate floor. "And how about you stay away from Benson Winters?"

The non sequitur threw her off balance. "Really? I mean, *really?*" *Oh, great comeback, Kat.*

"Considering the man put one hundred percent of the blame on you for your affair—told the media you tricked him into coming to that hotel room—he seemed pretty damned friendly today. Why is that, I wonder? Not that it takes much thought or imagination. It's clear to me that he was lying through his shiny white teeth about being innocent and tried to throw you under the bus to salvage his run at the Senate. No one could be that friendly toward a woman who totally screwed over his life. I guarantee he doesn't greet his ex-wife the way he did you."

"Maybe because she wrote that tell-all," Kat shot back. "That alone would have put paid to his bid for the Senate, even if we hadn't been accused of having an affair."

He turned to confront her, taking up far too much of an elevator car that seemed to be shrinking by the second. He even seemed to be using up too much of the air, taking far more than his fair share. "So, I repeat. Stay the hell away from the man. I won't have your ex-lovers ending our engagement before it's even started."

Fury ripped through her. "How, in any way, shape or form is that meeting my fault? It was sheer coincidence that we bumped into him. And just for the record? He's *not* my ex-lover."

"Bull. I know the truth, Kat. I was married to Jessa, remember? She gave me chapter and verse about you and

Winters. Not to mention what I witnessed with my own two eyes." Heat rolled off him, raising the temperature in the close confines of the elevator. "Nor do I believe in co-incidences, not when it comes to you two."

"Well, start. Because that's all it was." She didn't bother addressing his comment about Jessa. What was the point? He'd never believe her. Instead, she planted her hands on her hips, fighting to remain cool and calm. She didn't bother with composed this time. She didn't have a hope of attaining it. "And FYI? We're likely to run into him again in the future. He may not be a senator, but he is a renowned businessman who will undoubtedly receive invitations to some of those high profile events you want us attending. In fact, I'm shocked we haven't run into him before this."

He took a step in her direction, leaning in. He towered over her, despite the added inches her high heels afforded. Everything about him exuded pure masculine strength, lethal in its ability to devastate every one of her defenses. Beneath his anger she caught a surge of hunger, a silent roar of need that tugged at her, stirring an answering need.

"I don't want you talking to him," Gabe insisted. "It defeats the entire purpose of our engagement."

"Do you think I don't get that? I'm not stupid," she informed him. "I understand precisely what sort of threat Benson poses. Just like I get your need to stake your claim, to warn other males away from what you regard as your property. Well, newsflash, Moretti. I'm not your property."

"Yet," he snapped. "You're not my property. *Yet.* I'm sure you understand how important it is to change that small detail from perception to fact. Which is why I need to do this…"

He fisted his hands in the collar of her wool coat and yanked her onto her toes. Then he took her mouth in a kiss that exhilarated every bit as much as it devastated. The emotions she'd attempted to hold at bay crashed down on her, swamping thought and reason and all inclinations but one. Consummation. Now. She wrapped her arms around Gabe's neck and thrust her fingers deep into his hair, dragging him closer. Then she opened to him, gave him everything she possessed before taking with a demanding greed that left him groaning in pleasure.

His hold shifted from her coat to cup her face, tilting her head to give him better access to her mouth. Butter. He really was like butter, melting on her and over her and in her. She felt her knot of hair loosen and slide down her back, and couldn't help laughing against his mouth. She didn't understand why he always tugged her hair free, but for some reason he didn't like it confined. He shoved her coat from her shoulders, leaving it to pool at her feet. Then he was kissing her again, the demand growing with each passing second, the blistering heat inching toward unbearable levels.

Kat had no idea what might have happened—though she had a nasty suspicion it involved the floor of the elevator and the emergency stop button—if the subtle ding warning that the doors were about to open hadn't brought her to her senses. With a soft gasp, she yanked herself free of his arms an instant before the doors parted, leaving her the most exposed and vulnerable she'd felt since being discovered naked in Benson Winters' hotel room.

Gabe swore beneath his breath and swiftly stepped in front of Kat to block the scrutiny of an elderly woman who stood near the elevator doors, clearly about to enter. Neither woman had recognized the other—yet. With luck, the few extra seconds he could provide Kat would give her time to recover her poise.

"Matilda, this is a surprise." He leaned against the elevator doors to hold them open, blocking the interior of the car with his broad shoulders. Behind him he heard a swift, horrified gasp. "If you're here to see me, your timing is perfect."

As always, Matilda dressed impeccably. A silk Italian scarf in a wash of ocean blues accentuated eyes the soft turquoise of a Caribbean sea, while her winter-white wool suit provided a stunning complement to hair of the same shade. "I'm here to determine whether or not the rumors I've heard are true. I can scarcely credit they are."

"That depends on what you've heard."

He'd given Kat as much time as he could. Turning, he swept her coat from the floor of the elevator and fit his hand to the small of her back. He ushered her from the elevator car, careful to act as a solid bulwark separating the two women.

"Katerina!" Based on Matilda's shocked look, she hadn't noticed her granddaughter until that moment. Equally apparent was her abrupt and profound awareness of what Kat and Gabe had been doing during their elevator ride. She took a wobbly step backward and Gabe caught her arm in order to steady her. Her gaze flashed from him to her granddaughter, a certain desperate intensity lurking in her expression. "Then it's true? The two of you are involved?"

Even more gut-wrenching than Matilda's reaction was Kat's expression. The utter devastation and bittersweet longing with which she regarded her grandmother threatened to tear Gabe apart. "Gam," she whispered, and he could practically hear her heart break over that single word.

Once again, they were the center of all eyes. "Why don't we continue this discussion in my office?" he suggested.

The instant they were closeted behind the heavy barrier of his oak door, he assisted Matilda into a chair in the sitting area near the wet bar. "I have brandy." He gave Kat a subtle jerk of his head. "It's in the decanter on the left. Would you pour your grandmother a small glass?"

"Thank you," Matilda murmured. "I'd appreciate that."

To his surprise, Kat hesitated. "Your doctor won't object? It's safe for you to have a drink?"

Matilda stiffened and to Gabe's surprise she, too, hesitated. Her gaze flitted to the windows just over his shoulder, fixing on the wintery sky, laden with dark, heavy rain clouds. "At this point, it hardly matters," she said, and shivered. "I can feel the cold all the way to my bones. To be honest, I could use a small sip of brandy."

He took a seat across from her, studying her closely, examining her for any changes in the six months since he'd last run into her. It had been at an art exhibit for a small museum where she served as docent. She seemed more tired in comparison, a bit frailer, perhaps. But her gaze still burned with a power that defied the weaknesses of old age. Keen intelligence glittered there, while strength and experience lined a face more handsome than beautiful. And yet, he could also see the vulnerability, a perfect match to her granddaughter's.

"I'm sorry to hear you haven't been well," he told her.

"That's a polite way of putting it."

"It's serious, then."

She lifted her shoulder in a dismissive shrug and smiled calmly. "Does it matter? After all, life is a terminal illness, isn't it? From the moment we're born, we march inevitably toward death. It just comes down to when."

Crystal chattered in jarring disagreement. "Sorry," Kat murmured. "I seem to be all thumbs today. Must be the cold." She approached, offering her grandmother a small snifter of pale brown brandy, tinged with the tiniest hint of red.

For a moment their gazes locked and Gabe could feel the tension vibrating between them. He could see the words

bottled between them, words neither dared speak for fear
of what might escape. The risk of what might be said—or
the even greater risk of what remained unsaid. And yet it
hovered there, darkening the air with painful emotions, still
unresolved. Of accusations and declarations. Of regret and
recrimination.

But most intense of all was the helpless yearning ema-
nating from Kat. The way she reached for her grandmother,
the offer of brandy as intimate as a touch. And he saw something similar in Matilda's expression, in the gentle manner
in which she took the snifter, the unnecessary brushing of
hands during the exchange. The way they both attempted
to make the lingering of fingertips look pragmatic and de-
tached when everything about them brimmed with intense
emotion and need.

Then the moment passed, never to be recaptured, leaving the words unspoken and the emotions tightly contained.
Matilda sipped her brandy and Kat returned to the wet bar
to pour two more drinks. He noticed she poured herself a
double, and accepted the tumbler she offered. No lingering
of fingertips with him. And there sure as hell weren't any
soulful gazes. Deliberately, he caught her hand in his and
pulled her down beside him before turning his attention to
her grandmother.

"So, what brings you out on such a cold, blustery day,
Matilda?"

She didn't answer right away, but simply regarded them
over the rim of her snifter, taking in the way he held Kat's
hand. "I already told you. I came to discover the truth. Now
I can see for myself that you are involved."

"Gam, please," Kat whispered.

Gabe wasn't quite sure whether she was asking for per-
mission or approval, or perhaps was offering an apology.

But Matilda ignored her, keeping her gaze fixed on him, instead. "Is it serious?"

"We're engaged," he replied gently.

"That seems rather sudden."

"It is," he agreed. "But when it's right, it's right."

Now she did spare Kat a look and he realized why she'd ignored her granddaughter up to this point. She was afraid. Afraid she'd shatter if she spoke to Kat directly. Sure enough, she turned back to him, holding on by a thread. "You're engaged, despite what happened five years ago? Despite what she did to Jessa?"

He waited a beat, then shrugged. "Jessa and I never would have married if it hadn't happened. She'd have married Benson Winters instead."

"Perhaps," Matilda surprised him by whispering, heavy doubt underscoring that single word. Her fingers tightened around the brandy snifter, blanching white beneath the pressure. "I should tell you I always hoped you'd marry my granddaughter. Once upon a time I thought I would try my hand at matchmaking. It seemed to offer such nice symmetry when it came to Heart's Desire. But…" She shrugged. "Events got in the way."

Intrigued, he asked, "You were going to try your hand at matchmaking with me and Jessa?"

Matilda shook her head. "Not Jessa. Kat. It was always my intention to give her Heart's Desire."

Kat jerked in surprise and Gabe chose his response with care. "Well, as it turns out, you were right, though no matchmaking needed, apparently."

A ghost of a smile touched Matilda's lips. "Yes, I can see that. It's all worked out on its own. I'm relieved since Kat loved that necklace from the day she first set eyes on it." Her gaze flickered in Kat's direction, clung, then shifted back to Gabe. "I suspect it's part of the fabric of who she is. I also suspect it's part of the fabric of who she's become."

The observation gave him an odd jolt. Heart's Desire was also part of the fabric of who he was and who he'd become, and he couldn't help but wonder how the cloth that formed his life compared to Kat's. "Why not just sell the necklace to me, outright?"

"I have my reasons." Her tone sounded a shade defensive and she swept a hand through the air in clear dismissal. "Besides, now that you're engaged, it's no longer an issue. You'll have the necklace soon enough. At least, your wife will."

"Gam, the necklace belongs to Gabe," Kat broke in. "I have no objection if you sell it to him. As you say, once we're married, it won't matter, right?"

"I won't sell the necklace," Matilda retorted. "I don't need or want the money. I promised I'd leave it to you after I was gone, Katerina, and that's what I intend to do. I honor my promises, just as I taught you to do. What you choose to do with the necklace afterward is entirely your affair."

"Oh, Gam." Kat left his side and crouched at her grandmother's feet and dared to gather an arthritic hand in hers. "I don't want the necklace. I just want you. It's all I've ever wanted."

Tears glistened in Matilda's eyes. "I have my reasons for what I'm doing," she repeated. She caressed Kat's cheek with gentle fingers before her hand fell away. "But maybe…Yes, maybe there's a better way. Instead of leaving the necklace to you in my will, why don't I give it to you as a wedding present?"

It took every ounce of Gabe's self-control not to swear out loud while Kat shot a quick, panicked look at him from over her shoulder. "Matilda—" he began, though he suspected it was far too late.

Before he could say another word, she set her brandy

aside with a decisive click of crystal against wood. "Yes. Yes, this is the perfect alternative. A much happier alternative than a deathbed bequeath." She stood, tucking her handbag under her arm and adjusting her scarf. "When is the wedding?"

"We haven't—" Kat began, also standing.

"Soon," Gabe overrode her. "Very, very soon."

"Excellent. Sooner is better for me, all things considered." Matilda paused, and for the second time a heartbreaking vulnerability clung to her. "You...you will invite me once you've set a date?"

Kat spared Gabe a helpless look before nodding. "Of course. I wouldn't dream of getting married without you there."

Matilda gave a brisk nod. She took a single step in Kat's direction before catching herself, but Gabe could see the effort at restraint fighting the longing to make amends with her only surviving grandchild. Kat's chin trembled and then set in a slant remarkably similar to her grandmother's. She deliberately stepped forward and enclosed Matilda in a tight hug. Only Gabe saw the anguish mirrored on both women's faces. And then the moment ended and Matilda walked from his office, her spine set in a rigid line.

Kat turned blindly in his direction. It wasn't until she focused on him that the realization hit her. She caught her breath in a silent gasp. "Oh, Gabe. If she won't give us the necklace until we're married, what are we going to do now?"

He laughed, the sound without humor. Did she have any doubt? "You know damn well what we're going to do. We're going to marry."

Five

Kat shook her head. "No. No, we can't." A hint of her earlier panic swept through her words. "I'll talk to Gam. I'll convince her to give us the necklace for an engagement present, instead."

Gabe lifted an eyebrow. "You think she'd agree?"

She hesitated, and he could see her debating whether or not to answer honestly. "Probably not," she finally confessed. "But it's worth a try. I just don't understand why she's so set on giving it away instead of selling it."

"Something else you can ask her. And something else she can refuse to explain."

Kat's shoulders sagged. "I'm sorry, Gabe. You know it was never my intention for everything to get this far out of hand. We don't have to marry. We can string out the engagement until—" She broke off, her breath quickening. "Until after Gam is gone."

"She looked remarkably spry for someone on her death-bed."

Kat flinched. "Please."

He tilted his head to one side, studying her. "You were serious about the reason you proposed this ludicrous agreement. This really is all about Matilda, isn't it?"

"Yes." Fire flashed in her pale green eyes. "I told you I'd do anything to reconcile with her and I meant it."

"Even to the extent of marrying me?"

She nodded. "If there's no other option." It was her turn to study him. "I gather that means you're equally determined to get your hands on Heart's Desire?"

"I'll do whatever it takes." He took a step in her direction and tugged her into his arms, reveling in the helpless heat of her body against his. "Kat, it symbolizes love, a love that went hideously wrong. Of a love that started with a single touch."

"The Inferno?"

"The Inferno," he confirmed.

She frowned, splaying her hands against his chest. "You were going to explain that to me. Explain what The Inferno is and how it works."

"It'll be clearer if I demonstrate."

And then he did.

Kat's lips were like silk, yet sweet and a shade tentative. For some reason her hesitation drew Gabe in, made him desperate to break through her reserve and have her surrender to him. To give him everything she possessed without holding back. He didn't want to storm her defenses the way he had in the elevator. This time, he wanted it to be her choice. This time, she would acknowledge the uncontrollable desire that gathered them up in a whirlwind of need and exploded into The Inferno. It was the only way to make her understand what was happening between them.

He sensed her teetering on the edge, trembling on the brink of letting go. It would only take one little nudge and she'd tumble once again. He nibbled at those lush lips, teasing them apart. With the softest of moans, she opened to him. And still he held back, silently demanding she choose. She could admit that she wanted him or she could step away. But he refused to force the decision, refused to have her accuse him later of taking advantage of the passion that seared all senses and destroyed all sensibility.

He kept his arms loose around her, so she could back away any time she chose. Instead of pulling free, she snuggled closer, pressing those impressive curves tight against him. Her hands slid up his chest and around his neck, skating into his hair. He didn't know how much longer he could hold on, his need almost painful in its intensity.

"Gabe, please."

Just those two little words, barely audible, yet ripe with longing. And then he felt the give of her body, the sweet yielding of years' worth of defenses. His arms tightened, molded her against him, sealing her to him. They didn't rush, but slowed. Didn't feast, but savored. Immersed themselves in the heat, inch by delectable inch, instead of throwing themselves onto the pyre.

Not that it made any difference. The need built, just as it had from the moment they'd first touched. Soon it would overwhelm. For some reason Gabe didn't want that to happen this time. Instead, he wanted to simply flow with her, testing the newness and delighting in the discovery of what made her different. Special.

The one.

Those two simple words crashed down on him, the weight of all they suggested as heavy and overwhelming as the urge that demanded he take Kat in every way possible. He allowed the kiss to ease, to soften, to ever so tenderly end, before he pulled back and rested his forehead against hers.

Why her? Of all the women with whom he could have shared this instant connection, why did it have to be Kat Malloy? It was a betrayal of all he believed. All he held dear. Of his late wife, Jessa. Of the clear-cut lines he'd drawn in order to overcome his past and separate himself from the man who'd sired him, as well as the taint of his Dante heritage. Instead, that heritage had connected him to the last woman he would have chosen and stirred emotions he'd never thought himself capable of experiencing.

She wasn't the one. He didn't want her to be. As for The Inferno… Gabe refused to accept his grandfather's claims that he would be forever mated to this woman, heart and soul, for the rest of his life. He controlled his own destiny, chose whether to turn left or right. Chose how he conducted his affairs, both business and personal. Chose whom he permitted into his life and for how long. Though he'd allow Kat access, it sure as hell wouldn't be forever. Not after the way she'd betrayed his late wife. Just holding her, wanting her, this uncontrollable drive to possess her in every conceivable way, felt like another betrayal, one of the worst sort. And yet…

He couldn't resist this woman.

She stared up at him, her eyes shrouded in bewilderment. "You stopped. How could you stop when I—"

Couldn't? Was that what she'd intended to say? Her breath escaped a shade too fast and rich color suffused her cheekbones. It took her several seconds to pull herself together. "You confuse me. You really do."

"You asked me to explain The Inferno. I thought a personal demonstration would clarify what it is far better than any number of words."

It was the first thought to enter his mind and he went

with it. He released her and took a step back, allowing cool, rational thought to chill the primal heat seething between them. It helped, but nowhere near as much as he'd like. Unable to resist, he touched her again, stroking the back of his hand along the soft curve of her cheek. She shuddered. And he wanted. No. That struck him as too innocuous a word. He didn't simply want. He yearned. He craved. Every fiber of his being demanded he take her in order to fill the ravenous hunger clawing at him. And he resisted that hunger with every fiber of his being, knowing all the while he resisted the inevitable. This woman would be his. It was only a matter of time.

His hand lingered on her skin, drew a scorching line from cheek to jaw. "This… This is The Inferno," he murmured. "Or so I presume."

Kat leaned into Gabe's touch, seeming to draw comfort from the contact. "Well, I've heard it called many things, but Inferno is a new one on me."

He continued to paint her face with his fingertips, searing each curve and angle into his memory. "It's what the Dantes call it."

She stilled, her expression closing over. This time she stepped away from him. "The Dantes. You mentioned them before. Do you mean the Dantes who designed your mother's necklace? The same company I hope to work for someday?"

"Yes." He didn't want to have to discuss them, but didn't see any other option. "I'm related to them."

She turned from him ever so slightly, withdrawing even more. He felt the loss and almost reached for her, catching himself at the last instant. "I didn't realize."

He shrugged. "Very few know. It's not something I often discuss."

"You've lost me." She wrapped her arms around her waist. It seemed a telling gesture but Gabe couldn't quite hone in on why it concerned him. "Why would you keep your connection to them a secret?" she asked.

"Because it's not one I care to acknowledge." She remained silent and he sensed she was waiting for him to decide whether to say more or simply end the conversation. For some reason, he felt compelled to explain. "My mother had an affair with Dominic Dante. At the time of my conception—a very married Dominic Dante."

A small frown touched her brow and he wondered whether his bastard status bothered her, whether she would change her mind about marrying him now that she knew. "And the family has never accepted you?" Then she softened, taking a step in his direction. "Oh, Gabe, I'm so sorry. That's just wrong."

And once again, he'd misjudged her. Her concern for him couldn't have been any clearer. He read it in her eyes, heard it in the tone of her voice, felt it in the quick, spontaneous squeeze she gave his arm.

"Until recently, the Dantes didn't realize my sister and I existed. To be honest, they still don't know about her," he continued.

She gave him an odd look. "Sister?" She shook her head, not bothering to hide her confusion. "Wait a minute. You have a sister?"

"Lucia. We're twins." Was that hurt he caught flickering across her expression? Why? It wasn't as if they were close friends. Hell, the only place they experienced any sort of closeness was in each other's arms. "There's no reason you should have known, Kat. You were out of the country when Jessa and I married, which was the only time you could have met Lucia. And over the past three weeks, you and I have been careful to avoid intimate conversations in case it led to other intimacies. Although I expect that will change in the near future."

Kat blew out a sigh. "And I thought I kept my cards close
to my chest." She scooped her hair back from her face and
Gabe suppressed a grin at the irritation flitting across her
expression. She always kept herself so carefully put together,
wearing her cool, remote façade like a suit of armor. He liked
the idea of stripping her of that armor, bit by bit, and seeing what hid beneath. "Why don't you start from the top?"
she suggested.

"My mother was a jewelry designer at Dantes and had an
affair with Dominic. When he married someone else, she
transferred to their New York office. They met again years
later and had a one-night stand that resulted in our conception. When she discovered she was pregnant, she left the
company to work for Charlestons, a then-competitor, before
moving to Seattle about the time we were born."

"Did Dominic know your mother was pregnant?"

"No, not then. Eventually, he tracked her down and found
out about Lucia and me. It was right before our sixteenth
birthday." Memories swamped him of his father, an older,
larger version of himself, with a charm that made him almost irresistible. At least, he'd proved himself irresistible
to two members of his family. After watching his mother
pine for his father for so many years, Gabe had been less
enchanted by the arrival of the Dante "prince." But his sister... "Lucia was thrilled. She bought into the whole fairy
tale gig. The prince was going to marry the princess and
carry us all off to his San Francisco castle where we'd be
one big, happy family."

"Since your last name is Moretti, I assume that never
happened."

Gabe shook his head. "And who knows if it ever would
have. A few months later, my father died in a sailing accident, along with his wife. His death destroyed my mother."

"And Lucia?"

Compassion underscored her question, a compassion he itched to openly reject. "It left scars," he replied. He thought about Lucia's current job working for Primo, and the naked longing he'd seen in her expression. "Some still haven't healed."

"But you never bought into the fairy tale, did you?"

It was a shrewd guess. "Never. I'm not a Dante. I'll never be a Dante."

"Except for one small detail," she mentioned.

"Which is?"

"The Inferno." A hint of exasperation colored her words. "You keep saying this Inferno business comes from the Dantes. So, what is it, exactly?"

They'd come full circle, an irony that didn't escape him. "The Inferno is an infection. Or perhaps an affliction." He stared at his palm and ran his thumb across the surface. The tingle remained, the slight burning itch he'd experienced ever since first touching Kat. For some reason it seemed to intensify the desire that never left him, that constantly gnawed at him, demanding he allow himself to be consumed by the flames of what this hellish Inferno had sparked. "Or, more likely, another fairy tale."

She groaned. "Do I really have to drag it out of you?"

He took a deep breath and got to the point. "According to my grandfather—" Suddenly realizing what he'd said, and the fact that it caused Kat to raise an eyebrow, Gabe grimaced. "Technically, he is my grandfather."

"I didn't say a word."

"You sure thought a load of them." He waved off her attempt to respond and let her have it. All of it. "According to Primo, the Dantes can tell their soul mate with a single touch."

She held up her hand, palm out, a frown tugging at her brow. "That touch? The one that caused my palm to burn?"

"Yes. They call it The Inferno."

Her frown deepened, not that he could blame her. "How long does it last?"

He simply looked at her before dropping a single, shocking word between them. "Forever."

"For—" Kat's mouth fell open and she sank into the nearest chair. "You've got to be kidding."

"I didn't say it was real. I'm just telling you what my grand—*Primo*—said. It's another fairy tale," Gabe emphasized. "Just some silly family legend. But since I'm not a Dante, it doesn't apply. Not that it would, even if I were a Dante." Frustration ate at him, and bled into his voice. "Damn it, Kat. It's not real, okay?"

"A legend," she repeated. She shot him a look from blazing eyes. "As in, this story has been around for generations. Usually legends which have been around that long have some basis in reality."

"Right, reality." He couldn't keep the cynicism from creeping into his voice. "Let's examine the reality of this particular legend. Two strangers touch for the first time and instantly know they belong together for the rest of their lives. That's what you want me to accept as 'real'?"

She scrambled for an explanation. "That, or some version of it. More likely some version, like a chemical reaction when a Dante touches a woman they're attracted to. Maybe Dantes have more acidic skin, or more basic, or their skin contains an excess of some chemical that others don't normally possess. I mean, how should I know?" She closed her mouth and snatched a quick, steadying breath. "So, seriously. How long does this thing last?"

"I told you. According to Primo, it lasts forever."

"And according to you?"

"I figure it'll take a few months to work out of our systems." He offered a cool smile totally at odds with the heat smoldering within. "About the length of our marriage, I'm guessing, assuming we move forward with our devil's bargain."

He caught that hint of vulnerability he'd witnessed during their first meeting. Now, as then, it unsettled him on some visceral level. He didn't want to believe it genuine. She'd had an affair with a man engaged to her cousin, whereas his mother had slept with a married man. He'd never blamed his mother for that affair, had understood that she'd been helpless to resist his father. Had Kat felt that way about Benson Winters? How could he condemn one, but not the other?

"You believe that if we sleep together this Inferno will burn itself out?" she asked, that hint of vulnerability continuing to twist something he kept buried deep inside.

"Yes."

Her lashes swept downward. "And if it doesn't?"

"It will." He reached for her, lifted her out of the chair and pulled her into his arms. In that moment he realized he didn't give a damn about her past, only her immediate future. And what the hell did that say about him? Maybe that he was more his father's son than he cared to admit. "Don't think for one minute that whatever we're experiencing, whether Inferno or chemical reaction, is going anywhere. It's lust, Kat. A simple hormonal or pheromone response. You want me and I want you. End of story."

"An itch?"

"Exactly. We scratch it and after a while it goes away."

"Just like that."

Gabe couldn't help smiling at the snap in her voice. "You're offended."

"I guess I am," she admitted. She lowered her gaze for a moment before looking at him again, her expression reflecting an unwavering determination. "I don't like being compared to an itch. Nor do I appreciate being made to feel like a case of poison oak you'd like to cure at your earliest convenience. And I certainly don't intend to sleep with you in order to take care of your little problem."

"You want me."

To his surprise, she nodded, not backing away from the truth. "I'd be lying if I said I didn't. But that's not enough for me. It never has been. It's not who I am."

"So you were in love with Benson Winters?" He found the idea unsettling in the extreme.

"Not at all."

His eyes narrowed. "That was an aberration? Or are you telling me your affair changed you?" He put the final two words in air quotes, which might have been a mistake based on the flash of anger that swept across her face. "That you've learned your lesson and will never again allow yourself to be drawn into an affair to satisfy an itch?"

"I don't owe you an explanation for what happened with Benson," she informed him crisply. "It's none of your business."

"It is if we marry."

"No, Gabe. It's not." She stepped away from him. "You and I have a business arrangement, pure and simple. That's all it is. For some reason we've allowed physical desire to sidetrack us. But I, for one, don't intend to make that mistake again. This isn't about lust, or sex or even The Inferno. Our relationship is about Heart's Desire and my reconciling with my grandmother. That's it."

The reminder brought him up short. "And just how do you plan to prevent us from getting sidetracked again?"

"I don't plan to prevent it. I plan to ignore it," she stated simply.

Yeah, right. Look how well that had worked so far. "And I've explained why that's not possible," he retorted. "You want your reputation restored so your grandmother will accept you. I want Heart's Desire. To get what each of us wants, we're stuck with a long-term engagement at the very least, possibly even a marriage. It's already strange enough that I would marry you—of all people—after what happened between you, Winters and Jessa. You don't want to give anyone additional reasons to peek behind the curtain, particularly not your grandmother."

"You want the world to believe we're lovers? Fine. We'll just have to do an impressive job faking it." She gathered up her purse. "Thank you for lunch, Gabe. It was…interesting. I'll be in touch tomorrow. Maybe we can coordinate our calendars and pencil in some more lunches and dinners and that sort of thing. Dates." She edged toward the exit. "Public dates that are, well, conducted in public. Where we don't need to be alone. Ever."

"Sure." He stopped her retreat with a hand to her arm. "One quick thing before you go?"

She paused. Lifted one of those elegant eyebrows. "Yes?"

"Just this…"

He didn't give her any warning. He simply wrapped his arms around her and pulled her close. He waited just long enough for her to open her mouth in protest before sealing it with his own. He sank in, mating her tongue with his, telling her without words that her plan to conduct a celibate marriage had a snowball's chance in hell of succeeding. She silently argued the point for an entire ten seconds before conceding defeat.

She fell into the embrace. No, that suggested something far too passive. A surrender. She didn't surrender so much as a single inch. Instead, she attacked, gave as much as she took. Her tongue swept inward with a swift, sweet thrust, dueling with his. He savored her taste all over again, finding it just as delicious as before. She gave his bottom lip a quick nip, then soothed it with a gentle caress.

All the while her clever hands tripped across his body in open exploration, pausing to wander over the ridging of his chest, before gliding around him to trace the hard planes of his back. She wrapped him up tight while she consumed him, her breasts full and heavy against him, while her hips moved in tiny, urgent circles that threatened to drive him insane with the need to take her. And still those restless hands couldn't seem to settle, never quite satisfied until they finally slipped back to his chest and arrowed downward, skating past his belt buckle to cradle the heavy weight of his erection.

For some reason she froze, as though she'd found far more than she'd bargained for. Okay, fine. That just meant it was his turn to do a bit of exploration. He found the zipper to the Christmas-red dress she'd painted on and dragged it downward, allowing his fingertips to follow the path of her spine to the sweet indent just above her backside. He slid a single finger along the lacy elastic band of her panties and felt her shudder in helpless reaction.

"Gabe, please." The words escaped in a helpless moan.

"Please stop?" he teased. "Or Gabe, if you stop I'll have to hurt you."

"Yes, that one. The stop and I'll have to hurt you option."

His laugh escaped, deep and intimate and filled with dark promise. "That's what I thought."

More than anything, he wanted to strip away her clothes and simply drive into her, right then and there. But with his office door providing no more than a flimsy barrier between them and the outside world, he didn't dare. Combine that with the fact that he didn't keep condoms in his office and it added up to right time, wrong place. He snatched another kiss, intending only a quick taste before releasing her. Somehow it deepened, drifted from one moment into the next. If he didn't find a way to get her to his office apartment—and fast—he really would say to hell with it and spread her across his desk in order to seal their commitment to one another.

Forcing himself to end the kiss, a heroic effort considering how desperately she struggled to prolong it, he wrapped an arm around her and ushered her toward a staircase at the far end of the sitting area. The climb to the penthouse seemed endless. She hesitated at the top of the stairs, and stared at the large, sprawling apartment. Floor-to-ceiling windows showcased a stunning sweep of Seattle and the Bay, before wrapping around to encompass Mt. Rainier. The snow-covered peak loomed over the city, making one of its startling appearances against the mid-December skyline.

For some reason, she eased back a pace, shaking her head. She clutched her loosened dress tight against her chest. "No, not here."

Her abrupt turnaround caught him by surprise. "What's wrong, Kat?"

"Not here," she repeated. "Not where Jessa…"

He understood then. "Jessa never stepped foot in this apartment. I didn't even own this office building when we were married. I purchased it more than a year after she died."

Kat closed her eyes in relief, her breath escaping in a soft laugh. "I guess it seems ridiculous to you."

"Not at all." For some reason he was driven to reassure her. "I only use this place when I've been working late and rather not face the drive home. If it makes you feel any better, I've never made love to a woman here before. Any woman."

"Keeping business separate from personal?"

She left the question hanging between them and stepped away, crossing to stand in the flood of sunshine arrowing through the windows. She rubbed her arms as though chilled. Of course, that might have something to do with her dress gaping open in the back, exposing the lovely width of her shoulders, the endless expanse of flawless skin that curved inward to a narrow waist he could encircle with two hands before flaring into shapely hips. It always came as a shock to realize how petite she was, perhaps because she had such a huge personality. Well, that and the mile-high heels giving her the illusion of height. Gabe came up behind and wrapped his arms around her, tucking her against the warmth of his chest.

She relaxed into him, her head settling into the crook of his shoulder. "I guess since, technically, I fall under the heading of business, they're still separate."

He bent his head, his mouth brushing her temple. "Just to clarify, I've put together hundreds of business deals over the course of my career. Not one of them involved what we're about to do."

He felt a laugh ripple through her. "I have to admit I'm relieved." She turned to face him, her hands resting against his chest. "Gabe…"

And there was that defenselessness again, that gut-churning uncertainty that brought out every last protective instinct he possessed. He'd always been the protective one in his family, the one who stood in front of his mother and sister and attempted to absorb the blows aimed their way. Not that he'd succeeded. But at least he'd been there for them every step of the way. He should protect Kat, too. Maybe he would have, if the need to have her didn't override all instinct except one. And that instinct demanded he join them in the most basic and elemental way possible, a mating that had bound man to woman since the beginning of time.

"Don't," he urged. "Don't back out. Not now. Not when you know damn well what we're about to do is inevitable. Whether it happens today or tomorrow or next week or next month, it will happen."

"We've only known each other a matter of weeks. That's no time at all," she protested.

"If ours were a normal arrangement, I'd agree with you. But it isn't. Not only are the circumstances—well, frankly—bizarre. But so is our reaction to one another." He captured her chin, the soft curve centered in the palm of his hand directly over The Inferno's burn. "Tell me the truth, Kat. Have you ever experienced anything like this before?"

She didn't hesitate. "Not even close. But that doesn't mean we have to jump into the fire."

"Too late. The fire's already jumped into us. All we can do is let it consume us."

He saw it first in her crystalline green eyes, the quiet acceptance. "I didn't plan this."

"I know. Neither did I."

Her gaze never wavered. "I also know if you could have picked someone to experience The Inferno with, I'm the very last one you'd have chosen."

He didn't deny it. Couldn't. "I suspect, if we were honest with each other, we'd have both chosen someone else. But it doesn't change the fact that it's happened. We can deny it. We can try to ignore it. We can fight it. And yet, here we are, unable to resist going where The Inferno leads."

"Damn Dantes," she whispered.

He laughed. "Now there we're in total agreement." His amusement faded. "So, what's your decision, Kat? Do you continue to deny it? Keep fighting? Ignore whatever the hell this is? Or do you surrender to the flames?"

Her smile held a bittersweet quality. "I think that decision has already been made, don't you?"

"You're killing me, Kat. I haven't even touched you—not really. Not the way I intend to. And you're already experiencing regrets."

"Only because this is going to change everything."

He didn't disagree. How could he when it was the truth? "Nothing about this situation is easy."

He expected tears, but he didn't see any hint of them. And he couldn't help remembering her claim that she never cried. Ever. Instead, sorrow lurked in her light green eyes. For some reason the pain it hinted at impacted far harder than it should have, than even tears would have. He shouldn't care. Didn't want to care. And yet, in that moment, if he could fix whatever had hurt her, he would have.

"According to my grandmother, the Chatsworth family excels at difficult," she said with a lightness that missed its mark. "I'd hoped our association would prove the exception to the rule."

Gabe shook his head. "I'm not easy. Neither are you. And our history pours more turmoil onto an already tumultuous relationship."

"Sleeping together won't make our relationship any less tumultuous," she pointed out.

He shrugged. "I think The Inferno has already made certain of that."

She nodded and with that simple inclination of her head, he knew she'd made her decision. She stepped closer, the sun caressing the sparks of fire buried in the darkness of her hair and intensifying the bright red tones of her dress. She lowered her hands to her sides and gave a graceful shrug. The dress slipped from her shoulders and drifted downward to settle at her hips. He'd expected to see her wearing black undergarments again. But she wasn't. These were a creamy white, delicate and virginal and sweetly feminine, at total odds with the sophisticated dress she wore.

She gave a rolling shimmy of her hips and the dress took a long, slow slide to her feet. She stepped from the pool of silk and slipped off her heels before approaching. When had she become so tiny? And when had her appearance changed to mirror her undergarments—delicate and virginal and sweetly feminine? It was an illusion. It had to be. But it was an illusion that filled Gabe with a burning desire. To take her. To brand her with his possession. To be the one. The first, the last. The only. He surrendered to the fantasy, knowing full well that's all it was. A fantasy. Soon enough reality would intrude. But until it did…

He reached for her and she swept his hands aside. She didn't want him to touch her? Fine. He'd play by her rules. For now. She came to him and tugged at the knot of his tie, sliding it from around his collar and tossing it aside. Next, she pulled his shirt free from his trousers and worked her way down the row of buttons. Her hands spread across his chest, sculpting the warm, lightly furred skin, trailing her fingertips in agonizing circles downward across the ridge of muscles. She made short work of opening his belt and unzipping his trousers. And then she stripped him, saving his boxers for last.

Instead of removing them, as well, she turned and gave the apartment a cursory look, settling on the doorway leading to the bedroom. She headed that way, the high cut of her panties exposing buttocks that were round and lush and as bitable as ripe, white peaches. She paused at the threshold of the bedroom to give him a single glance over her shoulder. Her hair spilled over her shoulders like dark flames, licking across the creaminess of her shoulders and cupping the sweet curve of her breasts. She was the goddess of temptation, personified. And he couldn't help recalling that Até was also the Greek goddess of folly and despair, that she'd caused the downfall of many a man, usually through his own hubris.

How incredibly fitting.

Then she said, "Coming?" in a voice that made promises that nearly brought him to his knees.

Six

That's all it took, just that single, sultry word. Coming? Oh, hell yes, he was coming. Gabe made a sound from somewhere deep inside, from the very core of him. It was part growl, part exclamation. But it was wholly a claiming, a statement of sheer, masculine possession.

He went after her, charging across the room. He never slowed, simply scooped Kat into his arms and entered the darkened bedroom. In two seconds flat he had her tossed onto the bed, pale, silken limbs splayed across the bronze duvet. Her hair framed her face, and her lovely, sculpted features fought to appear impassive. Yet they revealed their secrets to anyone who bothered to look—really look. Vulnerability lurked in the forest-draped shadows of her eyes, while passion sculpted her lush mouth. Hesitation softened the lines of a determined chin, at direct odds with the urgency revealed by the taut planes of her cheekbones.

He came down beside her, tracing a fingertip from eyes to mouth, chin to cheekbone. "So much conflict."

"Is that what you see?" she whispered. "Is that all you see?"

"You want me."

"True."

"But you don't want to want me."

Her mouth trembled into a smile. "Also true."

"I guess that pretty much defines our relationship."

Her eyes fluttered closed and her breath came in a soundless sigh. "Are you trying to talk me out of this?"

Hell, no! Still… "I don't want any regrets afterward. No recriminations about not waiting until there's a ring on your finger." he replied, surprised by how gentle he sounded. For some reason she brought that quality out in him. "I'm trying to be honest, Kat."

Her lashes flickered back upward and she gave him a calm, direct look. "Not here. Not now."

Her comment surprised him and he lifted an eyebrow. "You want me to lie to you?"

"I want to say yes, lie to me." She caught her lower lip between her teeth, thinking about it. Then she sighed. "But, I'm afraid that would be a mistake," she admitted reluctantly.

He couldn't blame her. After all, he wanted the fantasy over reality, too. "Tell you what… Why don't we focus on the 'want' instead of the 'don't want.'"

"I'd like that very much." But instead of reaching for him, she levered herself up onto her elbows. "What do you say we also make a bargain?"

He groaned, not sure whether to laugh or strangle her. "*Another* negotiation?"

"Just a small one." She pinched two fingers together in demonstration. "I think the one thing we both can agree on is that we want each other sexually. As you said, we may have fought it, but if we're dead honest, we'll admit we can't resist the physical desire we're experiencing."

"I can't argue with that."

"So, let's take that one step further. Instead of lying about what we want, what if we agree that this is the one place we'll always be honest with one another? The one place where, no matter how painful, we won't lie?"

"Naked."

She nodded. "In every sense of the word."

He leaned across her and opened the drawer of the nightstand table and removed one of the condoms he'd only started keeping there these past three weeks. Had he been hoping this moment would come...or planning? He tossed the foil packet onto the bed beside them so it would be within easy reach when the time came. Without another word, he cupped her face and kissed her, telling her loud and clear just how much he honestly wanted her and how little the "don't want" factored into the equation. Her lips parted and their tongues began a teasing parry. Her kisses were divine, leisurely and playful.

But it wasn't enough. Not nearly enough.

There was so much more he wanted from her. So much more he wanted to offer her. Desperation filled him, a nearly uncontrollable urge to strip away the flimsy bits of silk and lace covering her and mate their bodies in one swift, hard taking. But something held him back. Maybe it was those scraps of innocent white, with their tiny feminine bows decorating the deep cleft between the cups of her bra. More bows perched on the flare of her hips, looking adorably sweet on a woman who epitomized European sophistication. The dichotomy gave him pause, as did the nervous tension that exuded from her.

After a moment's consideration, he decided to go with his instincts. This was their first time together. There would be plenty of occasions for faster, more exuberant encounters. But this afternoon, he'd take his time. Build toward that ultimate peak, slow caress by slow caress. Kiss every inch of that delectable body. And he'd begin with the soft, sweet center. Always a delicious place to start.

He lowered his head and pressed a string of kisses across the warm sweep of her abdomen, inhaling her feminine perfume. She shuddered in surprise and arched her spine a few inches. He smiled against her stomach, pleased to catch her off guard. He planned to keep her that way. She was a woman who liked to be in control. Well, not here. Not now. He wanted to devastate every last defense and have her fully participating, without any controls. With total loss of control.

He stroked her sides, his fingers teasing at the bows riding her hips. He felt the slight quiver of her belly beneath his mouth, the brief tensing in anticipation of his stripping away her panties. Instead, he skated upward to trace the contours of her bra. Again, he felt the shudder of reaction, the uncertainty and confusion he'd roused.

"Gabe, what are you doing?" she finally gasped.

"Playing." He lifted his head to look at her. "I can't seem to decide which ride I want to go on first."

She froze, clearly not expecting his levity. Apparently sex had always been serious business for her. Sad, really, when it was so much damn fun. Then she chuckled, relaxing against his hold. "Playing, huh?" She planted her hands on his chest and allowed her palms to rumble downward across his abdomen. "I think I'll go for the roller coaster."

He cupped her breasts and pressed them together within the confines of her bra. "I've always been rather partial to the bumper cars."

She allowed her gaze to drift downward and settle at the telltale bulge pressing against his shorts. "Somehow I thought you'd go for the sledgehammer. I bet you ring the bell every time."

"For you, I'll do my best." He teased the tiny triangle covering her womanhood. "Shall we start with the Tunnel of Love, or end there?"

She wrapped her arms around his neck and tugged him into her embrace. He fit against her, perfectly melded, male to female. His key to her lock. "Start there. End there. So long as you ring my bell along the way, I'm willing to go on every ride there is."

He smiled to see how much their silliness had relaxed her, how comfortably she settled against him. How the faded rose of the afternoon sun painted her in carefree colors. The worries that had burdened her melted away and she lingered in the moment, safe within his arms, within his bed and within their growing rapture. He could read the pleasure in her pale green eyes, see it in the happy tremble of her mouth, hear it in the laughter that had become part of their first sexual encounter. He reveled in it all, shutting out the darkness, along with the past. None of that mattered. Not here. Not now.

They made a game of stripping away the last of their clothes, of exploring one another's bodies. There was a sweetness to their teasing, a gentleness that permeated voice and comment and touch. And yet, all the while, tension built, the flicker of need lurking behind the lightheartedness they both knew would eventually explode into flames and sweep like wildfire into their encounter. Despite their awareness, it caught them both by surprise when it finally happened. One moment they were laughing at how he'd turned her body into an arcade game, and the next...

Gabe stilled, the laughter easing, dying. Vanishing. A ray of sunshine flickered across Kat. Winter gave the light a soft, remote quality, framing her in that softness and attempting to paint her into someone distant and untouchable. But it couldn't. She possessed too much vibrancy, her coloring streaked with touch-me passion rather than touch-me-not pastels.

Heaven help him, but she was beautiful. Fire crackled in her hair and seemed to catch in the earthy green of her eyes. A smile hovered on her lips, easing from amusement to a womanly perception. Eve becoming. She reached up to cup his face and he felt the slight tremble of her fingers. He turned his face into the palm of her hand, pressed his lips to the center where The Inferno first struck.

Now when he traced her body, he did it with intent, putting into practice what he'd learned while playing. She was extra sensitive right around the nipples and on the bottom slope of her breasts, and he lingered there until she trembled in his arms, the breath hitching in her throat. He'd also discovered she shuddered in ecstasy whenever his fingertips skated along the back of her thighs, that desire cascaded off her and she instinctively opened to him whenever he touched her there. He found if he tugged at her lower lip, taking it in a gentle love bite, she'd plunder his mouth with uncontrolled urgency. She was self-conscious about her backside, considering it too generous, though he found her bottom about as perfect as a bottom could be. And the kisses he placed on the little dimples just above all that lushness drove her insane.

Inch by inch, he explored each and every part of her, determined to build the fire into a conflagration that would be unlike any she'd ever experienced before. He drove her ever upward until he realized that he hovered on the brink every bit as much as she did.

He snatched up the condom and handed it to her. "Put it on me," he said. "I want to feel your hands on me."

It took her three tries to tear open the foil packet. And she had him teetering on the edge of control with the slow, teasing way she went about the task. First, she pretended to get the angle wrong, then claimed she'd tried to put it on inside out, before finally sheathing him, slowly unrolling it until he couldn't take it another second.

He lowered himself on top of her, poised at the warm, moist heart of her. "Wait, Gabe," she whispered, pushing against his shoulders. "I don't think I did it right."

"No more teasing," he told her. "Not now."

"But—"

He stopped her protest with a slow kiss and thrust inward, breaching the tightness at the same instant he breached her mouth. She stiffened, squirming against him in a way that almost had him finishing before he'd started. He gathered himself, determined to bring her as much pleasure as she brought him. Slowly, he pulled back, before driving into her, burying himself deep within. There he paused, though he thought it just might kill him, waiting for her to become accustomed to the joining. And all the while, he found those areas that gave her the most pleasure. Her stiffness eased, melting away, and her arms tightened around him. She opened more fully to him, lifting upward, searching for a rhythm.

It amused him that they weren't instantly coordinated. He'd have thought that two fairly experienced people would get it together a little faster than they were. But maybe that was The Inferno's fault. Maybe the urges that swamped them, that threatened to overwhelm them, were so intense they didn't allow for expertise, just gratification in the fastest, most basic way possible. Then the rhythm caught, amplified, became something he'd never experienced before, something that sank inward and connected on a level he didn't realize existed. It transcended all that came before, sang into the now, and made promises for what would come in the fullness of time. He saw the burgeoning of whatever seed had been planted reflected in Kat's eyes, saw that same connection.

Then something changed.

She bowed upward, her gaze locked on his, filled with shock and disbelief. Filled with innocent delight. "What have you done to me?" The words escaped in a thready whisper. And then tears filled her eyes, tears she'd denied possessing. They slid down her temples and burrowed into the dark embers of her hair, glittering with the rawness and purity of rare fire diamonds.

And then she came utterly undone, her climax slamming through her. It drove him straight over the edge and he fell. Fell hard.

Fell into innocence.

Gabe turned from the window and stared at Kat. Late afternoon sunshine splashed across her sleeping form. Another image transposed over the current one, an image of how she'd looked in Benson Winters' hotel bed. But the image was all wrong. It tilted. Fractured. Splintered into pieces that would never be whole again. She hadn't been Sleeping Beauty after the awakening. The Sleeping Beauty from five years ago had never known the prince's kiss...or anything else.

It explained a lot about their lovemaking, including the way she'd fumbled with the condom. She hadn't been teasing, dragging out the moment in order to increase his pleasure. She'd been inexperienced and attempting to conceal it from him. It also explained why she'd wanted to wait until they were married, something he'd denied her.

He lowered his head. He'd been the one to push, to insist they make love here and now. The image of her looking at him in response, her haunting, haunted eyes filled with quiet acceptance cut deep, as did the memory of her bittersweet smile. Other images came to him, deepening the cut. Her reaction when she'd thought he'd brought her to a bed Jessa might have shared with him. Those damn virginal undergarments. Even her surprise at his playfulness in bed. Why hadn't he seen? Why hadn't he understood? Why hadn't he protected her, if only from himself? He'd been the one to awaken her, and now that he knew what to look for, he could see the difference. Feel the difference.

What he'd assumed was fantasy had been reality. And if that were true, then it also meant that reality was… Well, not what he'd assumed, he knew that much for damn sure.

That still didn't explain how she'd ended up in that hotel room bed all those years ago. Could Winters have been right? Had Kat attempted to seduce him that night? No, that didn't make sense. Unless he was complicit in that seduction, he'd never have greeted her so warmly at lunch. Nor would he have asked to meet with her again. Gabe thought it through, attempting to use the dispassionate logic that had aided him throughout his life. But somehow he couldn't remove himself from his emotions. Not this time. Not when it came to Kat.

There were any number of explanations for her virginity, including… An image came to mind, of Jessa arriving on his doorstep in tears, begging him to go with her to a hotel room where she'd been told she'd find her fiancé in bed with another woman. At that point he'd been no more than a friend. After they'd found Kat, his relationship with Jessa had swiftly become something more. He turned from the memory, unwilling to examine that particular possibility. Which brought him back to the woman currently gracing his bed.

One thing he knew for certain. His was the only bed Kat had ever been in. And his was the only bed she'd be in for a long time to come. He retreated to the living area and re-

trieved his cell phone from his trousers. The series of calls
didn't take long. The one to Primo met with delight and instant approval, the one to Matilda met with almost identical
enthusiasm. After that, it came down to simple pragma-
tism—arranging for the flight, the hotel rooms, the necessary license. Amazing what money and connections could
accomplish in such a short span of time. Once finished, he
returned to the bedroom—and to the bed.

Gabe eased down beside Kat, warming her with his body,
gathering her within the shelter of his embrace. In sleep her
barriers were nonexistent, her vulnerability sculpted into
every line of her body. He swept a tumble of hair from her
face and leaned in, wakening her with a slow, passionate
kiss. She moaned softly, still half-asleep, opening to him.
Giving herself without restraint or hesitation. Gifting herself.

Her lashes fluttered and she opened her eyes, dark and
slumberous and edged with passion. "Is it morning?" she
asked, her voice blurred and husky.

"Dusk."

She laughed softly. "I'll never sleep tonight."

He swept a lock of hair from her face. "I can think of a
few things we can do instead," he gently teased.

"I don't doubt it."

Ah, there she was. Not gone at all. The prickly defiance,
the dry irony, it just hadn't fully awakened. "We need to
talk."

She stiffened, regarding him with a familiar wariness.
"About what?"

"Let's see… Life. Death. Taxes." He paused a beat. "The
fact you were a virgin. Explain that to me, Kat."

He had to hand it to her. Even though warm color swept
across her cheekbones, she continued to fix him with a direct gaze, not so much as blinking. "I'd really rather not explain anything."

"I'd really rather you did." He unleashed a hint of steel. "In fact, I'm afraid I must insist. And since you were the one to bargain for honesty when we're in bed together..."

"Damn it." She glared at him. "Bed Honesty was supposed to work in *my* favor, not yours."

Bed Honesty? He would have laughed if it weren't so painfully serious. "Yes, most unfortunate. For you." He hooked her chin and tilted it into the wash of fading sunlight. It stripped through artifice and laid her bare. "How is it possible that you were having an affair with Winters and yet came to my bed untouched?"

She shrugged. "It's a miracle?"

"Or, you weren't having an affair with Winters."

"That's certainly another possibility." She led with defiance. It bled into every part of her from expression, to voice, to the rigid tension of her body. "You may recall I did tell everyone at the time."

"And no one believed you." He fought against the impact of that, along with his own culpability. But it wasn't easy, not when he'd contributed the most to her condemnation.

"The evidence was rather damning," she conceded.

"Winters claimed you tried to seduce him."

"Yes."

"But if that were the case, why was he so friendly toward you at the restaurant?" That single question continued to nag at him.

"Maybe he realized I'd been set up."

"By whom?"

Her mouth tightened and emotions cascaded over her. Anger. Betrayal. Disappointment. Hurt. "You know who set me up, Gabe. You just don't want to believe it. No one did, not even my grandmother."

It struck him then that not once had Jessa intruded into his time with Kat. Not as a regret. Not as a comparison. Not even as a shard of guilt. But she swept between them now, like an unforgiving arctic wind, scouring the landscape— or in this case the bed and its occupants. "She was my wife. You're asking me to believe—"

"She wasn't your wife at the time," Kat cut in. "And I'm not asking you to believe anything. I don't give a damn what anyone believes or doesn't believe. I know what happened. I've lived with it for five years. I've lived with the condemnation, was called a whore. Accused of trying to steal my cousin's fiancé. Accused of wrecking Benson's reputation, not to mention his hopes for a Senate seat."

"I don't understand something, Kat. Why would Jessa set the two of you up? It doesn't make sense."

"What does it matter, Gabe? She can't tell us. And any explanation I might offer is sheer speculation. Not that it's any of your business."

"It is my business if Jessa's involved." He cupped Kat's cheek, his voice deepening. "And it is if you're involved. Because as of this moment, I'm involved, too."

She pulled free of his hold and escaped the bed, only to look around in bewilderment, no doubt wondering where she'd left her clothes. Giving up, she crossed to his closet and yanked out a chocolate-brown robe. She pulled it on and knotted the sash around her waist. It was miles too large, making her appear even more defenseless than when she'd been wearing nothing at all.

"I don't want to talk about it anymore," she announced, turning to face him.

"You mean, you don't want to tell me the truth. That's why you left the bed."

Kat glared at him, scooping her hair from her face with both hands. "Okay, fine. I don't want to tell you the truth— not that there's any great truth to reveal. Besides, it's not like we're married."

"That's about to change."

Wariness draped her more thoroughly than his robe. "What are you talking about?"

"I've made arrangements for us to fly to San Francisco. We leave first thing in the morning. I've already made arrangements to stop by Matilda's and pick her up. We can also swing by your hotel so you can pack a bag." He left the bed and approached, snagging the collar of his robe and reeling Kat in. "In two days' time, you will be my wife. And then we'll be returning to bed, at which point you will tell me what I want to know. Every last *honest* detail." He leaned in, his mouth a breath away from hers. "Even if it means keeping you there until you do."

And then he sealed his promise—or was it a threat?—with a kiss that had The Inferno erupting like Vesuvius, consuming them in endless heat.

Kat sat in a leather captain's chair of Gabe's corporate jet and stared out the small port window while they streaked toward San Francisco. He'd been so solicitous with Matilda, settling her into the small onboard bedroom after they were safely airborne in order to ensure she didn't get overly tired during the flight.

One thought occupied her above all others. How did Gabe know she'd been a virgin? The only possibility she could think of was that her lovemaking had been so amateurish and unskilled there hadn't been room for any other possibility. She cringed from the thought, especially when she considered how he'd shut down in the wake of that final, blistering kiss.

She'd hoped knowing the truth about her and Benson Winters would help their relationship. Instead, it did just the opposite. Gone was the playful man who'd taken her to bed. Gone was the passionate man who'd made her his.

Gone was even the tentative accord they'd struck in order to accomplish their joint goals. Instead, she faced a man she didn't know, a man so barricaded within himself that she had no idea how to break through to the Gabe who'd made her first sexual experience so shattering.

Even though every instinct urged her to protest the speed of their marriage, she didn't dare. After all, it was what they both wanted, even if it struck her as happening far too fast. She spared Gabe a swift glance. He'd buried himself in work, his face set in taut lines. Something was wrong, something more than the swiftness of their impending wedding. For some reason, he'd set himself on a course, refusing to waver from it.

So, what had happened to cause that fatalistic grimness to settle over him like some sort of dark shadow? Was it simply that she'd been a virgin? That didn't make sense. Granted, due to his history he tended to be protective. Maybe even overly protective. That still didn't explain the rush. Not really.

She shifted in her seat. Fine. If he wouldn't volunteer the information, she'd ask. And if that didn't work, she'd demand. And if *that* didn't work, well she'd just have to seduce it out of him. Drag him off to anyplace with a mattress and use their Bed Honesty agreement to force the truth from him. Did it make her a horrible person that she hoped he'd refuse to speak until the seducing and dragging commenced?

"Gabe, I wish you'd reconsider our marrying so quickly," she finally broke down and said. "No one will believe it's real. And I don't want Gam to suspect it's related to the necklace."

"She doesn't. Hell, Matilda and the Dantes already believe it's genuine. And soon, everyone else will follow suit."

"I don't understand," she pressed. "Why? Why are they

suddenly so quick to accept that it's real? And why will everyone else believe it, too? What's changed?"

He hesitated so long she didn't think he'd answer. Then he admitted, "What's changed is who I am. Once the media discovers I'm—" He broke off, a muscle jerking in his cheek. "Once they discover I'm a Dante and that we've been struck by The Inferno, they'll have no choice but to believe. Especially when my father's family steps forward to support the union."

He'd shocked her right down to her tiptoes. "You're going to tell people?" Why did the thought fill her with such apprehension? "I thought you didn't want anyone to find out about the connection. I thought you despised the Dantes."

"I do." He lifted his gaze to her, his eyes tarnished with bitterness. "But it will explain the speed of our marriage."

She didn't like this. Not his plan. Not how badly it seemed to impact him. And especially not how deeply it scored him on a personal level. "I still don't understand," she said uneasily. "How will announcing your relationship to them explain the rush and make it all acceptable? Why should it matter that we've experienced The Inferno? And more importantly, why do we have to rush into marriage instead of waiting a few months?"

He set aside his papers with a sigh. "I keep forgetting you've been out of the country for the past five years."

She regarded him in surprise. "Did something happen during that time that relates to all this?"

"The Inferno happened," he replied. "All this nonsense became public a few years ago when one of my father's sons, Marco, staged some sort of media event to prove his wife could tell him apart from his twin, even blindfolded, all thanks to The Inferno. It was reported in just about every scandal sheet out there, and even hit some of the more respected news sources. If I announce publically that I'm a

Dante, and admit we were struck by The Inferno when we first met, no one will question the speed or validity of our marriage, especially with a wall of Dantes at our back."

"The Dantes are going to support us in this?" If so, it could mean only one thing. He'd gone to them. He'd asked for a favor.

"Yes. That's why we're marrying in San Francisco, so the Dantes can publically throw the weight of their name behind us."

She understood then, both the cost and her own culpability. She'd gone to Gabe, been the one to suggest this insane engagement. And it had been her grandmother who'd put a potential marriage on the table by promising to give them Heart's Desire as a wedding gift. Her actions, as well as Matilda's, had put him in his current predicament, and her heart broke for him. He'd sacrificed himself for her. For their marriage. And she had the odd feeling it wasn't just for Heart's Desire. For some reason, his decision to move forward so rapidly and to involve the Dantes had to do with what happened between them in bed yesterday. She just had to uncover what, and more importantly, why the rush?

"Oh, Gabe," she whispered. "You didn't. You didn't go to the Dantes."

His mouth compressed. "It's the only way."

"No. It's *not* the only way. We can wait, just like we planned. Wait to see if Matilda won't change her mind." She leaned forward and touched his knee. "Gabe, please don't do this, not unless you're using it for an excuse to initiate some sort of reconciliation with your father's family."

He returned his attention to his papers, though he flipped through them far too fast to truly absorb what he read. "It's done, Kat," he stated with finality. "Besides, it's no big deal. I've simply arranged for the Dantes to support our marriage.

Best of all, there will be very little for us to do. Primo is taking care of most of the wedding details for us."

She struggled not to wince at his calm, indifferent tone. "Will your grandfather be attending?"

A short, harsh laugh escaped. "Oh, not just Primo. The entire family. You'll get to meet all the Dantes, all the ones who have denied my existence since the day I was born. And you'll get to know who and what I am. What I came from. What I reject." He regarded her grimly. "And most of all, what I'm grateful I never became."

She allowed the words to wash over her, to recede, realizing he was hellbent on this course of action and that nothing she said would cause him to deviate so much as a single step. Keeping her voice calm and pleasant, she asked, "Is Lucia attending? She's the one I'm most interested in getting to know."

His indifference vanished and he smiled with genuine affection. "Yes. You'll get to meet Lucia." His smile faded. "But I should warn you, she's working undercover for Primo. He doesn't know who she is and I want to keep it that way. I don't want her hurt again. She's been hurt enough for one lifetime."

So, protective. But then, she'd caught that same reaction each time he'd mentioned his mother and sister, and even at odd moments, toward her. "She's working for Primo? I'm surprised, especially after all you've told me about your past."

"It came as a surprise to me, too." Gabe shrugged. "I only found out recently."

Kat took a moment to consider, the answer obvious once she thought about it. "She wanted to get to know her grandfather, didn't she?"

"Yes."

She saw it then. The wound. The pain from what he perceived as a betrayal. His determination to conceal it. He was a lion with a thorn in his paw—perhaps one she could help excise. "I guess she doesn't share your feelings toward the Dantes," she commented idly.

Of course, he saw right through her. "Leave it alone, Kat."

She pressed a little harder, searching for the thorn and realizing it was buried deep. "You must have been hurt when you found out. It must have felt like a betrayal on some level."

"What part of 'leave it alone' didn't you understand?"

But she couldn't leave it alone. She decided to go in fast and yank hard. "Gabe, I'm sure Lucia wasn't trying to hurt you. Nor is she saying that you aren't enough. It's natural that she'd be curious about her father's family."

The thorn popped free, causing the lion to roar in reaction. Then he swiped at her, claws extended. "Let's see if this won't stop you from talking."

He heaved himself out of his seat and reached for her. Yanking her into his arms, he took her mouth in a hard, fierce kiss, allowing his anger free rein. If he thought it would intimidate her, he was mistaken. She gave him back kiss for kiss, making hers just as demanding as his. Dear heaven, but she wanted him, every bit as much now as before they'd made love. Maybe more, since she knew what to expect. Understood how it felt and what it did to her. To them both.

She dragged her mouth from his, pressing frantic kisses along his jaw line. "Gabe, please."

He groaned. "Please stop? Because I don't think I can."

"I don't want you to stop. I want you to make love to me."

"Make love," he repeated. He closed his eyes and leaned into her, simply holding her. "Don't call it that. I don't want to hurt you, but I will if you try to turn this into something it isn't. It's not love. It's sex."

"Or The Inferno?"

To her surprise, he didn't instantly deny it. Instead, he blew out a sigh. "What the hell does it matter what we call it? I just know it won't last. You need to understand that."

"What does that have to do with the speed of our marriage?" she asked uncertainly.

He glanced down at her and for the first time she saw a crack in his defenses. "Because I didn't stop when you asked me to," he replied cryptically.

She frowned in confusion. "I don't understand. I didn't ask you to stop."

His expression softened and he tucked a strand of loosened hair behind her ear. "The condom," he reminded her. "It came off, sweetheart. You told me you hadn't gotten it on right and tried to stop me. I thought you were teasing. But you weren't."

Her confusion turned to shock. "You think—" She broke off, struggling to breathe. "You think I'm *pregnant?*"

Seven

Gabe nodded. "Pregnancy is a serious possibility. So we marry sooner rather than later, particularly if you want to reconcile with your grandmother. You've only just begun to reestablish your relationship with her. I don't want my taking you to bed to sabotage that. Better she think we married because of The Inferno, than suspect it was a shotgun wedding."

The possibility wiped every single thought from Kat's head, but one. Pregnancy. A baby. Gabe's baby. The mere thought that she could be carrying his child made her lightheaded. Images flashed through her mind. A dark-haired son with eyes of liquid gold. A baby nursing at her breast. Gabe protectively cradling a child they'd created. Gabe, The Inferno burned out, caught in a trap of her making.

Oh, dear God. She couldn't do that to him.

Kat yanked free of his arms. "No. That's not possible. I'm not pregnant, not after just one mishap."

Instead of replying, Gabe simply lifted an eyebrow at the absurdity of her response.

"Okay, fine," she said. Her hands darted through her hair, destroying the sleek knot and finishing the job Gabe had started. "It's a possibility. But a remote one, right?"

"If you say so, I'm not willing to take the risk. We need to marry, anyway, if I'm to get my hands on Heart's Desire. This just put an expiration date on our engagement a little sooner than expected."

"How can there be an expiration date when we weren't actually engaged? I mean, it's not like you even proposed. Not really. In fact, I think I'm the one who did all the proposing." Aware her voice had risen, she snatched a deep breath, struggling to regain her self-control, an almost impossible task. Everything seemed to hit at once, overwhelming her. "Oh, Gabe. What are we going to do?"

"We're going to take it one step at a time."

She nodded, steadied by his calm response. "And the first step is getting married."

Gabe laughed, though she didn't catch so much as a trace of humor in the sound. "Wrong. The first step is dealing with the Dantes and the preparation for our wedding."

"And that's a bad thing?" she asked uncertainly.

He hesitated. "That's a complicated thing."

Kat quickly discovered just what he meant by that when they were met at the airport by a private car carrying Primo. He puffed on a fragrant cigar, releasing a tiny wreath of smoke that practically jittered with nerves. After being introduced to Matilda, he turned to Kat. The shock of his resemblance to Gabe dissolved beneath the enthusiasm of his European-style greeting, a tight hug and a kiss on each cheek. Fortunately, her years in Italy had accustomed her to the exuberance of many of its compatriots and she returned the embrace with a natural generosity.

"It's a pleasure to meet you," she told him.

"And you." He stepped back and held her at arm's length in order to get a good look at her. "So. You are Gabriel's Inferno mate. The Inferno has been most generous in its choice for my grandson."

Kat couldn't prevent a blush. "Thank you."

He glanced toward Gabe and grinned. "No greeting for your Primo?"

To Kat's surprise, Gabe stepped forward and embraced his grandfather. She could practically see Primo's nervousness evaporate beneath the hug. "Thank you for meeting us. And for taking care of the wedding details."

"It is my pleasure to do this for you. I welcome the opportunity." He slapped Gabe on the back. "Come. We go to meet Nonna."

Ah, complication number one, Kat realized. They were ushered toward the car, Primo insisting Matilda sit beside him with Gabe and Kat facing them. She was impressed with how gentle he was with her grandmother, teasing slightly, but always respectful, despite the fact that they were of a similar age. Maybe Gabe had warned his grandfather about her precarious health. At Matilda's insistence, they dropped her off at Le Premier. It didn't take them long to get her settled in her room before continuing on to Primo's home in Sausalito, working their way through the crowded city streets toward the Golden Gate Bridge.

"Who will be there?" Gabe asked abruptly.

Primo offered immediate reassurance. "It is only Nonna for now. We will not overwhelm you with all your many brothers and cousins, nieces and nephews until the ceremony. But I warn that your grandmamma is not happy about this meeting." He thumped his chest with his fist. "Not like your Primo, who is delighted to have you with your family where you belong. She is more like you, Gabriel. She is not certain she wishes to acknowledge the connection."

"Then why force it?" he asked, his voice stiff with pride.

"Because you are the son of my son," Primo answered simply. "You are also the son of her son. She will see this the moment she sets her eyes on you. She will see her son reborn in you and these reservations will vanish like the morning fog."

"I am not like Dominic," Gabe said, withdrawing into winter's embrace. "Nor will I become some sort of replacement for him."

"No," Primo replied with a hint of sadness. "This you will never be."

He turned his attention to the sights they passed, giving Kat a guided tour along the way. At long last, they reached the ferry terminal and trendy shops clustered near the harbor and took a winding road that zigzagged high into the hillside. The car dropped them off outside a large wooden gate of a spacious home overlooking Angel Island and Belvedere. Primo opened the gate and ushered them through to a large yard overrun with dormant gardens. Though they were held tight in the clutch of approaching winter, Kat could tell they'd be spectacular come spring. In place of flowers, someone had decorated with fairy lights, holly, Christmas wreaths and garlands.

"Welcome to my home." Pride blended with the flavor of Tuscany to accent Primo's voice. He gestured toward the decorations. "When it grows dark, it is quite beautiful. Not too much, not too little. Just right, *capito?*"

When Gabe remained stubbornly silent, Kat answered for them both. "I'm sure it's spectacular."

She glanced at the man who would soon become her husband, tempted to give him a swift elbow to the ribs, only to discover her mistake. He hadn't fallen silent due to rudeness, but out of respect. He fixed his full attention on a woman who sat at a wrought iron table beneath the protective embrace of a mush oak. With that single exchange, the two spoke volumes to one another and the atmosphere thickened with tension.

Primo followed Gabe's gaze and grinned, oblivious to the growing friction. "Ah, and there is Nonna, waiting for us with hot chocolate." He paused, beaming in delight. "Look, my boy. Is she not the most beautiful of women? Never have I seen anyone who can lighten my heart and make it dance with such joy. But then, you have discovered this with your Katerina, yes?"

Gabe replied by taking Kat's hand in his. "Your wife is beautiful, Primo." He glanced down at Kat, a hint of concern reflected in his gaze. "She also looks scared to death," he murmured beneath his breath. "When she's not glaring at me, that is."

"I'm sure you'll find a way to win her over, as well as reassure her," Kat replied softly. "To protect her from hurt."

His hand jerked in hers. "Protect her?" he repeated.

She couldn't help smiling. "Isn't that what you do? Isn't that what you've always done?"

"I've tried, but—"

"She's angry at her son, not you," Kat whispered. "And she's frightened because she doesn't know how to handle this situation. She's afraid you'll bring harm to her family. She just needs to know that you don't intend to hurt them. And you don't, do you?"

"That depends."

"Gabe… I know what it's like to lose my family, to be cut adrift and have no one. Absolutely no one. I would give anything to have my grandmother back in my life." The words seemed torn from her, filled with trembling passion and heartache. "You have that chance, right here and now. I'm begging you, don't let it slip by."

They didn't have an opportunity for further conversation. Primo ushered them forward. He must have picked up on the emotions swirling between his wife and grandson, and puffed nervously on his cigar in response. The instant Nonna's gaze arrowed in on it, he gave a choking groan and whipped the cigar from his mouth, burying it in the nearest mound of rich, dark soil. "How could I have forgotten? I must be as worried as my Nonna looks," he muttered.

"We will speak of this later, old man," Nonna stated crisply. "When we are alone and I do not disgrace you in front of—" She broke off, no doubt at a loss for how to describe them. Family? Friends? More likely, enemies.

"This is Gabriel," Primo hastened to introduce. "And his wife-to-be, Katerina Malloy."

Nonna inclined her snowy head in a gracious nod, all the while hostile, hazel eyes inspected them critically. There was a spark of anger there, along with something that wavered on the cusp of rejection. And yet, Kat also saw a stunning helplessness, a sorrow that deepened the lines of a face graced with the sort of bone structure that gave Nonna a beauty that would undoubtedly last until the day she died. She turned the full power of that look on Gabe and her mouth compressed, but not from anger, Kat suddenly realized. If anything Nonna attempted to keep her lips from trembling. As though to confirm it, tears welled into her eyes and slid silently down her cheeks.

It was too much for Gabe. He broke from Kat's side and dropped to one knee in front of his grandmother, gently taking her hands in his. "Don't," he murmured. "If my presence causes you this much pain, I'll leave. It was wrong of me to come here. To ask this favor of you."

"Hush, *nipote*." Nonna slipped her hands from his and

gathered his face, lifting it to hers. Then she kissed him. "Forgive a foolish old woman who believed that because my Dominic did wrong, what he created was wrong, as well. If I'd looked with my heart instead of my head, I'd have seen this, for I have always had the sight. I have always seen what others cannot or will not."

Gabe shut his eyes, fighting desperately to shore up his barriers. But it was a losing battle. They crumbled beneath her compassionate regard. "You need to know I despise him for what he did to my mother," he confessed. "My own father and—"

She shushed him again. "How could you feel anything else when you were not given the chance to know him as a son should know his father? But now you have found us. At long last you have come home to become one of us. A Dante."

He shook his head. "I'm not," he denied. "I'll never be a Dante."

She laughed, the sound like the warmth and cheer of Christmas holding at bay the cold rawness of a barren winter. "How illogical you are. How can you not be what you have always been?"

"I'm a Moretti," Gabe stated through gritted teeth. "And I am the most logical person you will ever meet."

She gave a dainty snort. "And these Morettis, they have welcomed you? They have provided for you what the Dantes have not?"

He didn't answer immediately, not until she pinched his cheek, making him feel all of five. "No," he admitted. "My mother's family disowned her when they discovered she was pregnant and unmarried."

"My poor boy." Tears welled in her eyes once again and a ferocity grew there, a blistering determination. "No matter. After all these years, we have found you, Gabriel. We will never disown what belongs to us."

He stiffened in open rejection. She'd touched on the one point he found most unforgiveable. "That's not true. You turned your back on us after Dominic died. You knew we existed, but you refused to acknowledge us. You may not have disowned us, but you did reject us."

Nonna shot an alarmed look at Primo. "Is this true? You have known about Gabriel since we lost our Dominic?"

"What is this? What is this?" He hastened to Gabe's side. "You think we have turned our back on you? Who told you such a lie?"

Gabe hesitated, unwilling to set a match to the turmoil that swirled across the surface of their conversation like a toxic slick of crude oil. He spared a swift look in Kat's direction, who offered a nod of encouragement. He understood the unspoken message. The time had come for total honesty. "He told us you knew. My...my father. That you wanted nothing to do with us."

It took a moment for his words to sink in. The instant they did, Nonna rocked back and forth, tears welling in her eyes and sliding down her lined cheeks. "Oh, Dominic. What have you done? Why did you keep this from us? Your son was an innocent. He needed his Nonna and Primo, and you never told us."

Unable to help himself, he took his grandmother in his arms and simply held her. Then he felt the strength of his grandfather's arms around them both. There was no longer any question about whether or not he *should* be one of them. He knew the truth in that moment. He *was* one of them.

Only one person remained on the outside. He turned to Kat, reached for her. She tried to evade his grasp and he understood why. She considered herself an outsider. But he wouldn't allow it. She needed family as much as he did. He overrode her incipient protest and drew her in. He couldn't quite explain it, didn't dare analyze it, but the instant her warmth and strength joined them, it felt right. The circle melded, became complete. They were bound in some inexplicable way, united in pain and loss, yet found. Accepted. Loved.

There was no awkwardness when they broke apart. Somehow his grandparents wouldn't allow it. "So," Primo said. "It is done. You are one of us."

Gabe spared his grandparents a sharp glance. "You really didn't know about me?"

"I only recently was made aware. Your cousin Gianna told me about running into you during her visit to Seattle, mentioned how much you look like Severo. We knew by then that Dominic had had an affair with your mother, but had only recently suspected that she might have become pregnant as a result. I began looking into it after Gianna found you."

"Family is everything to us," Nonna said with quiet simplicity. "We never would have turned from you if Dominic had told us of your existence."

Gabe heard the ring of truth in her voice and nodded. "Thank you."

Primo stood at Nonna's side, a united front. "I will have my car take you to see my assistant. Lucia has volunteered to be your wedding planner. She will help arrange for the marriage license. Then, while she takes your bride to pick out her wedding gown, Sev has agreed to meet you at Dantes Exclusive to select the wedding rings." He offered a tentative smile. "This is agreeable to you?"

"Sev's going to meet with me?" More than anything Gabe wanted to refuse. But he couldn't. Not when his grandmother watched him so anxiously. They were doing everything possible to reach out. The least he could do was meet them halfway, especially since he'd approached them. "Sure. Not a problem. We were bound to meet sometime."

"It will not be easy for either of you," Primo said. "But it is long past time the two of you know each other as brothers. Try to remember that he is an innocent in all of this, as well. And he feels Dominic's betrayal of his mother as keenly as you feel it for yours."

"There's one difference." Gabe took Kat's hand in his. For some reason, the touch of those warm, slender fingers offered him an unexpected solace, one he hadn't anticipated, but didn't hesitate to accept. "He grew up with the Dante name from the day he was born. I didn't."

Kat fell in love with Lucia the moment they met, amazed to discover Gabe's sister possessed a personality as different from Gabe's as her appearance. While her brother tended to keep his emotions on ice—except for the occasional volcanic explosions—Lucia's face revealed every thought and feeling, from the apprehension of their first meeting to the delight of discovering a kindred spirit. It all came through in each gesture and intonation.

What amused her the most was when Lucia and Gabe balled their hands into fists and linked index fingers before embracing. "It was our private signal to each other and to our mother," Lucia explained afterward. "Sort of an unwritten code to let the other know we're there for them and that we love them. That we have their backs."

Obtaining the marriage license didn't take any time at all, though it soon became clear that Primo had pulled a few strings in order to get them preferential treatment. The only awkward moment occurred when Gabe caught a glimpse of her application.

"That's your birth date?" he asked in an odd voice.

"Yes." She gave him a puzzled glance. "I'll be twenty-five in a couple months. Why?"

"You were only twenty when...?"

She appreciated that he didn't finish his question in front of a curious Lucia. "Technically I was nineteen. How old did you think I was?"

"Not nineteen." His mouth compressed. "I didn't realize Jessa was so much older than you."

Kat glanced at his information. "I've got news for you. She was older than both of us."

He immediately shook his head. "That can't be right. She told me—" He broke off. "Maybe we'll save this discussion for a later time."

"What's the point?" she asked quietly. "After all, it won't change anything."

For once, he didn't have an answer. When they were finished with the paperwork, they split up, Gabe heading for Dantes Exclusive, while Lucia took charge of their shopping expedition. Her natural exuberance had faded and Kat couldn't help but wonder if she'd finally realized who Gabe was marrying—or rather, what she'd been accused of five years ago.

Sure enough, she broached the subject, her tone unnaturally clipped. "You're Jessa's cousin, aren't you?"

"Yes." Kat didn't bother to expound. Offering any sort of explanation seemed futile. Lucia caught her bottom lip between her teeth, clearly debating whether or not to speak her mind, which would have been amusing under different circumstances. "You might as well go ahead and say it," she said kindly.

"Okay." Lucia snatched a quick breath and blurted, "I hated your cousin. I know I shouldn't speak ill of the dead, but I thought she was all wrong for Gabe. If she hadn't died in that car wreck, they'd have been divorced by now. I guarantee it."

"Uh—"

Kat didn't manage more than that small squeak before Lucia launched into speech again. "And she'd have taken my brother to the cleaners before she finished with him. Not that she'd have had to. He'd probably have given her anything she wanted just to get rid of her." She made a face. "Okay, maybe not anything. He would have done everything in his power to get his hands on Mom's necklace, assuming Jessa inherited it. Not that she would have let it go easily. Knowing her, she'd have used Heart's Desire to get *her* heart's desire which was every last penny Gabe possessed. Lord, I hope you're not like her." She turned a fierce glare on Kat. "Because if you are, I'm not holding back this time. I will find a way to take you down."

It took Kat a moment to process the flood of information, before admitting, "Gabe and I are marrying so he can have Heart's Desire and I can reconcile with my grandmother. The marriage is just temporary."

"Oh." Lucia's brow wrinkled. "Well, that's not going to work."

"Why?"

"Don't you know?" She tossed a grin in Kat's direction. "How can it be temporary when it's clear to anyone with half a brain you're crazy about each other?"

From that point on, Lucia and Kat became firm friends. It felt odd. It also felt good. She'd never had anyone treat her with such immediate and spontaneous affection. There'd always been barriers before, even during her time in Italy. Of course those barriers were of her own making. After the scandal, she'd been cautious to the extreme, afraid to open up to anyone in case they hurt her the way Jessa had. Somehow, Lucia had a way of sweeping past all that, as good at opening up others as she was at opening herself to them. And yet, Kat didn't have a moment's doubt that her secrets were safe with Lucia.

"We certainly have our work cut out for us," Lucia said, sweeping into the first bridal shop. She ticked off on her fingers. "There's the wedding gown, of course. The veil. The undergarments. Shoes. Something gorgeous and sexy for your wedding night. A few extra outfits to throw in just because."

"I don't need a few extra outfits."

Lucia shot an admiring glance at the dress Kat wore. "Probably not, but what the hell, right? And once we have your wedding gown picked out, I'll know what sort of flowers to order."

"I think I hear my credit card whimpering."

"Don't be ridiculous," Lucia protested. "The Dantes are paying for everything."

"Oh, no, they most certainly are not," Kat shot back. "I won't allow it. And I guarantee, Gabe won't, either."

Lucia frowned in genuine concern. "You can't refuse. You'll break Primo's heart if you do."

"I'm afraid he'll just have to live with a broken heart," she stated in her most implacable voice. "It'll mend."

Not that her tone cut any ice with Lucia. She swept aside Kat's comment as though it were inconsequential. "You don't understand. He won't be disappointed, he'll be offended. And if you offend Primo, you offend all of the Dantes." She shrugged. "It's an Italian thing. Offend one, offend all."

Damn. After five years in Italy, she should have anticipated that. "Gabe will not be happy."

"Gabe will have to learn to live with his unhappiness, especially considering where he's going right now," Lucia said tartly. "His meeting with Sev won't be easy. My half brother has issues when it comes to my mother, and with Gabe in particular."

"Why Gabe in particular?"

Lucia hesitated and a profound sadness crept into her expression. "I suppose it would be with both of us if he knew I existed." She pretended to give her full attention to the designer gowns on display.

"Lucia?" Kat prompted gently.

"I think it's because of The Inferno," she confessed softly.

"You've lost me."

She spared Kat a swift look over her shoulder. Her eyes darkened, the teal-blue reflecting endless pain. "If Cara Moretti was Dominic's Inferno soul mate..."

It only took Kat a moment to connect the dots. When she reached the logical conclusion, she winced. "What does that make Sev's mother?"

"Exactly. *Not* Dominic's Inferno soul mate. That's why I can never have any sort of meaningful relationship with my half brothers. The fact that Dominic never truly loved their mother would always stand between us."

Primo's car dropped Gabe near the Embarcadero, in the heart of the financial district. He'd been directed to a smoked glass door etched with the initials DE, and used the call button nearby to announce himself. A buzzer immediately sounded, releasing the door lock and allowing him access to Dantes Exclusive.

While the outside appeared unassuming, the interior was anything but. An understated opulence permeated the reception area, echoed by a staff member dressed in an elegant suit and tie. He gave a start of surprise, bordering on shock at Gabe's appearance, no doubt due to his close resemblance to Sev. Then he offered a polite greeting and escorted Gabe to a private elevator that went directly to the penthouse level.

Clearly, he'd been expected. He stepped off the car into a massive room that could have been mistaken for a private residence. His shoes vanished into the thick, dove-gray carpeting that gave the area a lavish, yet intimate feel, echoing what he'd experienced at Dantes corporate office building.

The employee gestured toward a glittering wet bar at one end of the room. "Would you care for a drink?"

He might just kill for one, Gabe decided. "No, thanks." He'd also be damned before he accepted anything else from the Dantes.

"Mr. Dante will be right with you," his escort said—warned?—before stepping back into the elevator and leaving him alone in the room.

Gabe wandered deeper into luxury where plants and elaborate fresh flower arrangements gave the area an added warmth. Divans covered in gray and white pinstripes dotted the room, along with silk chairs in a rich ruby-red, all with glass tables placed in front of the sitting areas. The tables were a bit higher than normal coffee tables, with overhead spots throwing circles of blazing light on each table, leaving the chairs and couches in soft shadow. No doubt the tables had been specifically designed to showcase Dantes' fabulous gems for some of the company's more exclusive clientele.

A door opposite him opened and a man entered the room. Gabe didn't have a single doubt this was Sev Dante. Based on Gianna's reaction when she and Gabe first met, as well as the DE employee just now, he'd been anticipating the resemblance, assuming they would look quite a bit alike. But he didn't expect to meet someone who could have passed for his twin. Sev spared him a single shocked glare, then paused by a wet bar, splashing amber liquor into two glasses. He approached and offered one of the drinks.

"If you're experiencing anything close to what I am, I'm betting you need this as badly as I do," Sev said.

"Hell, yes," Gabe answered, accepting the tumbler.

They both took a swift swallow, then continued to eye one another with undisguised dislike. "So, who goes first?" Sev asked. The question held the unmistakable slap of a challenge.

Gabe didn't hesitate in snatching up the gauntlet. "I will. Just so you know, if I had any other choice, I'd have been just as happy never meeting any of you. I don't want anything from you. Ever."

"And yet, here you are, expecting us to acknowledge you," Sev shot back. "In my book, that's wanting something."

Gabe's mouth tightened. "Okay, fine. I want something."

"And just so you know, if Primo hadn't insisted on my being here, I'd have been just as happy never meeting you, too." Sev bared his teeth in a rough semblance of a smile. "I can also categorically state—just so we're crystal clear on the subject—that not only don't I want anything from you, I wouldn't accept anything from you if I were on my deathbed and you possessed my only hope for salvation."

Gabe thrust his nose toward one identical to his own. "See, there's where we differ. I *would* accept what you possessed. I'd just make damn sure I found a way to make you suffer for your generosity."

Sev's nose thrust out another inch, as did his chin. "Excellent idea. Since you're the one who needs what I have, let's see if I can't make you suffer before I give it to you."

They both hesitated. Gabe broke the confused silence. "Okay, I gotta admit," he said. "I don't understand a word of what we just said."

"Neither did I," Sev concurred. "But I think what we both mean is that we despise each other and would be only too happy to make life as miserable as possible for the other person. Does that sum it up?"

Ah, good. A negotiation. The familiar territory put him on sound footing and also made him realize just how off-balance he'd been this entire time. "I think we have the bare bones laid out. And I have some suggestions where we can take it from there."

"You want another drink while we put some flesh on those bones?"

"Only if we stop speaking in metaphors."

"Thank God."

Sev added a couple fingers to each glass and eyed Gabe over the rim. "Considering how happy we all were not having to deal with each other's existence, why step forward now? What's changed?"

Gabe rubbed his thumb across his palm. "If it weren't for this damn Inferno, I wouldn't be here. But I don't have any choice, not if I want to protect Kat."

"Your bride-to-be?" At Gabe's nod, unholy amusement glittered in eyes identical to Gabe's. "You two experienced The Inferno when you first touched?"

"Yes."

"And how will it help to have the Dantes acknowledge the connection—"

"For want of a better word," Gabe inserted smoothly.

Sev growled. "You'd prefer a different word? Fine. How about *bastard*? There. Is that a better word?"

Gabe shrugged. He'd heard the word used in reference to him so often, it no longer had the power to wound when someone attempted to use it like a weapon. He'd learned to deal with what he was years ago. To accept his illegitimacy in a way his mother and sister never had. "Do you think calling me a bastard changes anything? That I'm offended? Hurt?" He gave a harsh laugh. "I've got news for you, Sev. I *am* a bastard. And do you know why? It's because that's what our father made me."

"You think I don't know that?" Sev shot right back. "Not a day goes by that I'm not aware of your existence and the implications of that existence."

"Oh, man, I feel for you." Sarcasm ran roughshod over Gabe's response. "Poor you. Having to deal with the fact that you've got a bastard brother. Try living it. Then come crying to me."

"Hell, hotshot. You're the one standing square on Dante property, hat in hand. If anyone's crying…"

Gabe saw red. He acted without thought. Spinning around, he heaved his glass at the nearest wall. It exploded with a high-pitched crystalline shriek, and splattered shards of glass and amber liquid across the pristine wall and floor beneath. The Scotch bled downward, as though weeping bitter tears. He gulped air, stunned by his utter lack of control. He struggled against the white-hot fury whipping through him, shoving him closer to the edge than he could ever remember being shoved, knowing the least wrong word would push him into the seething abyss.

He swung around to face Sev. "I'm not here for myself, you ass. I want nothing from you. I'm here for Kat. To protect her. As far as I'm concerned, you can take the Dante name and shove it."

"Jealous?"

Eight

That single taunting word stripped through years of denial. Laid Gabe bare. How had Sev done it? It took all of two minutes in the same room together before he'd nailed Gabe's one weakness and broken through the iceman façade to what seethed beneath. To what he'd fought so hard to suppress…and failed.

And he'd hit on the single key vulnerability Gabe had spent his entire life attempting to deny. Taking a deep breath, he forced himself to open that locked door and stare at what he'd hidden inside. To confront the truth from an adult's perspective and deal with what a child had buried so many years before, desperate to conceal that truth from anyone and everyone. He stiffened his spine and met Sev's gaze squarely, allowing the ugliness free rein. After all, what did it matter what this man thought of him, so long as he protected Kat? After what he'd done five years ago, he owed her at least that much.

"Yes. Yes, I am jealous." he whispered. The gut-wrenching pain slipped free of his iron grip and he released it, unable to contain it for another second. "You have what my mother and sister would have given anything to possess. You've lived a life we'll never know. Do you blame me for wanting to turn my back on what was denied me? For despising the man who created us, then deserted us?"

"Sister?" Sev demanded in shock. "You have a *sister*?"

Damn, damn, *damn*. That's what happened when he lost control. "A twin," he reluctantly admitted.

"Does Primo know?"

"No. Not yet, and I prefer to keep it that way until she's ready to tell him, herself."

"Is she… Is she—" Sev broke off and shook his head.

Was that concern Gabe heard? It sounded almost protective, which struck him as utterly ridiculous. Why would Sev feel the least bit protective toward Lucia? Unless… Unless they were more alike than he cared to admit. It was an unsettling thought. "Is she…what?" he asked suspiciously.

"I want to say, is she okay. But how can she be?" Sev sighed. "How can any of us be okay with any part of this?"

"She wasn't okay for a very long time," Gabe found himself admitting. "But she's…coping."

Sev fell silent. "I found out about Dad's affair right after his death. There were letters." He grimaced. "I didn't know until recently that the affair had resulted in children."

"And if you had known?"

He didn't hesitate. "I'd have told Primo right away. He and Nonna brought us to live with them after our parents died. Of course, I was in college by then, but my brothers…" A hint of a smile drifted across his mouth. "Knowing Primo, he'd have taken you and your sister in, too. Raised us as a family. Knocked our heads together until we learned to accept each other."

Gabe returned the smile, amazed by how natural it felt. "From what little I know about our grandfather, I suspect you're right."

The muscles ridging Sev's jaw tightened. "Dad loved her, you know. Your mother. Our father loved her in a way he never loved my mother." The confession came hard, almost as hard as Gabe's admitting he'd been jealous of Sev and his brothers. "Maybe you can understand it a little better now that you've experienced The Inferno. My brothers and I, we were the product of his marriage. But we were never the product of his heart."

Gabe swore beneath his breath. "Still, you bear his name."

"True. But you and your sister and mother owned his heart." His mouth tightened and bitter grief darkened eyes identical to Gabe's. "So it would seem we both are jealous of something the other possesses."

It was a bizarre thought, one that twisted how Gabe saw himself and his family and the Dantes. "So, what now?"

"Maybe now we simply accept what can't be changed and move on. Maybe figure out what we can change in the future." Sev allowed that to sink in before deliberately switching the subject. "Tell me how our name will protect your bride-to-be. Kat, is it?"

"I need the Dantes to acknowledge the connection so she won't be vilified in the press."

Sev frowned. "Why would they do that?"

"She was unjustly accused of having an affair with her cousin's fiancé. Benson Winters? He was a senatorial candidate at the time." Sev nodded his recognition of the name and Gabe continued. "She was found in bed with him."

Sev's expression closed down. "She was caught in bed with him, but she's innocent." He paused a beat. "You're sure?"

He spoke in a noncommittal tone, but Gabe could hear

the doubt leaching through the words. "It's a little hard to have an affair with a man when you've never slept with anyone before," he retorted.

To his surprise, Sev stepped right over the line from doubt to immediate acceptance. "Well, who was the son of a bitch who accused her? And why the hell would he do something like that?" Anger stirred in his gaze with the sort of protective rage Gabe found all too familiar. It disconcerted him to discover one more similarity between them. "And why the hell haven't you beaten the living snot out of him?"

"Because I'm the son of a bitch who accused her."

"You." Sev's eyes narrowed and Gabe suspected he teetered on the edge of personally administering the beating he'd recommended. Apparently that protective streak came from the Dante side of the family. Who knew? "Why? Why would you do that?"

"Because I found her in his bed. I don't have all the facts about what happened. Yet," he added. "And obviously, there's more to the story than my attempting to right a wrong. There are reasons—reasons I'd rather not go into—for our needing everyone to accept our marriage and believe it's genuine."

"Which I assume it is." Sev tossed back the last of his drink. "At least, it is if you two have been hit with The Inferno."

Gabe didn't bother to correct him. The Dantes would discover the truth on that score as soon as he and Kat divorced. But maybe he could obtain a more realistic explanation for The Inferno before that happened. "As long as you brought up the subject…"

Sev laughed. "You have questions about The Inferno."

"I asked Primo, but—"

"Our grandfather has strong opinions on the subject."

"I gather you don't agree with those opinions?" It came

as a relief to discover Sev didn't buy into the fairy tale. "So, you're just humoring him?"

"You want me to say that The Inferno will go away. That it's not real."

"It isn't real."

Sev laughed in genuine amusement. "That's what I thought until it hit me the first time Francesca and I touched. That's what my brothers all thought until it happened to them. Just as it happened to all four of our cousins. Almost all of us fought it. And every one of us lost the battle. Face it. If you're a Dante, you're stuck with The Inferno."

"I'm not a Dante!"

Sev shook his head in disgust. "That's what I planned to tell you. In fact, I'd intended to make it clear with my fists, if necessary." He shrugged philosophically. "Looks like we're both wrong. You're a Dante whether you want to be or not. Hell, whether *we* want you to be or not."

"Look, it doesn't matter what you call me. Not really. Once Kat and I are married, we'll be out of all your lives," Gabe insisted.

"Sorry, but it won't be that simple," Sev warned. "You're not a Dante one minute and then not one the next. It's all or nothing. Primo and Nonna won't allow it to go down any other way. As much as I hate to admit it—" He stuck out his hand. "Looks like we're brothers."

Gabe stared at the hand Sev offered for an endless moment. Instinct warned that if he accepted it, everything would change. His life would never be the same again. He'd become a different person. He'd be accepting something he'd spent his entire life denying. Granted, it was his choice. But once the decision had been made, it couldn't be undone.

He looked into Sev's eyes and saw himself. Saw the same tawny eyes which had been passed from father to son through the generations. Saw the same passion and fierce determination. The same protectiveness. Saw features cut into harsh lines by a life fully lived, filled with both happiness and pain. Saw himself, the good as well as the bad.

He stared again at the hand being offered. Accepting it would forever alter him, take him from being a Moretti...to becoming a Dante. And he knew which he wanted, which he'd always wanted, if he'd been honest with himself.

Without any further hesitation, he took his brother's hand.

Kat woke on her wedding day to a fierce wind and a leaden sky unleashing a torrent of rain. She stood at the window of the suite Primo insisted on booking at Le Premier, a five-star hotel on Nob Hill, and struggled against disappointment. The rain made her think of tears. And though she claimed to never, ever cry—despite a single aberration the first time Gabe made love to her—she couldn't deny feeling a tiny bit tearful when she stared out at the gray, wet curtain blanketing San Francisco.

Her grandmother joined her at the window. "It rained on my wedding day, too."

"Did it bring you bad luck?"

Matilda laughed, and for the first time in more than five years it came with a familiar ease. For some reason the sound had those tears Kat held at bay welling into her eyes. "Not even a little. Your grandfather and I looked like two drowned rats when it was all said and done. But it led... Well, it led to a very special wedding night."

Kat bowed her head. "Gam, I'm sorry. I'm so sorry I hurt you."

"Hush now, child. It's not you who should apologize, but me. You wrote to me the entire time you were gone, kept in touch while I allowed pride to get in my way. Allowed moral outrage to hold me apart from you for five lonely years instead of following my heart and accepting that you were young and foolish and made a dreadful mistake. Forgive me if it takes a little time for me to be the grandmother you deserve." She gathered Kat close. "But no matter what, always remember that I love you, Katerina."

"I love you, too, Gam." She burrowed against the woman who'd been mother, grandmother and confidante, and inhaled the familiar scent of her, a powdery fragrance lightly accented with rose. It was like coming home, even if everything had changed. Even if she couldn't quite regain the relationship they'd once shared. "I don't want to lose you. Not after I just found you again."

"There's still time." She gave Kat a final hug. "I brought Heart's Desire with me. I thought maybe you'd like to wear it today."

Kat pulled back and smiled in delight. "I'd love to wear it. It would mean the world to Gabe."

Matilda crossed the room and removed a velvet box from her purse. She gripped it tightly, hesitation disturbing the even tenor of her expression. "This marriage…it's all happened so fast. You…you do love Gabe? That is the reason you're marrying?"

Oh, dear. She didn't want to lie to her grandmother. But she couldn't admit the entire truth. She didn't dare. "I realize it's fast. But Gabe explained to you about his connection to the Dantes, right? And he explained about The Inferno, what it is and—" For some reason she couldn't prevent a blush. "And how it works?"

A small smile touched Matilda's mouth. "I have to admit, I find it terribly romantic. Not that I consider myself the romantic sort. But to feel that sort of love from the first moment you touch… And best of all it was with Gabe. I adore him, you know. I always have."

Kat approached her grandmother and offered her most reassuring smile. "Then you can trust him to do what's right."

Matilda released her breath in a sigh, clearly relieved. "Yes, yes. Of course." Fortunately, she didn't pick up on the fact that her original question had never been answered. She handed Kat the box. "I have to admit I haven't seen the necklace in quite some time. If I'd known the wedding would happen so soon, I'd have had it cleaned for you."

Kat carried it to a small table covered in a linen runner and shifted a lamp closer so it spotlighted the center section. Then she spread the necklace beneath the high-powered light. The diamonds burst into flames.

"It really is spectacular," she murmured, then frowned, leaning in.

Something wasn't quite right. She studied the necklace more carefully and realized that not all of the stones contained the same flash and glitter she would have expected from fire diamonds, or that she remembered it having five years ago. Her frown deepened. Was it possible that they weren't all fire diamonds? She peered closer, wishing she had a loupe. Were they even real diamonds? Could the original design have combined regular stones with those unearthed in the Dante mines? Her stomach clenched. It was possible, wasn't it?

Possible, maybe, but highly improbable.

One way or another, she needed to find out and fast. Until she uncovered the truth, she didn't dare wear the necklace, not in front of countless Dantes, all of whom could spot a fake a mile away. And what about her marriage to Gabe? If the necklace was a fake—or missing a significant number of the original diamonds—would he still be so quick to marry her? Or would he wait in order to verify the necklace appraised…and determine whether or not she was pregnant?

Okay, okay. Stay calm. It was an old necklace. It was entirely possible that thirty or more years ago the Dantes didn't use fire diamonds, exclusively. Francesca! Francesca would know. Kat would simply solicit the opinion of Sev's wife. As their top designer, she'd be able to determine the authenticity of both the necklace and the stones. Until then...

She glanced at her grandmother and forced out a smile. "You know, it occurs to me that if I wear this necklace the Dantes might recognize the piece, as well as its significance. It might not be the most diplomatic decision to wear jewelry Dominic gave to someone other than his wife, even if she was Gabe's mother. I wouldn't want to risk damaging his relationship with his family now that they're on the verge of a reconciliation."

Matilda frowned. "I hadn't considered that." She gave it a moment's thought. "Perhaps you could give it to him to-night as a wedding gift?"

"I think that's an excellent idea," Kat replied, relieved beyond measure. "Or possibly as a Christmas gift. What do you think?"

"I think he'd appreciate that, as well. If you wait until Christmas, you'd have time to get it cleaned," Matilda pointed out.

An old-fashioned doorbell rang, putting an end to their discussion, and Kat quickly stowed the necklace in the suite safe while Matilda went to open the door. Lucia entered in her role as wedding planner, the female half of the Dante contingent in tow, there to assist with the pre-wedding prepa-rations. To Kat's frustration, Francesca wasn't one of them, having agreed to cover babysitting duties in order to free up the others.

It was interesting to discover that Gabe's sister possessed his same attention to detail, along with his ability to man-age and direct. In no time, she had everyone scurrying to tackle all the endless tasks necessary to get a lot accom-plished in a very short period of time. Kat debated whether or not to escape the organized chaos in search of Gabe and warn him of her suspicions about the necklace. But Lucia put a swift end to that possibility when asked, oh so casually, about his whereabouts.

"He's not here, and don't even bother asking where he is. None of us will tell you."

"Well, of course not," Gianna added with a mischievous grin. "You can't see the groom before the ceremony. It's bad luck."

The women all burst out laughing, one of them explaining, "Gia had a confession to make to her husband, Constantine, one that couldn't wait until after the ceremony. So she invaded the groom's room, despite risking very bad luck. It's become a family joke."

"I promise I won't invade Gabe's room before we're married," Kat began, "but—"

"You can't call him, either. Primo took away his cell phone. I think he's probably the only one who could have gotten Gabe to cough it up, too," Lucia whispered with a grin. "I wish I could have seen that."

So, that cut off her only other avenue of contact. Kat spared a glance toward the windows. "Seems like the weather really has brought bad luck."

"Rain is not bad luck," Nonna insisted. "*È buona fortuna.* It brings you good luck. It cleanses all the bad from your past. Rain is also a sign of fertility. Babies. It brings you the baby."

"Is she going to have boys or girls?" Gianna asked. She winked at Kat. "My grandmother has the eye. She hasn't gotten a single one wrong, yet. So, which is it, Nonna? Boys or girls?"

"Yes," Nonna said placidly.

The women all laughed. "There you have it," Gianna's mother, Elia said. "You're either going to have a boy or a girl."

The women turned their attention to laying out her gown and veil, and setting up stations for makeup and hair. On the far side of the room, Gianna and Matilda had their heads together. Based on the snatch of conversation that accompanied their laughter, they were comparing wedding day stories.

Nonna beckoned to Kat, waiting to speak until she'd come close enough not to be overheard. "You wish to know what you will have?"

Kat shrugged. Why not? "Sure."

Nonna touched just beneath the knotted sash holding Kat's robe closed. A hint of color touched her cheeks. "I did not wish to say in front of the others since you and Gabriel should not have made this baby before saying your vows." She gave a shrug of resignation. "But what is done is done. Soon you will be married and your son protected from the life Gabriel experienced."

Kat choked. "I'm…I'm pregnant?" Her voice rose in a breathless squeak and she sank to her knees beside Nonna's chair. "You mean, *now?*"

Gabe's grandmother chuckled. "This is usually what pregnant means. You are not far along. The spark is so very tiny, I almost missed it. Just the barest of flickers. But strong. Stubborn. A fighter."

"A son." She grappled with the concept. "You said it will be a boy."

"This first one, yes. The two that follow will be girls. Twins. With pretty reddish hair like yours, but with their father's golden eyes. Your son, he will have your eye color." Nonna smiled. "I see you do not believe me."

"I—" Kat shook her head. "I don't know what to believe."

"I am not offended. In time you will see I am right and then you will not question." She frowned. "You are upset. Does this not make you happy?"

Kat bowed her head. "It makes me very happy," she whispered. "But I'm not sure whether it will make Gabe happy."

Nonna appeared astounded at the suggestion. "Why would Gabriel not be happy?"

"Because it means he'll be stuck with me."

"Stuck with...?" She shook her head and called to her daughter-in-law. "Elia, *che cosa significa* 'stuck with me,' eh?"

"*Intrappolati.*"

Nonna turned a sharp gaze on Kat. "You and Gabriel, you have experienced The Inferno, yes?" At Kat's nod, she smiled in relief. "Do not worry about this stickiness. The Inferno, it will unstick you."

"You mean, it goes away?"

Nonna laughed. "No, no. It never goes away. You just do not feel sticky. You only feel love. It is like *il bambino*. It must have time to become. You marry Gabriel and you will have all the years God blesses you with to become. *Capito?*"

Oh, Kat understood, all right. She just wasn't sure she believed. But the plans Gabe had set in motion were moving too fast to stop. Her hand slid low on her abdomen, settling over the baby Nonna claimed rested there. If she really were pregnant, she couldn't stop the marriage, even if she tried. Even if Heart's Desire was a fake. If Gabe so much as suspected she carried his baby, he wouldn't rest until he'd placed his ring on her finger in order to make absolutely certain his child didn't experience the stigma he had growing up. Still, she hated the idea of tying him to a marriage he thought temporary.

And yet, throughout the rest of the morning she caught herself cradling the spark of new life she and Gabe may have created.

A baby.

* * *

The wedding was everything Kat could have wanted, and then some.

She wore a gown that she and Lucia had fallen in love with the second they'd seen it, a delicious blend of elegance and romance. The women helped hook her into the lacey, fitted bodice, exclaiming that it made her waist appear miniscule. They smoothed the skirt of the gown around her, one that flared out in a wide bell with a dramatic chapel length train. To her stunned delight, Nonna provided an antique tiara, studded with fire diamonds, clearly from Dantes personal collection. The tulle veil attached to the tiara and swept to the floor, framing her in softness, the scalloped edges trimmed with lace that matched her gown.

There'd been heated debate among the women over her hair, but she'd held firm, quietly insisting that she wear it down. It was how Gabe preferred it and as soon as she explained that, they swiftly shifted gears, discussing the exact style that would suit both the veil and her facial structure. In the end, they pulled the sides back and up and curled the rest, allowing it to tumble down her back and shoulders. Then they wove a narrow silver beaded ribbon through the strands, anchored with bits of mistletoe and holly, a reminder that Christmas was right around the corner, only ten days away.

By the time they left for the chapel, the rain had subsided and the sun beamed through a series of large, puffy clouds. The ride from the hotel took no time and the women assisted Kat with her gown so it wouldn't get damp during the climb to the stone chapel topping the hill. They left her in the garden on one side to await the start of the ceremony, while assisting Matilda to her seat in the chapel. Kat stared out at the glorious view of the bay and its islands, along with the distinctive red arches of the Golden Gate Bridge, struggling to remain calm and focused while nerves tried to get the better of her.

Maybe if she hadn't realized the necklace might be a fake… She glanced toward the chapel wondering if she could sneak in and speak to Gabe before the ceremony. Tell him about the necklace and give him the option of changing his mind. Before she could follow through on the thought, Primo joined her, looking dapper in his tux, puffing on his signature cigar.

She spared the chapel a final look of regret before turning her attention to Gabe's grandfather. "Thank you for offering to walk me down the aisle," she said.

"It is my pleasure. You look…" He shook his head, emotion welling into his eyes. "You look the way a bride should on her wedding day. Radiant, yes?"

She could feel her smile tremble at the edges, bordering on the tears she refused to let fall. "Thank you."

He took her hand in his. "You are nervous. It is understandable, but there is no need. You will discover this for yourself in the fullness of time." He gave her hand a fatherly squeeze. "Whether you realize it or not, you both love each other."

Kat instantly shook her head. "No, not after such a short time. It's not possible."

"It is fear that keeps you from admitting the truth. Gabriel is afraid you will betray him the way his father betrayed his mother, choosing to marry for financial gain instead of following his heart. Then when Dominic never returned to claim the child he had created out of wedlock, Gabe lost all ability to trust. It is why he continues to hold himself from his Primo and Nonna. But, you…" He hesitated, then shrugged. "I see your fear, but do not know you well enough to guess the cause."

"I'm afraid to trust, as well," she confessed. "I've also been betrayed in the past."

"You are afraid Gabriel will betray you?" Clearly, the thought astounded him.

She instinctively shook his head. "He just wants to protect me."

"Ah." Primo regarded her with a wealth of tenderness and wisdom in his antique gold eyes. "And you do not want him to confuse protectiveness for love."

"Yes." He'd summed it up in a nutshell.

"Gabriel is a Dante. He will always feel driven to protect those he loves. It is part of the fabric of who he is." Primo leaned forward and kissed her forehead. "So if he protects you, it is because he loves you."

Kat wished she could believe him. Considering Gabe had done everything in his power to protect Jessa, including destroy the woman he now intended to marry, she had her doubts. Despite what his grandfather claimed, he couldn't love her, not after so short a time. Therefore, he wasn't attempting to protect her out of love, but due to some other misguided notion. Maybe he was only marrying her out of guilt, to right a wrong. She flinched from the thought.

The chapel bells sounded, a joyful pealing that heralded the start of the ceremony. Primo gently covered her face with the veil and offered her arm, escorting her to a vestibule where Christmas scented the air. It had been decorated in a mix of snowy white ranunculus and red roses, poinsettias and garlands of cedar boughs. Someone handed her a cascading bouquet that mirrored the Yuletide decorations surrounding her, tied together with a silver beaded ribbon that matched the one wound through her hair. Lucia, maybe? Then, the bells faded on the crisp winter air, the sweet sound of a string quartet replacing them, joyfully announcing the arrival of the bride.

For a split second, panic set in and Kat couldn't move. What was she doing? Had she lost her mind? She'd only known this man a few short weeks. How could she contemplate marrying someone after mere days of acquaintance, despite what happened whenever they touched? It was wrong. It went against everything this ceremony stood for.

It was bad enough that she'd fallen into bed with Gabe, had surrendered herself heart, body and soul whenever he took her into his arms. But to compound the mistake by marrying him, especially when he believed it would give him his Heart's Desire? She couldn't do it.

She'd figure some other way to reconcile with her grandmother. They were halfway reconciled already, weren't they? As for Heart's Desire, she'd simply insist her grandmother give it to him, especially if it proved to be a fake or missing a significant portion of the original diamonds. She didn't need or want it. And the possibility of her pregnancy? How would she handle that? She closed her eyes, fighting to breathe. Why, oh why, had she chosen a fitted bodice when any second now it would squeeze the very breath from her lungs?

Primo urged her forward and she teetered at the threshold of the chapel, on the verge of bolting. The aisle stretched in front of her, an endless flow of snowy white, accented with bright red rose petals that led straight to Gabe. She stared at him, knowing that all he had to do was look at her with those demanding tawny eyes and she'd pull a Cinderella.

He stood ramrod straight, at an angle to her. Then, almost as though he sensed her desperation, he turned his head and their gazes collided. She could never explain what happened then. With every instinct she possessed clamoring that she run, a tiny tendril of emotion pushed its way upward from deep inside. Despite being so small and new, it held her immobile, forcing her to look, really look at Gabe. So, she did.

She witnessed a similar dawning in his expression, a

look of stunned disbelief, as though he'd never truly seen her before. Where before his gaze carried a hint of tarnished resolution, now it changed. It was as though the sun rose in his eyes, bright and golden and filled with warmth that invaded every part of her. She saw a bottomless well of desire. Not the hunger they'd shared the night they made love. But something more reverent, something that made her palm itch and pulsate.

Then he slowly raised his hand against the dark palette of his tux and formed a tight fist, his index finger lifting free to curve into a hook. It was almost as though she heard him say the words: *I have your back. I'm here for you. I'll protect you.* That one simple gesture snagged hold of her, linked her to him. Every bit of tension drained away and she moved toward him without hesitation. Her heart filled with hope, and something else. Something she couldn't quite identify.

And when he took her hand in his, index fingers linked, that small, persistent tendril blossomed. Became. She recognized it then. Her fear faded and she took a chance, opening herself to it, allowing it to fill her, deep and powerful, until it became a permanent part of the very warp and weft of her being.

Love.

She realized in that moment she loved Gabe Moretti and knew with an unwavering certainty she would love him for the rest of her life.

Nine

The endless round of photographs left Kat teetering on the edge of a total meltdown. Who knew? Who knew that she'd handle the ceremony with aplomb—with the exception of that one teeny, tiny panic attack beforehand. She also breezed through meeting an endless kaleidoscope of Dantes, even managing to match names to faces. Of course, it helped that she quickly picked up on their unique characteristics and created private nicknames for each.

There was Gabe 2 (Sev). Silver Tongue (Marco). Spock (Lazz). Rambo (Nicolò). Then came the cousins. The Protector (Luc). The Wolf (Rafe). The Dragon (Draco). Okay, that was a bit obvious, but it fit. And finally, The Princess (Gianna), who possessed all the best qualities of Kat's personal nickname for her and none of the less admirable traits. She had a slightly more difficult time remembering the wives' names, with the notable exception of Francesca. But then,

Francesca was also a jewelry designer, someone Kat hoped to one day work with.

Kat managed it all with aplomb. But the photographer utterly defeated her, driving her to the brink of insanity, first at the chapel, and then at Le Premier, during the reception hosted by the hotel. Finally, Gabe stepped in and, with a few terse words, arranged for a brief interlude of privacy. He guided Kat to an elegant divan off in one corner, and circled behind her. Leaning in, he massaged her shoulders.

"I think I'm going to melt," she murmured, her eyes drifting closed.

"You're doing fantastic. Better than I would have in your shoes."

She chuckled, sticking out a foot, the four-inch spikes glittering like fairy dust. "You couldn't wear my shoes. No man could."

"Considering the height of those heels, they'd be tough to run in. When you walked into the chapel and realized what you'd gotten yourself into, I thought you'd give it a try."

She winced. "You noticed?"

"I took one look at you and realized I should have posted guards at the door." He leaned in to whisper, "Of course, if you'd bolted, I'd have been about three seconds behind you."

She tilted her head back to smile up at him. "I doubt you'd have gotten far. I think the Dantes would have tackled you."

"Tackled me and beat the living crap out of me." She caught a hint of reluctant humor lurking behind the words. "And enjoyed every minute of it, too."

"Boys will be boys," she said lightly.

He circled around to sit beside her. "Just remember, once they'd finished with me, they'd have gone after you."

She laughed. "Probably to congratulate me for my good taste in dumping you."

Unable to help herself, she reached for him, desperate

for the reassurance of his touch. The instant their hands met, heat flared. Gabe bent to kiss her. And then Kat's eyes closed and she surrendered to the embrace, allowed it to overcome logic and common sense. To sink inside of her and nourish that tendril that had blossomed during their wedding ceremony.

A whir and flash interrupted them and Gabe tensed. He lifted his head and shot a single glare at the photographer, who scurried off. "I'd go after him, but I have a feeling I'm going to want a print of that one."

A keepsake of their temporary marriage? Hope filled her. Maybe it would turn into more than a temporary marriage. Maybe, given time, he'd discover what she had. That, despite the short time she'd known him and despite all that continued to stand between them, she'd fallen in love with him, knew to the depths of her being that he was the one. The only. Her soul mate.

Gabe leaned in. "I have something for you." He'd lowered his voice to an intimate level that shut out everyone and everything else. "I was going to give it to you during the ceremony, but decided to wait until tonight. But somehow this seems like the right time."

Something soft and feminine stirred within. "What is it?" she couldn't resist asking.

"It's an engagement ring." He reached into an inner pocket of his tux and removed a black velvet ring box with the distinctive DE logo imprinted on the outside. He gave a soft laugh. "I should have given it to you before we married. But, like everything else in our relationship, we've gotten this backward, too."

He flipped open the lid and removed the ring. Taking her hand in his, he slid it onto her finger where it nestled against her wedding band. Kat's breath caught. It was a stunning piece, clearly one of Francesca's designs. An impressive cushion-cut fire diamond topped the platinum filigree, accented on either side with a swirl of smaller fire diamonds that contained an almost pink cast, lending a fiery color to the flames that made the Dante diamonds unique in the world.

"Oh, Gabe." Her breath escaped in a rush. "It's stunning."

"It's part of Dantes' Eternity line." An odd quality crept through his voice. "They're all named, which I didn't realize when I chose it. Sev's wife, Francesca, designed all of the pieces for the line."

"Yes, I can tell." It also looked somewhat familiar. And then it hit her, caused a cascade of disparate emotions to flood her, longing and guilt, hope and shame. She moistened her lips, driven to say, "You know, in some ways it reminds me of Heart's Desire."

He hesitated for a fraction of a second. "There's a reason for that. Sev told me Francesca based the design on photos she'd seen of Heart's Desire."

She dared to look at him, saw something that went beyond mere passion stirring in his Dante eyes. "What's it called?"

"My Heart's Desire."

He's surprised her. "So similar? Is that why you chose it?"

He shook his head. "I chose the ring before Sev told me the name. Bizarre coincidence, don't you think?"

She had to tell him the truth. Now. Granted, it wouldn't change the fact that she went through with the marriage instead of giving him the option of cancelling it. But at least they could start their marriage off with all the cards on the table. "Gabe…"

Before she could say another word, Francesca approached. She bent to kiss Kat, offering Gabe an apologetic smile. "You look so happy off to yourselves I hate to interrupt. But, Primo wanted to speak to you privately. I'd be happy to keep Kat company in the meantime. We can talk about jewelry design." Her chocolate brown eyes gleamed with amusement. "I find it intriguing that your mother was a jewelry designer and that you're also married to one. It has such a nice symmetry to it, don't you think?"

Gabe's hand slipped from Kat's shoulder just as the opportunity to confess all slipped away. "That it does." He stood. "If you'll excuse me, I'll go see what Primo wants."

Kat waited until he was out of earshot before speaking. "Actually, I was hoping to discuss something with you before we returned to Seattle. I wondered if you'd give me your opinion."

Francesca perked up. "Is it jewelry related?"

Kat nodded. "It's about Heart's Desire. I'd like you to look at the necklace."

"You have it with you?" Excitement blossomed in her expression at Kat's nod. "I'd kill to see an example of Cara Moretti's work. We have photos of her designs, but none of the actual pieces."

"Would you be willing to take a quick look now? It's in the safe in my suite." She spared Gabe a glance, concerned to see he looked even grimmer than when he'd left them. Whatever Primo was saying, it clearly packed an emotional punch. "We probably have time to run upstairs before we're scheduled to cut the cake."

The two slipped from the ballroom and took the elevator to the suite. Someone had cleaned the rooms in the few hours since she'd last been here. All the feminine clutter and chaos had disappeared, replaced by flowers, chocolate and a magnum of champagne resting in a bucket of ice. Soft music played in the background. It was the perfect romantic stage for a dream wedding night.

Beside her, Francesca sighed. "It's stunning. Maybe you should duck out of the reception and have Gabe come directly up here."

"Tempting." Or it would be if she hadn't seen how grim Gabe appeared when she'd left the reception. "Why don't I get the necklace?"

Kat retrieved the velvet case from the safe and once again spread it on the linen covered table beneath the spotlight of a lamp. She stepped aside so Francesca had an unobstructed view. Endless seconds ticked by.

"Do you have a loupe with you?" Francesca's question sounded tense and riddled with concern.

"No."

"Nor do I." Francesca spared Kat a swift look. "You see it, too, don't you? That's why you asked me to take a look."

"The diamonds…" Her throat had gone so tight, she could barely get the words out. "Some of the stones are fake."

"I won't know for certain until I get a good look at it. But, yes." Francesca touched several of the larger stones. "These aren't fire diamonds. I can say that much definitively. In fact, I seriously doubt they're diamonds, at all."

Kat closed her eyes. How was it possible? And what was she going to do? If the necklace was fake, even partially fake, she'd have to confess all to Gabe. And once she did… "Francesca, I need to know. You of all people will be able to tell if this is—" The words dried up and it took her a moment to gather herself. "I need to know whether any of this is real. Is this even Cara Moretti's necklace?"

Francesca took her time examining the piece, her calm professionalism aiding Kat in recovering her own poise. "I've seen pictures of Heart's Desire." She spoke with authority. "The necklace itself appears genuine. But some of the stones have clearly been replaced. I can't say for certain how many until I have an opportunity to give it a thorough examination."

"I need to know what happened." And even more vitally, "I also need to find out when the stones were sold, if that's possible."

"Absolutely. Try not to panic." She gave Kat a swift hug. "All of our stones are photographed and laser-etched with codes so we can keep track of them. I don't know for certain whether these were encoded, but so few loose fire diamonds ever hit the market, that I can guarantee we'll be able to trace any that have. If the individual stones were removed from the necklace and sold, chances are we can get the pertinent details for you. We might even be able to contact the current owner and buy them back. Then your necklace will be as good as new."

Kat nodded, forcing out a grateful smile. "Thanks." There was only one problem with Francesca's scenario. She couldn't afford to buy back those original diamonds. She didn't even want to consider how much money might be involved. She returned the necklace to its case and handed it to Francesca. "Please call me when you find out what happened."

"Hey, no more worries, okay? Not today of all days." She held out her hand. "Come on. Let's get back to the reception. You have a cake to cut and a wedding night to look forward to."

The rest of the reception passed in a blur. Afterward, Kat had a vague, hazy memory of cutting the cake and feeding a tiny piece to Gabe. She vividly remembered the moment he took her into his arms for the first dance, though. The power of his hold. The feel of his hard, strong body moving against hers. The tenderness of his touch. But when the last note died, it was the kiss he gave her which became forever etched in her memory, a kiss that—if circumstances had been different—might have turned her hope into certainty that their temporary marriage would become a real one.

But how could it? How could he possibly feel anything other than trapped? *She'd* been the one to approach him with this devil's bargain, knowing full well he'd do anything to get his hands on Heart's Desire. *She'd* been the reason he'd gone to the Dantes for help and been forced to openly acknowledge his relationship with them—to admit to the world he was a bastard. And *she'd* been the one to surrender to him, to remain silent about her inexperience. If she'd been more upfront, perhaps he'd have taken better precautions and she wouldn't be...

Pregnant.

If Nonna was right and Kat carried Gabe's baby—granted, a big if—it would change everything, including their relationship. Would he suspect she'd set him up? Would he believe she'd scammed him, especially once he learned the truth about the necklace? She closed her eyes, fighting the panic crashing down on top of her.

"What's wrong?" Gabe's voice slid over and around her, deep and husky, filled with concern. "More bridal jitters?"

"It's all happening so fast." She fought to draw breath. Somehow her gown had shrunk again. "Maybe we should have waited."

"Got it. I think I can solve your problem."

The band slipped seamlessly into another number and Gabe swung her to the edges of the floor and then out through the nearest exit. Wrapping an arm around her waist, he urged her toward the elevators. People they passed smiled indulgently, some calling out good wishes. The car arrived after a few moments and those waiting stepped aside, allowing the newlyweds to make the ride to their suite in privacy.

Kat opened the door with her key card. Before she could step foot across the threshold, Gabe swung her into his arms and carried her into the suite. He took in the setup with a single, all-encompassing glance and headed for the doorway leading to the bedroom. He didn't stop until he reached the bed. Together they took the fall, allowing the soft mattress and even softer duvet to absorb the impact.

Though the curtains were open, sheers muted the light cascading through the windows, leaving the room in soft pastels. He smiled down at her, cupping her cheek and tracing her bottom lip with his thumb. "Have I told you how beautiful you look?"

She managed a smile. "You're looking pretty fine, yourself."

"Okay, that didn't work." His eyes narrowed. "Maybe we should clear the air about a few things. We're in bed. And you know the rules when we are."

Uh-oh. How could she have forgotten? "I'm beginning to hate Bed Honesty," she complained.

"Tough. Time for another honest conversation. Now tell me the truth." His mouth compressed. "Not that I don't already have my suspicions."

Oh, God. He knew. Knew about the necklace. Knew she loved him. Knew she was pregnant and he was trapped with no easy way out. "Gabe—"

Kat stared at Gabe with such a look of panic, he couldn't bring himself to make the moment any worse for her. "You want to work for Dantes," he supplied for her. "Or should I say, you want to work with Francesca. That's why you two went off together."

She blinked in surprise. At a guess, he'd thrown her and it took a second for her to switch gears enough to respond. "With everything that's been going on, we never got around to discussing my career aspirations. I guess I've also been avoiding the subject because—"

"Because you were afraid I'd think you were using my relationship with the Dantes to help you get a job with them," he filled in for her.

"Now that you mention it, I wouldn't be surprised if you thought that. Maybe even suspected I'd planned it from the start."

"Not a chance."

She shook her head. "I don't understand. Why not?"

"Because no one, not even Jessa or Matilda, knew I was Dominic Dante's son. Hell, most of the Dantes didn't know until recently. And I was careful to keep the connection very, very quiet." He lifted an eyebrow. "Unless you somehow found out?"

She met his gaze and answered with absolute sincerity. "I had no idea you were a Dante until you told me. Nor do I want you to ask them for a job on my behalf. If Dantes hires me I want it based on my talents alone."

"Agreed." He paused a beat. "So, we have that cleared up, yes?"

"Yes."

The brevity of her smile warned he'd only uncovered part of the problem. Thank God for Bed Honesty. "But, apparently we haven't cleared everything up. So, what's next?"

"Nonna. Nonna said…" Kat snatched a quick breath, then gave it to him straight. "Nonna said I'm pregnant."

He couldn't help himself. He laughed. "It's been, what? Three days? After only three days, Nonna can tell you're pregnant?"

"It does sound rather ludicrous when you put it that way," Kat admitted. "But everyone says she has the eye."

He brushed her veil back from her face. "I think you've been living in Italy too long."

"Gabe, seriously. What if I am?"

"We discussed this on the plane," he replied with a shrug. "We're married, aren't we?"

"Well, yes."

"If you're pregnant, we'll figure out how best to raise our baby. If that means staying together…" His voice hardened, turned implacable. "Then we stay together. But I won't allow a child of ours to experience what Lucia and I did growing up. Our son or daughter will know both its parents. Clear?"

"It's just that everything's hitting us so fast. We haven't had time to adjust to one issue before another knocks us over. And there's something else." A hint of desperation crept into her voice. "It's about Heart's Desire."

He shook his head, adamant. "Right now I'm not interested in anything but you and me and the fact that this is our wedding night." To his surprise, he discovered it was the absolute truth. Nothing mattered right now, not even his mother's necklace. "Got it?"

"What about five years ago?" she protested.

"Stop." He gave her a slow, impassioned kiss. "I know where you're going with that one and I'd rather you didn't. There won't be anyone in this bed tonight but the two of us. We'll have time to deal with all the other issues tomorrow. But not here. Not now. Just let it go, okay?"

He kissed her again, slowly lifting her to a sitting position, pleased to feel the tension slip from her body and see the worry ease from her brow. So far, Jessa hadn't come between them, at least not in bed. He intended to keep it that way. Whatever had happened the night he'd found Kat in Winters' bed, he hadn't uncovered the full truth. There was something hidden beneath the surface, something that involved his late wife. He'd been so quick to protect Jessa, he hadn't bothered looking deeper at the time. That would have come, he didn't doubt it for a moment. But she'd died two short years into their marriage, when only the first few troubling clouds had appeared on the distant horizon. When suspicion had been no more than a tendril of doubt.

Now the past had collided with the present, taking him in a new direction, one he found far more intriguing than memories from that other life. He dismissed all thought of anyone other than Kat, not the least surprised at the ease with which he did so. How could it be otherwise when he held in his arms the most beautiful woman he'd ever known? She was his wife now. She was the one he was honor bound to protect. And that's just what he'd do.

Gently, he unhooked her wedding gown and eased it from her shoulders. It dropped to her waist, exposing the daintiest bra he'd ever seen, barely more than a wisp of lace. Her skin seemed to glow against the delicate scrap, her breasts filling the cups to overflowing while the skirts of her gown and petticoats mushroomed around her. He found the bra closure and released it. She smiled up at him from where she sat, curled on the bed. She exuded feminine mystery and enchanted allure, looking like a half-naked sea nymph rising from a foaming sea of silk and tulle.

Just as she'd stripped him the night they'd first made love, now it was his turn. He took his time, peeling through her wedding garments, layer by layer, until all that remained was the tulle veil edged in lace. It cascaded over her, softening her nudity and making her all the more bewitching.

"I wish I could take a picture," he murmured.

"Don't you dare. I've had more than enough pictures taken today, thank you."

"None like this."

"You're right. Nor will there be any."

He grinned at her tart response. "I guess I'll have to rely on my memory."

Then his smile faded and he felt the tug of The Inferno, the odd, insistent certainty that he would carry this image of her for the rest of his life, labeled, "My wife on our wedding night." And he sensed there would be other images that would become fixed there. Kat, swollen with his child. Kat, their child nursing at her breast. Kat, tearfully watching their children heading off for their first day of school. Kat, proudly watching those same children graduating. Kat, cradling their first grandchild. Kat, snowy haired and aged, and still the most beautiful woman he'd ever seen. The images formed a kaleidoscope in his head, dizzying in their scope.

Silently, he removed his tux while she watched, her lovely eyes the same shade as new growth. A new beginning. He shed the last of his clothes and came down beside her, parting the edges of the veil that separated her from him. Where before he'd seen possibilities—a misty future stretching before them—now he saw only this woman and this instant of his life, the moment finely honed. He steeped himself in it, absorbing it, relishing every second, every small step and subtle tick of the clock.

The first time he'd made love to her there had been a newness to their touch, laden with a hint of uncertainty. When he took her in his arms this time, it was with a man's knowledge of how best to satisfy his woman. He'd already discovered some of her endless secrets, just as she had discovered his. It brought a deeper intimacy to each caress. To the slow, drugged kisses. To those places known only to him which would bring her the greatest pleasure.

"Gabe…" Kat smiled against his skin, touching his flat, male nipples with the tip of her tongue and threatening to send him straight over the edge. "I know what I want this time."

He released a groan that was half laugh. "Tell me it's the same thing you wanted last time."

She smiled her woman's smile, the one that caused The Inferno to pound and burn and demand. "That, too. But I also want…" Her lips drifted close to his ear and she whispered a suggestion, one that took his breath away. "Can we try that?"

"Everything. Everything and anything," he promised.

"It might take a while."

"We have all night. Hell, we have all of tomorrow, if that's what it takes to satisfy you."

"I think it just might."

They spent the entire next day in bed, rarely far from each other's arms. It was a time apart, a time where two became one. In body. In heart. In soul.

Sometimes they came together in humor, as they had the first time they made love. Other occasions, Gabe made love to his wife with heartbreaking urgency, as though desperate to cling to their rapidly dwindling time together, time which slipped by like raindrops through cupped fingers. They both sensed something looming on the horizon, a consequence to their changing the terms of their contract before the issues between them had been resolved.

The last time they came together, was in the deepest part of the night, when ghosts lurked in the shadows and the heavy silence spoke volumes. Kat clung to him, shuddering beneath his touch, the air so saturated with desire he could practically taste it. Instead, he tasted her. She was beyond sweet, beyond spicy. It was as though someone had discovered the perfect flavor, one made specifically for him and only him. And that flavor was Kat.

He cupped her breasts, finding the most delicious of nectars beneath his tongue. The catch of her breath and the pounding of her heart gave a voice to her taste. His hands skated lower and now he could feel her flavor, as well as hear and taste it. Feel the honey of her skin, how it flowed beneath his fingertips, rippling and undulating. And then he reached the core of her, where sweetness mingled with spice. The very center of what made her a woman, the full-bodied richness that belonged to his wife and only his wife.

And he consumed her, lost himself where all their senses joined. Came alive. Began and ended and began again. Her cries of release shattered the darkness, sent the shadows fleeing and turned night into something dazzling and radiant. And then he took her again, melding their bodies, mating them in a moment so perfect it would always live inside him.

Even when it finished, it didn't end. She turned to him, still part of him in sleep, her body mated with his, his essence still warm within her body. Words hovered on the tip of his tongue, words he longed to speak but had never given voice to. Almost he said them. But they wouldn't form. It was as though some final barrier held them fast. But that didn't change the fact that he knew. Knew what he felt for Kat. Knew it was real and permanent and forever.

Gently, ever so gently, he took her hand and curled it into a fist. And then he linked her index finger with his and let his heart speak the words that wouldn't become.

Gabe, Kat and Matilda returned to Seattle the next day. Based on the vague air of apprehension that seemed to descend the farther they distanced themselves from San Francisco, he suspected she felt exactly the same way he did. She was waiting for the shoe to drop, waiting for the fairy tale to shatter and for reality to intrude on what had been a beautiful interlude, but one that couldn't last.

Of course, he didn't expect his own sister to be the one to drop that shoe, or for it to be two days before Christmas.

Gabe's private line rang and he picked it up automatically, pausing just long enough to make a notation on the contract in front of him before speaking. "Moretti."

"Gabe?" Tension rippled through his sister's voice. "Are you there?"

He came instantly alert. "Lucia? What's wrong?" Because something was definitely wrong.

"I just heard something about Mom's necklace." She paused, as though bracing herself. "Were you aware the Dantes have it?"

That stopped him cold. "Wait. Wait one damn minute. How the *hell* did they end up with it?"

"Kat gave it to Francesca the day you were married." A long sigh came through the phone. "I gather from your reaction you didn't know."

"No, I damn well didn't know. I didn't even know Kat had it on her." Though now that he thought about it, she'd mentioned something about the necklace on their wedding night. Had that been what she'd wanted to tell him? "Why the hell didn't she give it to me?"

Another long, uncomfortable pause. "Maybe because the necklace is a fake," Lucia admitted. "At least, that's what the Dantes are claiming."

Gabe felt himself turn as cold and icy as the snow spitting earthward outside his window. "A fake," he repeated.

"Okay, maybe not a fake exactly. But Francesca said some of the diamonds aren't real."

"They were sure as hell real when I sold it to Matilda. We had it appraised."

"Well, they're not—anymore. Listen, they've put a private detective named Juice on the case. From what I've heard about him, he'll get to the bottom of it."

"Did Kat know it was a fake when she turned it over to them?" He shoved the question out through gritted teeth. When his sister didn't immediately respond, he pushed harder. "Answer me, damn it. Did she realize it was a fake when she gave it to them?"

"I'm sorry, Gabe. Yes, she knew." Lucia hesitated before asking, "What are you going to do?" Apprehension riddled her question.

"Get to the bottom of it from my end."

"Don't hurt her!"

"I'm not going to hurt her," he snapped. Reconsidered. "Much."

Gabe hung up without another word. Shoving back his chair, he crossed to the bank of windows and stared out at the sprawl of buildings through the curtain of pelting snow. Damn, damn, *damn*. He'd come so close. So incredibly close. For the first time in memory, he'd trusted someone, unconditionally. Had bought into the fairy tale he'd always cautioned Lucia to resist.

It was those eyes. Those sweet, innocent eyes, as dewy and unspoiled as spring leaves. She seemed so genuine. So sincere. Appeared to succumb utterly to The Inferno. Even worse, she'd been wounded, much as he had, sharing his wariness, his inability to trust. And yet, the two of them had trusted. Despite all that stood between them, they'd given themselves, heart and soul, to one another.

Fool. Idiot. She was conning him. And instead of seeing through the con as he'd normally have done, he'd been led right into her trap by parts of him that had no business making any decision other than how often and how long. He should have demanded to see the necklace. Had it examined by an expert. How could someone with his experience have neglected to follow the most basic of business procedures?

Because he'd wanted to believe. He'd wanted Kat, even rushing her into marriage. Well, now he had her. The real question was...

What the hell did he plan to do with her?

Christmas lights flickered up at him from the street below, twinkling gaily, symbolizing a deep-seeded belief,

filled with profound meaning. One that encouraged faith
and hope and peace. He rested the palm of his hand against
the glass, felt the stirring of The Inferno, felt the throbbing
pulse of the powerful connection he'd forged with Kat. And
he heard a small voice, at the core of his being, insisting he
was wrong. Insisting there had to be a rational explanation.

A voice that insisted he trust the woman he loved.

He closed his eyes and fought the pain and disillusion-
ment that had shaped his life into one of caution and distrust.
And he realized he had a choice. He could trust—against all
odds—and move forward. Or he could take a step back and
return to the safety of his world before Kat had swept into it.

He opened his eyes and made his decision.

Ten

Kat's cell phone rang and she retrieved it from her pocket, her gloves making her fumble a bit. She yanked them off and stuffed them in her pocket, glancing at the display. Francesca's name flashed and she felt her nerves stretch taut. "Merry Christmas!" she said, hope warring with dread. "Are you all set for the big day?"

"Almost." Francesca's voice matched hers—one attempting to conceal her distress beneath a bright, shiny wrapping of enthusiasm topped with a pretty little bow of forced cheerfulness. "Just one or two last minute gifts to wrap and…" Her breath exploded in a sigh. "Oh, Kat. I'm so sorry. But it's bad news. Not all bad, but definitely not good."

Kat kept moving, lifting her coat collar against the spate of snow swirling down from a leaden sky. For some reason it became more of an effort to put one foot in front of another. "How bad?"

"I'll give it to you straight. You were right. Some of the

stones are fake. But here's the good news. The necklace, itself, is genuine. So are most of the stones."

"How many are fakes?"

"Six." A significant pause. "The largest six, I'm afraid."
Six? So many! Kat fought to speak coherently, to form
even the simplest of sentences. "Have you been able to track
the stones?"

"We have. There won't be any problem at all restoring the
necklace." Francesca's voice took on a soothing quality. But
it ended up having just the opposite effect. "Primo's making arrangements to buy the diamonds back as we speak."

Dollar signs flashed before Kat's eyes. "For how much?"
The question came out low and thready. She cleared her
throat. "I know you can't give me an exact figure. But ball-
park."

The figure had her knees threatening to give out. She
stumbled to a stop in front of a department store window,
decked out for Christmas. She stared at the scene, some
tiny portion of her brain still functioning enough to take it
in. Fake snow rained down over a storybook setting, complete with a traditionally decorated tree and a toy train mer-
rily steaming along its track. Overhead, snowflakes swirled
earthward, mirroring the scene in the window. They hit her
exposed skin and she shivered at their icy touch. The fore-
cast called for a white Christmas. It seemed they were about
to be proven right.

"Kat? Kat are you still there?"

"Yes, Francesca. Thank you for letting me know. Keep
me updated, will you?"

Something in Kat's voice must have given her away. "Try
not to worry," Francesca urged. "I'm sure Primo will work
something out with Gabe."

"No. No, this is my problem. *I'll* work it out with Gabe."

"If you say so. Have a good Christmas," she said gently.

"You, too."

Kat spared the window a wistful glance, longing for the dream it represented. No wonder her grandmother hadn't wanted to sell Gabe the necklace. How could she when she'd sold off a number of the diamonds. But why? Because of her illness? Or had she lost her money sometime over the past few years when the economy had gone south? What had compelled her to sell some of the diamonds? And why not approach Gabe and sell the necklace to him, intact? He'd have paid whatever she'd asked. He'd made no bones about that.

There was only one way to know for certain, not that it would change anything. She should have told Gabe about her suspicions. Told him before they ever married that she suspected the diamonds in Heart's Desire had been replaced. By not doing so, it made her look very, very guilty. Would it be the final straw for him? Would her silence make it impossible for him to trust her? She hit a hot button on her phone, the one she'd designated for Gabe. He answered immediately, almost as though he'd been expecting her call.

"Is there any chance you can cut out early and meet me at my grandmother's?"

"I think so. Problem?"

She sighed. "I'm not sure, yet. I'm on my way over there now."

He didn't waste time on idle chitchat. "Be there in twenty."

Kat pocketed her phone. Snow drifted down around her, a bit heavier than it had been just five minutes before. Even though it was only midafternoon, the curtain of snow made it appear much later, muffling sound. She stared at the window display, seeing her ghostly reflection mirrored there, as well as the cityscape behind her. For an instant, it felt as though she were enclosed in a soft globe that held time at bay, locking her between two worlds—the life she'd led before Jessa had chosen to destroy her world, and the one she'd built with Gabe. Now those two worlds were colliding, the old shattering the new, and she was helpless to prevent it from happening...unless a miracle occurred.

For some reason, despite all odds, a tendril of optimism took root. It was the season for miracles, wasn't it? Maybe, just maybe, she could still straighten everything out. Maybe, just maybe, she wouldn't lose Gabe in the process.

The reflection from Christmas lights flickered in the window, twinkling gaily, symbolizing a deep-seeded belief, filled with profound meaning. One that encouraged faith and hope and peace. Kat rested the palm of her hand against the glass of the window display and felt the stirring of The Inferno, felt the throbbing pulse of the powerful connection she'd forged with Gabe. And she heard a small voice, at the very core of her being, urging her to go to him. Tell him everything.

A voice that insisted she fully open herself to the man she loved.

She closed her eyes and fought the fear that had shaped the past five years into ones of caution and distrust. And she realized she had a choice. She could put her trust in Gabe and move forward. Or she could take a step back and return to the safety of her world before he'd first touched her.

She opened her eyes and made her decision, turning resolutely toward her Heart's Desire.

Gabe swept into Matilda's parlor like an avenging angel, his black snow-dusted coat swirling around him. One look at his expression and Kat's prayer for a Christmas miracle died an early death. She didn't know how or when, but he'd heard about Heart's Desire. And there wasn't a doubt in her mind that his discovery spelled a fast and painful end to their marriage.

She released her grandmother's hand and stood. "Gabe…"

His gaze rested for a brief instant on Matilda, before snapping in her direction. He stared at her, his golden eyes tarnished into darkness. "I believe you have something to tell me."

She nodded, unable to look away, trapped within that fierce bleakness. "First, you should know that I gave Francesca your mother's necklace to examine."

"When?"

She flinched at that single, biting word. "The day we were married."

"Why?"

She spared her grandmother a brief, anguished glance. "Gam gave me Heart's Desire the morning of our wedding and suggested I surprise you by wearing it."

"But you didn't wear it." His smile reflected the wintry coldness outside. "I would have noticed if you had."

She swallowed—hard—and gave it to him straight. "Some of the stones didn't look right to me, so I told Gam that, given its history, wearing it in front of all the Dantes might not be the most diplomatic option."

"Clever." It didn't sound like a compliment.

"I then asked Francesca to examine the necklace during our wedding reception. She…she agreed with me. Several of the stones weren't fire diamonds."

"Do you mean to say, Heart's Desire is a fake?" Matilda demanded in a shocked voice. "That isn't possible."

"The necklace, itself, isn't a fake," Kat hastened to reassure. She crouched beside her grandmother's chair, relieved to finally escape her husband's implacable gaze. "But some of the diamonds aren't real."

"They were real when I sold the necklace to your grandmother," Gabe stated, folding his arms across his chest. "It was certified by an expert. So, if there's a problem now, it's happened since the sale."

"And I'm telling you that's simply not possible," Matilda protested. "Other than to have the necklace cleaned and re-appraised a few years back, I haven't touched it."

Kat twisted her hands together and frowned. The engagement ring Gabe had given her during the reception bit into her skin, the sharp pain a tiny reflection of what she'd soon face when her marriage ended. Why didn't her grandmother simply admit the truth? After all, it was her necklace. If she chose to sell off bits and pieces of it, that was her prerogative.

"Gam... You must know that six of the diamonds have been replaced."

Gabe stepped forward, shrugging off his coat and tossing it over the arm of a nearby chair. "But you don't know, do you, Matilda?"

She shook her head without speaking, pressing her trembling lips tightly together.

Kat rocked back on her heels, and stared at her grandmother, stunned. "Wait a minute. I assumed— But, if you didn't sell off any of the diamonds, then who...?"

"There are—were—three logical possibilities," Gabe replied. "I also assumed Matilda was responsible, which would have explained her reluctance to sell me the necklace these past few years. There are two problems with that scenario."

Matilda lifted her chin in a proud gesture. "Which are?"

"Why sell off the diamonds one by one, when you knew I'd have paid you a bloody fortune for the thing?" His rationale echoed Kat's.

"And the other reason?"

He smiled with surprising kindness. "I only have to look at you to know your shock isn't faked. You really didn't know there was anything wrong with the necklace. If you had, you wouldn't have dared give it to your granddaughter to wear at our wedding. It would have been far too risky with so many experts around, any one of whom would have spotted the fake diamonds."

Kat slowly stood to face her husband. "You said three scenarios. If it wasn't Matilda, then who else?" A bitter chill settled over her. "Me, I assume."

"Oh, definitely you, my love."

Matilda stiffened. "Gabe, no. She couldn't have—"

He spared Kat's grandmother a look of regret. "The only other possibility is Jessa. Those are the only other logical options." His returned his gaze to his wife while continuing to address Matilda. "You told me Kat loved Heart's Desire. That it helped shape who and what she's become. Maybe it helped her more than you realize."

"Is that what you truly believe?" Kat demanded.

"Tell me, my dear wife. How did you support yourself in Italy? How have you been able to afford designer clothes and footwear? Maybe when you realized you were going to lose everything to Jessa you decided to help yourself to a few of the choicer stones. Such perfect symmetry, isn't it? Using the fire diamonds to pay for your training in jewelry design? Selling them off one at a time in order to finance your education. To pay for your daily expenses, along with a few luxuries you couldn't live without, like those sexy little shoes you're currently wearing."

"I worked for everything I own," she snapped, bristling with defiance. "I worked three jobs at times, every day, all day, without any outside help. Everything I've accomplished in the past five years, I've done on my own."

"If you say so."

"I say so."

He lifted a shoulder in a noncommittal shrug. "Then we'll move on to option number three. Jessa."

Her name hung in the air between them. Matilda seemed to shrink in on herself. "Jessa?" she asked fretfully.

"It's the only other logical option. No one else had access to the necklace, did they?"

Matilda shook her head. "No," she whispered.

"Then it's either Kat or Jessa, and I don't think there's much question about who it is." He allowed the words to settle before continuing. "After all, it was Kat who attempted to seduce Benson Winters. Kat who betrayed her cousin. Kat who adored Heart's Desire. Kat who couldn't stand the idea of it going to Jessa."

"Stop it, Gabe." Kat stepped between him and her grandmother. "Leave her alone. If you want to come after me one-on-one, fine. I'm ready for you. But not Gam. I won't let you hurt her."

"I'm just trying to get your grandmother to consider the situation logically. For her to figure out what I already know."

"And what do you know?" she demanded, fighting tears. "Or rather, what do you *think* you know?"

He tilted his head to one side. "Surprisingly, there's very little thought involved. I suppose that's why it took me so long to understand."

Kat stared at him, utterly confused. "Okay, now you've lost me."

"I hope not."

Then he looked at her. Just a simple look. For an instant she couldn't bring herself to interpret that look—like Gabe—found it difficult to align logic and reason with what her heart was telling her. He was saying something to her. Something she didn't understand, but which caused her palm to throb in response. She rubbed at the burning itch, felt the heat of The Inferno flare to life. She hesitated, her hand slipping to cup her abdomen, cradling the spark of life she suspected lived beneath her palm. And that's when certainty swept through her.

She didn't know why he was painting her with the guilt brush. She simply knew that he didn't believe it for one little minute. He continued to regard her with an implacable expression and she realized he had no intention of explaining. No intention of reassuring her. She either trusted him or she didn't. She made him wait an endless thirty seconds. Mean of her, true. But hey, he'd given her a few queasy minutes, too.

She stepped closer to him, until they stood no more than a foot apart. She still held her hand over her abdomen, over the baby sleeping there, and she slowly formed a fist. And then she crooked her index finger.

His eyes closed for a split second and she literally felt the tension break over him like a tidal wave, before dissolving. Ever so gently, his hand formed a matching fist and he linked fingers with her. The Inferno pulsed between them, sweeping through her veins like the sweetest of wines.

"I'll reimburse you for the diamonds," Matilda said quietly. "But only if you agree this matter ends here."

Kat returned to her grandmother's side and gave her arthritic hands a gentle, reassuring squeeze. "It's all right, Gam."

"No, it's not all right," Gabe retorted. "Either you are guilty or Jessa is. I want Matilda to tell me which one it is. I think she knows. I think deep down she realizes that she made a horrible mistake five years ago. That's why she asked you to come home. And that's why she claimed she was dying."

"I am dying," Matilda retorted. Then she ruffled the air with a sweep of her hand. "I may have exaggerated how soon that might happen. But as I told you. Life is a terminal condition and I'm a good piece closer to the end of that life than to its start."

"Oh, Gam, why?" Kat asked, shaken. "Why would you do such a thing? Do you have any idea how frantic I've been at the idea of losing you?"

Tears gathered in Matilda's eyes. One escaped, running along a deep rivulet time had carved into her face. "I was afraid you wouldn't return unless you thought I was dying. Even then, I wasn't entirely sure you would come."

Kat gathered her grandmother up in a tight hug. "Don't be ridiculous. Of course, I came back. I love you. You're all the family I have left. Why do you think I've continued to write to you all these years?"

Matilda's chin quivered for an instant before she regained control. She shot Gabe a hard, direct look. "Kat would never have done anything to Heart's Desire. Never. She cherished that necklace, thought it was the most beautiful thing she'd ever seen. She'd sooner cut off her arm than do anything that would devalue it."

He closed his eyes, understanding crashing down on him. "That's why you refused to sell it to me all these years, isn't it? Because Kat loved it so much."

She nodded, more tears tracking down her cheeks. "It was my last connection to her."

"And Jessa?" he asked quietly.

Matilda sighed. "She came to see me the day she died. She was furious because I'd told her I still intended to give the necklace to Kat. I wondered…" She bowed her head. "I wondered if she thought by marrying you, I'd eventually change my mind and leave it to her."

Gabe appeared startled. "I never expected you to give it away. I always hoped to buy it from you."

She waved that aside. "Jessa had other plans." She hesitated, guilt settling like a shadow on her face. "I have a confession to make about the day she died. I…I've always blamed myself for her death. Maybe if we hadn't fought about the necklace, she wouldn't have driven so recklessly."

Gabe refused to let her get away with it. "It was her choice. Her decision to drive the way she did. And she paid the ultimate price for that decision."

It was then Kat realized he no longer retained any protective feelings toward Jessa. That somehow, at some point, he'd stopped believing in her…and started believing in Kat. That whatever love he'd felt for his first wife had evaporated, his allegiance transferring, for good. Light caught the fire diamond gracing her engagement ring and released the inner flames. They burst free in an arc of brilliant color, as though confirming her prayer that maybe…just maybe, she'd been given a Christmas miracle, after all.

She must have made some sound because he spared her a questioning glance before continuing. "But I can tell you with absolute certainty that Jessa sold the diamonds."

Kat started. "How do you know?"

"I called Primo on my way here. Asked when the stones were sold and if they could identify the seller. There's no question it was her."

Matilda's mouth dropped open. "You knew that when you walked in here?"

Gabe nodded. "But I needed you to figure it out for yourself, to realize Kat was the innocent one."

"Well, I can't say I approve of your methods," she informed him sharply, "though I will admit they're effective."

"I apologize, but it seemed the most expedient way to force everything out into the open." He approached and leaned in, planted a kiss on her wrinkled cheek. "If you don't mind, I'd like to take my wife home. I guarantee I owe her an apology as well."

"Count on it," Kat muttered.

He spared her a swift smile before returning his attention to Matilda. "Since tomorrow's Christmas Eve, why don't we swing by and pick you up? You can stay at our place for the night and celebrate Christmas Day with us."

Matilda returned his smile with a tremulous one of her own. "Thank you. I'd like that."

"And don't worry about the diamonds. All you have to do at this point is stay healthy. Kat would like her grandmother around for a nice long time." He gave her a naughty wink and whispered, "Long enough to become a great-grand-mother a few times over."

The drive to Medina took twice as long due to the weather. As far as Kat was concerned, it felt endless, es-pecially since she and Gabe had a number of issues still to resolve, none of which she cared to discuss in the car while creeping across Evergreen Point. By the time they arrived home, night had descended and the house and grounds were covered in a soft blanket of white. They entered the silent house and he led the way to the study. It created an odd symmetry to create a final resolution here, mere steps from where they'd first discovered their Inferno connection.

The room was lit by firelight from the stone fireplace. In the bay window a Christmas tree twinkled gaily, the roman-tic setting no doubt courtesy of Gabe's housekeeper Dennis before he'd left for the evening. Gabe grabbed some cushions from the sofa and tossed them onto the floor in front of the tree so they could watch the fire while they talked. Drawing Kat down beside him, he wrapped his arms around her and pulled her close. Cupping her face, he leaned in and kissed her. She reached for him, clung to him.

Several long minutes passed in passionate silence before Gabe pulled back slightly and stared down at her. "Truth time."

"Bed Honesty?"

He shrugged. "Considering I plan on making love to you here, I think this qualifies as a bed for our purposes." He smoothed her hair back from her face. "Tell me about Jessa so we can finally close that door."

"Some of it's speculation, and some of it's based on what Benson told me," she warned. "He called a couple of days ago to apologize for misjudging me. He said it took him a little while, but he finally realized I'd been set up as much as he had."

"Still, I'd like to hear your version of what happened."

She sighed. "You have to know that Jessa and I didn't enjoy a very close relationship. Some of it was our age difference. Some of it was her resentment over the bond I shared with Gam. Whatever the reason, Jessa and I were cordial... but distant. And then Benson happened."

"I know she met Winters when she worked on his campaign."

"Yes. They released the news about their engagement right after he announced his candidacy. His numbers experienced a nice bump as a result. It began to look like he had a real shot at winning."

Gabe's brows pulled together. "So what went wrong? The tell-all his ex wrote didn't come out until after the scandal with you broke."

"I asked Benson about that," she confessed. "He said his campaign manager received advance notice that the tell-all was coming and warned Jessa. Said the book would put his ability to win in serious jeopardy. He claimed she didn't take it well."

"You think she decided it was time to cut her losses and move on?"

Kat nodded. "It would explain a lot. A week later she called me, said she wanted to create a closer relationship, wanted us to be more like sisters than cousins, especially since we didn't have any family other than Gam. She suggested a girl's night. She rented a suite so we could have dinner, wine, massages."

"Even though you were underage?"

She winced. "Well...yeah. I think that was probably part of the appeal. The naughtiness of it all. Remember, I was raised by a very strict grandmother." She closed her eyes, the dispassion in her voice at odds with the pain ripping through her. "Like a fool, I went," she whispered.

Gabe tightened his arms around her. "It's over. It can't hurt you anymore." He feathered a kiss across her brow. "I assume Jessa drugged you? And arranged for Benson to drop by?"

She nodded, shuddered. "I woke up to find myself in bed, naked. You were there. Benson was there." Her chin trembled, and she took a moment to gather her self-possession. "And the media showed up almost immediately after."

Gabe closed his eyes. "The things I said... I can't apologize enough. Jessa told me you'd always been jealous of her, had set out to seduce her fiancé. I believed her, was so certain she was the wronged party." He rested his cheek against the top of her head. "And instead, she'd decided Winters was on his way down and this was her clever way of bailing before that happened."

"She couldn't just dump him. It would have made her look bad. Plus, she already had her sights on a replacement for Benson. You were making quite a splash by then, very much on the way up. And she played on your protective instincts by painting herself in the role of the victim."

"Why use you?"

"Because I was young and foolish enough not to question her motives," she admitted with gut-wrenching honesty. "And because I stood between her and Gam, or rather Gam's money. And more important, Heart's Desire."

He lifted her chin and forced her to look at him. Tears filled her eyes, tears she desperately attempted to control. "You can say it, Kat," he told her gently. "You can finally say the words. And this time, someone will believe you."

The tears escaped, sliding down her cheeks. It took three tries before she managed to push out the words. "I didn't do it." She closed her eyes and surrendered to the tears. To lance a wound which had tormented her for five long years. To finally release all the pain and bitterness. "I didn't do it. I'm innocent."

He simply held her while she cried it out. Held her as though he'd never let her go. When the tears finally ended, he wiped her face, nodding in satisfaction. "Much better."

And miraculously, it was. "One problem resolved?" she asked with a watery smile.

"It was never a problem, just a question I needed answered so we could start our marriage with a clean slate, without the ghost of Jessa hanging over us. I can't apologize enough for my part in what happened all those years ago, Kat. For not realizing Jessa set you up."

"You weren't to know. She was always good at manipulating people."

"Shall we move on to the next issue?" He reached above her head and nudged a pretty golden bell with his finger. Its bright peal silvered the air, reminding her of the bells that had sounded on their wedding day. "Why didn't you tell me when you first suspected something was wrong with the necklace?"

She shrugged. "It was only a few hours before the ceremony and your family arrived within minutes of my discovery. They were all quick to inform me that Primo had confiscated your phone so I had no way to contact you. Besides, I hoped I was mistaken about the necklace." Her brows drew together. "Not that I was."

"When did you know for sure?"

"When I brought Francesca to our suite after the wedding." She glanced hesitantly at him. "You were talking to Primo, remember?"

"Vividly."

"She pretty much confirmed my suspicions." Kat shifted restlessly. "Maybe I should have stopped the ceremony and discussed the problem with you. I certainly considered it."

"I think what you were actually considering, was running."

She laughed, the sound husky from her crying jag. "True." She gazed at him uncertainly. "So what do we do now? You married me so you could finally get your hands on the necklace. Everything that's happened instead isn't at all what you bargained for."

"True." He cupped her cheek, stroking his thumb just beneath her bottom lip. "And I'm afraid our original deal can't be fully consummated until you've replaced the diamonds."

"Do you have any idea what they're worth?" she protested. "I'll never be able to afford to replace them."

She couldn't read his reaction. Once again, his expression turned impassive. "In fact, I'm counting on it."

She shook her head. "I don't understand."

"I figure it'll take you, oh, fifty or sixty years to pay off what you owe me for those diamonds."

A tendril of hope speared through her, a brilliant lightness and joy. "You think I can do it that soon?"

He shrugged. "Probably not, especially if I tack on interest."

"So, I'm stuck with you?"

He smiled down at her. Where before she'd been unable to catch any inkling of his innermost thoughts, now she saw a wealth of love and tenderness. "I'm afraid there's no choice. You are stuck with me. At least until the deal is fully consummated."

"In fifty or sixty years?"

"As you said, probably longer."

Slowly, she formed a fist with her hand, curling her index finger. He mimicked the gesture, linked their fingers together. "I love you, Gabe Moretti," she whispered.

"I love you, too, Kat Moretti. I think I have from the moment we first touched. I know I have since the moment I made love to you." He feathered a kiss across her mouth. "Do you agree to my demands?"

Her eyes fluttered closed and she pursued the kiss, deepened it. "Without question."

He pulled back a tantalizing few inches and offered a teasing smile. "Now for our final problem."

"Which is?"

He cupped her abdomen. "What to name our baby."

She slid her hand on top of his, this time linking all their fingers. "You really think I'm pregnant?"

"According to the Dantes, there's a very real possibility."

"So what do you want to name him? Nonna said it was a boy," she hastened to add.

Gabe hesitated, abruptly serious. Very serious. "Primo made a suggestion on our wedding day."

It only took her a moment to make the connection. "That conversation you had when Francesca and I went upstairs?"

"Yes."

"What name did he want us to consider?"

"Dante." For an instant Gabe's voice failed him. "Only, he wasn't suggesting it for a first name, but for a last. He asked if I'd consider taking his name, either by legally changing it or through adoption."

"Oh, Gabe." Her heart broke for him. She knew at one

point in his life, he'd have given anything for his father to have done that for him. "What did you say?"

The sun rose in his eyes, turning them a shattering gold. Before, a shadow had always tarnished their brilliance. But no longer. He gathered her hand in his so their palms bumped together, then melded, Inferno against Inferno. Heat rushed through them, a sweetness and joy that eclipsed all that had led them to this moment.

"Assuming you have no objections," Gabe replied. "I said we'd be honored to become Dantes."

"You won't become a Dante just because you change your name." She drew him down for another slow, thorough kiss. "You were born a Dante, Gabe. You always have been and you always will be. Just as you always have been and always will be my Inferno mate."

He pulled her close and held on tight. "Just as you always have been and always will be my Heart's Desire."

The snow fell outside their window, a blanket of purity surrounding a heart of warmth. Christmas had arrived early. And its gift was the return of faith and unwavering trust. It had led them to each other. To a family they'd always longed to know. To a bright and shining future with the promise of a son. A son who'd experience his Dante legacy and bear the name Dante from the day of his birth.

It had started as a faint, wavering spark, one that had caught, held, becoming an Inferno. But at its heart of hearts, becoming something far more.

Becoming Dante.

* * * * *

"I have a proposal for you."

He leaned against the counter like a lazy puma. "How romantic."

"Not that kind of proposal." Her voice had a prim, school-mistressy snap that she instantly regretted. "A…business proposition."

"Perhaps we should go somewhere more private." His dark eyes added an undercurrent of suggestion to his words. He turned his head to the hotel clerk. "She won't be needing her room."

A surge of desire, tangled up with fear and anticipation and even—already—regret for what she was about to do, rose through her body like a flash flood. She lifted her bag higher on her shoulder. She was strong now. She could handle him. She'd have to.

"Why won't I need my room?" The question was purely for show, since they both knew the answer.

"You'll be staying with me. Just like old times."

Dear Reader,

I had always heard that the history of South Florida did not go back much past the invention of air-conditioning. When I moved here last year, I was surprised and excited to discover a tangled web of history involving conquistadors, pirates, Seminole indians, soldiers, tycoons and adventurers.

Hurricanes are a familiar aspect of life in South Florida, and I soon learned about the large number of shipwrecks off the coast, dating back to the early Spanish treasure fleets. Excavation is under way right now on several vessels, with probably the most well known being Mel Fisher's recovery of the *Nuestra Señora de Atocha*, with its huge stash of gold coins and silver ingots.

I began to imagine a hero who searches the seas for treasure. And what if my hero was the descendant of a pirate, whose ship had sunk with his ill-gotten gains? Throw in a feisty heroine determined never to fall for the hero again and it sounded like a brew as salty and tangy as a frozen margarita. I had a blast writing this tale, and I hope you enjoy Jack and Vicki's story!

All the best,

Jennifer Lewis

THE DEEPER
THE PASSION...

BY
JENNIFER LEWIS

Published in Great Britain 2013
by Mills & Boon, an imprint of Harlequin (UK) Limited,
Eton House, 18-24 Paradise Road, Richmond, Surrey TW9 1SR

© Jennifer Lewis 2012

ISBN: 978 0 263 90464 2
ebook ISBN: 978 1 472 00086 6

51-0213

Harlequin (UK) policy is to use papers that are natural, renewable and recyclable products and made from wood grown in sustainable forests. The logging and manufacturing processes conform to the legal environmental regulations of the country of origin.

Printed and bound in Spain
by Blackprint CPI, Barcelona

CHOICE OF
TWO
GIFTS!

A **treat** from us to **thank you** for reading our books!

Turn over **now** to find out more

Thanks for reading!

We're treating you to **TWO** fabulous offers...

2 FREE BOOKS

from your favourite Mills & Boon series plus have books delivered to your door every month!

Find out more and claim your free books at
www.millsandboon.co.uk/bookclub

or call 020 8288 2888 and
quote BOOKCLUB today!

Plus

15% OFF **

Your next order online with code
THANKSFEB at **www.millsandboon.co.uk**

CIFEB13

Jennifer Lewis has been dreaming up stories for as long as she can remember and is thrilled to be able to share them with readers. She has lived on both sides of the Atlantic and worked in media and the arts before she grew bold enough to put pen to paper. She would love to hear from readers at jen@jenlewis.com. Visit her website at www.jenlewis.com.

For Anne MacFarlane,
writer and critique partner extraordinaire

One

"It's pronounced *sin-cere*." Vicki St. Cyr leaned on the hotel counter. She was used to having her name mangled.

"Don't believe a word of it." The deep, rich voice in her ear made her start and spin around. Those familiar flashing dark eyes were settled firmly on the hotel clerk. "She's not to be trusted at all."

The young female behind the desk looked up, and her face took on that foolish sparkle of a girl suddenly confronted with the attentions of a handsome predatory male. "Can I help you, sir?"

"I'll let you know." Jack looked back at Vicki, and she felt her blood heat.

"Hi, Jack." Vicki realized, too late, that she'd crossed her arms defensively over her chest. "Fancy seeing you here."

"Vicki, what a surprise." His voice contained no more astonishment than hers. His gaze seemed to peer right through her carefully groomed exterior and flay bare a small part of her soul. If she still had a soul. "I hear you're looking for me."

She swallowed. How had he heard? She'd hoped at least for the advantage of surprise. But then Jack had always been two strides ahead of her. Why would now be any different? "I have a proposal for you."

He leaned against the counter like a lazy puma. "How romantic."

"Not that kind of proposal." Her voice had a prim, schoolmistressy snap that she instantly regretted. "A... business proposition."

"Perhaps we should go somewhere more private." His dark eyes added an undercurrent of suggestion to his words. He turned his head to the clerk. "She won't be needing her room."

A surge of desire, tangled up with fear and anticipation and even—already—regret for what she was about to do, rose through her body like a flash flood. She lifted her bag higher on her shoulder. She was strong now. She could handle him. She'd have to.

"Why won't I need my room?" The question was purely for show because they both knew the answer.

"You'll be staying with me. Just like old times." His broad, sensual mouth widened, like the habitual slight grin of a crocodile. He grabbed her bag off the floor and strode for the door. Vicki's faithless eyes tracked his tight behind, clad in faded denim, and the way his worn T-shirt hugged the thick muscle of his back.

"Should I cancel the room?" The desk clerk didn't take her eyes off him, even after he disappeared through the revolving door. "There will be a cancellation charge of fifty dollars because it's already—"

"Yes." Vicki put her credit card on the counter. What was another fifty on top of what she already owed? It would save a fortune over staying in this expensive boutique hotel. Two years of trying to "keep up appearances" had left her close to beggary. Lord knows she wouldn't be here otherwise.

But desperate times called for desperate measures, like daring to set foot in Jack Drummond's lair.

Jack was behind the wheel of his vintage Mustang when she got outside. The fierce South Florida sun beat down on the tarmac and threw dazzling diamond reflections off the custom jade-green paint job. The engine was already running and the passenger door open for her to get in. Did he know she didn't have a car? In the old days she'd have rented one and insisted on driving it just to keep the escape hatch open. Right now she didn't have that luxury. She climbed in and settled herself against the soft leather seat. "How did you know I'd be here?"

"My spies are everywhere." He didn't look at her as he pulled out of the parking lot and left the exclusive Ramona Beach Inn behind.

"You don't have any spies." She seized the opportunity to study his face. Skin tanned to a rich copper as usual, dark hair flecked with gold. "You've always been a one-man band."

"You've been hanging around the New York Drummonds." He still didn't turn toward her, but she saw the muscles tighten in his hand on the wheel. "Figured I was next."

Vicki drew in a breath. "I spent a relaxing few weeks with Sinclair and his mom. It was fun to catch up with old friends."

A smile twitched at the edge of his mouth. "You always have an ulterior motive. The fun is in figuring it out."

She stiffened. "My motives are very simple. I'm helping Katherine Drummond locate the pieces of a three-hundred-year-old family chalice."

"And you're doing this because of your passion for history?" This time he did turn to her. His smile deepened, beneath his bold cheekbones. "I heard you became an antiques dealer."

"The chalice has an interesting story."

"Oh, yes." His voice deepened into a throaty narrator's drone. "Three brothers, tossed by the stormy seas on their passage from bonnie Scotland, bid goodbye to each other in the New World but pledged one day to reunite their family treasure. Only then could the mighty Drummond clan regain the luck of their esteemed ancestors." He tossed a mighty laugh out onto the wind. "Come on, Vicki. That's not your style."

"There's a reward." Might as well come clean. Jack was more likely to be tempted by money than sentiment.

"Ten thousand dollars." He turned off the main road onto an unmarked and unpaved side road, fringed by spiky palms and tall scrub pines. "I've got junk worth more than that in the trunk of my car."

"It's twenty thousand per piece. I convinced Katherine to raise it. To attract the right sort of treasure hunters."

"Like me."

"Like me." She was gratified when he turned to look

at her. His dark gaze met hers and a jolt of emotion leaped through her. Old feelings, long buried, started clawing their way to the surface. She felt a shimmer of panic. "Not that I really need the money, of course. But if I'm going to look for an old cup, there might as well be a profit in it."

"And you need my treasure hunting expertise to claim the reward."

"You're the most successful treasure hunter on the Atlantic coast. I read an article about your new boat and all its expensive equipment. You're famous."

"Some would say notorious."

"And most likely the cup fragment is somewhere in your house." She'd found the first piece in the attic of his cousin Sinclair's Long Island mansion.

"If it's anywhere at all." His hand slid on the wheel as he turned down another unmarked road. The pines and saw palmettos ended as abruptly as the road, which descended suddenly to a beach. Jack swung the car to the left and parked near a broad wooden dock. A good-size boat, white with gleaming chrome rails, bobbed at the far end.

"Your dock looks different than I remember."

"It's been a long time." He was already out of the car and carrying her bag down the dock with feline grace.

"Not that long. There was a building here and a gate." And a bench where they'd once made love under a bright full moon.

"Gone in the last hurricane. Road keeps getting shorter, too."

"Must be frustrating to lose expensive real estate to the sea."

"Not if you enjoy change." He swung her bag into

the boat and turned to watch as she walked along the wood jetty. She hoped her own walk had a fraction of the swagger she admired in his.

He helped her onto his boat, where he'd already slung her bag. She walked around the deck to where a big, padded fighting chair held a commanding position. She perched herself on the seat and grabbed hold of the armrests. Jack had never been a slow driver. The boat lurched to a start and the propeller wash foamed beneath her feet as the engines roared into action. She braced her feet against the footrest as they leaped and bounced over the choppy water. Within a minute or so, Jack's island appeared over the horizon. Fringed with palms, no building visible, it looked like the kind of place you could get marooned and die. And she was going to be trapped here with Jack Drummond, unless she geared herself up for a long and bracing swim.

The dock on the island looked the same as the last time she saw it, years ago. Built of coral rock and carved in the elaborate style of some ancient and wealthy Drummond ancestors, it was flanked with two stone turrets that probably once concealed armed men. Maybe they still did, if tales of Jack's wealth were to be believed.

"Lost your sea legs?" Jack grabbed her arm when she wobbled while trying to climb out of the boat.

"I haven't spent much time on the water lately."

"Shame." His gaze hovered on her face and, to her horror, she felt her skin heat. How did he have this effect on her? She was the one who ate men for breakfast. He was just some scurvy sea dog from her past.

Does he still think I'm beautiful? The sudden thought stabbed her—a pang of insecurity.

*Who cares? You're not here to make him fall in love
with you. You need his help to find the cup and then
you can wash your hands of him forever.*

The old house on the island was obviously built more
as a fort than a cozy residence. Limestone walls rose
from behind the wild hedge of round-leaved sea grape
that separated the pale strip of beach from the interior
of the island. Only two tiny windows pierced the stone
block exterior, although the iron-studded doors were
thrown open to let in the morning sun.

"Is there anyone else visiting you?" The open door
shoved unwelcome thoughts into her brain. Another
woman? She hadn't dared to assume he was single. He
never was for long. Women swarmed Jack Drummond
like sharks to a flesh wound.

"We'll be alone." He strode ahead of her, sunlight
picking out golden highlights in his dark hair. Shadow
cloaked him as he entered the tall arched doorway into
his private sanctum.

Good. She didn't need competition at this stage. It
would be embarrassing flirting in front of someone else.
Trying to compete. She might have enjoyed that in the
old days, but she didn't have the brash confidence of
raw youth anymore.

The intricate colored-marble floor of the entrance
hall stood in lush contrast to the fortress exterior. Jack's
ancestors may have been pirates, but they also loved
beautiful things—expensive things—which might explain why they became pirates in the first place.

Jack looked as arrogant as ever. Even from behind
he radiated self-assurance, his broad shoulders set
easy against his powerful neck, his hair—too long, as
usual—curling almost to the collar of his T-shirt. Jack

didn't bother to conform to norms of fashion or try to fit in. He didn't need to. Born into a semicriminal dynasty of treasure hunters, he'd excelled in the family trade and made more money—legally—in the past five years than all his ancestors put together.

He filled a glass of water at the monstrous steel fridge and turned to her, offering it. "Too early in the day for champagne, but I'm celebrating your arrival all the same."

The twinkle in his eye disarmed her as she took the water. Was he really happy to see her? "The pleasure is mutual." She raised her glass of water. Let the flirting begin. "I've missed you, Jack."

"This is getting better every minute. I still can't figure out what you're after."

She smarted under his unromantic retort. He leaned against the broad pine table in the kitchen and crossed his powerful arms. Tiny golden hairs stood out against thick, bronzed muscle. She cursed herself for noticing.

"Isn't it enough to visit one old friend while helping out another?"

"Nope. And half of a twenty-thousand-dollar reward isn't enough to tempt the Vicki St. Cyr I know. Unless your financial situation has changed." His eyes narrowed slightly, and she felt their dark perceptive power.

She swallowed and stiffened but tried not to show her anxiety. The press hadn't yet sniffed out her father's sudden descent into financial ruin. The confusion created by his death from a stroke had provided a smokescreen. Her mom had slipped off to Corsica with a wealthy friend of her dad, and the only person left holding the empty bag was her.

"I can always find something pretty to spend ten

thousand dollars on." She played with her silver brace-let, which was probably worth about twelve dollars. "It's a curse to be raised with expensive tastes."

"Unless you're born gagging on a silver spoon. You've never needed to make money."

"I find it emotionally satisfying." If Jack knew she truly needed the money he'd be less likely to help her. He'd be unable to fight the urge to play with her, like a cat with a trapped mouse. "It makes me feel normal."

Jack threw his head back, and a great guffaw filled the kitchen, bounced off the stone surfaces of the walls and floor and echoed off the high ceiling. "Normal? You're probably the least normal person I know, and that's why I enjoy you so much."

"It's been a long time, Jack. Perhaps I'm more con-ventional than I used to be."

"I doubt it." A tiny smile pulled at one corner of his mouth.

"Why do *you* bother to make money?" Going on the offensive might be her best line of defense. "You could have lived comfortably on the ill-gotten gains of your ancestors, but instead you're out there every day trawling the oceans for gold doubloons as if your life depended on it."

"I get bored easily."

Vicki's stomach clenched. He'd grown bored with her. Eight magical months, then one day he was gone, off to pursue more elusive treasure and find a new dam-sel for his bed. "So you do. And what do you do with all the money you make?"

"Some of it I spend on new toys, the rest I just keep lying around the house in sacks." Mischief twinkled again in his eyes, which stayed firmly fixed on her.

She fought a sudden urge to scan the place for burlap bags filled with Spanish silver. "I have expensive taste in boats, especially my newest."

"I'd like to see it."

"Her." Mischief sparkled in his eyes again.

Vicki tensed as visions of a hard-bodied blonde crept into her mind. "Oh, your boat is female."

"They all are."

"Why is that?"

He shrugged. "Maybe because they drive us men crazy." His gaze lingered on her face, and she felt her skin heat. "But we love them anyway."

The word *love* made her jump slightly. Not a real jump, a jolt deep inside her. Either way, it made her feel even more off kilter than she did already. How did Jack Drummond manage to fluster her like no other man?

"So, this cup. It's part of your family history and probably stowed in a dusty corner of this old pile." She gestured at the stone walls around them. "Any idea where it is?"

Jack tilted his head slightly as if thinking. "No idea at all."

"Can we search your family records?"

"Pirates aren't known for keeping detailed records. It's harder to deny having stuff that's written down."

"People don't get as rich as your ancestors by being loosey-goosey with the books." She lifted a thoughtful finger to her lips. "I bet there are some old leather-bound ledgers somewhere."

"Even if there were, why would they bother to catalog a worthless old cup piece? They probably threw it away."

"A family heirloom? I think not." Though a shiver of

apprehension did cool her. People threw away priceless things every day because they didn't look like the stuff on department store shelves. "The Drummonds are far too proud of their auld Scottish ancestry for that. Look." She pointed at the old stone kitchen fireplace. Above the big opening where cauldrons once boiled was a big crest, its paint faded and peeling from the worn wood.

Jack smiled. "They did keep detailed records." His dark gaze studied her face. "And I've been through them all with a fine-tooth comb. No mention of a cup."

"It's not the entire cup. We found the stem up in New York. You'd likely have either the base or the drinking vessel, so it could have been described differently if someone wasn't sure what it was. Why don't we look together at the ledgers from the lifetime of the first person to own it, and see if anything crops up?"

"Oh, there's nothing of his. He didn't build this house. Never even visited the island as far as we know. He drowned in a wreck with all his possessions."

Vicki frowned. "Then who founded this island and carried on the family line?"

"His son. Swam ashore and took over the place. He was only fifteen at the time, but fought off anyone who came near with some muskets and shot he salvaged. Eventually he managed to rob and swindle enough people to rebuild the family fortune. I'm sure he was a sweet boy."

"I'll bet." She lifted a brow. Meanwhile her heart was sinking. "So if his father had the cup, it would have gone down in the shipwreck."

"Along with all his plundered booty and his latest child bride."

She sucked in a breath. Jack was playing with her.

He'd known the item she came here to search for was long gone before she'd even climbed into his car. Then again, he was an undersea treasure hunter. "Did it happen far from here?"

"Not far at all. The boy washed ashore here, clinging to a piece of spar. Can't be more than a few miles."

"So let's find it."

Again his rich, deep laugh filled the big kitchen. "Sure! We'll just throw out a fishing line and reel it in. People have been looking for that boat for years."

Her ten-thousand-dollar share of the reward started to shrink in her mind. "And why haven't they found it?"

He shrugged. "Who knows?"

"Come on. I know you must have looked for it."

"I did, early on. Truth is, these waters are filled with old wrecks, and I've always stumbled across something else to keep me busy. The combination of Spanish treasure fleets sailing regularly from Havana crossed with yearly hurricanes makes this area rich pickings for a treasure hunter."

"But you have better equipment now than you did then." Excitement started to prickle her skin. "I bet there was treasure on that ship when it went down."

"No doubt." Jack's eyes rested on hers, humor sparkling in their depths. "I never thought I'd hear you begging to go on a treasure hunt with me."

"I'm not begging!"

"Not yet, but if I don't say yes, you will be."

His arrogance made her want to slap him. "I'm simply asking."

"No." He turned and walked across the kitchen, then out through a door on the far side where he disappeared from view.

Vicki stood staring after him for a moment, her mouth gaping open like a fish. Then she strode after him. She spotted him in a long, stone corridor. "What do you mean, no?"

He turned. "I mean, no, I won't take you out hunting for part of some crazy old cup. Though I'm damn sure curious about why you want it so bad."

"What if the legend is true, and the Drummonds won't be happy again until the pieces of the cup are reunited?" She lifted a brow, trying to look nonchalant. It was a stretch.

Jack raised his own brow in response. "From what I can tell, none of us is really suffering right now."

"And none of you is happily married, either." Though his cousin Sinclair would be soon, largely thanks to her meddling.

"Maybe that's why we're happy." He shrugged and kept walking.

"Were your parents happily married?" She hurried to keep up.

"You know they weren't. My mom took my dad to the cleaners in the divorce. She even got this island."

His mom was a famous Nicaraguan model, now on her fourth or fifth husband. "See? Sinclair's parents weren't happy, either. It's his mom who's the driving force behind the search for the cup. She doesn't want her son to suffer like she did."

"How is old Sinclair? Still trimming his hedge funds into topiaries?"

"Sinclair is a very nice man, I'll have you know. And he's just fallen in love, too."

"There goes your theory about the family curse."

"Get this. He and his newly beloved were secretly

pining for each other for years—she's his housekeeper—
and it wasn't until they started looking for the cup that
they finally hooked up." She didn't mention her own
fairy godmother-esque role in shoving them together.

He reached a carved wooden door and rested one big
hand on the handle. "How sweet. What if I don't want
to fall in love?"

"Maybe you already have."

"With you?" His dark eyes twinkled.

"With yourself." How could he still look so handsome? You'd think all that sun and salt air would have
wizened him into a raisin. Instead he looked bronzed
and burnished like a fine statue from ancient Greece,
ready to throw a discus in the Olympics or besiege a
walled city. His body had filled out a little in the past
few years—all hard muscle, of course. Lucky thing
she wasn't as soft as she used to be or she'd be in danger of falling for him all over again. "Okay, that was
uncalled for. You're surprisingly modest, considering
your accomplishments. And I don't suppose you have
any shortage of women madly in love with you at any
given time."

"You're right, though." He looked thoughtful.

"You do love yourself?"

"No. That I've never fallen in love. Not really." His
eyes darkened and he looked as if he was about to say
something else but didn't.

She wanted to make a quip about how he'd been pining for her all those years, but she didn't speak, either.
Too much wishful thinking or something. "And you
think it's time you did?"

Still hovering outside the door, he rubbed at the muscle of his left arm. "I do want children."

Her eyes widened. Jack Drummond wanting a family? She didn't believe it. Maybe he was winding her up. "Maybe some will wash ashore in the next storm."

"You think I'm kidding, but I'm not. I like kids. They're fun. They bring a different perspective to everything, and they enjoy toys as much as I do."

Vicki laughed. "You're always full of surprises, Jack. So why don't you have any rugrats running around Castle Drummond?"

"Haven't met their mom yet." He held her gaze while he tilted his head. "At least I don't think I have." His voice contained the tiniest hint of suggestion. Was he playing with her? In that case he might be playing right into her hands.

"See? You need to find the cup so you can find Mrs. Right and start building your team. Let's look at some of those big complicated maps you love and see if we can figure out where the wreck is." She moved toward him. She could tell he was at least slightly interested, despite his protests.

"I see you know the way to a man's heart is through his nautical maps." He finally turned the handle and pushed open the door. "But first, let's go to bed."

Two

Jack walked into the bedroom, knowing Vicki would follow. She thought herself wild and unpredictable, but he knew better. She wanted that old cup for some reason and she was very determined in pursuit of a goal.

He couldn't resist turning to enjoy her expression. As expected, she'd walked coolly in behind him and was surveying the space. "Nice. Is that bed French?"

"Might be." The big oak monstrosity had been there since the house was built.

"I bet it could tell a few tales." She walked over to the headboard and examined the carved decoration.

"Lucky thing it's discreet." He swung himself onto the bed and relaxed, arms behind his head. "Come on in."

"You didn't seriously lure me in here in hope of seducing me, did you?"

"Hope springs eternal."

"I didn't know you were such a bright-eyed optimist."

"You have to be an optimist in the treasure hunting game. Eyes on the prize."

Vicki's almost-black hair was tied up in a messy bun, with tendrils falling about those adorable ears he still remembered nibbling. He let his eyes drift lower. She wore a black top that appeared to be made from pieces of ripped T-shirt, sewn back together. Knowing her it was probably from Paris and cost two thousand bucks. It hid her slender shape, but he knew that under its mysterious black layers was a lithe body with high, pointy breasts, and a stomach you could bounce gold doubloons off. A broad leather belt was slung across her hips, atop a pair of jeans that encased her long, slim legs. Desire crept through him, hot and relentless, like bootleg rum in his blood. "And the prize is tempting as ever."

"I see you haven't grown more subtle in your old age."

"Not much wiser, either. How about you?"

"I seem to get dumber every year." A smile tugged at her cheeky mouth. Vicki's lips were always dark, as if she wore lipstick, but he knew from kissing them that it was her hot blood close to the surface. "Otherwise, why would I be back here?"

"Because you couldn't get me out of your system." He narrowed his eyes and watched her reaction. Of course it was wishful thinking on his part. She'd probably forgotten him ten minutes after he left. He'd certainly hoped so at the time. Things had gotten way too intense and it was time to lift anchor and run for the open sea.

"You've been out of my system almost as long as the last dregs of nicotine from another one of my bad habits." She lifted her chin. "So don't get any ideas that I'm here for you. I'm just here because I *need* you."

"Be still, my heart." He placed a hand over it and wasn't surprised to find it beating faster than usual. Vicki must have that effect on any man. "Come lie next to me."

"No way."

"It's important."

"Nothing's that important." She'd crossed her arms in a defensive posture, and her hips tilted at a defiant angle. Sense memory flashed a moment of luscious recall—her hips pressed against his, arching higher, driving them both to a realm of beauty and madness.

"Not even finding your precious cup?"

"I fail to see how climbing into the sack with you brings me closer to my goal."

He raised a brow. "I always thought you were a lateral thinker. The thing is, you need to join me in bed to see how things lie."

She pursed her lips slightly and shifted her weight onto her other foot. Her pale violet eyes viewed him with intense suspicion. "I can see how things lie from right here."

"No, you can't." He glanced up at the ceiling. Time had faded and darkened the image. The plaster had cracked in places, but the fresco still showed the green shore of the island against the pale blue of the sea. "Come on. Hop up." He tapped the sheets. "So you can take a look at the old family map."

"What?" She peered upward, but he knew she couldn't see anything. The edge of the four-poster bed blocked any view of the painting unless one was literally lying on the mattress.

"Lazaro Drummond—the shipwreck survivor— painted the map above his bed, so that no one could see it but him."

"And his lovers."

He let a slow smile creep across his mouth. "Exactly."

Vicki walked toward the bed and climbed gingerly onto the opposite side. She settled herself on her back with her head on the pillow. He studied her for signs that she was uncomfortable—or excited—by being next to him on a bed. But no, she was entirely riveted by the painting overhead. She stared at it without speaking, almost without breathing, for a full minute. "I do believe this is the first real-life treasure map I've ever seen."

"They never do look like the ones in the movies." He enjoyed the fascinated expression on her face. How long had it been since he kissed that sassy mouth? Six years, at least. The urge to repeat history was rising in his blood.

"I keep looking for the X but I can't see it."

"The mermaid sitting on the rock. She's the X."

"Hmm." Vicki stared at it thoughtfully. She hadn't moved her eyes from the ceiling since the moment she lay down. "So the wreck is southeast of the island. Is there any kind of distance scale so we know how far it is?"

"If the size of the island is accurately drawn, it would be about two and a quarter miles off the northernmost inlet. That's what we Drummonds have always assumed anyway."

"And none of you has ever found it."

"Not yet." He shot her a sly glance.

She finally turned to look at him. Her pale eyes sparkled like diamonds. "That's why I'm here."

"I can believe you bring luck."

"Luck? How about my sharp mind?" She looked back up at the painting.

He felt as if the sun had shifted and thrown him into shadow. He wanted that bright, hopeful gaze on him again. "What will you do for me if I find it for you?" He made sure his voice held a purr of suggestion.

"Do for you? You'll get all the loot your ancestor stole and took to the bottom of the ocean with him. Isn't that enough?"

"There's never enough." He stared at her, willing her to bless him with her radiance again.

She turned to him, cheek resting on the soft pillow. "What else did you have in mind?" Dark lashes framed her eyes, giving them a smoky, sultry look. Her soft, pink mouth looked ripe with promise. He could easily imagine leaning forward a few inches and pressing his lips to hers.

Arousal thickened his groin and made his breath come faster. "I like having you back in my bed again." Her mouth twitched slightly, which was almost unbearably sensual. "If you'll stay with me here in my bed while we search, I'll plumb the depths of the ocean for you."

Her eyes widened. "That's a big ask."

"So's yours. I've got projects lined up that could keep me busy until 2050. You're asking me to drop everything and go fishing around on the bottom of the ocean for a wreck people have been hunting for more than 250 years. It won't be easy to find, that's for sure."

"You don't like things too easy, though, do you, Jack?"

He laughed. "No, Vicki, I don't."

"Then I can hardly just agree to your command, can I?" She sprang off the bed and strode from the room before he could even gather his thoughts, which were scattered and distracted by the sight of her tight ass in those fitted jeans.

She knew him too well.

"So where's the boat?" Vicki headed into the big living room, past the dark pieces of ancient furniture. Lucky thing she could still remember her way around somewhat. She tried a handle on one of the French doors, which opened out onto a broad, stone terrace.

"At the dock."

"Not the one we came on. Your super-high-tech treasure hunting boat."

"Ah. That's hidden."

"More valuable than the treasure it finds?"

"Something like that." Jack followed her out onto the terrace and squinted in the afternoon sun.

Damn but she'd been tempted to take him up on his offer. He had looked almost irresistible, lying there relaxed, heavy and sexy as hell, muscles sinking into the soft mattress, and that cool, curious look on his face.

But as she'd observed, he didn't like things too easy. He got bored quickly. Anyone wanting to keep Jack's interest better keep him guessing. And she'd already failed at that once, so the pressure was on.

"You trust me, don't you?" She smiled sweetly at him.

That lazy, puma grin sneaked back across his mouth. "At least as far as I can throw you." He took a step forward and her muscles tightened as she read sudden intention in his body. "Let's see exactly how far that is."

His arms reached out and she shrieked and ran—down the wide steps and onto a scraggly lawn. She ducked left and looked for an opening in the sea grape hedge, but it was too late. Jack's hands caught her around the waist and clutched her against him.

Breath flew from her lungs, less from force and more from the emotional impact of feeling Jack's big arms around her again. She braced herself, waiting for him to pick her up and hurl her somewhere. Instead, his grip only tightened and she felt his warm breath on the back of her neck.

Desire unfurled inside her, hot and liquid, darting through her veins and loosening her from head to toe. She could turn around right now and kiss him full on the mouth—but that would end the chase, and the chase excited him. "You wouldn't take advantage of a defenseless maiden, would you?"

"No way. But you? Sure." She could feel his grin radiating into the back of her brain. Still, his hands didn't stray from her waist. She found herself wanting them to.

"So you're not going to throw me?"

"Apparently I can't."

"Too soft?"

"Something like that. But it doesn't say much for how far I can trust you." He leaned in closer and his hot breath tickled her neck. "Though, strangely, I do trust you. You've never deceived me or led me astray." He sounded thoughtful. "At least not that I'm aware of."

"And I don't plan to start now." She wanted to move. Being so close to Jack, with his arms around her and her back pressed to his hard chest, was starting to mess with her mind. Worse yet, her body was starting to act up. Nipples thickening against her shirt, belly quivering, knees growing unreliable. If he hadn't already noticed, he might soon, and she'd rather die than have him know that he still had power over her.

"So, your precious ship. In some hidden cove, I'm guessing?"

"Nope, it's at the deeper dock." His hands pulled way from her waist slowly. Relief mingled with a surprise ripple of sadness. "Follow me." He pulled right away from her and set off across the lawn. Abandoned by his warm attentions, her skin felt cold. Still, she had to keep the dance going. It wouldn't work if he had his fill of her before they even got started. She was in control this time and she intended to keep it that way.

Jack's treasure hunting boat was dark blue, faded by the sun. It didn't look especially precious or expensive, but then probably the treasure it found didn't, either—at first.

Jack climbed aboard, muscles flexing beneath his faded jeans. "Done much diving lately?"

"Nope."

"Can you still remember how?"

"More or less." Jack had shown her how to dive years ago. Breathing underwater felt horribly unnatural and she'd been a slow study. She'd only fought past her fears out of sheer determination to prove he was wrong when he'd said she'd never do it. She wasn't too excited about doing it again. "Do we need to dive? Don't you have sonar to find the ship and a team of nano-robots to crawl the ocean floor for artifacts these days?"

He laughed. "That would take all the fun out of it." He reached down a hand and, with some misgivings, she grasped it and let him help as she climbed onto the shifting deck. "We sometimes use sonar to look for a wreck, though it doesn't always help. These funnels are used to blow holes in the ocean floor to expose stuff that's buried under the sand. After that, it's all about having sharp eyes and a lot of patience."

"You don't strike me as the patient type." She squinted in the sun. The boat was neat as a pin, every rope coiled to perfection and the surfaces scrubbed to eye-popping white.

"I'm as patient as they come." His slow, lazy smile challenged her to disagree. "I'll wait a whole lifetime for something if it's worth waiting for."

"Intriguing." She peered at the controls of the boat. It was probably not that much harder to maneuver than a car, should the need arise. "I suppose that's why you've never married."

"Who says I've never married?" His reply made her head snap up, which she bitterly regretted when she saw his smile broaden. "I only said that I've never fallen in love. But I'm touched that you care."

"So, have you?" She tried to look casual, walking to another part of the deck. The idea of Jack pledging himself to another woman for an entire lifetime made her stomach tighten. Which was ridiculous. Why would she care?

"Not yet."

Relief sank through her. Probably because she didn't need any more complications right now, like some dam-sel coming forward to claim that the treasure was half hers as a result of their divorce settlement.

"But I might have."

"If there was someone out there crazy enough to take you."

"I like crazy broads." His lazy gaze grazed her body, setting her skin on fire through her clothes and igniting a flash of irritation inside her.

"Why doesn't that surprise me?"

"Probably why I liked *you* so much." He hadn't taken his eyes off her, and his dark stare seemed to penetrate right through her. Why did she still have to be so attracted to him? You'd think that kind of thing would fade over time. She thought it had! But now that she was right here, only a few sun-scorched feet from him, all that long-forgotten desire was rising up like buried treasure—or junk—hidden beneath shifting sands.

"I don't think you liked me all that much." She walked to the prow of the boat, careful to keep her footing on the slippery surface. The deck rose and fell with the constant heave of the ocean, and she had to work slightly to stay balanced. "But maybe I'm wrong." She turned to him, feeling safer with slightly more distance between them.

"Maybe you are." His forehead was slightly furrowed, and his eyes rested on her for such a long time that she almost lost her footing and had to grab the rail around the deck. Was he thinking back to their whirlwind romance, all those sweltering nights in the Keys that one summer after college? She didn't think about it much, not anymore. She was over it.

Truth be told, though, she wasn't entirely over getting dumped at the end of their steamy romance. And if the spark between them should happen to get reignited, she looked forward to returning the favor.

The rise and fall of the ocean shifted the deck under her feet and her stomach was starting to feel queasy. If Jack knew, he'd make fun of her for not having her sea legs. "So, shall we plan to start the search tomorrow?" Then she'd have time to take a seasickness remedy in advance.

"I don't know." He stared out at the horizon, squinting out at the deep, blue unknown, sun blazing on his hard features. He was taunting her. He turned to look at her and her stomach lurched. "Did you think about my proposal?"

"I suppose it does make sense to spend time under the map together. To study it." Anywhere other than here on this lurching deck. She grabbed a handrail, trying to look casual. It was surprising how little movement it took to throw your inner ear off kilter. And what an unhappy effect that had on the stomach.

"It'll be like old times." His voice held more than a hint of suggestion.

Without waiting for an invitation, she clambered over the side of the boat—with some difficulty, which she attempted to conceal—and back onto the hard and very still dock. "Not really." This time she'd be in control of what happened, and when it ended.

"Leaving so soon? I was going to show you the sonar."

"I'll see it in action tomorrow." She marched up the dock toward the house, hoping she could make it back there and collapse somewhere fast. She didn't intend for Jack to see her in a moment of weakness. Like the predator he was, he'd have to pounce and play with her, and she wasn't quite strong enough for that.

Once she had the reward, though, she'd feel strong. Ten thousand dollars might not sound like much to her old friends, but it would be enough to sow the seeds of her new life. A life where she wouldn't have to depend on anybody but herself.

She heard the thud of Jack's feet hitting the deck. He was coming after her. A satisfied smile crossed her mouth. She made sure to add an extra ounce of swagger to her walk, knowing—or was it hoping?—that his eyes were tracking her hips like a laser beam.

He thought he'd achieved a victory by getting her to agree to sleep with him. Little did he know it had been her plan all along. She'd enjoy it, too. She hadn't chanced a sensual affair in almost a year. She'd been too busy dodging creditors and trying to hide her precarious financial situation. She certainly hadn't wanted to be in an intimate situation where she might have to open up to someone.

She wouldn't have to open up to Jack. His personal walls were as thick as the battlements on his ancestral home, and he never let them down. They could make love all night long and keep their hearts under lock and key. Hers had chains on it that weren't likely to break anytime soon, especially not for Jack Drummond.

His footsteps were gaining on her, and she fought the urge to walk faster. Instead, she slowed to let him catch up. "Is there any hope of dinner out here on your desert island?"

"I caught a big swordfish yesterday. We can grill it."

"I thought we weren't supposed to eat swordfish anymore now that we've poisoned the oceans. A friend of mine is pregnant and she said the doctor told her the toxins can affect your genes and damage your future children."

"My children might enjoy having three eyes." His grin cut a white slash across his dark face. "Are you worried about your own offspring?"

"I won't ever have children." She said it brightly. "So I can eat all the swordfish I want."

His smile vanished. "You can't have kids?"

She startled at the sudden change in his demeanor. Why did he care if she could have children or not? "Not can't, *won't*. I'm not cut out for motherhood. Too much wiping butts and drying tears for my taste."

He laughed. "Did your mom do those things?"

"No, she hired a nanny for that." She walked faster. This conversation was getting too personal.

"You could do the same." She felt his dark, penetrating gaze on her cheek.

"No, thanks. I'm doing my best not to turn out like my parents."

"Me, too. Unlike my dad, I intend to be alive at fifty." Something in his voice made her turn to look at him. His eyes were shadowed.

"I heard about his death. I'm sorry. It was a small-plane accident, wasn't it?"

"It was no accident." He marched steadily, eyes now straight ahead. The house loomed through the trees. "He'd been trying to kill himself for years."

The Drummond curse. Vicki remembered Katherine Drummond begging her to help her find the lost cup pieces and lift the curse that had dogged the family for centuries. At first Vicki had laughed it off, but the Drummonds certainly didn't seem to have much luck in life. They could make money all day long, but when it came to marriage or family harmony, or even simple contentment, they were a disaster zone.

"The awkward silence descends." Jack spoke softly, slightly mocking. "So, the swordfish it is. Let our children learn to play with the dark hand they're dealt."

"I'm sure it will be delicious." She regretted her quip about the fish. "I eat it all the time and love it."

"I remember it being your favorite." He opened a side door of the house, pushing at the big, tarnished brass handle. Something in the tone of his voice made her breath catch at the bottom of her lungs. What else did he remember? How she'd called him in the middle of the night just to hear the sound of his voice? The way she sighed when he kissed her neck?

The time she'd made the bitter mistake of telling him she loved him.

That last one wasn't a question. He probably would remember that, unless he'd repressed it somehow. That little slip of the tongue had sent him running.

She followed him into the cool, shaded interior. Things would be a lot easier if she could find this cup without his help. Just her luck, it had wound up on the bottom of the sea. Even if they could find the ship, it would be a miracle if the cup piece hadn't washed away, and then again, if it were recognizable enough for her to find it. This could well be a wild goose chase, and she couldn't afford to waste too much time on it. She should probably set a strict deadline for herself, with plans to jump ship if they hadn't found it within two weeks.

"You're quieter than you used to be." His words startled her from her thoughts.

"More going on in my brain, less coming out of

my mouth." She smiled and leaned against the kitchen counter.

"How enigmatic." He pulled a bottle of wine from a large rack against one wall. "Pinot grigio?"

"Sure." She watched his hands as he peeled away the foil over the cork. His fingers were precise and careful, no doubt good with fine detail and careful with precious relics. He plunged the corkscrew in with gusto—the kind of thrust with which he approached most aspects of life—and turned it aggressively. The muscles in his forearms torqued beneath the skin, revealing their power and stirring something primal inside her.

It had to be primal because it had nothing to do with modern-day common sense. Men didn't need strength to be successful in today's world. A good head for numbers and a dubious set of morals was a much more effective get-rich-quick kit.

Still, she admired the bulge of his biceps against the soft sleeve of his T-shirt as he pulled the cork from the bottle in a swift and brutal movement. The cork squeaked and popped free, leaving her heart beating slightly faster.

She distracted herself by admiring the interesting tile work on the wall behind the stove. No sense getting herself too aroused and invested in their evening plans. She might need to pull back at some point and she didn't want her own rampant desires to make that almost impossible.

Jack handed her a brimming glass of pale gold wine. "To treasure."

"Treasure." She smiled and lifted her glass. The wine tasted delicious, smooth, rich, cool and refreshing after the hot sun outside. "Jewels and coins and gold bars for you, part of an old cup for me."

"That doesn't sound fair." His dark eyes sparkled behind the lock of hair hanging down to them. "Maybe we'll have to find you a gold necklace or a stash of rings."

She held out one of her pale, bony hands. "As you can see, I'm not much of a ring wearer."

"You might change your mind, for the right one."

"Don't count on it." She glanced at her empty ring finger. She did not intend to live her life by anyone else's rules. "But I'd be happy to sell it for a handsome profit." She shone him a bright smile. "In fact, that's my intended future business, so it would be a nice jump start."

"I heard you were working for an auction house."

"That was my apprenticeship. Now that I know what things are worth, I plan to go out on my own." She sipped her wine again. "This is good stuff. Tastes expensive."

"You do know what things are worth." His eyes crinkled in a smile.

"You're funny, Jack. You always look so casual and act like you don't care about money, but you do enjoy the finer things in life."

"One of my many weaknesses."

"Hmm, makes me wonder what your other weaknesses are." Not a soft heart, for sure. Which is why he'd never fallen for anyone.

"A passion for a fickle mistress." He looked at her over his glass.

"The sea." She knew it wouldn't be a real woman.

He nodded. "Though she's been good to me."

"She's giving you all the riches she took from the

hundreds of men and women who've died off this coast over the centuries."

"I did say she was fickle."

"And obviously has her favorites."

A slow smile crept across his mouth. "Let's go sit where we can see her." He led the way out onto a veranda with a view out over the sea grape in the dunes. Blue and steady, the ocean lay before them like a velvet throw. She could hear the waves crashing on the beach, but couldn't see them because they were hidden by the dunes. Jack ushered her to sit on a sleek upholstered outdoor sofa. When she was seated, he eased himself down next to her and flung his arm casually on the back of the sofa behind her.

Her neck and shoulders prickled with awareness. Of course he was doing it deliberately. He wanted to taunt and tempt her. He had every intention of seducing her. And she might even let him, but not until they were at least on the way to finding the cup. Otherwise he might find he'd already got what he wanted and send her packing.

She twisted the stem of her wineglass in her hands. "Because there's a reward, there are probably other people looking. We need to move fast."

"We'll start tomorrow at first light."

"When is that?"

"Six or so is when you can start to tell the sea from the shore."

She cringed inwardly. Jack probably didn't even drink coffee in the morning. She usually started the day with her familiar newspapers and a hearty meal to ground herself before venturing out into the cold, cruel world. The prospect of having to drag herself out of bed and onto the sea without those reassuring comforts was frightening. And she'd better buy something for her stomach. If she'd known the cup was under the sea, she might have been better prepared. "Where's the nearest drugstore?"

"Headache?"

She hesitated. "Nope. I might need a little something for my stomach on the boat tomorrow." She avoided his eyes. "It's always good to be prepared."

"Don't worry. My larder's well stocked." His eyes twinkled. Maybe he'd give her a placebo so she'd be leaning over the edge of the deck, begging for mercy. "We can stay out at sea for days at a time. Weeks even."

"I'm not sure I'd survive weeks trapped on a boat with you, Jack."

"I suspect you could survive almost anything." His arm shifted behind her, and she tried to ignore the shimmer of response that slid through her body. "You look slender and insubstantial on the outside, but you're made of sturdy stuff."

"I hope so." She'd need to be to make it through this trial. Being this close to Jack was having a dangerous effect on her sanity. Which didn't make any sense. He was just another rich, handsome bozo and she had years of experience and training in dealing with them. "I guess only time will tell."

"You look different." His eyes narrowed. He studied her face for a moment while her pulse quickened.

"It has been six years since I saw you." Did she look older? Her dad had aged dramatically during his swift and private fall from grace. Hollows appeared under his eyes and cheekbones, and his skin developed a bluish undertone. "You, on the other hand, look exactly the same."

Not exactly. Time and the sun, working hand in hand, had made him look rugged and distinguished. His eyes still had that insolent flash to them, and his lip that disdainful way of curving upward so you couldn't tell if he was laughing with you or at you.

Did she imagine it or did his left thigh creep imperceptibly closer to her right one? She could almost feel the heat of it through her pants. The salt air filled her lungs and made her giddy.

"I don't know what exactly is different." His eyes rested on her face—her cheek, to be precise, because she was avoiding his gaze by staring at the horizon. "Something big, though."

She shrank a little under his inquisitive look. She was quite a different person than the brash, confident and empty-headed girl who'd partied and had sex on the beach with him that summer. Then she'd thought the world was hers for the taking and she was taking a vacation before seizing it. The years since had taught her that the world wasn't too interested in whether she wanted it and that the foundation of her life—the privilege and wealth afforded by her proud family—had been built on the shifting sands of illusion.

She certainly didn't intend for him to find out about that. No, they could laugh about that later once she'd made a name for herself and didn't need to rest on anyone else's laurels. Right now, though, she was hanging in thin air, and she intended to keep that a secret.

Which might be interesting, because she'd already committed to sharing a bed with him. Hopefully she wouldn't talk in her sleep.

Three

Jack grilled his delicious swordfish and served it with skewered grilled vegetables out on the terrace, where the evening breeze kept bugs at bay. They could see the lights of fishing boats and the occasional cruise ship in the distance, but all was stillness and silence on the island.

"It's so peaceful here." Vicki looked out over the dunes. "Doesn't it drive you nuts?"

"Maybe that's why I've always been nuts." Jack reclined in his chair. Lit tapers in the gnarled old candelabra on the table cast flickering shadows over his hard features. "I need it, though. Helps me recharge my batteries."

"Hmm. I can just hook myself up to my car engine by the jumper cables." She sipped her wine, then, realizing she'd had almost three glasses, pushed her wineglass out of reach. She was in danger of becoming tipsy. She'd better work on keeping her hatches more tightly battened.

"You still like living in the city?" Jack lifted his arms and placed them behind his head, giving her a breath-stealing view of his powerful biceps.

She swallowed and squinted slightly to obscure the view. "Yes. I think I love being another anonymous face in the crowd. I can't imagine living in a small town where everyone knows who I am."

"Sounds like you're running from something. Or someone."

"Maybe I prefer being out of reach." She smiled and made a conscious effort not to pick up her glass again. If only they could go to bed so she could stop trying to put on a bravely charming front. Then again, that might be leaping from the frying pan into the fire.

"Did you ever think about me, you know, over the years?" His voice was low, gruff.

"Certainly not. You dumped me, remember?" Her adrenaline level jumped. This had to come out sooner or later. Might as well get it over with.

"I always felt bad about the way I took off. Blame it on youthful immaturity."

She sneaked a glance at him. It was hard to read his expression in the flickering candlelight, but she imagined she saw a hint of sheepishness in his eyes. "Don't flatter yourself that I've spent the last few years pining over you. I've had far more traumatic relationships since." She inhaled the sea air.

"Have you? Did someone break your heart?"

"No way. Nothing in there but cogs and wheels. That's why I can jump-start my battery so easily." A sudden chill in the night air made goose bumps spring up on her arms, and she rubbed them. "Things may be a little rusty, but nothing's broken."

He chuckled. "I've got some oil for your rusty gears."

"I bet you do." She looked at him down the length of her nose. She had to work hard not to smile. It was almost impossible to be mad at Jack Drummond when she was in his presence. That came later, when she realized how he'd played her like a violin. "But you can leave it on your garage shelf. I like to think of my rust as a protective barrier."

"I'm feeling jealous." His annoyingly thick biceps flexed as he stretched. "I'm beginning to think I made a big mistake back then."

"One of many, I'd imagine." Again, she had to fight the reflex to reach for her wine. Shame she didn't smoke. It was hard not to fidget, but she worked hard to look cool and calm.

"You know it." That familiar lazy grin eased across his mouth. "But they've been fun, each and every one."

"Just think of all the fun we'd have missed out on if we'd fallen madly in love with each other and done something stupid like getting married." She hugged herself. It was getting colder. "That would have been quite the act of rebellion at the time."

He laughed. "Yes, your parents might have died of shock at the prospect of their princess marrying a beach bum."

"Until they realized how filthy rich you are. Then they'd have staged a brisk recovery and welcomed you with open arms. It would have all been very boring."

"I spared us that by running off like a coward at the first sign of emotion."

She froze. He'd just admitted it. That he remembered. *I love you.*

She'd said it loud and clear, for the one and only time in her life. She'd rather slit her own throat than ever utter those three words again. "Emotion? I'm not sure I was ever capable of one of those."

"Me, either. Inconvenient and messy things. Best left to those who don't have enough going on in their lives. Speaking of which, we should get to bed." His eyes flashed, creating a frightening jolt of response somewhere low in her belly. "Because we need to get up early in the morning, of course." His steady, dark gaze suggested more than sleep.

Suddenly her plan to enjoy the pleasures of his body seemed like the dumbest idea she'd ever come up with. Maybe because she was tired and all this talk of old hurts made her feel vulnerable. "Do you sleep in that same room, under the map?"

"Of course. It's always been the captain's bedroom." He grabbed the bottle and glasses from the table. She hesitated for a second before taking their plates and cutlery. She'd become used to being waited on hand and foot in Sinclair Drummond's house—by the woman he'd recently become engaged to.

"That map must be emblazoned on your brain by now."

"Hasn't helped me find the treasure, though."

"Maybe you're reading it wrong?" They walked back into the air-conditioned calm of the house. "Perhaps what it needs is a different perspective." She didn't want to speculate on how many women's eyes had stared up at that map over the centuries.

"I'll welcome your angle on it. I think we've read it every possible way it can be read."

"But you've never found the ship."

"The ship could be broken up and washed away by now."

And the cup gone forever. "It's out there. I feel it in my bones." She shot him a glance as they walked side by side down the hallway to the bedroom.

"I would definitely bet money on your intuition."

"You should. I hooked your cousin Sinclair up with his new bride. The moment I saw the way they looked at each other, I knew they were meant to be together."

"Were they dating?"

"Nope, she was serving him his morning coffee and ironing his linen napkins, but I made sure Cinderella went to the ball with her handsome prince and it's been all uphill from there." Well, mostly. No need to mention the part about his horrid ex-wife suddenly discovering she was pregnant. "He certainly believes in my hunches now."

"Then I'll bet on them, too, and put my equipment and expertise at your disposal."

He opened the door to the bedroom, dimly lit by wall sconces that cast a romantic glow over the old plasterwork. The bed looked much smaller than she remembered, its massive wood structure framing what was probably only a full-size mattress. "It's going to be a tight fit for both of us."

"All the better." His feral grin flashed for a brief second. Then a more gentlemanly expression returned. "I'll leave you to get changed while I lock up for the night."

"Lock up? We're on an island. Who are you trying to keep out?"

"Maybe you should ask who I'm trying to keep in."

He vanished before she could come up with a witty reply. Or any reply. Her suitcase stood silently in one corner, and she hurried to get changed into her pj's before he could come back and watch her undress.

She donned a bra and panties as extra armor underneath her white cotton camisole and lounge pants. Not that she expected him to do anything mischievous while she was asleep. That wasn't his style. There was absolutely nothing sneaky about Jack Drummond. If he planned to lay siege, he'd do it while she was wide-awake.

It was her own defenses she was worried about. She didn't want any part of her to start straying toward his side of the mattress, hoping for a casual brush against those thick biceps or one of those powerful thighs. Much better to keep everything strapped down and swathed in fabric.

She washed her face in the big onyx sink. The mirror was ancient, foggy and flecked with dark spots. When she caught sight of her reflection, it startled her. It was as if she'd seen a dream version of herself, pale and wan, lost in a strange world. She turned away sharply. When she walked back into the bedroom, Jack was there, casually stripping away his clothes and revealing his tanned physique. She made a valiant effort not to look, but it was hard because he faced the opposite direction and she had free rein to indulge an academic interest in seeing how his body compared to the one in her memory.

Favorably. She had to admire the way he'd filled out. Not a rangy, sunburned youth anymore, but a man in his prime. Broad-shouldered enough to carry the weight of the world. When his jeans slid down, she gasped at how pale his backside was. Obviously the only part of him that never got much sun exposure.

He must have heard her intake of breath because he turned his head. "I hope I'm not being rude by stripping off right here. You have seen it all before."

"It's your bedroom. You do what you like." She grabbed her phone from her purse, so she could distract herself by checking her messages, then walked to the bed and climbed in, with some difficulty because it was high. She slid under the covers and was gratified to find soft sheets there. Once again, only the best for Jack Drummond. She turned on her phone and checked her texts. Nothing interesting. Her gaze drifted up to the mural painted overhead. The green shoreline, dotted with palm trees, the blue sea, the crudely painted mermaid sitting on her rock. No one would call it a work of art. The fresco obviously hadn't ever been restored, either. Even the scant light from her phone picked out the uneven surface and revealed where tiny chips of plaster had flaked off. It was darkened by centuries of smoke from candles and pipes and who knew what else Jack's pirate ancestors had burned in here. It would be interesting to see what a good cleaning might reveal.

"How did you measure the distances on the map to know where to look?" She kept her eyes firmly off Jack as he walked toward the bed—still naked, as far as she could tell—and climbed under the covers.

"We started a few yards off the shore and kept moving out north at the same angle. It wasn't too scientific. In all honesty I put nearly two years into it and I'm sure I wasn't the first."

"One of your ancestors could have found the wreck and salvaged it." Her skin tingled with uncomfortable awareness that his naked body shared the same dark, small space with hers.

"Found it maybe. Salvaged it? Impossible. There's a steep shelf offshore and the wreck is somewhere outside the shelf. The water's way too deep for anyone without sophisticated equipment like oxygen tanks to explore. No way it could have been done before the twentieth century, and if it was that recent I'd know about it."

He rolled toward her, so close she could almost feel his hot breath on her skin. Her nerve endings pulsed and tingled—with the desire to leap out of this bed and save herself. She managed, with great effort, to keep her eyes on the low ceiling above the bed. What she saw there made her squint her eyes in an effort to focus more closely. In the dim half light from her phone the shadowy pits in the plaster stirred adrenaline in her blood. "Do you have a flashlight?"

"Sure." She heard him turn and reach behind him. "Keep one next to the bed at all times. We often lose power during storms."

She turned to take it and got a disarming eyeful of his tanned pecs. "Thanks." She climbed out from under the covers, careful not to accidentally dislodge them from any more of his bare flesh, and stood on the mattress. Holding the flashlight above her head, she shone it at the ceiling. "Interesting." Her pulse quickened and she moved her arm higher, trying to keep her balance on the squishy surface of the mattress, which was already thrown off balance by Jack's heavy form.

"What do you see?"

"The plaster has some tiny chips, but there's still color behind them. I think there's another painting underneath this one."

"You're kidding." She braced as he shifted the mattress by sitting up.

"You should already know I'm not the jolly jokester type." Gingerly she reached up and touched one of the indentations in the surface. She scraped the edge of the hole lightly with her fingernail—museum curators would shudder—and tiny fragments of plaster came away, but the surface beneath stayed intact. And was definitely pigmented. "I wonder if one of your sneaky ancestors covered up the real map with a misleading one to put someone else off the scent."

"If they did, it's worked very well. How do you remove the top layer?"

"It looks like someone slathered a fresh layer of plaster over a previous painting. If that's the case we should be able to chip it off. Look…" She pointed to the chip in the fresco. "There's a patch of blue underneath this green area. That's what makes me think there's another picture."

Jack rose to his feet, shifting the entire mattress in his direction. She struggled to keep her footing, but had to put out a hand and steady herself on the rock-hard muscle of his torso. Once she had her balance again, she snatched her hand back as if his skin had burned it. "Of course, chipping it off will destroy the painting. I know it's part of your family history."

"We Drummonds have far too much family history."

"There are ways of lifting it off, using glue and fabric to transfer it to a new surface, but we'd have to hunt down the materials and I've never done it before, so it would take some research and experimentation…."

"I'll go get a couple of chisels." Jack jumped off the bed, throwing her off balance again. She had to steady herself by thrusting her arm up toward the ceiling. Where her fingers met the surface she could swear she felt it crack slightly, ready to release it's grip on the ceiling above and fall away to reveal its secrets.

Jack had left the room, so she took a moment to heave a tiny sigh of relief. Instead of an awkward night beneath the sheets with him, it looked as though they were in for an interesting night of discovery.

Either that or she was about to destroy a Drummond family heirloom. She pulled her camera from her bag and took about fifty pictures of the painting from all angles, in case removing it should prove to be a mistake.

Jack returned a minute later with an armory of tools in a wooden box, and some khaki shorts—thank goodness—covering his man bits. She rifled through the box and chose an ancient flat-head screwdriver and a tiny hammer. "We want to use something blunt, so we don't chip right through it. Hopefully if we can crack the surface it will fall away like it's already started to do."

She started first, chipping gently next to one of the existing holes. Spider cracks crawled slowly across the plaster, a few millimeters at a time. She was barely breathing. This could all be a stupid mistake—someone might have just painted the wall a flat color before creating the map. She kept going, though, and after about two minutes, a tiny chunk of plaster no larger than a pinky nail fell to the sheets below. Underneath it was more of the rich indigo-blue color she'd glimpsed. "You'd better get a drop cloth for the bed or your sheets will get dusty." She spoke through a smile.

"Never mind that." Jack picked up the little hammer and began tapping. "I can't believe I've slept under this thing for years and never thought to look beneath the surface."

"Then it's rather a miracle that I came back into your life, isn't it?"

"Indeed it is."

Jack's arm ached from holding it over his head while tapping at the fresco. They couldn't risk being too aggressive and damaging the painting beneath, so it was slow going. As 3:00 a.m. rolled past, they'd revealed enough to see that there was indeed another map painted below in far richer and more saturated colors. This map showed only the shore of the island, a detailed outline with nooks and crannies and rock outcroppings. The rest of the painting, so far, was all indigo-blue sea. No sign of an *X,* or even a helpful mermaid.

"What do you think of all these white lines?" The blue ocean surface was crisscrossed with faint white hatch marks, which gave the appearance of ocean peaks and waves.

"Could be something to do with where the treasure is hidden. Or not." Vicki tapped away relentlessly at the plaster, which rained down on the bed, and sometimes on him, in a fine powder dust. "We'll know more once we can see the whole thing."

"How about a break?" His legs also ached from standing on the bed. It made the deck of a ship seem downright steady. But the sight of Vicki's lithe body, scant inches from his, kept his strength up enough to keep going.

"No way. We need to get out there tomorrow. There's a reward for the cup, remember?"

"How is anyone else supposed to find the cup when they don't even know it's under the sea?"

"They'll figure it out." She hadn't even glanced at him. Too wrapped up in her task. "Believe me, it won't be that hard. Something tells me there are books written about your ancestors and their treasure."

Jack shrugged. "I suppose. Still, the reward isn't large enough to draw the big treasure hunters."

"No, but the treasure is, and once other people start looking for it, they'll want in on the action. How would you feel if some metal detector hobbyist found it and claimed everything?"

"That might make me cry." He sneaked a sideways glance at her, and was rewarded by her turning to him. "But at least you'd be here to dry my tears."

"Don't count on it. I'll be out there cozying up to the finder." Her teeth flashed in a sudden smile that made his breath stick in his lungs. How could she still be so beautiful? The passing years had chiseled her girlish features to a fine perfection—high cheekbones and determined chin. Her eyes had a dimension he didn't remember seeing there, something wary and challenging that added depth to her proud beauty.

"So you'd ditch me for the winner."

"Wouldn't you do the same?"

"Probably." A grin pulled at his mouth. His arms, tired of all the chiseling, had fallen to his sides. "It's not easy talking to someone who knows me so well."

"Even after all these years, huh? I guess you haven't changed that much."

"I don't think I've changed at all." He put serious effort into not growing staid and boring like his former surfing buddies, with their McMansions and monster

SUVs. "And if you haven't changed, either, we're still a team to be reckoned with."

"Which is why we're not quitting on this fresco." Her arms were still raised and her tool tap-tap-tapping gently against the brittle plaster. Jack's eyes burned from the dust, but he was damned if he'd quit before she did. She wouldn't respect him, for one thing, and for some strange reason he didn't feel like analyzing, her respect was important to him. Suppressing a groan, he got back to the task, chipping away at his family history, when he'd much rather be stripping away Vicki's dusty pajamas and tasting the lush body hidden beneath them.

There'd be time for that later.

"I think this is some kind of code." Vicki murmured the words so low he could barely make them out. She'd stopped chiseling and was staring hard at the surface. "The white hatch marks. I keep seeing Roman numerals in them."

Jack stared at the pattern, which danced before his tired eyes. "Why would someone put hidden numbers on a map?"

"I don't know." She pressed a long, slender finger to the surface of the mural, smearing away the layer of dust left behind. The action pulled her T-shirt firmly across her delicious, pointy breasts, and he suddenly had to grab a bedpost to keep his balance. "Don't fall and hurt yourself."

The slight lift of her brow made him smile. Then he tried to focus on the painting again. He could make out vertical and horizontal lines that, when looked at with a forgiving eye, did look a bit like numbers. "I see what you mean." He reached up, partly to steady himself on the ceiling, truth be told, and partly to focus his tired vision on the spot he was trying to read. He made out a VIII. "This looks like an eight."

"And look, this is an *X,* it's just divided into two *V*s so it isn't so obvious."

"*X* marks the spot?" He squinted at the spot near her fingers.

"No way. That would be too easy. And look, there are loads of them."

"Great. I've always loved looking for needles in haystacks."

"Me, too." Her eyes were riveted on the painted surface. "There's a pattern to the numbers. When were lines of latitude and longitude invented?"

He shrugged. "We Drummonds are more into stealing history than learning about it."

"You can't fool me." Her bright gaze challenged him. Her whole face glowed with an excitement that he couldn't help feel beginning to tingle at the tips of his own fingers and toes. And some other, more private places. "You're a professional treasure hunter. I'm confident you know the histories of your wrecks better than you know what's going on in the world today."

"Is there still a world out there?" It was too much fun to torment her and watch the impatience and frustration flash in her eyes. "I try to avoid contact with it."

"Easy enough to do when you have your own island, I suppose." She shot him a glance. "But seriously, could these be latitude and longitude?"

Jack peered at the faint patterns of numbers. They did look like Roman numerals, which as far as he knew had never been used to write location coordinates. "They did use latitude and longitude in the eighteenth century, sure. They found their location using a sextant, which measured the angle of the sun to the horizon, so they could know where they were in relation to the equator, and a chronometer, which kept Greenwich Mean Time so they could figure out which time zone they were in by how far off their high noon was from London's." He let out a sigh. "Latitude around here is about twenty-six degrees—we're twenty-eight degrees north of the equator—and longitude is about eighty degrees west of London."

He peered at the painted hatch marks on the wall. They buzzed in front of his tired eyes. Then the number twenty—XX—popped out. Then VIII—the number eight. And IX—nine, then XIV—fourteen. "You might be on to something."

"Yes! Now all we have to do is write it down and find that treasure." The shine in her eyes made his stomach do a weird flip. It even made him keep his mouth shut about how it was bound to be a lot more complicated than that. For some reason he didn't want to disappoint Vicki. He wanted to make her happy.

Now, that was disturbing.

Four

Vicki sat on the prow of the boat, squinting at her pages of notes in the blazing early morning sun. Above them, thousands of cotton-ball clouds scudded across the vast sky and not one provided a lick of shade. No sleep and an army of nonsensical numbers marching through her brain had driven her half-mad.

And then there was Jack.

He was being so nice. So helpful. It was disarming and troubling. This was not the Jack she knew and loved/hated. She was beginning to think he might be up to something a lot more complicated than wanting to seduce her and dump her again.

"I still don't get what we're doing out here." He called from the deck where he was steering them… somewhere. "Those numbers don't mean anything that we can figure out."

"I hope coming out on the water will give us some perspective on the map." It had been her idea, queasy stomach and all. A flask of stomach-calming ginger tea sat by her side, and so far, so good. "It's right here in front of us somewhere. We have all the pieces. We just need to put them together."

Easier said than done, especially with the distraction of a barely clad Jack Drummond a few feet away, sun gleaming off his tanned, muscled form. She should probably just have sex with him and get it over with. That might be the only way to reduce the sexual tension pounding in the air like jungle drums.

He kept shooting sly glances at her, from beneath that dark lock of hair that dipped to his eyes. She tried to convince herself that she'd already rowed his rowboat and there was nothing to get excited about...but her memories of Jack in the sack unfortunately had the opposite effect.

Was he still the tender and passionate lover she remembered? Or had time hardened him into a more impatient or guarded bedmate? Curiosity made her skin tingle and she pulled her attention back to the stack of papers in her hand. Printed images of the ceiling fresco with its ragged coastline and wispy sprawl of Roman numerals.

They'd translated the numerals into familiar numbers as best they could, and Jack had pointed out that they weren't coordinates, at least not according to any system he knew.

They probably should have slept at that point, but the bed was covered with plaster chunks and dust and she didn't want to risk a discussion of where else they might sleep because his agreement to help her was contingent on her agreeing to join him in his bed. With her luck, they'd end up in a single bed with his chest as her pillow.

"Tired?" Jack must have seen her yawn.

"Not at all." She smiled briskly. Let him think she was a demon who didn't need sleep. "Nothing like a little sunlight and salt air to recharge my fuel cells."

"I couldn't agree more." His gruff voice held a hint of laughter. She resisted the urge to turn around because she didn't feel like being broadsided by a vision of his brawny body. "So where's the wreck?"

"It's out there somewhere."

The ocean was so vast. Opaque and impenetrable, its blue surface heaved under the boat. Maybe the wreck had been pounded to smithereens over the centuries. Or washed far out to sea in a storm. Or been found and stripped clean by one of Jack's more enterprising ancestors.

"What if it's a code?" Jack's voice jolted her from her train of depressing thoughts.

"Of course it's a code. What else could it be?" Adrenaline surged through her. Why hadn't she thought of that? She'd been so hung up on the latitude and longitude theory that it hadn't crossed her mind that the numerals had some other meaning. She peered at the pages with fresh interest, while trying to hide her sudden enthusiasm from Jack.

If the numbers were letters, there would be some that occurred more than others—*A,* for example. She scanned the pages. And sighed. Roman numerals were insanely repetitive already. Instead of having 1, 2, 3, 4, 5, 6, 7, 8, 9 and 10, they had I, II, III, IV, V, VI, VII, VIII, IX and X. A grand total of three characters: I, V and X. Her careful transcription contained no higher numbers like C for a hundred or M for a thousand. Words were hardly jumping off the page at her.

"Cracked it yet?" His teasing voice made her head jerk involuntarily in his direction.

"Almost." Great. Another eyeful of his bulging biceps as he pushed some button on the boat deck. "Maybe we should throw out a net and see if we can catch the wreck."

He chuckled. "Or maybe you're just hungry for more fish."

Her stomach lurched at the prospect. It was barely 8:00 a.m. She reached for her ginger tea and took a bracing gulp. She stared at her pages of numbers. Of course she wasn't even sure they were the right numbers. They'd tried to find gaps between the endless rows of Xs and Is and Vs and might have got some of them wrong.

There were a lot of IXs, though. And IIIs. She squinted at the page. If those corresponded to *a*'s or *o*'s or *e*'s... The rolling, lurching motion of the ship was not helping her brain power. "Maybe we should go back." She needed flat, hard land under her feet to figure out this mess.

"I thought you were going to use your feminine intuition to find the wreck beneath the waves."

"It's blown a gasket. And I need an egg sandwich. Let's head into town."

"Your wish is my command." The engine roared as he swung the boat around and headed for shore at an impressive clip. She grabbed up her papers to shield them from the salt spray. She watched his steady arms for a moment.

"I do like that about boats."

"What?" He squinted in the bright sun, a half smile tugging at his mouth.

"That you can just say, let's go to town, or to the Bahamas, or Madagascar, and all you have to do is rev the engines and off you go. No roads or rules or traffic lights."

"You're beginning to understand the pull of the sea." He watched her steadily for a moment until his gaze felt as if it was going to burn a hole in her. "No speeding tickets, either."

He floored the accelerator, or whatever you called it with boats, and suddenly they seemed to be shooting across the surface of the water, bouncing hard. She grabbed a nearby chrome rail and hung on for dear life as she felt her hair unravel and stream behind her in the wind. Part of her wanted to scream, and the rest wanted to let out a whoop of joy, as cobwebs fled her mind and adrenaline shrieked to every corner of her body.

By the time they reached the shore, she'd broken a sweat just sitting still—or attempting to—and she couldn't wipe the goofy smile off her face. "You're crazy."

"Always have been, always will be."

They had breakfast at an outdoor café with the decor of a truck stop and a million-dollar view of the ocean. Vicki scribbled on her papers, making notes and trying out code possibilities.

"I can hear your brain working from here." Jack relaxed in his chair with an iced tea.

"Is the ticking keeping you awake?" She didn't glance up. Something about the pattern of the Vs made her think she was on the verge of a breakthrough.

"It's more of a humming sound, like a laser."

She met his gaze. "Careful you don't get zapped."

"I might like it." Humor danced in his eyes. He was flirting again. Worse yet, she was liking it. Where was all the hatred and bitterness she'd hoped to feel?

Don't fall for him again. He'll only get bored and dump you.

Her mind knew the truth, but her body kept rippling with pleasurable tension. His broad, arrogant mouth was so annoyingly kissable. That confident sparkle in his eye promised heights of sensual pleasure she hadn't scaled since…the last time she slept with Jack.

Sunshine and lack of sleep were making her loopy. "I need sleep, and I mean *sleep,* or I'll never figure this out."

"Paloma will have tidied up the bed by now." His feral grin sent a shiver of…warning to her toes.

"You have a housekeeper?" Hard to imagine surf-bum Jack with staff.

He shrugged. "Sometimes I'm out on the water for a week or more at a time. The lizards would take over the house if someone didn't come in and fight back the forces of nature."

"I guess that's a hazard of living in a historic property."

"Built by pirates with no construction experience." He stretched, giving her yet another annoying view of his biceps. "Amazing it hasn't fallen down by now."

"I suppose if you can figure out how to keep a wooden vessel afloat on water 365 days a year, piling some rocks into a sturdy house doesn't seem so hard. I wonder if they buried any treasure in the walls while they were building."

Jack lifted a brow. "Maybe we should start chiseling around the window frames?"

"Let's find the wreck first." She lifted her bag onto her shoulder. "After I get some sleep."

To her surprise, Jack did let her sleep, alone in the luxurious comfort of fresh white sheets. Jack's silent and invisible housekeeper had removed every trace of plaster dust and left the room sparkling and smelling pleasantly of beeswax. When Vicki awoke, sometime late that afternoon, the newly revealed fresco hovered above her like a summer sky, its colors intense, unfaded by sunbeams and time. Why had someone covered it up? They must have wanted to hide the information contained in this map. Maybe they had it committed to memory and needed to conceal it from greedy family members or servants until they found the time and means to retrieve it.

She could easily imagine the various Drummonds not trusting each other. They seemed like a pretty tormented family. Maybe there was a curse that needed to be lifted.

Speaking of which, where was Jack? Her ears pricked as she listened for sounds of him. As far as she knew, he hadn't come near while she was sleeping.

She slipped out of bed and walked over the cool tiled floors into the hallway. "Jack?" No sound of him. She really should enjoy the solitude while she had it. What was she doing trying to hunt him down and bring him back to torment her?

She climbed up on the bed with her phone. Fifteen missed calls, all from the same number. Why couldn't this jerk get the hint? She'd never even been out on a real date with him. Leo Parker had cornered her at an art opening and sweet-talked her with promises of a dinner at Nobu. The dinner was delicious, the company not so much. When he'd sidled up to her at an auction she was attending, with an invitation to dinner at Annisa, she'd found herself too hungry and impoverished to resist. It wasn't hard to make conversation with him—all you had to do was nod while he talked about himself. The tricky part was getting away from him at the end of the night.

Maybe he thought she was playing hard to get? She really shouldn't have accepted his invitation to the U.S. Open. She didn't even like tennis that much. But with money so tight and her valiant efforts to keep up appearances taking a toll, she figured it would at least give her a story to tell at all the art openings she attended nightly to eat the free hors d'oeuvres and cozy up to the rich art lovers she hoped would be her future clientele.

He'd turned into an octopus behind court number eight. Lips like raw fish and arms of steel. She'd managed to fend him off with a sudden coughing fit and threats of a virulent sore throat, but since then he'd called at least once a day. Staying at Sinclair's house on Long Island had kept him at bay, and she'd assumed coming to Florida would lose him for good.

Most people would have taken a hint by now. That he hadn't was troubling.

Reluctantly, she listened to his plea. "Hey, babe, haven't seen you around lately. We could catch the new *South Pacific* and go out for a late bite…." He droned on. Grrr. If only he was charming and handsome. Or at least one of those. And she didn't like musicals, either.

You led him on. She could hear her friends' accusatory voices in her head, even though she hadn't told any of them about him. Maybe she was embarrassed to stoop so low for a free meal. And now she was here leading Jack Drummond on for the chance to win a reward that would once have been pocket change to her.

Did this make her a strumpet? It probably would if she was actually sleeping with them. Or even kissing them. She shuddered at the memory of Leo's cold, wet, sloppy attempt. A fumble from Jack, though...

She let out a sigh and deleted the rest of her messages. Nothing important. Life was happening back in New York as usual. The rich getting richer, the poor getting screwed out of what little money they had. She couldn't wait to work her way back into the former group. Which was the *only* reason why she was here right now.

Where was Jack? She headed out to look again. The sunset blazed through the kitchen windows, casting a mellow golden light over the expensively refurbished stone counters and the huge industrial appliances. Lights had come on in the hallways—subtle sconces embedded in the limestone walls—but that seemed to happen by magic or automation. "Hey, Jack. Where the heck are you?"

No answer. She cruised through the living room where a pair of patio doors stood open to the outside, no screen. No wonder he had lizards on his ceiling. Outside the open doors the salt tang of the sea greeted her and a breeze whipped her hair, but there was no sign of her host.

Barefoot, she picked her way over the prickly grass and down some stone steps to the dock nearest the house. His boat was gone. He'd abandoned her here on this island in the middle of nowhere.

Suddenly, the golden fingers of sunset, spreading across the dark, still, ocean, looked downright spooky. She glanced over her shoulder. What was she expecting? The ghost of a peg-legged pirate? She sucked in a breath and suppressed a shudder.

Jack was probably in the arms of some well-stacked barmaid, like all his salt-caked predecessors. What did she care? She only wanted him for his expertise, so the quicker she could get out of here, the better.

She went back to the map and stared at it, her stomach growling. There were a lot of numbers, but none of them very high. In fact she hadn't seen a number higher than twenty-five.

An idea flashed into her mind. If each number corresponded to the place of a letter in the alphabet—if III was the letter *C*, say, and VII was the letter *G*…

Frantically, she grabbed a fresh sheet of notepaper, then scrolled back and forth through the alphabet, translating the numbers again using this new system. Slowly and painstakingly, a message from the past emerged on the crumpled sheet of paper in front of her.

Start at dawne and rouwe due north from Deade Men's Cowve to the baneyan tree. Set course east northeast and row ye three score strokes. Swing thy prouwe to the horizon and row five score strokes towarde the sunne, where the north spalle of the island meets Raster's Docke. Keepe them close as ye row seven score strokes east southeast. Hold thy oar alofte at noone and it shall point to that which ye seek forty fathoms belowe.

* * *

When she reached the end, she stared at the paper and let out a long exhale. She felt like leaping into the air…for a split second. Then she realized how insubstantial the directions actually were. Dependent on the position of the sun and the angles of the boat to the shore, they might not yield the same results at all after three hundred years of geologic change.

On the other hand…

How could Jack abandon her like this? She climbed off the bed and made her way to the kitchen, where she managed to forage together a turkey wrap so he wouldn't return to find her bleached bones on his patio. Three score strokes. A score was twenty, so three score was sixty. But surely strokes by a big man would be different than strokes by a scrawny cabin boy, and how would she know which was right?

Let's just assume Jack's ancestors all looked exactly like him. Burly, brawny and badass. She sighed. She needed Jack and a rowboat. And he was busy under a barmaid.

She couldn't wait until she was independent and didn't have to depend on anybody for anything.

It was nearly dawn when she heard the sound of a boat engine in the distance. She wondered whether to pretend she'd been asleep the whole time and hadn't noticed he was gone, then decided she couldn't be bothered. Instead, she marched to the dock and waited there in the moonlight with her hands on her hips like a neglected wife.

He watched her from the deck. "Nice to be welcomed home by a beautiful woman."

"I'm glad you came home. I thought I might be marooned here forever if you got hit by a bus."

"I don't think there's been a bus near here since the 1960s."

"What a relief. And I cracked the code. Now all we have to do is go dig up the loot."

Still in the boat, a cardboard box in his arms, he paused. "Where is it?"

"Under the sea, of course. Off a spall and three score strokes here and there. We'll find it." And she turned and marched back to the house, hoping her backside looked sexier than his barmaid's.

"I went to visit a friend." He put some items in the fridge from the box he'd brought in.

"That's what I figured."

"Not that kind of friend." He looked amused. "Were you jealous?"

Embarrassed that her voice or face had apparently given too much away, she only risked a shrug. "It's your life."

"My friend is an old fisherman who's been catching dolphin and sea bass off these shores for fifty years."

"Dolphin? That's disgusting."

He laughed. "What we call dolphin is what you Northerners call mahimahi. It's a fish that swims with the dolphins."

"Well, that's clear as clam chowder." She crossed her arms over her chest again, not at all sure if she believed the fisherman part. "Did you stay up all night singing sea shanties?"

"I wanted to ask him if he'd ever seen traces of the wreck or bits of spar that could be from it. He said he never has."

"How encouraging."

"It might be. If it's buried beneath the sand or locked into encrusted coral it might be more or less intact—missing cup parts and all."

"Except that we'll never find it."

He poured himself a big glass of orange juice and swigged it, his Adam's apple throbbing rhythmically. She tugged her eyes from the sight of his powerful hand holding the glass. She needed that hand to tug on some oars. "Not without my cannons, no."

"Cannons? You're going to lob cannonballs into the surf?"

"Nope. These are high-tech treasure hunting cannons. They blow air with force and rip holes in the seabed, exposing all the goodies hidden under it."

"Boys and their toys. And how many hours did it take you to find out that your friend hadn't seen anything floating in the water?" She instantly regretted her pathetically catty question.

Jack grinned. "I like it when you're jealous. I see sparks flashing in those mystical eyes of yours. Gets me going."

"I hate you."

One brow lifted slightly. "Getting better all the time. I'll have to stay away longer next time."

"I'll swim ashore."

"I bet you would." That annoying twinkle of humor lit his face. "And you'll have to take these with you." He pulled a big stack of papers out of the cardboard box. "It appears you had some mail forwarded."

She felt her face heat. "I needed to send it somewhere. I used your address because I wasn't sure where I was going to stay."

"Or because you knew you were going to stay with me."

"Nonsense. But I did come down here to see you, and I figured you wouldn't mind." This was getting worse and worse. She didn't want to admit that she literally had no fixed address now. Her mail and subscriptions followed her like a pack of stray dogs behind a gypsy camp.

He riffled through her morning papers. "The *Wall Street Journal?* The *New York Post* and *Women's Wear Daily?*"

"Just trying to keep abreast of certain trends." The lifestyles of New York's rich and famous, to be precise.

"Most people would use the internet."

"I'm traditional in some ways. I like to get newsprint on my fingers while I enjoy my morning coffee."

He laughed. "You're an old-fashioned girl in many ways, Vicki. One more thing to love about you."

She tried to look steely and unconcerned as she took her papers from him. She'd kept her familiar subscriptions going through her first couple of moves, assuming she'd soon be settled. Once she knew the routine it was easy enough to arrange for them to follow her on her travels. They were a turtle shell of familiarity in her ever-shifting and far-too-mobile world and she hated to start the day without them. Already she was dying to flip to Page Six and see if anything about Sinclair Drummond and his new fiancée, Annie, had crossed the pages. If she did one good deed in her lifetime, it was forcing those two to see they were meant for each other.

"Do you want to hear what the map says or not?" He didn't seem to care one way or the other.

"Sure. Mushroom omelet?"

"Why not." She pulled a folded paper from the pocket of her pants. "Here's what your crusty old ancestor wrote." She looked up, and was further annoyed to see Jack pulling out a pan and retrieving ingredients from the fridge instead of riveting his attention to her words. As she read, though, he turned and frowned with gratifying concentration.

"What the heck is a spall?" he said, after a long pause.

"I looked it up. A spall is something that has broken off. So maybe a little chunk of land off the end of the island?"

"There isn't one."

"Maybe it's under the sea now." Why was he arguing with her over this minor point? "More importantly, where's Dead Men's Cove?"

"Thataway." He tilted his head toward the fridge. "I found another skeleton embedded in the rocks there the other day. The old family story was that shipwreck victims were washed into the cove by the current. I now suspect it's where they buried their enemies."

She shivered. "Lovely people, your ancestors."

He dropped quivering raw egg onto the bubbling oil, and she watched as it hardened into a solid, golden mass. "We're a proud and solitary race, who don't take well to interlopers." He winked.

"I'd better watch my back, then." She dragged her eyes from his once again. His wink had sent a little frisson of sensation darting across her midsection. Which was ridiculous. She distracted herself by pulling plates from a shelf and hunting around for cutlery. "What about Raster's Dock?"

"Whatever it is, it's long gone. There was an old

homestead just up the coast with a spit of rock, like a jetty, in front of it. Maybe we'll assume it's there for the sake of argument."

"Do you have a rowboat?"

"Several score of them." He grinned. "How many is in a score anyway? I'm guessing you looked it up."

"Twenty." She glanced out the window. "We'd better hurry if we're going to make it by dawn."

"Don't worry. We have another forty-five minutes. We're a lot closer to the equator down here than you're used to. Dawn doesn't wake you up in the middle of the night, even in summer."

She took her plate, now freshly decorated with half the omelet, and dug her fork right into it. She was glad she'd managed to avoid another night in Jack's bed. She was beginning to think it could be far too risky to enjoy his charms. They might have the same effect as "just one drink" on a former alcoholic. "Let's hurry."

Five

Jack's broad back flexed in the light from the electric lantern as they tugged the rowboat from its dusty grave in the disused boathouse. Nets and buoys and fishing rods of every size and description lined the walls and crisscrossed the sandy floor.

Vicki tried not to break a nail as she helped him lift it over an old crate filled with tangled rope. "When did someone last use this, 1964?" The rowboat was an indeterminate color, somewhere between beige and pink. "And what makes you think it will still hold water?"

"She's a trusty one. I use her all the time."

"That's not what this layer of dust is trying to tell me. When would you ever need to row somewhere?"

"When I don't want anyone to hear me coming." He turned back to her and shot her a sly grin.

Which made her stomach do a crazy flip.

She grabbed one end of the boat and peered into its depths. "Great. This is your sneaking-up-on-unsuspecting-maidens craft. I hope there aren't too many condom wrappers in the bottom."

He chuckled. "Nope. Don't see any. Maybe we'll have to put a couple in there."

He didn't turn around to see her faux-shocked expression. "In your fantasies, Jack Drummond."

"Indeed." He hoisted his side of the boat higher, no doubt to further unhinge her with the sight of his powerful physique. "A man's allowed his dreams. One of the few rights and privileges no one can take away from us."

"Hmm, you're right. I'm surprised there isn't a tax on steamy male imaginings."

Now she had an eyeful of his burly chest as he walked backward—without looking, she could tell his eyes were entirely on her—out of the old boathouse and down onto the beach.

She tried to glance past him, out to where the sky was brightening every second, even though the sun hadn't peeked over the horizon yet. "How long will it take us to row to Dead Men's Cove?"

"About three minutes, once we're afloat. It's pretty calm today."

They shoved the boat out into the water and carefully climbed in while it rocked in the quiet surf. Her feet were bare and the bottom of the boat felt dusty and splintery. Jack rowed and she sat up in the bow, trying to remember the words she'd written down as it wasn't yet light enough to read.

"This is Dead Men's Cove," said Jack quietly, as they rounded a small spit of land just as the first white-hot sliver of sun peeked over the horizon.

"Row due north from Dead Men's Cove to the banyan tree. Where's the banyan tree?"

Jack tilted his head back the way they came. Vicki looked through the predawn gloom to see a huge, gnarled tree rising above the sea grape near the beach. "Let's go."

He swung the boat around with minimal effort, bare chest shimmering gold in the first rays of sun. Couldn't he have worn a shirt? This was distracting and she needed to focus all her attention on following the details of the directions. "How old is that tree?"

"Dunno. Been there almost forever, I guess." His muscles contracted and released as he pulled on the oars, sending powerful ripples across his hard belly. She tugged her focus to the spreading branches of the tree again, but her gaze shifted inexorably back to the vision of his strong body at work. Apparently, she had been manless for too long.

"When we get to the tree, you row east-northeast."

"The tree is inland." He glanced over his shoulder at it.

"Go as close as you can get and then turn."

His broad hands gripped the oars with force. Why was she paying attention to his hands at a time like this? They had only a few minutes to find the location before the sun would be in the wrong place until tomorrow. "How do you know which way east-northeast is?"

He chuckled. "In my blood."

"You probably have a compass somewhere near your solar plexus." She glanced at it for a moment—flat, hard stomach, beaded with trickles of sweat—then looked hard at the horizon. She could see a boat in the distance, and another farther to the south. She wondered if any of them could guess their strange changes of direction were due to three-hundred-year-old instructions.

As they neared the rocky coastline by the tree, he swung the boat around ninety degrees and rowed farther out into the ocean. "One, two, three…" Sixty strokes. She kept count, glad of something to do while Jack put his entire body weight into propelling the rowboat through the shining water. "Sixty. Now row toward the horizon."

With little visible effort, Jack swiveled the boat again and started pulling for the dividing line between sea and sky. Again she counted, this time to one hundred, the words beating an eerie rhythm with the splashing of the oars, out in the quiet world of the open sea.

She peered back at the shore. *To where the north spalle of the island abuts Raster's Docke.* The end of the island was cloaked in trees right to the water. The shoreline behind it looked similarly featureless. Was this where their quest would end? "Eighty, eighty-one, eighty-two…" She kept the count going, staring at the island, looking for a sign, for anything. There was no spall and no dock, with or without extra *e*'s. "Ninety-nine, one hundred. Stop!"

Jack brought the boat to an impressive stop by spinning it in place. "We're supposed to be at the place where the north spall of the island abuts Raster's Dock, but were out in the middle of nowhere."

He squinted at the coastline. "Those rocks there, you can barely see them now, but at high tide they're exposed and look like the remains of a jetty. I'll bet anything that's Raster's Dock. Don't know about the spall, though. There's nothing under the ocean there.

If there was, I'd have run aground on it at some point when I was a kid."

"Damn." Vicki chewed her lip and glanced about. "We're obviously supposed to stare at how they line up as you row east-southeast."

"What if the spall isn't a spall anymore, but is part of the island? It could have been built up by sand shifting in a storm." Jack stared hard at the wooded tree canopy. "Never bothered crashing my way in there, though, so I don't know."

"Let's pretend it is and give it a try." The end of the island didn't quite line up with where the rocks started. "I think we need to shift thataway a bit." She jerked her chin to the right.

"North-northeast, ma'am. I'm on it." Jack smoothly turned the boat and pulled at the oars. "I see it. Look at those tall trees—or trees on taller land—now they're lining up with where I know the rocks are. What next?"

"Don't pretend you don't remember! *Keep them close as ye row seven score strokes east-southeast.* That's one hundred and forty." She didn't have to tell him to hurry. He'd already shifted the boat and pulled hard on the oars, and the boat seemed to leap across the water at his touch. Timing was crucial. A minute too late and the sun would be in the wrong place as it hit the oar to point to the shipwreck.

"One thirty-nine... One forty!" He spun the boat again to stop its forward momentum, sending her lurching against the hard wood. "Hold up an oar."

Jack hoisted the dripping piece of wood into the air, bracing it with his arms against the bottom of the boat. Its long black shadow pointed right at Vicki, making her scoot to the side, rocking the boat. With her out of the way, it tapered over the edge of the boat and pointed its long dark finger toward the land.

"Do you suppose that means it's right here?" Vicki peered into the murky depths over the side. Deep and dark, the ocean revealed no secrets.

"Unless they're playing a joke and it's actually buried on the island." Jack peered at the now-distant palm-fringed shore. "We've never looked right here, though. The other map said it was about half a mile to the south." His face wore an expression of intense concentration mingled with barely controlled excitement. "There's something compelling about the way it uses points on shore to line us up. It feels like the way a seaman would think."

Vicki glanced about. Nothing but shimmering ocean in every direction. "How do we mark our position so we can find it again? We can't exactly plunge a stake in."

He pulled a black contraption from his pocket. "GPS. I'll plug in our coordinates." His fingers worked the buttons. "We could mark it with a buoy, but no need to put a big shiny *X* on the spot for everyone else to see."

"I like the way you think, Cap'n Jack."

His quick grin caused her blood to heat. Or maybe it was just excitement that they might be right over the wreck of the sunken ship. "Do you think there are skeletons down there?"

"Undoubtedly." His grin broadened with a hint of menace. "How are your scuba skills?"

"Rusty." She didn't like breathing underwater at the best of times, but especially not if she was sharing space with a bunch of barnacle-covered dead pirates.

"Maybe we should forget the whole thing and go lie

on the beach." He peered at her under a lock of sun-streaked brown hair.

"No way!" She shoved him slightly, causing the boat to rock, and both of them to laugh. "I'm afraid to leave, though, in case we can't find our way back to this spot."

"Don't worry. I have it programmed into my seafaring brain as well as my GPS. I could find my way here in the dark. Let's go back and get the gear."

Jack rowed back to shore, describing the moment he'd found the last wreck he'd pillaged. How they'd seen one end of an anchor poking out of the seabed, then the encrusted end of an old cannon. It wasn't until they were back on dry land that Vicki realized she'd never even thought about being seasick.

They returned under the steam of Jack's powerful outboard motor, carrying scuba diving gear. When they reached the spot indicated by the directions in the fresco, Jack killed the engines. "Let's look around."

"We just jump right in?" She peered into the murky, featureless depths.

"Nope. We'll let the sonar do that for us." He lowered a line over the side of the boat, bearing a piece of equipment he called a towfish. "Now we trawl along real slow and look for something interesting." Up on the bridge, they stared at a wishy-washy black-and-white picture on a monitor as the boat moved. Vicki stared at the screen, but to her, it all looked like a bowl of undersea oatmeal.

"Hold up." Jack peered at the image. "Something's down here."

"That was easy."

"Don't get cocky. It could be an old car." He maneuvered the boat around. "Let's go in for a closer look." Vicki squinted at the wavering gray image, willing it to be the shattered remains of a great wooden vessel. Jack punched buttons and moved with effortless calm to bring the boat around while scanning the surrounding area. "Can't see much, but in my experience the distention of the surface makes it worth exploring."

"What does that mean in English?"

"It's bumpy, so there might be something under the sand."

"Let's get our shovels and pails and get to work."

"My sentiments exactly, but don't dive in just yet." He swung down from the bridge and strode to the rear of the boat, where he maneuvered two big cylinders down into the water. "These will blow the prop wash down onto the sand, and hopefully move it, so we can get a better look at what's under there." The engine roared and the water around the boat turned murky with churned-up sand as their wake streamed down the tubes.

"How are we supposed to see anything in this water?"

"We have to wait for the sand to settle." He winked.

"Won't it cover everything up again?"

"Maybe." He switched off the engine, then with a pleasant smile he stretched out on the deck, torturing her with the sight of his chiseled chest. Why couldn't they be somewhere cold and miserable so he'd have to don a wetsuit? She turned the other way to distract herself. She'd worn dark sunglasses so she could stare right at him without his knowing, and the aftereffects of a morning's ogling were wreaking havoc on her sanity.

A sleek white vessel sat still in the water out toward the horizon. "Is that a fishing boat?"

"Sometimes." He hadn't even looked. "Sometimes it's a party boat. Owned by Iago Knoll."

"The corporate raider? What's he doing down here?" She squinted at the boat, looking for the tall, arrogant silhouette she knew well from New York.

"Same as everyone else. Looking for some fun in the sun."

"That's not what I'm doing here." She crossed her arms over her chest, which was covered in SPF 50 sunblock and a T-shirt over her swimsuit.

"Not yet." He flashed that wicked grin at her again. "But we'll give you time."

"No way. I'm far too much of a New Yorker to enjoy lazing around in the sun."

His deft fingers checked the connections on his scuba equipment. "Who said anything about lazing? Surfing, sailing, kayaking, deep-sea fishing—no need to be a deck-chair potato down here."

"Sounds exhausting. I'd rather be pounding some hot pavement." She jerked her eyes from his hands to her own scuba equipment. Jack had already checked it over and she trusted his judgment more than her own. "All this sun and salt air is making me dizzy." *And you're not helping.* The water around the boat was clearing. "How long until we can jump in?"

"Anytime you like. Sometimes it's fun to be down there as the mist of sand recedes and reveals what you're looking for."

"A cup base sticking up out of the sand like Excalibur."

"You think it's the base?"

"It's not the stem because Sinclair has that. So it's either the cup—the most exciting part, and probably the easiest to find—or the base. So I'm guessing it's the base."

"Calculated pessimism. That was never your style." He heaved his tanks onto his back.

"I've learned from experience."

"Apparently you've been having the wrong experiences." He peered over the edge of the boat. "The sand is settling."

"I'm going in." Might as well get the first dive over with before she lost her nerve.

"Go for it."

The warm, eerie silence of the underwater world enveloped Vicki as she plunged beneath the surface. Her flippers propelled her lower, and she reminded herself that it was okay to breathe. She heard, or rather felt, the impact as Jack slid into the water behind her, flipped and dived for the seabed.

The sun above brightened the water, and she looked around, trying to gain her bearings in Neptune's unfamiliar kingdom. But she needed to go down into the murky depths where the sun barely filtered through the water. She held a flashlight in one hand, and a pointed steel rod in the other. Jack said that was the best tool for rooting about in the sand. She supposed it would also work as a deadly weapon should the need arise.

He had a metal detector and something that looked like a claw, and he was already a good ten yards below her. She pumped her legs trying to keep up, as she didn't fancy being lost and alone down here in this blue underworld. Jack's strong thighs powered him effortlessly through the water, but she was almost panting into her respirator by the time she neared the ocean floor. He scanned the sand with the detector, and she peered around for a place to start poking her ridiculous stick.

The propeller wash had carved out a shallow irregular bowl in the sand, and as her eyes accustomed to the dim light—and she figured out how to turn on her flashlight in underwater slow motion—she saw an item over to the left of the indentation.

Must be the cup base, she teased herself. Down here in the vast, dark water, the idea of finding one single three-hundred-year-old artifact seemed ludicrous. She'd anticipated a little rummaging in Jack's attics and then her work would be done. This situation had spiraled right out of control.

She approached the object and poked around it gently with her stick. It didn't budge, and with a little determined burrowing she discovered that it was large and the rest was buried beneath the surface. The mysterious item was encrusted with barnacles or other sea life, but there was definitely something solid underneath them. Probably a 1967 Chevy.

She flashed her light at Jack in the agreed-upon signal and he swam over. He ran his metal detector over the object a number of times, then turned and gave her a thumbs-up.

If only she'd learned American Sign Language when she had the chance. They dug around together and the more they dug, the deeper the object got until Jack gave her the signal to surface.

Rushing toward the light felt like coming back to life after a sojourn in the underworld. Once afloat, she pulled up her mask and took off her respirator. Jack popped up beside her and pushed his respirator aside to reveal a big grin. "Damn, girl, you're a magic charm!"

"You think this is it?"

"It's a cannon."

"How can you tell?"

"See one, you've seen them all. Looks like the right era, too. I think you've finally found the lost treasure of Macassar Drummond."

Maybe it was the excitement shining in his eyes or maybe it was the scuba gear, but he suddenly looked exactly like the Jack Drummond who'd stolen her heart and left it in pieces. She struggled to ignore the mess of sensations running rampant inside her—while staying afloat in the water by paddling her flippers. "It's a shame you have such a boring name when your ancestors have such good ones."

He grinned. "Isn't it? I'm going to make sure my son has a name you can really hang your hat on."

"How can you be sure you'll have a boy?"

"The Drummonds always have a boy. That's why we're still here. If we had girls they wouldn't be Drummonds." He seemed to float effortlessly in the water despite the heavy tanks.

She wished she could turn and stride smoothly away, but that wasn't going to happen. "Guess there's too much testosterone in the Drummond blood."

"Too much something, for sure." The sun gleamed off his bronzed face. "But maybe you're about to find the cup and change all that. Let's get back on deck and do some more digging electronically."

He went back to the sonar and used something called a magnetometer to zero in on places to dig. There were several pockets of matter that showed up on the equipment, begging to be investigated. They dived again and turned up two broken glass bottles and an almost-intact plate, all encrusted with sea life but clearly recognizable.

"My God, we've found it, haven't we?" Vicki gasped for air as they surfaced again. The sun was setting behind them over the land, casting its burnished glow over the sea.

"You found it, babe. I'd never have done it without you. That map would have stayed hidden up there for another two hundred years or more if you hadn't had the bright idea to chisel away at the ceiling above my bed."

They climbed back on the deck. Jack was too excited to go back to the house. He insisted on making dinner on the boat so he could dive by moonlight overnight. Vicki protested until he showed her the cornucopia of goodies inside his fridge. After a dinner of chilled shrimp with mango salsa and coconut rice, they sipped Jack's special "diver cocktail" made of pomegranate, orange and lemon juice. She suggested that because she certainly wasn't heading to the briny depths in the dark, she should be allowed a cold beer, but he explained that because alcohol and diving didn't mix, he didn't allow booze on board.

So she couldn't even blame alcohol for what happened next.

Six

"Damn, I didn't realize how much I've missed you." Jack lolled against a floatation device on the deck. Water drops still glistened on his tanned stomach, although his high-tech trunks looked dry.

The moon cast a lazy silver glow over the whole scene and the warm evening air caressed Vicki like a hug. Which wasn't helpful because she was already battling a sensual languor at the end of their long, high-octane day. "You missed being bossed around by a crazy broad?"

"Sure, who wouldn't?" His lips cracked to reveal those ridiculously white teeth. "And when she's as crazy beautiful as you, it's impossible to resist obeying her commands."

"What if I command you to take us to Monte Carlo?"

"I'd be delighted." His sleepy gaze challenged her. "Though we might run out of fuel on the way."

"Excuses, excuses. What do you do for fun, Jack Drummond?"

"I'm doing it right now. Lazing on my beloved boat with the woman of my dreams."

She laughed, but his words plucked at some long-forgotten string inside her. Then she reminded herself he was just teasing her. "With treasure sparkling away hidden in the sands below us."

"It doesn't get any better than this."

"I guess you're an easy man to please."

"Or I've managed to organize the perfect life for me."

She envied his contentment, and damn, it made him attractive, too. "I intend to organize the perfect life for me when I get back to New York." She could already picture her apartment, maybe with a view of the water or of Central Park, once she made her first few big deals. Well-heeled clients would visit her tastefully decorated pad to discuss trophy items they needed to add to their collections—a Matisse, perhaps, or a small Rodin for the garden.

Jack jolted her from her thoughts by lifting himself from the deck and joining her on the deep, upholstered bench with its view over the silvery water. The skin of her thigh sizzled slightly as he sat down right next to her. "So why aren't you there right now, making your dreams come true?"

"I need to find the cup first."

"I know you're trying to convince me that you're hell-bent on saving the Drummonds from a future of misery, but I don't think you're that charitable. You told me you want the reward, but it's small change in the grand scheme. Unless you really, really need that small amount of money for some reason." His eyes narrowed and he leaned toward her.

Her stomach clenched, partly at the ugly realization that he now suspected she was strapped for cash, but mostly at the blood-heating closeness of him.

"I know your dad died, and I'm sorry."

"Thanks." She was getting more flustered by the minute. This was way too personal.

"But that should mean—and I apologize for being crude—that you'd be rolling in it by now. Did something happen to the family war chest?"

Vicki's mouth was stuck half-open. No one knew about her personal financial ruin. Nobody. All the lost money had been hidden in an offshore interest, which made it impossible to prove or claim back once it had been swindled away. She'd spent the past eighteen months hustling to maintain the friendships and contacts she had without letting them know she was living from hand to mouth.

"You're very quiet, Vicki Sin-cere. I'm beginning to suspect that you're flat broke." His eyes twinkled with a mixture of amusement and genuine concern that ate at her insides like acid.

What could she say now? She couldn't lie to Jack. He'd see right through her and laugh his ass off.

So she leaned in—it was only a few inches—and covered his taunting mouth with her own. Their lips locked instantly, and a rush of fevered confusion, desire and long-forgotten passion roared through her like a flash flood. Her arms wound around him, and she felt his hands sliding around her waist, pulling her close.

A sigh fled her mouth, into his, and she couldn't stop

it. She couldn't stop the kiss either. It took on a life of its own, powering her entire body, as she reeled from the force of his desire striking hers and making sparks that rained down over both of them.

Her nipples thickened beneath her swimsuit and goose bumps flashed over her thighs. She clung to him, inhaling the fabulous scent of Jack Drummond—sea, salt air and that indefinable dash of raw healthy male that made him utterly irresistible.

Their kiss deepened and she found herself sitting in his lap, lips still locked to his. His big hands squeezed her backside, making her squirm with pleasure. Her chest rubbed against his, her hard nipples rasping against his washboard abs and sending hot flames of arousal leaping through her. He tasted like heaven, rich and warm and oh so familiar. The years since their last kiss evaporated as if they'd never happened.

As if she'd never said *I love you* and ruined everything.

That thought stilled her tongue inside his mouth and sent a stark clarity shooting through her brain. She pulled back just enough for their lips to part, which felt agonizingly painful.

"Hot damn," murmured Jack, once her mouth cleared his. "I've missed you even more than I thought."

Me, too. She managed not to say it. All these unsaid words must be building up inside her like a dam about to burst.

His rock-hard erection jutted against her thigh, and she looked down at it and laughed, glad of the distraction from her roiling emotions. "I guess you are happy to see me."

"Happy to hold on to you, as well." His arms were

still around her, and he hugged her gently, affectionately. Her heart did a double backflip and she closed her eyes to avoid his gaze.

"I guess I must be getting loopy from lack of sleep or something." She pretended to stretch. Jack's lips touched hers, sparking an electric pulse of passion which made her eyes jump open.

Sure enough his dark, penetrating gaze was fixed right on her. "Believe me, sleep is the very last thing I have on my mind right now." His wicked, predatory grin stretched across his handsome face.

Desire flared deep inside her, hot and low, like the rumblings of an underground geyser. Could it really hurt that much to have a quickie with Jack? They were both here in the middle of nowhere. They were practically naked already. And let's face it, they'd done it before and it was really, really good.

She couldn't kid herself, right at this moment, that having sex with Jack Drummond would do anything at all to get him out of her system. It was likely to have the opposite effect.

On the other hand, she was a grown-up now, with responsibilities and pressures and a life to get back to, not some foolish girl with too much time on her hands.

Worst-case scenario—she'd be filled with regret and have to nurse a broken heart for a few months. Right now that seemed worth it.

She licked his lips like the top of an ice-cream cone. His grin widened. He licked back, and the tickling sensation reached deep inside her, to her feminine core. He let out a low growl, like a curious puma, which made her smile and only aroused her more. "I feel like I'm relapsing into an old addiction."

"And there's no cure."

She didn't have to voice her agreement. Her body said it all. Her fingers explored the contours of his chest and stomach as he peeled her swimsuit away. The warm evening air caressed her bare breasts, closely followed by Jack's hungry mouth. She sighed and arched her back as he licked her nipple to a tight peak.

The stubble of his chin tickled her skin, increasing the amount of sensation building all over her. As he rose to kiss her mouth again, she ran her fingers through his thick hair, pulling him closer and kissing him with six years of pent-up passion.

The chemistry between them was explosive as always. One glance at Jack and her self-control headed for the nearest exit. One touch and she was lost. The feel of his arms around her released the tension she'd been carrying around like a shield and she sensed herself falling out of reality and into the private world they'd always shared.

She was dimly aware of the ocean around them, its gentle swells lapping around the edges of the boat. She could feel the warm evening air crowding around her, humid and sensual, caressing her body like a soft blanket, even as Jack eased her swimsuit down over her legs leaving her stark naked on the upholstered bench.

She opened her eyes enough to tug at his boxers, then opened them wider to enjoy the view as she pulled them down over his hair-roughened thighs. His arousal was unmistakable, bold and proud like everything else about him. Their eyes met and they laughed, both naked and insanely turned on, with only the big, pale moon as a witness.

They were both standing now, and Jack stepped to-

ward her slowly, drinking in her body with his eyes as
if it was the last sip of fresh water left on a long ocean
voyage. He settled his hands on her hips, claiming her.
His fierce kiss almost shook the breath from her body.
She flung her arms around his neck and cleaved herself to him, skin to skin, from her lips down to her toes.

Her insides quivered and throbbed, already anticipating the feel of him inside her. His thick erection
pressed against her belly, teasing and tormenting her
with the pleasure that lay ahead. Just when she thought
she couldn't stand it any longer, he lifted her onto the
bench and moved over her.

He stroked her hair and murmured her name as he
entered her. She lifted her hips as he filled her, drawing
him deeper. "Oh, Jack." His name escaped her lips as
she welcomed him back into her body, into her heart.
She'd never met another man who moved her the way
Jack did. All her beaus since had been a pale second
best and her romantic encounters lackluster and unsatis-
fying. After Jack Drummond, every other man seemed
a wan shadow whose petty needs and foolish conversation bored her.

Jack always managed to reach right into her core and
wake her right up. She let out a moan of raw passion as
he touched a place deep inside her that hadn't known
feeling or sensation since she last saw him. She writhed
underneath him, letting herself fly into a realm of passion she'd almost forgotten.

I love you, Jack. The ghost words haunted her, driven
by memories of that passionate era in her life all those
years ago. She knew she couldn't love him now. Too
much water had flowed under the bridge and they were
both different people with different agendas. Still, the

thought swirled around her head as they moved together in a hypnotic rhythm.

His big, warm body wrapped around hers and made her feel fabulously safe and protected, although even now she knew she should feel the opposite. Jack Drummond had always been her danger zone, the place where she easily waded out of her depth and into unknown territory. He was the rock upon which her heart ran aground and became beached, only to survive scarred and damaged.

Those thoughts popped up in her brain like tiny clouds in the blue sky of a perfect sunny day. Like those passing clouds they didn't cast even the smallest shadow on her intense enjoyment of making love with Jack. Somehow it was soothing, a kind of release, to know she was getting in over her head. She'd trod so carefully in her life lately, been so afraid of making mistakes and revealing too much. At least now she knew she was hurling herself headfirst into trouble and, dammit, she was going to enjoy every sweet, soul-wringing second of it.

They moved together like a seasoned pair of dancers executing a spectacular routine they'd built and practiced together, adding new flourishes that gave each twist and turn a touch of unexpected magic. Her first climax led almost seamlessly to a second, and then a third, as she and Jack scaled new peaks of unimaginable pleasure on almost every surface in the boat. When they finally lay in each other's arms, spent, sweaty and unbelievably satisfied, she could barely believe she was still on the same planet she'd inhabited as the nervous, secretive and edgy Vicki she'd been earlier that day.

Perhaps it made a difference that she'd left the predictable solidity of dry land behind and now floated on the vast, wide ocean. She hadn't felt a trace of sea-sickness. Apparently her sea legs—or were they flippers?—had kicked in. But the real change was allowing herself to open up to Jack, physically at least, and step back into the exotic world of pleasure and passion they'd always shared.

"Vicki, Vicki, Vicki." Jack rasped her name with his last ounce of strength. "I'm beginning to remember why I ran away from you."

"Oh, yeah?" She lay propped up on one elbow. Tendrils of dark, damp hair clung to her face, which the sun had already started to work its golden magic on. "Getting bored already?" Defiance flashed in those violet eyes, challenging him.

"Not bored, no. Never bored." Thoughts were hard to come by in his present state. Especially with Vicki's long, lithe body stretched out on the padded bench in front of him, clothed only in pale moonlight. "Overwhelmed, maybe."

Vicki wasn't like other women. Once she fixed those piercing pale eyes on you, or slid those slender fingers into your hair, or maybe even glanced at you the right way from across the room, you were done for. Or he was anyway.

He drew in a long breath and watched his chest rise. His body felt as if it belonged to someone else. He himself was floating somewhere about three feet above it in a fog of sensual and sexual bliss. And they weren't even touching anymore.

"You have magical powers." He met her bright gaze. "I wish."

"You must. How else could you find a lost ship that my ancestors, and a whole host of other people, have been hunting for centuries? And in less than a day."

"Fresh eyes."

"Yours certainly are fresh, and an intriguing shade of pale mauve, but that doesn't explain their perceptive powers."

She licked her lips, sending a shot of sensation to his groin that almost blinded him. "When you look at something every day, you don't really see it. You've been sleeping under that fresco for so long that it's just a ceiling to you. I had to stare at it for a while, and get lucky with the way the light was hitting it, and I could see that the surface wasn't entirely stable. Frescos should last a thousand years or more, but only if they're applied the right way, with the artist painting into fresh wet plaster. Yours was faded and flaking, so I thought it was worth a second look."

"I doubt a scurvy pirate worried much about the archival quality of his work. It could have just been done badly. How did you know there was another painting underneath?"

"You'd be surprised at how often there's another painting underneath the ones that pass through the hands of auctioneers and galleries. Like pirates, artists are a bunch of penniless scavengers forced to make do with what they can lay their hands on." She smiled that seductive, almost-feline smile that sent his blood pressure into overdrive. "And my hunch turned out to be a lucky one. Anyone could have figured it out, if they had a chance to look at the fresco, but your ancestors were clever enough to hide it away where only their most intimate companions would see it."

"If my forbears had spent their nights with cleverer women, they'd have found the ship and its treasure long ago."

"I shudder to think who or what your ancestors were sleeping with." Her eyes twinkled with humor. "Have any of them ever left this island for good?"

"My dad, but that was by judicial edict, not choice. He'd already gambled or drunk everything else away so it was the last thing he had left to hand over to my mom when they divorced."

"Where does your mom live now?"

"Miami." He smiled. "South Beach. She and her new husband enjoy parties more than hunting for pirate booty."

"Lucky her. She escaped and lived to tell the tale."

He felt a smile creep across his mouth. "Which begs the question, will you manage to do the same?"

Something flickered in her eyes. Despite the darkness, he could see her quite clearly. The moon was almost full and the sky clear and bright. The water around them reflected its platinum rays, painting them both with an eerie light that made the scene look like an old black-and-white photograph.

"Only time will tell."

His question spooked her, because she swung her shapely legs down to the floor and reached for her now-dry swimsuit. Lust sneaked up around the edges of his brain again as she pulled it on over her slim body. Then she wrapped a towel around herself and stood staring out over the water, where the first bright shimmers of dawn licked at the horizon. "Can we go back now?"

He suppressed the sigh that filled his chest. He'd have liked to stay out here for a week with her, with no one to disturb them and the outside world no more significant than a flashing message light on his phone. "If you insist, m'lady."

"I do." She shot him a smile. "A girl needs to powder her nose now and then, you know."

He chuckled at the idea of Vicki powdering her nose. Although who knows, maybe she did? He heaved himself up, grabbed his trunks and headed for the bridge, comforting himself with the thought that the cup—if it was ever there in the first place—must be very well hidden in the sand and coral rock and could take a good long time to find.

They slept in late in their shared perch under the fresco. Vicki awoke first and sat bolt upright as the memory of the last day and night flooded back into her sleep-refreshed brain. Okay, so they'd slept together. No biggie. Not like it was the first time or anything.

But damn was it beautiful.

She slid carefully off the bed so as not to wake him. A quick glance behind her revealed that he was as dangerously handsome as she remembered. Worse yet, his eyes were cracked open and he was watching her.

"Worried I'll try to make a run for it?"

"Nope." His mouth hitched into an arrogant smile that made irritation and desire shimmer through her. "Too far to swim."

"Go back to sleep. I want to be alone." She didn't look at him as she said it and she hoped she sounded stern. She did need some time to herself to process what was happening. There was nothing worse than getting swept along a tide of events and finding yourself washed up somewhere you never expected and couldn't get back from.

She'd showered before getting into bed, so she grabbed some panties and a sundress from her stash in the chest, along with her phone, and slipped out of the room.

Once out of their shared space, she allowed herself to lean against the wall and take a deep breath. What a night. Other men didn't make love to her like Jack. What was different? He held her with such passion and conviction. It was almost hard to believe that he didn't love her. Maybe he threw himself into everything like that?

She pried herself off the wall and wandered to the kitchen, where she helped herself to a glass of orange juice. The tart liquid puckered her tongue and made her shiver. Jack Drummond. Again. Had she really expected at any point that she could manage to avoid having sex with him? It came as no surprise that his boat was well stocked with a variety of condoms, not that she needed them. She didn't leave that kind of thing to chance and was already protected.

At least her womb was protected. Her heart, not so much.

Two friends had left messages on her phone, wondering where she was. She hadn't told anyone about her jaunt down to Florida. She hadn't wanted anyone to know what she was up to in case she chickened out. Or failed.

Seventeen missed calls, all from the same number. Leo Parker. Seventeen times he'd called and not left a message? Did he think she couldn't tell he was stalking her like some nut job from a horror movie? Except that he wasn't scary—more sad and lame. She was half-tempted to call him back and tell him exactly what she thought of him. But it didn't pay to make enemies, especially in her world, where everybody knew everybody. She'd tick him off, then find out that his aunt was a top curator at the Met.

Her ears pricked at the sound of feet padding down the corridor toward her. A puma on the prowl. She cursed her body's instant response to the nearing presence of Jack Drummond. How did he have that much power over her—again?

It's just lust. He's big and bold and male, and you've been deprived of sexual satisfaction for too long. Yeah, that was it. "Couldn't stay away, huh?" She challenged him with a hard stare as he entered the room.

It took tremendous effort to keep her eyes off his bare, bronzed chest, which was ridiculous as she'd had ample opportunity to grow bored with it on the boat yesterday. Maybe it was just her connoisseur's eye for well-formed *objets*.

"Nope." His confidence was adorable and infuriating at the same time. Jack Drummond never felt the need to sneak around or try to play it cool. He was simply... Jack. "And I thought I'd better make you breakfast. You don't look like you know how to cook."

"I hate cooking."

"I remember. That's why I'm going to make you waffles with papaya from my backyard."

Her stomach betrayed her with a fierce rumble. "Apparently my body says that would be fantastic."

His smile made her heart squeeze. Why did he have to be so nice? Arrogant, sure, obnoxious, too, but beneath the sun-scorched surface Jack Drummond was a straight-up nice guy.

Unless you needed to depend on him. She reminded herself that he valued his independence—his freedom—above all else, and anyone who forgot that for even an instant would learn the hard way, sooner or later.

But she wasn't going to make that mistake again.

They spent the day out on the boat and in the water digging around in the sand. Having determined that there was definitely a full ship there, and it would be a big project to unearth it, they decided to call for reinforcements. Jack phoned around to his crew, swearing them to secrecy. He grew silent after the last phone call.

"Dirk says he just got a call from Lou Aarons wanting him to dive for the same wreck." An uncharacteristic furrow had appeared in his tanned brow.

"Impossible. No one knows it's there."

"They didn't until now, but it's easy enough to spot when someone's up to something. We probably never even noticed one more helicopter in the air or another boat not far off while we were diving. People know my boat, so if it's anchored in one place for too long, they start to make assumptions."

Vicki chewed her lip. Could someone else really dig the cup right out from under them? In reckless moments she'd imagined she might ask for a cut of any gold coins or bullion they found, and now she was at risk of losing even the small reward she needed so badly. "Can we stake a claim to the site?"

"Sure, but it takes time. No one's going to come blow our boat out of the water, but they can start searching the same area. In wrecks, the debris scatters far enough that your cup fragment could be half a mile away. That's why the team will help. They know how to get the seabed up and poke around in there fast. We'll go ashore and get some supplies, then we can stay out on the water day and night until we find what we need."

Vicki wondered exactly what Jack needed. It wasn't the cup fragment, for sure. He was probably excited about finding his pirate ancestor's stolen goods. She had to admit that she was pretty excited about that, too. The prospect of fondling eighteenth-century emeralds almost took her mind off the intense sensations and emotions last night had awoken in her.

They headed to the local marina for refueling and Jack went into a boat repair shop to buy some parts. Vicki went into a small market and stocked up on basic food supplies and gallon jugs of water. She had just loaded them on the boat and disembarked to go find herself a cappuccino when she heard footsteps behind her on the wood planking of the quay.

"What a surprise." A male voice with a distinctive and highly recognizable sarcastic undertone. Leo Parker.

She spun around, out of alarm as much as recognition. "What are you doing here?"

"On vacay with my old mate Iago. Know him? He owns Viscaya Investments."

She shrugged. She'd heard of him, and none of it was good. "Oh." How could she get away from him? This time, if he asked her to dinner, she'd be sure to answer with a firm *no*.

"Didn't you get my messages?" His rather low forehead furrowed beneath his mop of coiffed blond hair.

She shook her head. "I lost my phone. Had to buy a new one." Hopefully her nose wasn't growing. If it was, she deserved it for stringing him along in the first place. Had he tracked her down here? Her gut clenched.

"Oh, that explains it." He smiled that annoying vacant smirk she'd sworn never to subject herself to again. "Iago's gone back to New York for a few days, so I have his house and boat to myself. I was thinking you could join me for some R & R."

She glanced around. No sign of Jack. Her gut was sending out all kinds of warning signals right now. What world of delusion did this guy live in? "I can't, I'm afraid. I'm here with a friend and we're really busy." Annoyingly she couldn't go into any detail as this idiot would be quite capable of telling everyone he knew and inadvertently or otherwise drawing the attention of every treasure hunter on the East Coast.

"I'm sure you can make a little time for me, Vicki." The way he said her name made a little shiver creep up her spine. His watery pale blue eyes fixed on her in a steely stare she didn't remember seeing before. "Because I know more about you than I've let on."

She froze. What could this jerk know about her? She'd been careful to reveal absolutely nothing about herself while eating expensive dinners with him. "I really have to go." She gestured back at the boat she'd just left. She didn't even want to tell him she was going into the deli for coffee or he might take it as an invitation. Where was Jack? The boat shop was way over on the far side of the marina, a big hangar of a building, and he was probably still inside it.

"I know about your dad's bankruptcy."

She swallowed. Her father had never declared bankruptcy. The complexity of his investments—or perhaps the illegality of some of them—made that impossible.

He'd simply gone broke. But to say anything at all would confirm what he apparently knew—her family was wiped out financially and so was she. "I don't know what you're talking about."

He laughed, an ugly stuttering sound. "Let's not play games, Vicki. You need money. I have money. We enjoy each other's company, and we have a lot in common." He held out one of his limp, pale hands. "Come out for a nice dinner with me and we'll talk over some plans."

She recoiled and a wave of panic rose through her. "I can't go out to dinner with you now or ever again. I'm engaged to marry someone else." She said it loud and firm. And it wasn't until the words had left her mouth that she noticed Jack, climbing out of a red-and-white boat only a few yards away.

Seven

Vicki didn't know where to look. She wanted to run fast and far. Had Jack heard her entire conversation with Leo? She'd rather die than have him know she was flat broke. He'd pity her, and that would be a fate worse than death.

He'd obviously heard the last part because he walked toward them, slid a proprietary arm around her waist and squeezed her. "Everything okay, angel?"

The odd, affectionate term made her blink. "Uh, yeah. I was just heading back to the boat." She supposed she should introduce Leo, but because Leo was obviously a nutcase, he might take that as a cue to invite himself to dinner at Jack's house. Being rude seemed more sensible.

"Jack Drummond." He thrust the arm that wasn't around her waist toward the shorter man. Apparently

Jack couldn't resist digging deeper. "Are you a friend of my fiancée?" He dug her ribs a little bit on the last word.

She felt color rising to her cheeks—and that didn't happen often.

"We are friends. I had no idea she was engaged." Leo looked flustered, probably wondering why she hadn't mentioned this before.

Jack's gaze scorched the side of her face. "It was a very sudden engagement. We don't even have our rings yet. We've loved each other for years, of course." Jack wasn't doing a good job of hiding the humor in his voice. "Vicki's come to live with me here on my houseboat."

If she weren't trying to prop up this pretense, she'd have slapped him and said she'd rather live in a tent in the Gobi than on a houseboat with him. Instead, she said, "I've always loved the water," and managed a simpering smile.

She could feel a chuckle of laughter rising in Jack's mighty chest, which was pressed against her side.

"Well, little lady, we'd better get back on the boat so you can rustle us up some dinner." He squeezed her again. She fought the urge to shove him off the dock into the water. "It was nice meeting you, Mr.…"

Leo apparently realized he hadn't managed to introduce himself. "Parker. Leo Parker." His voice sounded a little shaky. This was not going at all according to plan for him, thank goodness. Jack was cheeky to insist on getting his name.

Hmm, maybe he was jealous?

That thought brightened her dark mood.

Leo Parker shrank away, and Vicki heaved a sigh of relief as Jack guided her back to the boat. Once safely on board, she turned to make sure Leo was nowhere around. She saw his dejected form climbing into a large black SUV in the marina parking lot. "Hey, I never got my coffee."

"That guy had no idea we were engaged." Jack turned to her, eyes sparkling with amusement. "Funny thing is, neither did I."

"That guy's a creep. I was trying to get rid of him." Did Jack overhear the part about her father going bust? She certainly wasn't going to ask. "I hope he didn't follow me down here."

"How could he know where to find you?"

She shrugged. "I did get my mail forwarded. And Katherine Drummond obviously figured out I was coming because she told you. You found me pretty easily." She glanced over. The SUV was still sitting in the parking lot. Maybe Leo Parker was in there, watching them on the boat deck. She shuddered. "Maybe he installed a tracking device on me last time I was foolish enough to accept his invitation to dinner."

Jack didn't look at all jealous. He was probably thinking she must be very lonely and desperate to date the likes of Leo Parker. He'd be right, of course, but she didn't want him to know that. "I suppose if he doesn't take a hint, I'll have to defend your virtue." He started the motor and looked amused by the prospect.

"Thanks for your support. He's staying with Iago Knoll, so he's not going anywhere just yet. Yuck." She shivered again.

"Why did you go out with him?"

"I didn't know he'd turn into a stalker."

"I suppose that is hard to predict." They pulled out of the marina. Jack's reassuring presence comforted her when she took a last glance at the marina—and saw that SUV was still there. "But he doesn't seem like your kind of guy."

"What exactly is my kind of guy?" She crossed her arms over her chest. Jack's infuriating arrogance was a nice distraction right now.

"Me, of course." She could only see him in profile, but she didn't miss his mouth curving upward slightly.

"Very sure of yourself, aren't you?"

"I suspect that's one of the things you find attractive about me." He didn't turn around to catch her expression. He didn't have to. No doubt he knew she'd be fuming, and thinking he was right.

"Don't get a big head. I'm only after your muscular body."

"And my world-renowned treasure hunting skills." She saw one eyebrow lift.

"Yeah, that, too. Are we going back to the site tonight?"

"Nope, first thing tomorrow we're picking the crew up here and heading out there as a group. You'll get to meet the guys."

"Great. Are you going to introduce me as your fiancée?"

His booming laugh gave her all the answer she needed.

In bed that night, she toyed with the prospect of rejecting him before he could reject her. Because the idea of their being engaged was so plainly laughable—and really, it was—then their relationship had an expiration date which was fast approaching. Someone was going to get dumped, and this time she was determined it wouldn't be her.

But when his big hand settled on her waist, a thick curl of lust unfolded low inside her, and her resolve faltered. Why should she deny herself the simple and healthy pleasure of having steamy-hot sex with the best lover she'd ever known? A sensible woman knew when to take advantage of what was on offer. Just because she relished sex with him didn't mean she was falling in love. She could enjoy the pleasures of the flesh, then walk away without a backward glance.

Right?

That night held a few dangerous moments, like after her third orgasm, when her mind began to play tricks, and fantasies of living happily ever after with Jack stalked the edges of her imagination. Then again when she let herself drift off to sleep in the safe embrace of his big, strong arms. For once she didn't feel as though she had to fight anyone or anything, or worry about what tomorrow would bring. Jack was in charge and he had it covered. His team of brawny experts would dive off the boat with their high-tech search equipment, and she could probably kick back with a virgin margarita and watch pelicans circle overhead. She'd be stuck on the boat, likely with no cell phone signal and no appointments or plans or rich people to suck up to. Which sounded ideal.

Right now she was Jack Drummond's willing prisoner—or was he hers? This whole thing was her idea anyway. Being marooned on Jack's boat was a welcome vacation from real life and she might as well make the most of it.

* * *

Jack's crew included four men ranging in age from early twenties to late fifties. All seemed excited and happy to be there. Jack gave her full credit for locating the wreck and treated her with the same demeanor as the rest of the crew. Which should make her feel relieved and happy. All she really cared about was finding that old piece of barnacle-encrusted cup and getting the heck out of here to claim the reward for it.

Right?

They headed out for the wreck site in two boats. When they got there, they anchored the smaller one and gathered on Jack's main boat to prepare for the dive. They were all on deck checking their equipment when Jack moved up behind her, slid his arms around her waist and kissed her cheek.

She gasped. All four of the men could simply lift their heads and watch. Embarrassment flashed over her, mingled with indignation. Was he showing off? Proving to them that he could have any woman he wanted with just the touch of his sturdy finger? Not one of them even glanced up. Maybe Jack always brought a broad along on treasure hunts for good luck, like the figureheads on old wooden boats.

She wanted to slap him away and mock him for being unable to keep his hands off her. To save face and show them all that she wasn't yet another pathetic woman drooling over the great Jack Drummond.

Instead, she found herself melting at the touch of his lips on her cheek, the warm circle of his hands around her waist. And when she kissed him back, her eyes slid closed and she forgot all about the men, and the sea and the sun and the sunken wreck and the missing cup and Leo Parker and all that other mess that cluttered up her brain. Nothing existed but her and Jack, locked in a passionate embrace and kissing each other as if it was the last thing they'd ever do.

He pulled back first, leaving her blinking and breathless in the sunlight. She stepped back too fast, trod on an oxygen tank and had to grab his arm to steady herself.

"You diving?" His brusque question ignored all that went before.

"Sure." Suddenly she didn't want to be the mascot sitting on the boat waiting for the menfolk to come back. "Let's get going." She tried to distract herself with checking her scuba gear and strapping it all on. Jack had moved to the other side of the boat and was going over some details of how to map out the wreck with one of the crew. Much better to be under the water keeping busy than sitting up here mooning over a man with a proven record of breaking her heart.

The dive lasted all day, with a raucous break for kebabs, which one of the guys had brought in a cooler and barbecued on a hibachi right on the deck. The whole crew was obviously stoked about the wreck.

Mel was the oldest, with years of commercial fishing experience before dipping his feet in the treasure hunting world. Silver-haired but with the tanned body of a young man, he found humor in everything. Jovial Greg regaled them with stories of a recent deep-sea fishing trip in the Bahamas with a famous music producer and his supermodel wife who thought fishing was murder. Luca was a handsome Italian with a rich accent and a flirtatious manner that might have been diverting if she wasn't already too sensually on edge for that kind of thing. And Ethan was an enthusiastic college kid who thought every piece of equipment and technique was the coolest thing ever. They all treated Jack with a reverence that would be impressive if it wasn't so annoying.

"Vicki's my lucky charm." Jack smiled at her through a bite of kebab during lunch. "I think the wreck was waiting for her arrival to reveal itself."

"Ships do have their feelings." Mel smiled at her. "Any old sailor will tell you that. And now she's rising up right into our hands to welcome us." They'd blasted away more of the sand to find the wreck in surprisingly intact condition. "Almost like the sleeping beauty's been lying under her blanket for three hundred years waiting for us to come wake her up."

"Vicki's most interested in one-third of a family chalice that went down with the wreck. At least we assume it did. It could be on a shelf behind the bar of a tavern in Kingston, Jamaica." Jack winked at her. "But even if we don't find that, we'll be rewarded for our work." He nodded toward the plastic bins already filling with items retrieved from the ship. Right now it looked like a bunch of unidentifiable rocks, all glued together with coral and who knew what else. But she'd heard them exclaim over coins and buckles and pieces of weaponry, so there were probably emerald rings and pearl combs and plenty of other treasures in there somewhere.

"Lucky we got out here so fast. Look who's over there." Greg nodded his head to the south where a large, white boat was clearly visible.

Mel chuckled and shook his head. "Lou Aarons. Always one step behind. I swear that guy just watches where Jack's boat goes and starts digging nearby."

"Let old Lou have our leftovers." Jack grinned and

took a swig of iced tea. "There's no need for us to be greedy when we have this kind of bounty at our fingertips. As long as he doesn't get Vicki's cup." He flashed a glance at her.

Her insides quivered like a subterranean jellyfish in a riptide. Already she couldn't stop thinking about tonight, and all the things he might do to her in the privacy of their shared bedroom. But she attempted to look calm and collected. "And don't forget that it probably doesn't look like a cup. It might be the base. So any unidentified metal objects you find, please show them to me even if they look totally useless."

They all agreed, and Mel told a story about a twisted old piece of encrusted metal he'd found that had turned out to be an ancient pre-Incan breastplate made out of nearly a pound of solid gold.

They dived all afternoon, and had filled ten large plastic tubs with "finds" before calling it a day just before sunset. Ethan was to sleep overnight on the boat and guard the site while the others returned to shore in the smaller boat. Jack and Vicki dropped the three remaining crew members off at the marina and headed back to the island, taking their booty with them.

Even though her body was tired from all the diving, Vicki's mind was crackling with excitement to examine the items that had been pried from the sea's grasp after nearly three hundred years of entombment. Even the prospect of getting naked with Jack paled in comparison to shining a bright light on the mysterious treasures in those plastic tubs.

"We need to keep them wet." Jack had half filled each container with salt water, making them unwieldy to unload from the boat. "We don't want them exposed to oxygen in the air until we know what we're dealing with."

"Aye-aye, Cap'n."

"I'm beginning to think you're part seal. You don't have any problem diving for hours along with the rest of us who do it all the time. And what happened to your seasickness?"

Vicki shrugged. "I have to admit I'm enjoying myself. Makes a big change from pounding the streets of Manhattan trying to make a deal over a Peretti brooch."

She pulled a concretelike lump with visible metal protrusions from one of the tubs. "How do you tell what anything is?"

"This big lump is called a concretion. We usually start with either a chisel or an X-ray machine, depending on how delicate and possibly valuable the items are. In this case I vote for the X-ray."

The X-ray machine was portable, and Jack set it up like a camera to focus on each object as they placed it on a taped *X* on a glass-topped table in his living room.

"Here *X* does really mark the spot." Vicki's stomach tingled with excitement as she placed the first heavy, wet concretion on the table. "What's the strangest thing you've ever found in a lump like this?"

Jack held the X-ray machine up and she moved well out of the way while he took the image. "A full set of solid gold teeth inside a skull."

"Eek! I shouldn't have asked. I guess that was pirate fashion back in the day."

"Probably held up better than the more popular wooden teeth." He put the X-ray machine down and scrutinized a monitor. "Hmm."

"What?" She moved around so she could see the

image. Several long, wavy shapes stood out against the textured background. She could see some curved masses, too.

"Could be knives. That looks like a mug. We might have found the kitchen."

"Could be a good place for part of an old chalice to be stored." She sneaked a glance at him.

"Yeah, as if it could be that easy." He chuckled. "There's definitely some interesting stuff in here, so this is when we get out the chisels. But we'll save that for later."

They ate baked ziti that his housekeeper had prepared and left for them to reheat, then they x-rayed several more concretions. One held some small round shapes that Jack recognized as coins, but he didn't seem excited enough to liberate them. Probably old coins weren't even thrilling to him anymore. A man only needed but so much treasure. There were plenty of shapes that looked as though they could be part of an old cup, which was either encouraging or quite the opposite, depending on how you looked at it.

As they neared midnight she found herself growing impatient for the next activity on her agenda—bedtime with Jack.

"I think we should get some sleep." Vicki's voice made Jack glance up from the monitor.

"Is it late?" He lost all track of the time when they made a new find. The adrenaline rush that accompanied discovering buried history could keep him awake for days.

"To most people, yes." She didn't look tired. She did look gorgeous. "I'm going to hit the sack."

"Okay." He adjusted the brightness on the monitor. Something in there was quite unusual. Delicate and multifaceted—like a piece of jewelry, perhaps. Too early to tell, but still... Maybe he could take the time to chisel delicately at this one.

"Aren't you coming?" Vicki hovered in the doorway. She was dressed in a long, thin T-shirt—and some tempting black underwear he'd noticed when she bent over to pick up the concretions—and looked very inviting.

"In a while." The mysterious object tugged his attention back to the monitor. Gold had a certain quality to it in an X-ray image. At least it did to him. Smoother, lighter than silver. He could spot it almost by instinct.

"I might get lonely." Her soft words jerked his head up from the screen. Vicki had summoned him to bed. This was new. Up until now he'd been doing all the flirting and chasing—which had been so worth it—and expecting only prickly reluctance in return.

Apparently now it was his turn to be seduced. "In that case, I'd better come with you." He switched off the equipment and followed her down the hallway. Her slim hips had a seductive swing to them that set his blood pumping. Even eighteenth-century gold paled in comparison to the swaying body of a beautiful woman beating a path to his bedroom.

And what a woman. He'd been keeping an eye on her diving equipment himself, to make sure she was doing everything right, but his caution had been unnecessary. Vicki could take care of herself. She'd fit in perfectly with the guys, and dived like a professional, with no complaints and an enthusiasm that rivaled his own.

In addition to being beautiful, she was smart and

sharp and funny. He even enjoyed her frosty barbs and cutting glances. In fact, he liked them better than the simpering and mewing of the more typical girls who crowded around him in bars begging for tales of treasure.

Vicki, Vicki, Vicki.

He followed her into the bedroom, and paused to savor the view as she pulled her T-shirt off over her head. The black panties were scanty, with a design that revealed more than it covered. If they were designed to deprive men of their powers of speech, then they worked like a charm.

She climbed up on the high bed—a move that sent blood rushing to his groin—and lay there, eyes half-closed in a seductive expression.

He ripped off his jeans and T-shirt and strode across the room, excitement percolating in his veins. He kissed her lips softly, then rougher, taking the kiss deeper until that first sweet moan of pleasure escaped them.

He teased her body with his mouth, feathering kisses over her breasts and belly, then licking her sex until it pulsed with anticipation. His own arousal was almost unbearable. Vicki's long, elegant fingers plucked at the skin of his back and roamed through his hair with abandon, while her sighs filled the air like music.

His level of arousal could probably be measured in degrees Fahrenheit by the time he finally let himself enter her. She was so eager, gripping him and tugging him closer, pawing him and kissing him, her eyes closed tight.

When he filled her, she said his name over and over, as if trying to convince herself it was really him. He needed no convincing that he was with Vicki St. Cyr, the most compelling and confusing and original and wonderful woman he'd ever had the pleasure to know. Part of him despised his weakness in being afraid of her power and passion all those years ago. She was a force of nature, like a tornado that sucked up everything in its path.

At least back then she was. Now she was quieter, cooler, more subtle. But perhaps no less forceful, like a riptide hidden beneath the surface, silent and invisible until the unwitting swimmer has been sucked halfway to the horizon.

These thoughts rolled in his mind as their bodies rolled on the bed. He'd been afraid of her then, although he'd rather have died than admit it. She was so sure of herself, so aware of her power over men and everyone else. Her confidence—her arrogance—had been a core part of her charm. No one dared to argue with her because they knew they'd lose. Playing with Vicki was like playing with a baby tiger or an open flame—you never knew quite when it would turn on you and leave you hurting.

So he'd done the cowardly thing and saved himself by running away.

He'd tried to lose himself in the soft embraces of other women. Tried to distract himself with work and travel and new exciting projects. For a long time he thought he was over her. Then he'd heard she was coming to town and got so impatient to see her that he tracked her down to the hotel. She'd swept back into his life like a sirocco, turned it upside down and reminded him of why he'd been so wary of her in the first place.

Why did she come back? Her excuse of finding the

cup and claiming the reward only made sense if she was desperate for money. Which was hard to imagine.

Vicki's tongue shot into his ear and he gasped with raw sensation, driving deeper inside her and rolling again until she was on top. If a quest for cash brought Vicki back into his life, it certainly hadn't brought her back into his bed. She was every bit as hot and hungry for him as he was for her, and not shy about showing it, either.

When he shifted back on top, he kissed her face through the damp tendrils of her hair, drinking in her heady feminine scent. This woman drove him crazy in the best possible way. He increased the pace until he felt her climax take her by storm, and finally let go of all the agonizing but pleasurable tension building inside him.

They drifted back to the soft pillows together, chests heaving and skin moist with perspiration. Having Vicki in his bed felt so right. He opened his eyes to see the bright fresco she'd revealed. He'd slept under it for years with no idea it was there, just like he'd been sleepwalking through life without her.

Was Vicki back for a reason more profound than simply finding an object? Maybe she'd come back into his life as a sign that it was time for him to…

The words *settle down* crossed his consciousness and made him shift uncomfortably on the mattress. Then he wanted to laugh. Life with Vicki St. Cyr would be anything but settled. She was as restless and easily bored as himself, always chasing new pleasures and mysteries.

Life with Vicki St. Cyr…

Was that the life he was meant to live? The question rang in his heart and he found himself letting it vibrate there. Did she feel the same way? Her feelings were hard to determine as she was secretive and wily by nature.

Her eyes were closed, long dark lashes resting against her soft clear skin. Then she opened them and pierced him with that relentless violet gaze.

Did she know what he was thinking?

Her thoughts were a mystery to him as always. He wasn't usually inclined to look beneath the surface of things unless there was treasure there. But Vicki intrigued him and he wanted to plumb her secrets depths and enjoy her hidden facets.

Then her eyes closed again. She was tired after their long day. A protective instinct filled his chest. He needed to make sure she got a good night's sleep and didn't exhaust herself. She'd been pale and gaunt when she arrived, and sun and sea air and good food—and the invigorating sex, of course—were already working magic on her, but he'd better make sure she didn't overdo it.

Vicki shifted slightly, and blew out a soft breath. She seemed so relaxed now, all her defenses down. A smile played across her delicate features, and he could see her eyes moving beneath her eyelids, so she must be dreaming.

Was she dreaming about him? He hoped so because the dream looked like a good one. A tiny chuckle rose in her throat and she leaned toward him—still fast asleep—until their noses were almost touching.

She opened her pretty, dark pink mouth and another soft sigh brushed his skin. Then she murmured something, very quietly, like it was a secret. No one was meant to hear it.

But he did, and her words caused his blood to still in his veins.

Eight

Vicki woke suddenly, disoriented by the bright sunlight. A quick glance at the bed revealed that Jack was gone. What time was it? She climbed off the bed and checked her phone. How could it be 9:20? They were supposed to head back to the wreck at first light.

Slipping a T-shirt over her nakedness, she opened the bedroom door and peered down the sunlit corridor. "Jack?"

"Good morning, senorita." A short, dark-haired woman shot out of the room right next door to her, making her jump. Jack's housekeeper. "You must be Vicki."

"And you must be Paloma. Jack's always talking about you." After watching Jack's cousin Sinclair fall madly in love with his own housekeeper, she had to admit relief that Jack's was old enough to be his mother.

Uh-oh. Did this mean she was jealous?

"It would be funny if I wasn't Vicki, wouldn't it?" She wished she had more than a T-shirt on. It was painfully obvious what she and Jack had been up to last night. Paloma had probably witnessed a lot of morning-after scenes and she hated being a stereotype.

She wanted to ask if Jack had left on the boat, but didn't want to admit that she didn't already know the answer.

"Jack told me to let you sleep in. He said you worked too long and hard yesterday." Paloma took on a bossy tone that was strangely reassuring. "He also told me to make you a huge breakfast, then let you do whatever you like with all the rocks and stuff in the living room." She shook her head. "Why he can't do that in the workshop, I don't know. Seawater isn't good for wood floors."

"No, I don't suppose it is." So Jack had left her alone with the treasure. She could spend her day whittling pirates' toothpicks out of the hunks of coral rock. Normally that would pass for a pretty interesting day, but somehow she felt hurt that Jack had abandoned her here. Maybe this was a subtle message that the team moved faster and more efficiently without her.

Or maybe this was the beginning of the big brush-off.

"Do you have grapefruit?"

"Of course we do." Paloma smiled. "And I baked fresh biscuits. How about I scramble some eggs to go with them?"

"Sounds heavenly." Her stomach growled in agreement. So what if Jack wasn't here. She could use a break from overexposure to his tanned and brawny physique. And an afternoon nap might be a welcome luxury, as well.

After breakfast she wandered outside to look for the ship in the distance. She couldn't see it, though, so it must be just over the horizon. The day was warm, with sensual, languid weather, perfect for relaxing in a hammock. But she couldn't resist being the first person to handle items that had gone down with the wreck, for the first time in hundreds of years.

She booted up the computer they'd used the night before and found the files of the X-rays, then printed them all out. Although the missing cup piece didn't seem all that riveting when compared to the prospect of looted Spanish gold and stolen jewelry, she figured she should at least scan the images for anything promising.

On the third image something caught her eye. A delicate filigree of metal entwined deep in the concretion of sand and coral. Her heart pounded as she scrutinized the shape and made out what looked like the outline of a large and elaborate necklace with the chain still attached.

She located the big chunk of seabed labeled with the same number as the image, and the tray of chisels Jack had shown her. She kept the rock in its plastic container, marinating in a few inches of seawater. No need to risk it crumbling to dust, and it would probably make less mess to keep the water contained. As Paloma vacuumed somewhere in the distance, she took a medium chisel to the lump of sandy rock.

The crust was surprisingly hard, and when it broke it tended to shatter into large chunks. She switched to a smaller chisel for more precision. The last thing she wanted was for Jack to return home and find she'd dented or broken a priceless antique. Eventually, she found a rhythm and refined her technique, and sometime around noon, the long-lost piece started to emerge from its stony tomb.

She saw a chain-link first, and immediately switched to the finest chisel on the tray, removing the sandy accretion almost grain by grain.

Gold. The chain was unmistakably made from its era's most precious metal. Untarnished by its long burial, it gleamed in the reflected sunlight shining through the window as if it had been waiting all this time to show itself.

Quite thick, the links were bent and twisted but all intact. The pendant attached to the chain was also gold, dented and squarish in shape, and looked as if something was missing. It had no gems. Possibly Jack's coarse ancestors had pried them off and traded them in a game of dice.

She laughed. She should be mad that Jack had ditched her, but she couldn't be. This was too much fun.

After Paloma left for the day, she indulged in that nap she'd fantasized about. She swung gently from a hammock strung beneath two palm trees on the lawn in the shade of the ubiquitous sea grape. Her dream drew her into a sensual realm not unlike last night's antics in bed. Apparently her brain and body couldn't get enough of Jack so they had to conjure him even when he wasn't here.

Disturbing. And it did not bode well for her easily forgetting him when this affair was over.

Jack returned shortly after dark. She'd rummaged around in the kitchen and found a casserole Paloma must have started in the slow cooker. She set the table and poured two glasses of wine, then lit the candles above the fireplace and took time to fix her face and hair so he'd be pleasantly surprised to see her rather than annoyed she was still underfoot.

He walked into the foyer and smiled as soon as he saw her. "We missed you." His words touched her. So did the rough hug he gave her. His T-shirt was damp with sea spray. His skin smelled delicious and she had to fight the urge to lick him.

"I missed you, too. Just a little. But I kept busy."

"I'll bet you did. Find anything good?"

"Of course. I've piled the stash on that funky dresser in the living room." It seemed entirely appropriate for pirate treasure to be strewn here and there about an eclectic house, rather than catalogued and stored in plastic containers in a lab. Although, being fully aware of the crucial importance of a detailed provenance for each piece, she'd taken pictures at every stage of her chiseling and labeled each item with a catalog number. The Smithsonian would be proud of her. "I found a necklace, four musket balls, a fork, two rings and a jug. And that was all in one lump o' stone."

"Impressive." He grinned and held her closer. His hands cupped her backside, and he laid another kiss on her cheek.

A smile sneaked across her mouth. "I bet you didn't find as much stuff without me there for luck."

"You must have been there with us in spirit because we found a mother lode. Probably the cabin where the women sheltered from the storm."

"There were women on a pirate ship?"

He shrugged. "If you were a strapping, testosterone-fueled brigand, wouldn't you want a few ladies with you on your voyage?"

"Maybe one." She lifted an eyebrow. "Do you prefer a ménage?"

"No way." He kissed her other cheek. "I'm a one-woman man."

One woman at a time, but not for long. She tried not to let her thoughts show on her face. "Well, that's a relief. I got dinner ready, although I can't take any credit for cooking. Paloma seems like a good woman to have on your pirate ship."

"She's my secret weapon."

"How does she get here?"

"I have an old sea-dog friend ferry her out here from the marina at nine every morning and take her back at one."

"I'm glad to know that. I was beginning to think there was magic involved. She made a casserole." She gestured toward the dining room as casually as she could. "I was about to dollop it into bowls and sling it on the table." She tried to make her hospitality sound as inhospitable as possible. She didn't want Jack to think she was going soft in her old age.

Jack paused in the doorway when he saw the lit candles and sparkling glasses of wine. "Quite the elegant repast to come home to."

Maybe you'll miss me when I'm gone. The thought stayed in her mind. It was a foolish one because he could just as easily get Paloma to set the table for him. If he wanted a housewife, she was the last person in the world she'd recommend for the job.

Would he miss her? She wondered if he'd missed her the first time. Did you miss someone if you were the one who left? Probably not. Your ears would still be ringing with all the reasons you couldn't wait to get away from them.

She served out the casserole—it had a delicious wine scent—and sat down. Jack raised his glass. "To sharing my table with a woman who'd be the envy of my ancestors."

"They're all around us, aren't they?" She glanced about the large room with its high ceilings. If this were a more typical stately home, there would be large oil portraits decorating the walls. The plaster walls of Jack's dining room were hung with ornamental cutlasses and the fireplace mantel bore a decorative pyramid of pitted cannon balls.

Jack shrugged. "If they were, wouldn't they have told me where to find the wreck?"

"Maybe they're more entertained by watching you search for it. Did you find any bodies?"

"Nothing. Just the artifacts that would have been on them." He took a draft of white wine. "Sometimes the bodies disappear without a trace, which I much prefer."

She shivered. "Those poor people. I wonder if the ship went down fast."

"It must have if there was only one survivor. It's pretty close to shore so unless Lazaro Drummond dispatched everyone else with his salvaged musket, there should have been more people who made it back. I don't suppose we'll ever know what really happened. As you've observed, pirates don't keep the best records."

"They want to hold on to their mysteries." She could relate to that. It seemed that the longer she stayed here, the more of herself she revealed to Jack. And that wasn't good. "So you think much of the treasure was in that room?"

He nodded. "Looks that way. It's not unusual for sea-
men to put all their most valuable possessions in one
locked room when a ship gets into trouble and they bat-
ten down the hatches. Then they know where it is and
can retrieve it quickly if the ship starts to break up."

"And surely they'd have kept it under lock and key
during the voyage anyway. I can't imagine a pirate trusting his own crew too far."

He lifted a brow. "You're wrong about that. If a pirate didn't trust a crew member he'd kill them as soon
as look at them. You couldn't go out raiding ships if
you didn't trust every last man—or woman—to defend
your life with his own."

"So there was honor among thieves."

"Most of the time. The rest of them ended up in Dead
Men's Cove."

After dinner she showed him her find and was
pleased that he seemed impressed with her extraction
techniques. He brought in the new tubs of findings, and
they x-rayed them. There was an abundance of good
stuff buried in the sandy lumps of stone.

"What if there are parts of several old chalices?"
She stared at a black-and-white image on the monitor.
"There might be such a thing as too much treasure."

"Then you take them all up to old cousin Sinclair's
place and see if they fit together with the one he has
there. How did they take the chalice apart?"

"From the look of the stem I'd guess the pieces just
slid into each other with a tight fit. It certainly didn't
screw in or anything crude like that. The stem part
had smooth ends. We thought it would be pewter, but
it turned out to be brass. The stem had some engraved

decoration on it, so I'd imagine you could find similar decoration on the other parts and line up the pattern."

"A puzzle."

"Exactly."

"And if you solve it, I and the other Drummond heirs can live happily ever after."

"Or have a slightly better shot at happily ever after than you do now." It was hard to imagine Jack in some off-into-the-sunset ending where he lived peacefully with one woman for the rest of his life. He'd be bored stiff within a year. At least this time she wasn't going to be the woman he grew tired of. She'd leave fast enough to guarantee that.

In the meantime, could it really hurt to enjoy a little more hot sex?

Jack switched off the monitor. "We should get some sleep."

"I agree." Her skin tingled with the prospect of pressing itself against his. He looked very tempting right now in dark cotton pants and a faded logo T-shirt, but he'd look even more irresistible after she peeled them off.

"You sleep in my bed. I'll go next door."

"What do you mean next door?" Shock propelled the words from her mouth. Was there some hot next-door neighbor he was in the habit of visiting for a nightcap?

"The bedroom next door." He turned his back to her and strolled for the door like the decision had already been made. "Then we won't get distracted by... you know."

I sure do. And I was looking forward to the distraction. "I'm not that tired."

"You will be if you don't get some decent REM sleep. Don't you want to come out on the boat tomorrow?"

"I do, but I'm used to an active nightlife." If only he'd turn around she'd have a chance of charming him, but he kept moving farther down the corridor. She hurried to keep up. Then realized what she was doing.

He was already walking away from her. And she was chasing him like a lost puppy. "Actually a night of peace sounds really good." Let him sleep alone if he wanted to. She lifted her chin. She didn't need him. She just needed his treasure hunting expertise. And frankly they'd already had plenty of sex.

Her body argued with her, especially the parts that were already pulsing and tingling in eager anticipation of intimate union with Jack. She told it to be quiet. "See you in the morning." She hesitated. "You will wake me up tomorrow?" It sounded pathetic, like a dog putting the leash in its mouth and coming to its master. Still, she would be hurt to be left behind again.

Which was a problem. How did her emotional health suddenly depend on Jack Drummond's whims and fancies?

"Sure, I'll wake you. It'll be early."

She'd hoped for a good-night kiss at the very least, but he disappeared behind the carved wooden door next to his own bedroom, and she was left in the hallway, alone.

She blew out a breath. What had happened? Last night he was totally hot for her. They'd had the most intense and pleasurable sex she'd ever enjoyed in her life. Then in the morning he'd sneaked off without her. And now...

Something had happened.

But what?

* * *

Jack woke Vicki for breakfast with a gruff "Time to get going." He didn't want to go into the room and see her gorgeous body wrapped in a sheet. Better to get out on the boat with the boys where he'd have other things to keep his mind off her charms.

Tonight they'd put some serious effort into unpacking those concretions and maybe the cup would be in there. With that in her suitcase she could be back on her way again.

And right now, that seemed like the best thing that could happen.

He heard her shower running and imagined warm water cascading over those long, slim legs that displayed such athleticism in moments of passion. Then he distracted himself by measuring coffee into the filter. The world was full of beautiful women. Vicki was just one of them.

And she was one he did not intend to hurt any more than he already had.

Her words still vibrated in his ears, sending shards of guilt through him. *I've always loved you, Jack. Always.*

His stomach contracted at the memory. How could history repeat itself like that? Worse yet, he'd been toying with the possibility that Vicki St. Cyr might actually be "the one." Lord knows he couldn't imagine growing bored with her. She seemed to fit right in with his life here and she even brought finely honed analytical skills. And there was that strange, hollow feeling in his chest when he thought about her leaving.

Then she'd talked in her sleep and all those wayward thoughts had reeled back and snapped shut like an automatic tape measure. He wasn't ready for the responsibility of someone depending on him for their happiness.

I've always loved you. What the heck did that mean? Had she been pining for him all through the past six years? What kind of a nightmare was that? He'd thought of her from time to time, sure, but mostly he'd kept himself busy swimming with all the other lovely fish in the sea. And there were a lot of fish out there he hadn't swum with yet.

Cad.

His mom would tease him. She thought it funny that his reputation as a ladies' man was so well deserved. Because his notoriety followed him around like a flock of gulls after a fishing trawler, women generally knew what they were getting into when they climbed into his bed. With his roving lifestyle he didn't have to make excuses for why he couldn't come over for pot roast on Sunday. Everything was easy, casual.

"Morning." Vicki drifted into the room, her long silky black hair tousled. She wore a navy blue bikini under a sheer white T-shirt with the word *DARE* written on it in black.

His gut tightened. She wanted him to want her. And he did. That was the worst part. How could you turn down something so delicious right in front of you?

But Vicki was no longer some kid he could chalk up to life experience. She was a mature and experienced woman who'd come back to his house and into his bed. She put up a tough front, sure, but if what she said was true, then she'd been carrying a torch for him for years and he'd just poured kerosene on it.

"Orange juice?" He tried to sound casual. Like he

wasn't deliberating about the history of their relationship in his head.

"I prefer pomegranate." She cocked her head, still confident and challenging.

"You would." A grin tugged at his mouth. Damn, he was going to miss her. "How about coffee instead?"

"That'll do the trick."

He made French toast for both of them, and sliced some papaya. She kept the chatter going with questions about how the concretions form around the debris of the wreck, and he explained how it helped treasure hunters out immensely by keeping all the pieces more or less in one place over the centuries.

Damn, she was beautiful. It wasn't just her violet eyes or her smooth skin or the raven's wing hair, it was her whole demeanor—deadly cool and fiercely passionate at the same time. He'd never met anyone like her.

What if he never did again?

Vicki was glad to get out on the boat and keep busy tinkering with all the equipment and chatting with the guys. It took her mind off Jack's sudden change of heart toward her. The other men all sneaked sideways glances at her and hung on to her every word—which she was used to. Jack, on the other hand, seemed busy poring over charts he'd printed out and typing notes into a computer.

She tried not to let it hurt.

Of course it was embarrassing that Jack had kissed her in front of everyone on the first day out on the boat. There was no way she could pretend she'd kept him at a cool arm's length. Maybe they were all wondering why he was suddenly so distant and preoccupied.

She found herself itching to don her scuba gear and head down into the quiet world of the ocean where there was no room for conversation or sideways glances or speculating about someone's body language.

Jack's muscled body was a constant torment, tanned and toned and right in front of her at every moment. That she no longer had license to touch it only made it more tempting and distracting.

"Vicki, don't forget to check your tanks. I meant to do it but I haven't had a chance." He glanced over at her, pinning her with his hot gaze.

"Thanks for reminding me." She noticed with chagrin that one tank was almost empty. So much for her being self-reliant and not needing him. "There are so many things to keep track of when you're diving."

"It all takes practice. You're pretty on top of things for a landlubber."

It hurt to hear him call her that. Which was ridiculous. Since when did she want him to consider her an old salt? She meticulously checked the rest of her gear and looked around for anything else on the boat that might need fixing. She didn't want his team to think she was a fifth wheel.

Even if she was.

"Vicki, do you realize what you've done?"

She glanced up in shock when the youngest team member spoke.

"What?" She glanced down at her scuba gear, wondering what else she'd screwed up.

"You've found what's probably the most well-preserved eighteenth-century wreck in the history of the area." He shook his head, sun-bleached hair tossing in the wind. "I don't know how, but the word is getting out and the vultures are circling. Look." He pointed at a helicopter in the sky. She hadn't noticed it before, being used to them in New York, but as she watched, it circled them in a lazy loop. "The TV reporters will be next. They love a good treasure hunt. It boosts the ratings."

"Is that good or bad?"

"Good if you're trying to raise high prices for the artifacts. Bad if you're still trying to extract them. Worst-case scenario—someone can try to shut you down by citing some ancient claim to the treasure."

"How could they do that when the original owners are long dead and gone?"

"Sometimes the crown of a country will claim the spoils. Spain and Portugal have both laid claim to lost ships from their treasure fleets, never mind that the ships went down five hundred years earlier."

"Do they ever win?"

"They do."

"That's crazy." She squinted at Jack. "But this ship belonged to Jack's ancestor, which makes things a bit more cut and dried."

"Except that Jack's ancestor was a known pirate. If someone could prove a right to the stolen goods..." He shrugged. "You never know what people will do when there's gold involved."

Vicki felt a little surge of righteous indignation as she glanced up at the helicopter, still drifting overhead in wide circles. It was white and blue, obviously private, with no markings other than the number printed on the fuselage. Someone was spying on them.

With her luck, it was probably Leo Parker. She wondered if he'd spread the word about her whirlwind "engagement" to Jack and if she'd return to New York and have to unravel a lot of complicated rumors about her love life.

Her stomach clenched at the prospect.

"Let's dive!" With his usual enthusiasm, Jack led the charge over the side of the ship. She donned her mask and followed. The warm water closed over her head, shutting out the noise of the helicopter and dimming the bright sunlight to a muted glow.

She dived, kicking with her flippers to propel herself down into the cool, shadowy depths. At least down here no one could tell that she was already nursing the festering beginnings of a broken heart.

Nine

"Vicki should go on air." The team sat around Jack's ancient oak dining table. They'd returned the previous evening to a long string of phone messages from various local and international media outlets, all wanting the scoop on their discovery.

And they'd spent another night in separate beds. Jack's rejection of her—coming so much sooner than anticipated—hurt so much that she was almost numb.

And very, very sexually frustrated.

Yet she still had to put on a brave face and act as though everything was just fine. "No, really, I hardly know anything about the history of the vessel or the methods you're all using. It would be much better if someone else did the talking."

"I'll speak, of course." Jack frowned at the collage of maps he'd printed from his computer. She couldn't read them at all. A jumble of numbers that made less sense than the crazy Roman numeral code she'd unraveled. "And I agree that Vicki should go on camera. She solved a puzzle that's had the Drummonds stumped for centuries."

Something in her gut told her that going on air was not a good idea. What if some bright-eyed reporter started digging around in her past and found out about her father's financial problems? It was almost a miracle that that had never hit the press in the first place. "If you tell them about the treasure map, they'll want to come to the house and take pictures. Probably better just to say you were digging around and stumbled across it."

"No way!" Ethan protested. "The treasure map is the best part of the story. I can already see the Hollywood movie version with Russell Crowe as Jack and Demi Moore as Vicki. It's a great story."

"Demi Moore?" Vicki had to protest. "She's more than twenty years older than me!"

"And still damn hot." Jack grinned. "Maybe I'll ask them if I can play myself opposite her."

"You go ahead." She lifted her chin. "And if you want reporters traipsing all over your private island, then you might as well invite them."

Jack frowned. "Hmm, that does go against a deep-rooted Drummond instinct for privacy. On the other hand, unlike my ancestors, I don't really have anything to hide."

"Your island might become a tourist destination." She lifted a brow. "They'll bring boatloads of eager vacationers out here to see the famous Drummond lair."

"And I can start a sideline selling T-shirts and fake scrimshaw." Jack leaned back in his chair and wove his fingers behind this head, giving her yet another infuriating view of his tanned and bulging biceps.

Her insides throbbed and pulsed with frustrated lust. It was beyond cruel of him to lead her on and tantalize her with the hottest sex of her life, then leave her high and dry like this. There should be a law against that kind of cold-hearted torture. "And mugs with your sunburned face on them."

"Hey, I like it." His grin widened. "Then the big question is, who do we call first?"

Vicki wanted to sigh and hold her head in her hands. Instead, she kept a poker face. "How about you start with the most local outfit and let the story grow from there." Then hopefully she'd be long gone before the coverage got out of control. If she didn't find that cup by the end of this week, she'd be leaving without it. They'd brought up so much stuff already that if it wasn't in one of the plastic boxes piled high around the house and workshop, it was probably gone forever.

And with everything else that was happening she didn't really care much anymore. There had to be easier ways to earn ten thousand dollars. It was a shame that she'd decided she was too proud to ask Jack for a finder's fee or a cut of the treasure.

"All right, we'll go with WGX. I went deep-sea fishing once with the head of the news department and he seems like a stand-up guy."

"Perfect." She rose from her chair. Of course he'd go with some old sailor-boy network connection. She couldn't wait to get back to her own world where at least she had some connections of her own. "If you'll all excuse me, I'm going to go chisel out some more treasure."

* * *

Jack felt like a jerk. Vicki was hurt. And why wouldn't she be? She'd finally let down her guard and fallen into his beckoning arms only to have him push her away.

After he'd enjoyed some downright legendary good times with her.

If only she hadn't said that stuff about always loving him. His chest clenched just thinking about it.

Luckily he didn't have much time to dwell on his own shortcomings because the crew from WGX had already descended and was trailing wires around his living room and setting up white-hot lights everywhere. Vicki had sequestered herself in the workshop. Even though she'd insisted that she shouldn't appear on camera, he took note of her rather glamorous outfit and carefully made-up face and suspected she would be hurt if he didn't shove her in front of the reporters.

So he certainly didn't intend to fail in that regard. Damn, she looked gorgeous. Her white blouse was translucent enough to make a man sweat. Dark jeans hugged her sinfully long legs, emphasized by high-heeled sandals. The more primitive parts of his brain—or maybe it wasn't his brain at all—urged him to wrap his arms around her and bury his face in her scented black tresses.

"Hey, Jack, is it okay if they shoot some footage of your boat?" The door had opened and an eager female reporter peered in.

"Uh, sure." He tried to snap his attention back to the chaos unfolding in his personal sanctuary. Two more young women entered the room and stared at the boxes of artifacts.

"Is this the stuff from the ship?" The one with long red hair lifted one of the plastic lids.

"Yes." Vicki hurried over and closed the lid. "And it can't be exposed to air because of oxidization." She gave the girl a stern look.

Jack wanted to chuckle. Vicki as schoolmarm— now he'd seen everything. He bet she'd be a strict mother who made sure her kids had impeccable manners, then she'd let them stay up and scare themselves watching a late-night movie.

"Jack, why don't you explain oxidization to these young ladies?"

His gaze snapped to them and he realized with a chill that he'd been thinking about Vicki's maternal qualities. Obviously he was losing his mind. Vicki had boldly declared that she didn't want children, and he had no reason whatsoever not to believe her. Not that it mattered. He and Vicki were far too volatile a compound to share space for long, let alone to reproduce.

At least that's what his brain kept telling him. His gut was singing a different song. "What do you need to know about it?" He looked from one girl to the other. They looked like college students and were probably interns. Maybe Vicki was dangling them in front of him like minnows to see if he'd take a nibble.

"How does water prevent oxidization from occurring?"

"It forms a seal around the objects as long as they're immersed."

"But water is part oxygen," the earnest blonde with the ponytail protested.

"I know, but that doesn't seem to matter." He shrugged. "I'm not a chemist, just a treasure hunter.

Whatever works, I do it, and I don't worry too much about the hows and whys." He smiled.

They nodded and one of them lifted another lid. "So we can look at these objects as long as we don't lift them out of the water?"

Vicki shot Jack a stern look. "Only if it's okay with Vicki."

"I think it would be better if we selected a few objects and concretions for you to videotape." Vicki sounded businesslike, which was quite a contrast with her rock-star attire. "This container here has the visible remains of an old cannon ball embedded in the coral, and several pieces of a glass bottle. Why don't you help me carry it into the other room?"

He watched her leave with the two girls. It had half killed him not to sleep with her last night. And the night before. It seemed such a cruel waste of a beautiful opportunity. He knew he'd never get another chance to share a bed with Vicki St. Cyr.

Not unless he intended to take up a permanent berth there.

Once again the wild and unreasonable prospect of a real relationship with Vicki assaulted his brain like strong drink. No part of the idea made any sense. Yes, they had more chemistry than the Scripps Institute and the sex was transcendental, but beyond that, they had almost nothing in common. She loved the New York social scene, going to parties, making deals, and he liked nothing more than to be out on his boat in the middle of the ocean where no one could find him.

But to be out in the ocean with Vicki...

That was a fantasy come true, and that there was

treasure involved, as well? He should pinch himself because he must be dreaming.

The door swung open again. "We're ready to roll tape."

"Coming." He wandered back into the living room. As he'd expected, Vicki had already taken center stage and turned on her familiar blitzkrieg of charm. She laughingly agreed to share the story of the treasure map and show it to them. He found himself watching with pleasure. Vicki was like an old-time movie star—Lauren Bacall, maybe, or Audrey Hepburn. You could stare at her all day and never get bored. At least he could.

How would he feel when she was gone for good?

As the crew dragged cameras and lights into Jack's bedroom, Vicki found herself regretting her rash promise to show them the map.

"So, uh, how did you come to see the map in the first place?" The smiling female reporter gestured to the ceiling above the bed. Her lacquered cap of blond hair didn't move when she tilted her head.

Vicki cleared her throat. "Jack explained that his ancestor Lazaro Drummond had painted the map there to hide it from anyone but his intimate companions."

"Are we to infer that you and Jack are intimate companions?" She was joking—sort of—but Vicki felt her cheeks heat.

"Jack and I are old friends. Very old friends, but that's all." The lie reeled effortlessly off her tongue. Was it perjury to lie on the local evening news? It must be some kind of crime. She hoped Leo Parker wouldn't see this. It rather undermined her other lie about being engaged to Jack. She could feel Jack's gaze on her from the far side of the room, and she wondered what he was thinking. He was probably relieved. He obviously regretted their "intimacy" or he wouldn't be sleeping alone in a different bedroom.

"Jack, could you join us over here?" The reporter looked up from the clip-on mic she was adjusting and turned to where he leaned against the wall on the far side of the room. "I think it would be fun if you both told us the story."

Vicki stiffened. Being close to Jack made her circuits go haywire. Too much loose electricity buzzing in the air. He ambled across the room, looking uncharacteristically awkward.

The reporter, an elegant woman in her early thirties, simpered at him. "Perfect! All right. I think we're ready to roll tape." There was some bustling around and a director appeared. No one actually said "action," but suddenly it was happening. "Jack and Vicki, you discovered the mural together?"

"Vicki gets all the credit." Jack's voice sounded gruffer and deeper than usual. He was so close that the hairs on her arm stood on end, as if reaching out to touch his arm. "She was lying in bed and she noticed pits in the fresco that were a different color."

Vicki swallowed. Did he have to mention that she was lying in bed? Why not say she was dressed only in skimpy lingerie, too? She decided to step in. "I was actually checking messages on my cell phone, and the light from the screen hit the fresco at an angle and highlighted the uneven surface."

The reporter gazed up at the ceiling. One cameraman was angled up toward the painting, and another kid was holding some kind of portable light.

"You must have sharp eyes. We have a lot of lights on right now, but it would be pretty dark under here otherwise."

"Well, once I noticed the unevenness, I asked Jack for a flashlight."

"Oh, so he was in here with you at the time?" The reporter flashed her perky gaze on him, a smile twitching at her painted lips.

"Uh…" Jack hesitated and glanced at Vicki.

"Of course. I'm hardly going to go rooting through his house looking for clues without his being present."

She watched Jack's chest fall in relief, which made sadness drift through her. He really didn't want people to think they were an item. Maybe he was already formulating dinner plans for him and Miss Microphone.

"So you came here to the house specifically to look at the map?" The reporter squinted slightly.

The lights and her intense scrutiny made Vicki blink. "Sort of. I was staying with some relatives of Jack's and they got me interested in the family history."

The reporter's eyes brightened and she leaned in. "I've heard some fascinating things about the Drummond family. There's a reward being offered for finding pieces of an old family relic. Is that what you were searching for?"

There was no way out. "Yes." Vicki sagged inwardly. This would only beat more treasure hunters out of the bushes. Although at this point that didn't really matter. She needed to get out of here, reward or no reward. "A chalice, which three brothers brought with them from Scotland. If the three interlocking pieces of the old cup can be reunited, it will bring luck to the family."

"What a romantic story." The reporter smiled at Jack. "Do you believe the cup exists?"

"I don't doubt it. Whether we can find it is a whole other story." He looked relaxed again. "But we're sure having fun looking for it. And Vicki's happy discovery of the treasure map led us to the wreck of my ancestor Macassar Drummond's boat. We've managed to salvage a lot of interesting material from the remains of his ship and have barely scratched the surface. I'd say we have years of rewarding work ahead of us."

"So the lost cup is already bringing you good luck?" Vicki saw the reporter's eyes dart momentarily to his muscled forearm. Of course she thought Jack was hot. Who wouldn't? The poor woman was only human after all.

"That's an interesting way of looking at it. I guess you could say it is bringing us luck." He smiled at Vicki. "And I have my old and dear friend to thank for it."

Vicki cringed inwardly. She didn't much like being described as "old" and "dear." Sounded like she might need a blue rinse or some new knitting patterns. "It's been fascinating for me, too. I'm an art dealer by trade, and interested in historical pieces." She managed a bright smile. Might as well get some decent publicity for herself out of this whole fiasco.

"Really?" Miss Microphone turned her glowing smile on Vicki. "Have you found anything yet that could be described as treasure?"

"We have. I put some pieces aside for you to see."

The reporter made a funny hand gesture that ground everything to a halt. Vicki sagged with relief now that the cameras weren't rolling anymore, and the crew started heaving and trailing their equipment into the

other room. Neither she nor Jack moved, so after about
two minutes they were left alone in the room, standing
right next to the bed.

"This was probably a mistake." He spoke softly and
with a hint of humor.

"But an unavoidable one." She had far too much
experience with unavoidable mistakes. Climbing into
Jack's bed might be her biggest one yet.

"We won't get any peace now."

"Just life in the modern world." She tried to look
cooler than she felt.

"This is the first time the modern world has been allowed to intrude into the Drummonds' hideout. Usually
it's where I come to get away from all that."

"Then I guess now you know how the rest of us feel.
Nowhere to run, nowhere to hide." She shrugged and
attempted a casual smile. It failed.

"There's always the open sea." Humor twinkled in
his eyes.

"I'm sure your pirate ancestors said the same thing."
A smile sneaked to her mouth. It was hard to stay too
serious around Jack. Maybe that was part of the problem. Why couldn't she just ask him why he'd gone cold
on her? That might make him think their fling actually
meant something to her.

And she didn't want him to think that even if it was
true.

Better to be glib and casual. "I suppose it's too early
in the day for a vodka gimlet." She winced at a loud
scraping sound from the other side of the door.

"Not if you're bold enough to drink one on camera."

She blew out. "I'm not as bold as I used to be. Five

years ago I wouldn't have thought twice. Maybe I am getting old and wise."

"You want to watch that. It might get boring."

"Maybe I'm already boring." Again she burned to ask what made him suddenly go off her. The sex had been amazing and Jack wasn't the type to fake an orgasm, even if it was possible for a man to do that.

"You'll never be boring, Vicki St. Cyr."

Then why won't you sleep with me?

The door flung open. "We're ready to start rolling again. We'd love you both to come talk about the stuff you found."

"Sure." She stretched. "I guess the gimlet can wait. God knows I've done crazier things than this stone-cold sober."

Jack laughed, which didn't entirely hide the odd expression in his eyes. If she didn't know better she'd swear he was looking at her with something akin to... tenderness.

But that was impossible. Pirates weren't tender and Jack Drummond was anything but sentimental. "Let's go manhandle the treasure."

It was well after dark by the time the crew finally left, which meant a lengthy and complex process of hauling their equipment back onto their rented boat in the dark. Jack seemed a little on edge, which she wouldn't have believed if she couldn't see it with her own eyes. His shoulders looked tense and a groove had appeared beneath his sun-lightened brows.

The crew had left her careful organization of the boxes and equipment in disarray, and she didn't have the energy to put them back. "When will the story air?"

They'd traded her imaginary vodka gimlet for a glass of chablis, and sipped it while standing in one of the French doors, looking out over the moonlit ocean. Peace had been restored, as long as you were looking outside the windows and not in.

"Tonight, I guess. I don't even know what time the news is on here."

"Don't want to let the outside world intrude on your sanctuary?"

"Not really. I don't watch TV much. I bet you don't, either." He moved close behind her, but not close enough to touch her. "I'm not sure either of us is good at sitting still for long enough to watch a TV show."

Her skin tingled at the feel of him so near...and yet so far. Why couldn't he just touch her, dammit? The wine wasn't helping. It heightened the sensual languor in the warm evening air and filed the edges of her well-honed inhibitions.

Made her long for a long, slow, seductive kiss.

She hugged herself because no one else was going to. "Cold?"

"No. I guess we should check the TV and see what kind of spin they put on the whole thing." At least if it aired today they wouldn't have time to ferret around in her past. And she couldn't stand still any longer with Jack hovering behind her. Her blood pressure was rising by the second.

"Yeah." He didn't move. And his body blocked the way back into the room. She could feel waves of heat rising off him. Or was that just her fevered imagination?

"Vicki." His voice had an uncharacteristic hesitant tone.

"Yes, I'm Vicki." She immediately cursed herself for

her snarky answer. How could anyone be romantic with her when she was such a prickly sea urchin herself?

"You sure are." He said it softly, then turned and went back into the room, leaving her standing alone on the edge of the darkness. Whatever intimate confession or utterance he'd been about to make would remain forever unspoken.

Fantastic. And she had herself to blame.

She peeled herself away from the door frame, her mind spinning with what Jack might have said. No wonder Leo Parker was the only man in hot pursuit of her right now. A guy would have to be crazy or stupid to chase after someone so difficult. She'd once thought Jack was crazy, but up close he seemed wonderfully sane. Leo was stupid and arrogant—maybe that was the only kind of man who'd ever be interested in her, because everyone else got scared off by her own arrogance and stupidity.

"Are you okay, Vicki? You're breathing a bit funny."

Emotions were welling in her chest. "I'm fine. It's just been a long day."

"You can go to bed if you want. I'll tell you what they say on the news."

She could go off by herself and sleep alone. In Jack Drummond's bed. The thought made her shoulders sag. She'd let some scenarios play through her mind when she decided to come here and look for the cup. Most of them involved Jack trying to get her into bed. Some of them involved her resisting. She'd never even considered the possibility that he'd keep her at a polite but safe distance. "No, thanks. I'll stay up for a while." All night if need be. If the cup was here, she'd find it. If she didn't, she was out of here anyway.

She had to leave or lose her mind. She'd been holding herself together and putting on a brave face for far too long. The promise of a bright future and her own self-confidence had buoyed her along. But now, here, she'd run right out of steam.

She closed the patio door and followed Jack into the den, where a huge sofa wrapped around three walls, so a group of people could stare together at the enormous flat-screen TV on the wall. Someday Jack would watch a football game with his future son in this room, and his yet-to-be-determined wife would probably bring them grilled shrimp and salsa—Jack wasn't really a chips-and-dip guy—and smile fondly at their masculine antics.

And she'd be off somewhere holding a loupe up to an eighteenth-century print to study the paper for foxing. Which was exactly what she wanted.

Jack had settled into the leather sofa, but she held herself against the wall near the door, poised for escape. He clicked past a colorful stream of junky television shows and belligerent commercials, finally settling on the local affiliate whose logo had been all over the house a few hours earlier. The news was under way. "Maybe we missed it." She didn't care much one way or the other. She just needed that cup for her own purposes.

"It won't be the headline story. There's no fresh blood involved, and we're only five minutes into the hour. Maybe it will be the feel-good story at the end."

She hugged herself again, then caught herself doing it and thrust her hands to her sides. She'd have to make her own feel-good story somewhere far away from here.

To keep herself busy, she poured them both a glass

of wine from an open bottle on the sideboard, then held hers untasted, afraid of its intoxicating effects. She already felt emotionally on edge, probably more so than at any time in her life, and the wine might do anything but steady her nerves.

"Here it is!" Jack sat forward as an image of his boat out on the water appeared on the screen to an excited voice-over about the new find. It must have been aerial footage from a helicopter, which cut to the bright gaze of the reporter who'd interviewed them.

"Local resident Jack Drummond has made another thrilling discovery, the sunken wreck of a three-hundred-year-old pirate ship just off our shores. And the best part is, the pirate was his own ancestor, Macassar Drummond."

Jack grinned, enjoying the story as the reporter rattled on about the history of the area and how the Treasure Coast had got its name from the regular encounters between laden ships and tropical storm systems along its palm-fringed shores.

Vicki started at the sight of herself when they cut to a shot inside Jack's house. She looked so serious and less glamorous than she'd imagined, even in her special on-camera getup. Next to Jack, who glowed like a Hollywood star on camera, she seemed small, rather insignificant, prattling on about history and provenance and cataloging techniques. It was a miracle they didn't cut her out altogether, but they did soon switch to some more-engaging footage of Jack on the bow of his boat, wind tossing his hair and the sun beating down on his bronzed skin, every inch the high-seas hero of the popular imagination.

"Well, that was harmless." Jack beamed as they cut

to a commercial and someone started shouting about amazing deals on a new Toyota. "I think we came off as quite a professional operation. Not bad for the scion of notorious pirates."

"It'll still bring all the backyard treasure hunters out of the woodwork."

"Can you blame them? Who wouldn't want in on a haul like this? Now that we've stirred up the silt there'll be coins and clay pipes and musket balls washing up on the beaches for years." He grinned. Obviously he didn't mind one bit that a bunch of strangers would share in the bounty. He was a much more generous and friendly soul than she. No wonder he wanted to cut her loose.

"I'm going to go root through a few more boxes."

"Still looking for that damned cup?" Teasing humor filled his voice.

"Don't come crying to me if you get to live happily ever after because I find it."

"I won't hold my breath. I'm off to bed. We need to get a very early start tomorrow so we can chase off any vultures that start circling."

"Great. See you tomorrow." She'd already left the room and headed down the hallway. She certainly wasn't going to stand around waiting for another embarrassingly polite explanation of why it made more sense for him to sleep in another room.

She switched on the computer and scrolled methodically through the files of X-rays, scrutinizing each one for any shapes that could be either a drinking vessel or a base. A white oval shadow on image number C53 made her pause. Tilted another way, it could be round. Which could mean it was a cup base or even the drinking vessel itself. Well worth investigating.

She rearranged the stacks of boxes to liberate number 53, then pulled out the dripping mass inside it, huge and heavy, and spread it on some damp towels on the floor. Starting with a small chisel and working her way down to a minuscule one, she scraped away the layers of sand and coral and encrusted sea creatures that had taken the strange object into their rock-hard embrace.

As she grew nearer to the mysterious object she'd seen on the X-ray, her blood started to pump harder. She had a real feeling about this thing, and her instincts were nothing to laugh at. People teased her that she could tell a real art object from a fake simply by the way the hairs on her neck stood on end in the presence of greatness, and something about this object was setting off her sixth sense.

If Katherine Drummond's story was true, she could be millimeters away from revealing part of a medieval chalice no one had seen for three hundred years.

It was metal, all right. She tried hard not to scratch the surface as she removed the layers of sandy grit. The silted material fell easily away, revealing the rim of a cup. She bit her lip, afraid to let her hopes soar. The inside of the cup was filled with grit, and she decided to chisel away at the outside first to get some idea of the age before she tackled its contents. Her careful work revealed a delicate etched pattern, emerging almost completely undamaged from its cement overcoat of seabed. And it looked just like the pattern carved on the stem segment they'd found at Sinclair Drummond's Long Island mansion.

I've found it. Elation mingled with unwelcome sadness. Now she could leave. She'd probably never see Jack Drummond again. What a relief. So why was her gut sending up flares of warning?

Ten

Still carrying the weight of its rocky contents, the cup was heavy and large as a man's fist. Vicki wrapped it in a hand towel, ostensibly to protect its surfaces, but mostly to conceal it. She wasn't sure why.

She packed the rest of box 53 away and mopped up the water she spilled, then, clutching the damp towel-wrapped bundle, she headed for the bedroom. She intended to leave without telling Jack. She'd plead exhaustion tomorrow morning and let him go off with the crew, then she'd call for a water taxi and make her way back to civilization.

He'd be none the wiser until he returned that night, by which time she might be safely back in New York, collecting her reward from Katherine Drummond. She'd send Jack his share of the reward once she was safely distant.

She crept along the corridor, praying he wouldn't wake. She didn't want to see him again. It was hurtful and humiliating that she still had feelings for him even after he'd rejected her again. Somehow even the nights alone on cool sheets hadn't chilled the fever of excitement Jack's presence stirred in her blood. If anything, they'd made it worse.

She opened her door gingerly. The old hinges tended to creak and if he was sleeping next door it could wake him up. Not that he'd want to have anything to do with her in the middle of the night. But it would be depressing that he didn't. Better not to have him stir.

She switched on the light, but it hurt her eyes, so she switched it off again. Her big duffel bag was on the dresser, and she unwrapped the cup fragment, then rewrapped it in some flannel pajama bottoms and shoved it deep into her bag. She'd have to remember not to heave it around too enthusiastically tomorrow.

She stripped off her clothes—no need to sleep in any protective armor—and headed for bed. To heck with her makeup; she'd wash it off tomorrow. She climbed up onto the high bed and lifted the covers, ready to climb in and sink down into the soft mattress.

That's when she discovered that the bed was already occupied.

Jack smiled in the dark as Vicki climbed into the bed. The light flicking on had woken him from a deep sleep, and he'd wondered if his sudden appearance back in his own bed might send her running.

She'd hesitated, sure, but then she climbed in and lay still. His skin hummed with awareness, even though no part of her was touching him. His fingers itched to reach out and spread themselves over her hips or around her waist, or to wind their tips into her hair.

But he hesitated. She'd seemed so quiet today, almost vulnerable, different than he'd ever seen her. Was that why he was here? He'd avoided her for two days because he didn't want to give her false hope.

False hope? Who was he to be so arrogant? The only evidence that she wanted a relationship with him at all was her unconscious nighttime ramblings. Maybe she was talking to some other Jack that had nothing to do with him.

An idea that set his nerves on edge.

But now that she seemed so…down, did he think his affectionate arms were the perfect prescription? His reasons for being here suddenly seemed foolish and callous. If she were pining away because he wouldn't sleep with her, wouldn't sleeping with her make that worse instead of better?

He sucked in a silent breath. This was all far too confusing. No wonder his relationships rarely survived the first year. The sea might get rough and unpredictable, but it didn't have hidden motives and inscrutable wishes that could swirl around and suck you under just when you least expected it.

Gingerly, he reached out an exploratory hand. It landed on Vicki's soft thigh. And she didn't slap it away.

He felt her breathing quicken, and his own matched its pace as he eased closer. Her scent heated his blood, intensifying as he buried his face in her hair. Her back was to him, so he bumped gently into the delicious curve of her tight backside, and paused to relish the rush of sensation.

Oh, Vicki.

She hadn't moved at all, but awareness pulsed from every pore. She had every right to play hard to get, after his hot-and-cold behavior of the past few days. His exploratory fingers touched the curve of her breast, and caught the rapid thud of her heart.

She turned toward him oh so slightly, just enough for him to press his lips to her cheek. From there they somehow climbed to her mouth as she rolled over and slipped her arms around him. His chest tightened as she held him, kissing him back.

I love you, Jack. I've always loved you. Her words, unspoken, hovered in his mind. Two phrases, uttered years apart, that had scared him right off. Right now they did nothing to dampen his fierce desire. If anything, they enhanced it.

I love you, too, Vicki. He didn't say it. Instead, he let the thought float in his mind, testing it out. It expanded, filling him with a strange lightness. His body felt good wrapped around hers. This was sheer physical pleasure he was comfortable and familiar with.

But with Vicki, there was always something more. An emotional component that threw him off his game and made him wonder if he was getting in too deep.

Which didn't make any sense, when deep in Vicki was such an awesome place to be.

Their kiss intensified as their hands roamed over each other. When he couldn't stand the building sensation anymore, he entered her. She let out a little whimper of pleasure, nails digging into his skin for an instant before she arched to take him deeper.

He moved over her slowly, floating in the sea of emotions that washed through him. The past two days he'd fought a constant, nagging urge to do just this—

lose himself in her. He'd had plenty to keep him busy, but nothing could keep his mind off her. Those nights alone in the spare bedroom had driven him half-mad. Vicki St. Cyr only a few yards away, wanting him in her bed, and him too…chicken to go there.

He laughed out loud at how ridiculous his behavior had been.

"Why are you laughing?" She breathed faster and faster, and sensation built between them like a wave heading for shore.

"Can't believe how stupid I am," he rasped. "For sleeping alone when we could have been doing this."

"I agree." She whispered the words in his ear, sending a hot sizzle of sensation to his core. "But intelligence never was your strong suit. You're more a man of action."

"True." Trying not to act on his primal instincts to bed Vicki over the past couple of days had half killed him. Finally getting to do what he'd craved all along felt so good he knew he could explode at any minute.

But he didn't. He held himself in check, moving slowly, shifting positions, enjoying the thrill of making Vicki gasp and moan as pleasure shot through her with the same crazy intensity.

Would she say it again? Right now she could say anything and it would sound just right. He and Vicki were meant to be together in some mysterious way. Even during their years apart, something had linked them. A mysterious thread of fate or destiny that had eventually pulled them back together.

"I hope you never find that cup." He breathed the words in between fierce kisses. Her search for the cup had brought her back into his life, and finding it might take her out of it. Right now that was inconceivable.

Her breathing changed slightly, almost like she was holding her breath, and their joint rhythm slowed. She didn't answer. Maybe he was in some realm where speech was no longer possible. That could happen during sex, especially the really good kind like this. He nibbled her ear, then licked it, something that had always driven her crazy.

She whimpered, then wriggled underneath him, inviting him deeper, and they drifted again into that driving rhythm that carried him out where speech, and even thought, became irrelevant. Then they rolled until she was on top and she rode him at a gallop until they both exploded into a climax that left him winded by his own spent passion.

Vicki, Vicki, Vicki. Could he stand to live without her?

Right now the answer was no.

Vicki heard Jack climb out of bed, but kept her eyes closed tight. It was still dark, but she knew he planned to reach the wreck before dawn to beat any treasure seekers who might have seen the news story. She held her breath when she heard him hesitate. Was he wondering whether to sneak out without waking her?

"Vicki, are you coming on the boat today?" That answered one question.

She pretended to half awaken from a groggy sleep. "Too tired."

"Sleep well, gorgeous." She almost opened her eyes when his lips touched hers in a soft kiss. Then she exhaled with relief when she heard the door close behind him.

Memories of last night flooded back, pressing her down into the mattress. Did Jack really have to come sleep with her just because he could? It was humiliating to have so little control around him. She had every excuse to give him the cold shoulder, but apparently even her shoulders couldn't resist him. Thank heavens she'd finally found the cup piece and could get the heck out of here with what little was left of her dignity.

A surge of excitement rushed through her at the thought of the cup. She couldn't wait to bring it to Katherine Drummond, and not just because of the reward. Katherine had placed so much hope in putting the cup back together, and the quest had helped her recover from a dangerous illness. She'd be so excited to hear that the family legend might actually come true.

Vicki stayed rock-still in bed until she heard the distant sound of Jack's boat leaving for the marina to pick up the others. Then she sprang into action. She needed to get out of here before the housekeeper showed up around nine, so she didn't have to answer any awkward questions. She'd already looked up a water taxi service on the internet—cripplingly expensive but she didn't have much choice—and she dialed them. A surprised-sounding man said he could be there in half an hour, and she didn't argue. That would still get her out of here around dawn without seeing Jack.

She showered and attempted to fix her hair in some semblance of a style, then dressed in an all-black ensemble that seemed suited to the somber task of escaping Jack's island.

There was no question of saying goodbye. What if he suggested that she stay awhile longer and she eagerly agreed? What if he waved her off, glad to have his private paradise to himself again? There were any number of possibilities, none of them good. At least this way she had the advantage of surprise.

She shoved her toiletries into her bag and zipped up the compartments. What would Jack think when he returned to find her gone? She wanted to feel a thrill of victory at finally being the one to leave him, but she didn't. He'd already picked her up and put her down and played with her like a plastic toy, so there wasn't much satisfaction in stalking away when he'd already proved he could do what he liked with her.

And she'd miss him. Maybe that was the worst part. She'd already missed his joyful energy in her life for six years. These past few days had reminded her of how much she enjoyed his company, and the zest and originality he brought to everything he did. There weren't too many men around like Jack Drummond.

None, in fact.

But maybe that was a good thing. She shoved her bag onto her shoulder and slipped her feet into her sandals, then went into the kitchen and made a quick turkey wrap for the road. She didn't have any appetite, so she shoved the wrap in a ziplock bag and stuck it in an outside pocket on her bag.

She couldn't resist sneaking a last, long look at the plastic boxes filled with recovered treasures from the bottom of the ocean. Seeing them all marinating there in their seawater gave her another pang of grief. How much fun would it be to stay here and unwrap each of them from their sandy giftwrap and watch the past emerge? Jack was so lucky—and brilliant, really—to have forged a life doing exactly what he loved. She admired and envied him, and that didn't make leaving any easier. She should hate him for the way he'd toyed with her, but she couldn't even do that. He was too likable—too lovable—so she'd have to settle for a lifetime of simmering resentment instead.

She wrote a note to Jack as a memo on the computer. At least there the housekeeper wasn't likely to find it and read it.

I'll be back in NYC by the time you read this. I found the cup piece I was looking for and I'll make sure you get half the reward. There's an old Chinese saying that goes "may you live in interesting times" and times are certainly always interesting around you. I think it's supposed to be a curse, so I won't wish for the rest of your life to be interesting because I do wish you all the best. XX Vicki.

Then she decided she'd rambled too much and said the wrong thing and she wanted to delete it, but if she fussed around too much maybe the water taxi wouldn't find the dock and she'd get stuck here trying to explain it in person. She agonized for a moment over what to name the document. *Goodbye* sounded too melodramatic, *Au revoir* implied that she'd see him again, *Laters* sounded too faux-casual, so she went with *Bye, Jack* and turned off the computer.

The sky had lightened somewhat by the time she headed for the dock Jack used for visitors. It was easy to spot from the shore and she raised a colorful flag she'd seen him use to attract the attention of the news crew's boat. Five minutes early, she heard the chugging of an engine, and a battered boat pulled up.

Instead of feeling a great weight lift as the grizzled captain helped her aboard, she felt it settle deeper into the pit of her belly. Once the boat's pilot had turned his attention to steering the boat, she looked back at the lush canopy of palm-topped sea grape that sheltered the infamous Drummond clan from the prying eyes of the outside world. What a magical place. Though Jack probably wouldn't ever find the perfect wife and have the 2.5 towheaded children of his dreams running gaily through the garden. Men like him usually left a trail of broken hearts—and fatherless children—scattered over the globe. For all she knew, he was no different already.

Her broken heart had almost mended from the first time he'd dropped it. This time she might not be so lucky, but never mind. She didn't have much use for a heart anyway.

Back in New York she holed up on her friend Zara's sofa on Prince Street. She could probably stay with Zara for a week on the pretext of looking for a new pad, but because Zara's huge loft was entirely open, the lack of privacy might start to unhinge her after that. She certainly wasn't going back to abuse the hospitality of Sinclair Drummond and his new fiancée. She liked the down-to-earth and practical Annie, and had immediately seen her as a match for Sinclair. But for whatever reason, Annie didn't seem to like her at all.

Sigh.

And there was the awkward reality of having to claim a large reward from a family friend. She'd have to pretend she would donate it to her favorite charity and just not mention that meant herself. Maybe that's why she still hadn't called to tell Katherine about the cup. Determined to get things moving, she picked up her phone and dialed the number.

"Vicki! I was wondering when you'd call. From the news stories I'm seeing, you obviously had no trouble finding Jack."

"Drummonds are easy to find because they stay in the same house for three hundred years."

Katherine laughed. "So true! And you found the cup on the newly discovered wreck?"

"It's a long story." She arranged to come out to Long Island and visit Katherine the next day. She would have been totally ashamed to admit that her chief motivation was to get her hot little hands on the twenty-thousand-dollar check. And she might not be in too much of a rush to get Jack's share to him. With all his millions he wouldn't mind waiting a month or so.

She took the train out to Long Island to avoid the expense of renting a car, and wasn't surprised when Annie met her at the station. Vicki greeted her with a friendly wave. "I see you're still the most helpful person in Dog Harbor."

Once again, Annie stiffened. She tried to take Vicki's bag and put it in the trunk. Vicki held on tight. "I can handle it. You're no stronger than me and you're not the housekeeper anymore."

"Did you have a good train ride?" Annie asked primly.

"No worse than usual. Annie, can I ask you to be completely frank with me?" She settled into the passenger seat.

"Okay." Annie looked anything but enthusiastic as she reversed out of the parking space.

"I can tell you don't like me, and I'm just wondering why." She looked at Annie, whose pretty, almost-strawberry-blond hair was loose to her shoulders for once.

Annie turned to her with a look that could only be described as distressed. "For one thing, I never know what you're going to say. And when you do say something, it usually throws me off guard. Frankly, you scare me a little." Annie's words had rushed out in one breath. She then realized that she'd reversed out and was blocking the street, and she swung the car around into the right lane.

"Oh." Vicki drew in a breath. "I'm sorry." She felt chastened. She didn't tend to worry all that much about other people's feelings. Maybe because she wasn't the world's most sensitive person herself. Often she didn't even notice when someone disliked her until someone else pointed it out. Even then, she usually didn't mind too much.

But somehow she wanted Annie to like her, and it hurt that she didn't.

"And you know what?" Annie continued, a slight frown marring her smooth brow. "It was weird being the housekeeper and waiting on people hand and foot. I had to be polite to everyone whether I wanted to or not. It's kind of stressful."

"And now you can be as rude as you like." Vicki raised a brow.

Annie laughed. "I don't think I'm capable of that. I'm too repressed or something. I think you and I are just opposites."

"Which is why I'd be disastrous with the lovely Sinclair and you're his perfect match. I could see it from the first moment I saw you together."

"How?" Annie sounded genuinely curious. "I didn't think we were all right for each other. I doubt we would ever have got together if you hadn't forced us into it."

Vicki looked sideways at her. "You can't fool me. Something had already happened between you."

Annie bit her lip. "Something...totally wild and unexpected and inappropriate and, well, eek!"

"And now it's turned into something wonderful and perfect and joyous for all concerned."

"And I have to give you credit where credit's due. I think I do like you after all." Annie smiled at her.

"I'm not even sure if I like myself." Vicki stared out the windshield. "Maybe I'll grow on both of us."

Katherine Drummond's pale eyes filled with tears at the sight of the cup. Still weak from a rare tropical illness, she sat in a polished chair at the dining table in her son's Long Island mansion. Sinclair stood nearby with his arm around his fiancée, Annie, and all attention was riveted on the artifact Vicki had pulled from her bag.

Tarnished and still somewhat encrusted with seabed, the cup didn't look at all impressive. Suddenly Vicki even wondered if it was the right cup. Maybe the pieces wouldn't fit together and her time would have all been wasted.

"Vicki, darling, I can't believe you went to such lengths to find this."

"It was all Jack's doing."

"How did you talk him into looking for it? I couldn't even get him to return my calls."

"I just had to fire up his treasure hunting instincts. It really wasn't hard. Shouldn't we make sure it fits?"

Katherine reached for the unimpressive-looking stem that sat in a fabric-lined box on the table in front of her. She squeezed it in her bony hand and looked at Vicki. "I know we still have to find the third piece, but I can't help but feel a sense of history being made right at this moment."

Vicki held her breath. How disappointed would she be if this was all a big mistake? Katherine hoped to end the Drummond family's long run of disastrous marriages and personal tragedies with this battered relic. That was a lot of hope to hang on one old cup.

She held out the cup and Katherine pushed the stem into the hole on the underside of the cup bowl. There was a grinding noise as remaining encrusted sand and mineral deposits scraped against metal. Vicki wished she'd taken the time to clean it more thoroughly, but she'd been impatient to come here and claim the reward.

"It fits." Katherine looked up at Vicki, tears glittering in her eyes. "Look, Sinclair." She held it up like a priest during Mass. "The legend is real!"

Sinclair raised an eyebrow. "Pretty cool."

Vicki wanted to laugh. Sinclair was so not the type to get fired up over a crusty old antique. His future wife wasn't, either. They were all wrapped up in plans for Annie to open a shop selling decorative home and garden items. Neither of them was at all worried about the impact of ancient curses and legends on their future.

Katherine twisted the cup in the light. "I wonder if you're supposed to drink a libation out of it?"

"I think you should wait until you find the third piece." Vicki stared at the cup, which visibly lacked its base. "Have you had any luck contacting the Scottish branch of the family?"

Katherine shook her head. "None whatsoever. It's very frustrating. I would be upset with James Drummond for being so rude, but apparently he spends most of his time in Singapore, so I'm not even sure that his Scottish estate is passing along my messages. I don't suppose you'd be willing to go there and track him down, Vicki?"

Vicki froze. "No, I'm afraid I really have to get back to my life in New York." The last thing she needed was to meet another tall, dark and debonair Drummond heir. They were all bad news as far as she was concerned. "Maybe you should visit him yourself?"

"The doctors won't let me travel. My immune system took such a beating they're worried that even a bad cold could knock me flat, so no air travel." She rolled her eyes. "I guess I'll just have to keep phoning and emailing James Drummond. Sooner or later I'll get through to him." Katherine turned the cup in her hands again. "But I feel a weight lifting already. I know we'll find the third piece. Look how happy Sinclair is." She glanced fondly at her tall, imposing son, who did glow rather sweetly with happiness.

Vicki felt even her hard heart swell with emotion. "I'm sure you will and I can't wait to see it all together. In the meantime, however, I'm afraid I must run. I wanted to bring you the piece I found as soon as possible, but I've been on vacation from my life for some weeks and I have a lot to do." She swallowed, hoping she wouldn't have to remind Katherine about the reward. She'd managed to conceal her lack of money all this time, but things were getting desperate. Her credit

cards were maxed out and she needed to pay them down
to get herself off the ground in New York.

"It seems rather a shame that the reward you talked
me into offering is going to people who already have
money." Katherine laughed. "I suppose you can always
give it to the needy."

Vicki managed a fake laugh. "Of course. I have some
pet causes." Like eating and having a roof over her head.
"And I'm sure Jack does, too."

"I saw the two of you on the news. I couldn't help
but notice that you'd make a lovely couple."

"How odd it made the news here." Vicki's swallowed. Her fling was supposed to be private and personal. Would others guess there was something between
them? "I thought it was a local interest story."

"It's one of the biggest finds of the century. It's nice
to see the Drummonds getting good publicity for a
change. Usually we're only in the papers when someone
crashes their plane into a building or disappears at sea.
Jack is very dashing. Don't you think he's handsome?"

"I guess." Adrenaline surged through her. Could she
just beg Katherine to write the check? "Kind of arrogant, but why wouldn't he be?"

"Why not indeed." Katherine smiled fondly. "Maybe
he'll find love now that the cup is being reunited."

Vicki felt ill. "Goodness, look at the time. A check
would be great."

Subletting a studio on Sutton Place was a coup. She
chose the tony address entirely for the snob factor. Although her building was right on the East River, her tiny
apartment was on the first floor and faced toward the
street. Still, it made for great letterhead and she could

walk down to the water and sip coffee looking out at Roosevelt Island whenever she wanted.

Writing a check for ten thousand dollars and mailing it to Jack Drummond didn't feel quite so hot. She'd hoped that once she posted it she could put that whole unfortunate episode of her life behind her. Then she found herself obsessively checking her bank balance—never a good thing to do—to see if he'd cashed it. And he didn't.

Did the check go astray? Was he too busy to visit an ATM machine? Did he suspect she needed the money and decide to treat her as a charity case? The possibilities danced in her brain even as she hustled to get her new business off the ground.

She hooked up with her first two clients through an interior decorator she'd met at a party. The first was a Brazilian shoe manufacturer who had a new Park Avenue pad with empty walls and needed to amass a lifetime's art collection in time for his daughter's engagement party in six weeks. The second was an advertising art director who'd just inherited several million and bought a Tribeca loft, and wanted to fill the space with contemporary masters. Could life get any better than that? She had plenty to do, calling around her contacts and attending auctions with an enormous budget to buy anything from Renoir sketches to Rikrit Tiravanija sculptures. With the commissions she'd already started to earn she'd be back in the black and on her way to financial stability by the end of the year.

Life was good. Except for that nagging hole that nothing seemed to fill. Sex didn't work, even with the delicious David from Sotheby's. The unfortunate truth that she craved a more substantial relationship really depressed her when she allowed herself to think about it. So she didn't.

Nearly a month had gone by since she'd returned. Should she call to see if the check got lost? Every time she picked up the phone, her heart beat so fast she wasn't sure she could sound normal, so she put it back down. Sometimes she jumped when her phone rang because she was so sure it must be Jack, calling to cuss her out for taking off without even showing him his own ancestral relic. But he obviously didn't care much one way or the other.

Then one night, the bleat of her phone startled her from her laptop, where she'd been perusing listings for an upcoming Christie's auction. It was him. This time she was sure.

"Hello." She cursed her hopeful tone.

"Vicki." A male voice, but not Jack's. "It's Leo."

Ugh. Her heart sank. "Hi." No encouragement. She'd love to hang up on him, but he was a bit too well connected for overt rudeness.

"When's the wedding?"

"The what?" She smacked her head when she remembered her pretend engagement ruse.

"You're not with Jack Drummond anymore, are you?" His voice had an edge to it that she didn't remember hearing before. He'd probably figured out she was lying. Especially if he'd seen the TV coverage.

"No. No, we broke up." Or were never together in the first place. "I have a call coming in on the other line. Can I call you back?"

"You won't call me back. You've never called me back."

Maybe you could take a hint from that. "Why did you

call?" Might as well get this over with properly. She'd be bound to run into Leo soon because they moved in the same circles, and a pointed conversation now could save an embarrassing scene later.

"I'm sorry it didn't work out with Jack Drummond, but now that you're single again, we could see *La Traviata* and grab dinner at Per Se."

This guy was scary. "I'm still in love with Jack." As she said the words, she knew they were true.

"He's an oaf."

"He's wonderful." Was she really having this conversation?

"Then why did you break up with him?"

"I didn't. He broke up with me." Now, that was the first lie of the conversation, except about the call coming in. Mercifully Jack never had the chance to dump her because she'd taken the reins of that carriage. Of course it had the unfortunate effect of leaving her wondering what might have happened if...

"Listen, Vicki. I've been very patient with you, but you're taxing even my vast reserves. I want to take you to dinner, and you *will* come."

"I won't." All this talk about Jack made her feel reckless.

"Don't forget that I know about your family's financial trouble. How would you like for me to go to the papers with that news?"

"Go right ahead." And she pressed End. Then blew out a long, hard breath. *Do your worst, Leo Parker.* She couldn't live with threats and secrets hanging over her head. She was good at what she did. So what if her ivory tower was in foreclosure? People would just have to take her as they found her.

* * *

The story broke slowly over the next week. A gossip column mention here, a blog there, an opinion piece about privilege and greed…and the results were disastrous. Her two clients ran in separate directions, leaving her holding the checks for three artworks she'd already purchased as the only salvage from her brief career as art buyer to the rich and famous. She retreated to her Sutton Place lair to lick her wounds and wait for the firestorm of gossip to die down.

"No one will even remember in a month." Annie had called to commiserate after seeing a story on *The Huffington Post*. "These things get people all excited and then they move on to some other new drama."

"I'm surprised anyone cares, but I suppose I knew they would, which is why I hid the truth for so long. Poverty is terrifying to the rich."

Annie laughed. "You're hardly impoverished."

"That's what you think." It was a relief to be honest. "I'm just good at keeping up appearances. I've been living from hand to mouth for nearly a year. Why do you think I spent so much time mooching around you and Sinclair?"

"I thought you liked us. I should have known better. What are you going to do?"

"I'll survive. What doesn't kill me, and all that jazz. Maybe I'll travel to Scotland in hopes of earning the rest of the reward."

"Really?"

"No." A banging noise made her jump. "I'd better go. Someone's at the door." That was odd. The doorman usually buzzed and announced anyone who turned up. She said goodbye and put down her phone.

Her gut flared with warning. Could Leo Parker have
come around to up the ante? He was obviously crazy
and vindictive and out to get her where it hurt. "Who
is it?"

"It's Jack."

Eleven

She opened the door and stood there like a mute for about thirty seconds. Jack Drummond in her doorway was not a possibility that had ever crossed her mind. "How did you find me?"

"I'm a treasure hunter." A wicked grin was already creeping across his mouth. His dark eyes sparkled with pleasure and he looked as if he was enjoying himself. "If it's worth finding, I'll find it."

She cursed the way her body already responded to his presence, prickling with awareness. "Why?"

"First, to tell you I don't want any part of the reward." He came in and shut the door behind him without asking.

"But you—" She wasn't sure what to protest about first: his refusing the reward or barging into her apartment. Being in close proximity to Jack was dangerous.

"Don't say it." He held up his hand. "I know you're short of cash, and you know I'm not."

Ouch. He pitied her. That was even harder to take than his pushing her out of his bed. Her skin crawled with humiliation. "I'm fine." Her protest seemed foolish now that everyone in the world knew her financial predicament. It was automatic, like a twitch. "And you need to leave."

Not a single muscle moved beneath his white T-shirt or the faded jeans that hugged his powerful legs. The worst part was how badly she wanted to rush into his arms and throw herself against that hard chest.

It took great effort to stand her ground. "Jack, I don't know what you're up to, but there's no good reason for you to be here and—"

"No good reason? You sneaked off with my family heirloom. I never even got a chance to see it." The mischievous gleam in his eyes belied his supposed anger.

"You never cared about that cup. Besides, I don't have it. I gave it to Katherine."

He sighed. "I know. I've just come from a touching reunion with that branch of the family. Sinclair and Annie do make a cute couple and I hear that you played millionaire matchmaker for them."

"At least I've done something right this year." Could she forcibly push him out the door? She was afraid of what might happen if she pressed her palms against his contoured pecs. Already the temperature in the room had shot up ten degrees.

"I miss you, Vicki." He spoke directly, no teasing humor. "I was happy until you came to visit."

"And I ruined everything. Story of my life." She threw up her hands, babbling, anything to break the tension in the air. "I have a knack for making people uncomfortable." She thrust her hands on her hips. Emotion built inside her, all the pent-up hurt and frustrated affection she'd never gotten to express. She'd been nervous about seeing Jack when she went down to Florida, and with good reason. She'd thought she could handle herself around him, and she'd been wrong. This time he'd left a wound too large and raw to heal. "You really have to leave."

"I'm not going anywhere." He stood there in the tiny foyer of her tiny apartment, looming like a colossus. "Why did you run off?"

"This is my apartment. I think I should have some say in who enters it." She crossed her arms over her chest, where her heart was slamming against her rib cage. "And I didn't run off. I simply left."

"Without telling me."

"I didn't want a scene." She lifted her chin.

"And you thought I'd make one?" Humor glinted in his eyes, sparking both fury and defeat in her chest.

"Maybe I was afraid you wouldn't make one." She shrugged. "I never should have slept with you again. It was a big mistake."

"It wasn't." He spoke softly, but his words grew to fill the whole apartment. "I thought it was at first. That I'd gotten in over my head. That's why I pulled back and went to sleep in the other room." He looked sheepish. "That's the only mistake that was made. I was an idiot and I apologize. I never wanted to sleep anywhere but right next to you."

Vicki trembled. Jack Drummond apologizing? Something very strange was going on. "Then why did you do it? Sleep in the other room, I mean." Curiosity overwhelmed her sense of self-preservation.

Jack hesitated. "You said something in your sleep that scared me."

"Was I muttering about sharp knives and revenge?" She lifted her chin. Embarrassing possibilities swirled in her mind.

He tilted his head slightly and looked at her through narrowed eyes. "You said you loved me."

Heat flooded her face. "You must have heard wrong." She'd said that six years ago, sure, but she'd rather cut out her tongue than make the same idiotic mistake twice.

He shook his head. "Clear as a bell. You weren't awake and I'm sure you didn't mean for me to hear it." He frowned. "You said you'd always loved me. It spooked the heck out of me."

"I'll bet. What a nightmare." She fought the urge to throw open the living room window and dive out. Had Jack come here to toy with her? A red-hot tide of pain and humiliation was rising to flood levels inside her. "And you came back here in hopes that you could have a good laugh over it with me?"

"No." He stepped forward, unfamiliar frustration written on his bold features. "I came here because I realized that I...I..." His brow creased. "I love you, too."

Vicki's jaw dropped. The words had emerged from his mouth slowly, deliberately, as though he really meant them. They echoed in her heart, but she still didn't believe them. "Are you messing with me because I didn't say goodbye nicely?" She cocked her head, sure he was going to start laughing any moment.

"I'm not good at this. I've had no practice. I'm the

descendant of scurvy pirates and my genetic heritage is telling me to throw you over my shoulder and head for the high seas. I'm miserable without you and I don't want to be miserable."

The intense expression in his brown eyes surprised her so much that she almost wanted to laugh, maybe just to relieve the tension crackling in the air like an electric storm.

She had no idea what to say. Thoughts whirled in her mind. Jack loved her. He'd come to New York to find her. He wanted to take her away with him. Could this be real?

"I want you to come back to my island. The whole place seems empty without you. Even my boat feels like something's missing."

"I don't belong there." She was trying to convince herself. She'd missed that cursed island every minute since she left it. And his big rambling house with its funky piratical layout. And the comfortable bed where his ancestors had slept under their treasure map. "I'm a New York girl at heart, and you know it." Would he believe it? She didn't. Still, he didn't mean this. Maybe he was just so pissed that she'd finally got the better of him that he thought he loved and needed her. If she said yes and came back with him, he'd tire of her once the thrill of victory wore off.

Jack took another step forward. "I don't think you are a New York girl at heart. I think you love adventure and discovery. You took to the water like a fish, and I know you enjoyed exploring the wreck and unwrapping all its treasures."

She shrugged. "Sure." It was hard to sound casual with her heart smashing against her ribs and emotion clawing at her throat. "But that doesn't mean I'm meant to throw up my whole life and run after you. I just started my own business." *Never mind that it's dried right up already.* "I need to get back on my feet and figure out what I really want."

It didn't matter if what she really wanted was Jack. She'd already learned—twice—how well that worked out for her.

Jack's muscles tightened. Probably unaccustomed frustration at not getting his way. He took a step forward and grabbed her hands. Emotion flashed through her, along with the physical sensation of his touching her skin. She struggled to hold herself steady and keep her expression neutral.

"I love you, dammit. I can't live without you. I want you to be my wife."

She couldn't move. He wanted to marry her? She couldn't imagine Jack married to anyone. "Have you lost your mind?"

"Apparently, yes. And there's only one way to get it back." Still clutching her hands, he dropped onto one denim-clad knee. "Vicki St. Cyr, will you marry me?"

She stared at him. "I must be dreaming. Or hallucinating. Maybe I have a high fever and have temporarily gone insane."

"That makes two of us, then." His chest rose and fell as he looked up at her. "I won't take no for an answer. You know we're perfect for each other."

"No one else could stand us." The sheer madness of the idea made it seem strangely logical. A smile struggled to cross her mouth.

"I love you, Vicki. I think I've loved you since I first met you. I was just too cowardly to admit it. I'm stronger now, and braver, and I've come to claim you." He squeezed her hands and stood up.

Eye to eye with him she suddenly felt weak, as though she could fall into his strong arms and rest there. Tears rose in her eyes and she fought to keep them from spilling. "I do love you, Jack. I have always loved you, although most of the time I've hated myself for it. I certainly didn't intend for you to find out."

His face brightened. "I'm glad I did. It knocked some sense into me. You know we need each other, don't you?"

She nodded. Then swallowed. "But we're both free spirits, Jack. That's why it's never worked out for us before." Mostly she was worried about his free spirit wanting to tack off into a headwind, leaving her behind, but it sounded less pathetic if she blamed herself, too.

"We can be free spirits together." His chest rose. "Why not? If you want to be in New York, then I can spend time here, too. It's easy enough to fly—or sail—back and forth. Then on weekends we can cruise to Madagascar or Brazil."

She laughed, finally, which released a huge bubble of tension. "That sounds so crazy and stupid that it actually makes sense." Her hands felt hot inside his. She longed to free them and grab hold of him. As if he'd heard her thoughts, he let go of her hands and wrapped his arms around her. The breath flew from her lungs as she grabbed him around his huge chest. "Oh, Jack, we're doomed, aren't we?"

"Yup. We'll just have to strap ourselves together like shipwreck survivors and hope for the best."

He pressed her cheek to his shoulder, mostly so she could get away from his fierce gaze. "I do love your island. It makes a good base for adventures." Already her mind was wrapping itself around this strange and wonderful new set of possibilities. "And it would be a fun place for children to grow up."

The silence was deafening. Had she really just said that?

"I'm not going to pressure you into having children. Any big decisions, we'll make together."

"We'd probably have to homeschool them." She lifted her head and found herself frowning at him. "Or we'd be stuck with someone else's schedule."

He nodded, eyes shining with emotion. "Whatever we do, I know it will be an adventure."

Their lips finally met and a tidal wave of relief crashed over her, mingled with the sharp excitement of kissing Jack.

His throaty groan suggested that he felt the same way. When they finally pulled apart enough to speak, he kept his strong arms locked around her waist. "I came to your bed that last night because I finally realized I was an idiot to waste one more night away from the woman I love."

Her heart squeezed. "You must have been pretty pissed when you saw my note the next morning."

"Poleaxed is a better *p* word for the way I felt. My first instinct was to run after you and drag you back, but my pride prevented me. Eventually it wore off." His rakish grin made her smile. "So here I am. I thoroughly deserved to be dumped and abandoned by you, and I promise I'll spend the rest of my life making it up to you."

"Sounds like a plan."

Epilogue

Six months later

"I'm amazed at how much insurance premiums drop when you tell them you're keeping the insured item on a private island." Vicki took a few steps back to get a better look at the pretty little Vermeer she'd picked up in Brugge. At least she was convinced it was a Vermeer. The gallery owner had attributed it to a minor Dutch painter, but it had a certain *je ne sais quoi,* and she was pretty sure she could convince the art world she'd found a lost painting by the revered master.

Jack lay on the big leather sofa, holding up a heavy and time-darkened musket. "Insurance. Now there's a concept."

"You don't keep any?"

"Don't have to when the stuff's all mine." He flashed

his pearly pirate grin. "And my reputation is my insurance. Everyone knows I collect muskets."

"And cannons."

"And cannon balls. And powder." He laughed. "But the stuff you bring home is prettier."

"Isn't she?" The picture showed a young woman, wearing not a pearl earring, but a tiny gold locket. She wondered what secret her locket held. A lock of her beloved's hair? A love note? Or maybe she was just getting soft in her old age. "I can't wait to find her a loving home. Preferably a very rich one."

He laughed. "I love your mercenary streak. Especially because it brought you back into my life."

"I donated Katherine's twenty-thousand-dollar reward to charity. I felt it was the right thing to do now that I'm back on my feet." She pointed to her red Ferragamo sandals.

"And such lovely feet they are. What charity did you pick?"

"A fund for starving artists, of course. Got to keep the pool of talent humming." She smiled. It felt so good to have money to give away again. Or just to have fun with. The shipwreck treasure was still being removed and cleaned and would bring in millions over the next few years. "Where are we going next?"

"That depends on what we're looking for—an old wreck or a valuable painting."

She lifted a brow. "Or a valuable painting disguised as an old wreck by the passage of time."

"We've had such good luck finding both already that it's hard to decide. Did they ever hear from the Scottish Drummond who supposedly has the base of the cup?"

"Not a word last I heard. He's some financial bigwig who spends all his time in Singapore."

"I'd have thought Cousin Sinclair might be able to launch an appeal to a fellow money man."

"I don't think Sinclair is all that interested. Those financial types don't appreciate quirky treasures and their mysteries the way you and I do."

"True. And as far as I know, James Drummond is still single. Finding his third of the cup could spell the end of that."

She laughed. "Maybe that's why he doesn't want any part of it."

Jack put down his musket and strode across the room. He slid his arms around her in that deliciously proprietary way that still made her gasp with excitement. "He doesn't know what he's missing."

"I don't suppose anyone does until love blindsides them when they least expect it." She ran her thumb over his rough cheek. "I certainly didn't think I'd fall madly in love again. Especially with the same man who broke my tender young heart."

"Lucky for me you're rash and impetuous enough to make the same mistake twice." He kissed her lips, sending a shiver of pleasure through her. "I love a woman who isn't afraid to wade into trouble."

"How do you do that to me?" She writhed as he nibbled her earlobe, sending shock waves of arousal dancing through her.

"I'm a keen student of your erogenous zones." He touched a thumb to her nipple through her thin blouse. It immediately thickened under the pressure. "I'm drawing a mental treasure map of them."

"That will lead you right to where X marks the spot?"

"Oh, I already know where that is." He growled softly in her ear, sending a rush of heat to her groin. "Let's go explore it right now."

Together they ran down the corridor, bare feet noiseless on the stone flags, and climbed onto the ancient carved bed where they'd spend countless nights making love under the secret map they'd found together.

* * * * *

A sneaky peek at next month...

Desire™

PASSIONATE AND DRAMATIC LOVE STORIES

My wish list for next month's titles...

In stores from 15th February 2013:

2 stories in each book - only £5.49!

☐ All or Nothing — Catherine Mann

& A Conflict of Interest — Barbara Dunlop

☐ Sunset Surrender — Charlene Sands

& Undeniable Demands — Andrea Laurence

☐ Bachelor Unclaimed — Brenda Jackson

& In His Brother's Place — Elizabeth Lane

Available at WHSmith, Tesco, Asda, Eason, Amazon and Apple

Just can't wait?

Visit us Online

You can buy our books online a month before they hit the shops! **www.millsandboon.co.uk**

0213/5

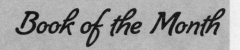

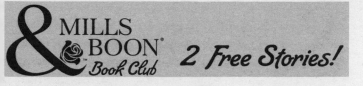

MILLS & BOON® Book Club — 2 Free Stories!

Get your free stories now at
www.millsandboon.co.uk/freebookoffer

Or fill in the form below and post it back to us

THE MILLS & BOON® BOOK CLUB™—HERE'S HOW IT WORKS: Accepting your free stories places you under no obligation to buy anything. You may keep the stories and return the despatch note marked 'Cancel'. If we do not hear from you, about a month later we'll send you 2 Desire™ 2-in-1 books priced at £5.49* each. There is no extra charge for post and packaging. You may cancel at any time, otherwise we will send you 4 stories a month which you may purchase or return to us—the choice is yours. *Terms and prices subject to change without notice. Offer valid in UK only. Applicants must be 18 or over. Offer expires 31st July 2013. **For full terms and conditions, please go to www.millsandboon.co.uk/freebookoffer**

Mrs/Miss/Ms/Mr (please circle)
_____

First Name
_____

Surname
_____

Address
_____

_____

                                        Postcode
_____

E-mail
_____

Send this completed page to: Mills & Boon Book Club, Free Book Offer, FREEPOST NAT 10298, Richmond, Surrey, TW9 1BR

Find out more at
www.millsandboon.co.uk/freebookoffer

Visit us Online

0113/D3XEb

Special Offers

Every month we put together collections and longer reads written by your favourite authors.

Here are some of next month's highlights— and don't miss our fabulous discount online!

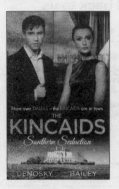

On sale 15th February   On sale 15th February   On sale 1st March

Save 20%
on all Special Releases

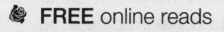
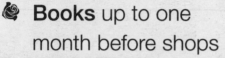

The World of Mills & Boon®

There's a Mills & Boon® series that's perfect for you. We publish ten series and, with new titles every month, you never have to wait long for your favourite to come along.

Blaze.
Scorching hot, sexy reads
4 new stories every month

By Request
Relive the romance with the best of the best
9 new stories every month

Cherish™
Romance to melt the heart every time
12 new stories every month

Desire™
Passionate and dramatic love stories
8 new stories every month

What will you treat yourself to next?

Ignite your imagination,
step into the past...
6 new stories every month

INTRIGUE...

Breathtaking romantic suspense
Up to 8 new stories every month

Captivating medical drama –
with heart
6 new stories every month

MODERN™

International affairs,
seduction & passion guaranteed
9 new stories every month

n o c t u r n e™

Deliciously wicked
paranormal romance
Up to 4 new stories every month

RIVA™

Live life to the full –
give in to temptation
3 new stories every month available
exclusively via our Book Club